Praise for Haw

"Hawk is intense from the get-go ... Each and every character has its own distinct and memorable personality, they're just begging for their own story. Patricia A. Rasey's fresh and exhilarating take on vampires is a must read."

— *Kimberly Rocha, Book Obsessed Chicks*

"A lot of the arcs started in the first book have some closure in this one along with a surprise at the end. Ms Rasey again does a perfect job of blending the life of a MC club along with the life of vampires."

—*Cindy 0, SnS Reviews*

"I'm really excited to meet the rest of the Sons and I hope we see more of them in future books ... Patricia A. Rasey is a wonderful story teller. Her stories are imaginative, unique and a blast to read. I thoroughly enjoyed Hawk and I'm looking forward to the next installment in the series."

—*Elizabeth, HEAs are Us*

"Hands down my FAVORITE READ OF THE YEAR!!! Yes this book was that good! Ms. Rasey took me on a ride at a hundred miles an hour downhill, didn't let up, didn't slow down! A ride I highly recommend!

—*Deana, Coffee Books Life*

Hawk
Sons of Sangue

Patricia A. Rasey

Patricia A. Rasey
patricia@patriciarasey.com
www.PatriciaRasey.com

Publisher's Note: This is a work of fiction. Names, characters, places, and
incidents are a product of the author's imagination. Locales and public
names are sometimes used for atmospheric purposes. Any resemblance to
actual people, living or dead, or to businesses, companies, events, institu-
tions, or locales is completely coincidental.

Book Layout ©2013 BookDesignTemplates.com

Ordering Information:
Quantity sales. Special discounts are available on quantity purchases by
corporations, associations, and others. For details, contact the email address
above.

Hawk: Sons of Sangue / Patricia A. Rasey – 1st ed.
ISBN-13: 978-0-9903325-1-0

Dedication

This one is for the Readers! I appreciate you patiently waiting for Hawk's story. It's for you that I have written it!

To Rasey's Rebels ... my small but awesome street team! Thank you for helping spread the word!

To the S.O.S. Role Players and Fan Page. You know who you are and every one of you are awesome! Thanks for entertaining me daily!

To my Beta Readers: Barb Auzins, Becky Martin, Suz Overmier, Michelle Boone, and Suzi Behar! For your patience in reading two chapters at a time!

To Lara Adrian and Kimberly Rocha, for your encouragement, belief in my story, and spreading the word. I love you both!

To my husband, Mark, as always for your love and encouragement. I love you more every day.

And last, and certainly not least, my Lord and Savior Jesus Christ for the talent that He gave me.

CHAPTER ONE

DARK CUMULONIMBUS CLOUDS THREATENED TO LET LOOSE. Cracks of lightning zipped across the horizon and lit the dark ominous skies, laying proof of the forthcoming storm. The likelihood of them making it to their destination before the promised torrential rains hit was looking damn nigh impossible. The winding road could be downright treacherous if the weather report was accurate with its forecast of possible flash flooding. Three to four inches in an hour could cause mud to wash down the mountainous terrain and then they would all be fucked.

Kaleb "Hawk" Tepes glanced to his right at the Sons of Sangue's Road Captain, Alexander "Xander" Dumitru, riding with him at the front of the pack, while the rest of the Sons followed closely behind. The strong winds whipped Alexander's jet-black hair beneath his skull cap against the collar of his shirt. Alexander would never hear him over the roar of the motorcycles' powerful V-Twin engines, so Kaleb nodded to indicate the impending storm. Alexander pointed up the road, then pulled back on his hand and gassed the engine, speeding ahead. Kaleb read his message loud and clear—Kane "Viper" Tepes needed them. Come hell or high water, the Sons of Sangue rose to action when one of their members was in trouble.

Growling at his twin's lousy timing, Kaleb followed suit and headed into the winding curves of Highway 101 traveling north

1

toward Seaside, Oregon. If they hurried, they might be able to make the edge of the small town up the coast in a little over three hours, providing the weather held out. Grayson "Gypsy" Gabor, the motorcycle club, MC's Vice President, who rode right behind the Road Captain, came up on Kaleb's right as Alexander pulled ahead. Grayson didn't look happy at having been called away on a moment's notice at what he considered a patsy's errand. Kaleb figured it had more to do with the fact his plans to get laid had been waylaid.

Then again, Grayson hadn't been a fan of Kane's since he had left the club six months prior without so much as a word of his whereabouts. That was until four hours ago when Kaleb received an urgent message from their puppet club the Sons had aligned themselves with, the Knights. Apparently, Kane had run into a spot of trouble in the coastal town and had asked for backup. The Knights thought the Sons would want to know.

Damn straight they would.

He thanked the fellow biker and told him to inform the rest of the Knights that the Sons would take care of their own. Kaleb didn't know what pissed him off more—the fact that Kane had contacted the Knights instead of his own MC, or that he had disappeared months ago without once contacting his twin. They were blood, for fuck's sake. He had a right to know what was going on with Kane.

Kaleb clenched his teeth against his rising ire. His anger would help no one, so his demand for answers would have to wait. First, his brother needed him and he'd damn well be there for him, no matter what the vamp had done.

The winds picked up as fat drops of rain fell from the sky, hitting his goggles and skull cap. Their luck was just about to run out.

Rounding a steep curve and about to hit the straight away, a pop sounded and Kaleb's rear tire started to shimmy.

"Son of a bitch," Kaleb said, pulling the unstable chopper to the side of the highway. He looked back to see his wide rear tire had blown a hole. Good thing it happened on a curve and not while he had the speedometer needle buried.

The rest of the Sons slowed to a stop as Alexander and Grayson circled back to see what the holdup was. Several motorcycle engines rumbled over the sound of the winds rustling through the ever-greens. Kaleb placed his goggles atop his helmet and let out a stream of curses. Talk about bad luck.

Alexander kicked the center stand down to his idling Harley Davidson, and stepped over the bike. "I think we're about fifteen miles outside of Lincoln City. Or we can keep heading north to Pacific City. Either way, it'll be about a thirty mile round trip. What do you want to do?"

Kaleb cursed again, kicking the flattened back tire for emphasis. "We don't know what kind of trouble Viper's landed in."

"Your call, P," Alexander said.

Rubbing a hand down his chin, he looked north as more fat raindrops hit the asphalt. Prospect Steven "Red Dot" Albu pulled his bike alongside Nicolas "Wheezer" Basil. Nicolas had been Steven's sponsor since the kid had been a hang around some six months back. He hadn't yet earned his patch. He got his nickname from his bright red hair that he kept cut short to the skull. Kaleb thought he showed promise and was a good kid.

"Wheezer, you and Red Dot head to Pacific City. See if you can round me up a tire. There's a motorcycle shop just this side of town. We need it back like yesterday."

Without questioning Kaleb's directive, he picked up his booted foot, kicked up the center stand, and headed down the road, Steven close on his tail. Kaleb watched the red taillights fade into the distance before he gave Alexander and Grayson his attention.

"You think we should call Viper?" Grayson asked.

"Whatever trouble he's into, he hasn't returned my calls. I tried contacting him right after I heard from the Knights. Left him a message but he hasn't called back. I don't know what the hell is going on. You'd think if he was in trouble, he'd answer his fucking cell."

"Maybe he can't," Alexander said, no doubt giving the previous president the benefit of doubt.

His twin and his old lady, Cara Brahnam, had up and hightailed it out of Pleasant shortly after Kaleb had killed Alec Furnar, an ancient primordial vampire with an ax to grind. Kaleb still awaited the fallout from his actions for that little mishap. Killing a primordial was strictly forbidden, not that the piece of shit didn't deserve it. But Kaleb wasn't about to let the bastard get away with his shenanigans. The primordial had not only put Kane at risk, he had threatened to take the life of the woman his brother loved. Kaleb hadn't approved of Kane's choice in partners, but then none of them had. Maybe that was Kane's reason for splitting. Either way, he should have stayed in contact with Kaleb.

An inhuman shriek sounded in the distance, followed by the sound of scraping metal against blacktop. His acute hearing picked it up as if it were mere yards away rather than it likely being a couple of miles up the highway.

Grayson's body went rigid, his nostrils flaring. "Son of a bitch."

Following Grayson's curse, the scent hit Kaleb's olfactory nerves. "Jesus."

There was no mistaking what every vampire in the pack smelled by now—blood. More specifically vampire blood. Kaleb took off on a dead run, heading in the direction Nicolas and Steven had traveled, knowing he could run nearly as fast as any of the motorcycles. Just then, the storm clouds cut loose and pelted Kaleb and his fellow brothers with rain. Rain poured from the heavens, drenching every one of them. The rest of the vampires abandoned their motorcycles alongside the road and followed Kaleb, knowing with the downpour they were much safer on foot than the slick tires of the bikes hitting tarmac.

It took Kaleb mere minutes to reach the gruesome scene. Two downed bikes and two sprawled, headless bodies. A steel cable stretched across the highway, red blood coating the surface. Nicolas and Steven's heads lay not far from the cable.

"Son of a fucking bitch!" *Who the hell?*

Kaleb glanced toward the thick forest, his gaze zeroing up the steep hill about two hundred feet, a flash of movement catching his notice. That's when it hit him, the scent of a primordial and the realization that it was supposed to be him. He normally rode at the head of the pack.

—

"I HAVE GOSSIP," TAMERA CANTRELL said as she entered the small living room to the townhouse Suzi Stevens had shared with her the past six months.

When Suzi had thought it best to leave behind Pleasant, Oregon and the Sons of Sangue, more specifically ... Kaleb, Tamera had taken her in. What the hell had Suzi been thinking? She could never truly run from the man. She could put several miles between them, and her thoughts would always conjure up the likes of Kaleb Tepes. She supposed only in death would her reflections of the man finally cease. At one time she had fancied herself in love with the cold-hearted bastard. That is until he fucked his way through a slew of donors, no doubt knowing how he'd hurt her in the process.

But she had been young and dumb.

No longer. Suzi knew Kaleb for the man ... vampire, he truly was. A self-centered jerk, who cared for no one other than his twin, Kane. Kaleb could rot in hell for all she cared. She fingered the vial of red blood that dangled alongside a red crystal, all suspended about her neck by a black leather cord. The necklace marked her as belonging to a secret society of donors, or rather food for vampires. She could never tell a soul or risk certain death. The society took their pledges seriously. Because of the donors, vampires could feed without fear of exposure. Without the anonymity, the sub-culture would be exposed, hunted down and exterminated. Vampires may have super strength and agility on their side, making it near impossible to kill them, but they were far outnumbered by the human race.

Suzi glanced up from her novel, placing the book on the side table beside her recliner. Her heart picked up its pace, knowing Tamera brought news about Kaleb. She could feel it like a sixth sense. Damn the traitorous pounding of her heart. No matter what her head said otherwise, her heart refused to listen.

"What is it?" she asked, trying to feign disinterest.

"There's been talk at the Blood 'n' Rave," Tamera said, being a donor herself and knowing the Sons firsthand. "Wheezer and Red Dot were killed tonight, beheaded on their way up north. Some rescue mission to help Viper that quickly went south."

"Who else was involved?" Suzi's heart beat so loudly within her ears that she could hardly hear a word the soft-spoken woman had to say.

The fiery, redhead stood about five-foot-ten on a curvy frame. Suzi often times found herself lacking in the beautiful woman's company. Where Suzi had size A-cup breasts, Tamera had an over-abundance, easily spilling out of a D. Men seemed to line up where she was concerned. Tamera hardly noticed, having no ego at all. If anything, she feared the scales tipped on the heavy side.

"All of the Sons had been on the mission."

"Hawk?"

Tamera shifted in her stance, looking to the hardwood planks beneath her size nine feet. She no doubt worried how much to disclose, knowing how hard Suzi had tried to put the past behind her. Suzi had even gone so far as forbidding the younger donor to even whisper his name if she had run into him at the Rave.

"Word has it he was the intended target."

Tamera glanced back up at Suzi, her gaze narrowing as she awaited Suzi's reaction. And though inside she had gone into full-blown panic mode at the idea of Kaleb losing his head, Suzi clasped her hands tightly in her lap and smiled.

"Then he wasn't hurt?"

"No."

"Did the Sons get to Viper?"

"No, not from what I was told. I think they called it a fool's mission."

Suzi thought about that. Kane hadn't been heard from since he and Cara left town following Suzi's departure. She supposed they had their own reasons for leaving. Turning Cara into a vampire wasn't supposed to happen. Suzi, however, was glad that Kane had chosen to ignore the stupid club rules and save her childhood friend from death's clutches, her throat having been slit from ear to ear. Without Kane's interference, Cara would have died.

"So how did it happen?"

"I was told a steel cable was stretched across the highway."

Suzi knew Kaleb, being the president, rode out front with the Road Captain. So why had Wheezer and Red Dot been the unlucky ones to come across the death trap first?

"How did Wheezer and the prospect wind up at front of the pack?"

"Hawk had a flat. They sent Wheezer and Red Dot ahead for a new tire."

"Jesus ... Hawk must blame himself."

"My source says he was still at the Rave as of about twenty minutes ago, downing all liquor in sight."

Suzi turned her wrist and checked the time on her watch. The Rave should've closed over an hour ago. Draven must've taken pity on the poor fool and kept the place open out of respect for the Sons. She contemplated on whether to make the fifteen minute trip into Florence or to leave the blackguard to wallow in his own self-misery. Shaking her head and rolling her eyes, Suzi knew there really wasn't a decision to be made at all. She needed to see for herself that Kaleb was okay. Besides, with his brother MIA, he might need someone to talk to, or so she tried to convince herself.

Fool.

Of course she was. But regardless, Suzi rose from the recliner and headed for her small bedroom, grabbing her purse and the diamond solitaire from the dresser top as an afterthought. She had purchased the engagement ring for just such occasions. Men tended to leave engaged women off their radar. In this case, it would be Kaleb's. Suzi needed to be smart and guard her heart, because Kaleb was the one vampire who had the ability to irreparably crush it.

Suzi shoved her feet into a pair of black leather flats by the door as Tamera watched. Kaleb had always been her biggest weakness, and Tamera knew that. But she would also know trying to talk Suzi out of going would be a waste of her breath. The thought of someone or something trying to hurt Kaleb was like a call to action. Not that she could protect him from harm, but she'd be damned if she stood by without doing anything.

Suzi had retired herself from donating, when she came to live with Tamera. Though no one ever left the donors. Once pledged, you're in the society for life. But a donor could decide to stop providing the nourishment. Her mind traveled back to the night she had made up her mind to leave and change her life once and for all. She stood in the parking lot of the Sons of Sangue's clubhouse, arguing with Kaleb over her spending time in his home, more specifically his bed. Kane had only meant to protect her and Cara Brahnam from a psycho primordial vampire wanting to kill Cara. He had no idea of the history she and Kaleb shared.

She had followed him into the night, proposing a perfectly doable living arrangement when he had shut her up with a kiss. And damn if that kiss hadn't done the job. Her toes had curled and left her breathless as he sped away on his chopper. That's when she knew she had to leave. Staying in Pleasant while he carried on with other women was no longer an option for her.

"So just like that, you're going to chase after him?" Tamera asked, bringing her thoughts back to their discussion.

Suzi sucked in a deep breath. "It's not like that."

"You positive? Because it sure looks like it. You forget, I know Hawk too. You're just setting yourself up to get hurt, Suzi."

"That would require me to care again."

Tamera laughed. "It's three in the morning. Heading off to the Rave doesn't already say that?"

Suzi knew the truth of it, but damn it she didn't care at the moment. She had to see for herself that Kaleb wasn't beating himself up for losing two of his brothers. It could've been him. And if she were honest with herself, then she'd admit that was the real reason she needed to see him ... because it could've been him. Losing Kaleb, and never having the option to see him again, scared the living hell out of her.

"I may be the biggest kind of fool right now, Tamera, but Hawk may need me."

Tamera shook her head. "Then you are a fool if you believe that. Hawk Tepes doesn't need anyone."

CHAPTER TWO

IVE EMPTY BOTTLES OF JACK DANIEL'S BLACK LABEL SAT ON the bar's scarred surface and he felt none of the damned alcohol. Fuck his vampire genes for regenerating at such a high rate that he felt the lasting side effects for no more than a few blessed minutes. His morose mood had chased most of the Sons away, all of them except for Alexander who sat at his right, booted feet kicked up on the bar and nursing an iced tea. He understood, in some capacity, how Kaleb felt because he would've lost his head as well had it not been for Kaleb's blown tire.

But rather than imbibing in alcohol—the man never did—he sat quietly sipping an unsweetened tea, lost in his own dark thoughts. The two hardly exchanged a word in the last couple of hours. Even Draven had retired to his office and allowed them their peace. Other than Kaleb and Alexander, the club sat empty, industrial music playing in the background. The ravers had gone home long ago after Draven had raised the house lights and closed the joint.

Kaleb swirled the last of the Jack in his glass before taking it to his lips. He downed the contents, feeling the burn in his esophagus. Sucking in a deep breath, he looked to the ceiling. Hunger gnawed at his gut. Maybe he should've taken advantage of the couple of donors who had braved his mood and approached him early on. In-

13

stead, he had sent them fleeing with a menacing growl. No one dared to approach him after that, which had been his intent.

"You going to sit here and drink another fifth?" Alexander asked, not bothering to look up from the condensation gathering on his glass. It wasn't an accusation, just an inquisition.

"What's the point?"

Alexander didn't answer, only shrugged and took another sip.

Kaleb ran a hand over his mouth and down his jaw. "You know Wheezer and Red Dot died because of my actions," he finally said, voicing what neither had since finding Nicolas and Steven lying prone on the asphalt.

Alexander slowly nodded, pursing his lips. "Yeah, but not much you can do about it now, is there?"

His anger rolled in his gut, mixing with the alcohol. Had he been a normal man, he would have been on all fours heaving his guts, or worse yet, dead from alcohol poisoning. But he wasn't normal, and the only way to kill him would be to stop his heart from beating by a direct shot or sever his head from his shoulders. At least Nicolas and Steven had not suffered. After the Sons had returned with an enclosed trailer and carted off the corpses, Kaleb had tried to reach his twin again with no luck. The Knights had taken their place and traveled to Seaside, but Kane was nowhere to be found.

The whole fucking thing had been a setup.

All for retaliation. Kaleb knew it with every fiber of his being. He had broken a cardinal rule and taken a primordial life. The punishment was death, and Nicolas and Steven had taken his place. It should have been him. Moisture gathered in his eyes. Son of a bitch, his self-loathing couldn't get any higher. He had made the decision to end Alec's life. He had taken on that responsibility.

"Why don't you head out, Xander. I don't need a damn babysitter."

"It's not your fault."

"It is and you fucking know it."

"Any of us would've done the same thing. That primordial deserved what he got. Maybe we need to let Mircea know that. I'd be willing to go to Italy on your behalf."

Mircea II of Wallachia, brother of his great grandfather many times over, Vlad III, was stepfather to Rosalee, the one responsible for this whole mess and his twin's mate, one Kane couldn't unsaddle himself from. Once a vampire takes a mate, it's for life. Kaleb's only regret? That he hadn't taken Rosalee's life along with Alec's. After all, the primordial had been acting on her orders. Rosalee had wanted Kane to pay for having her banished to Italy for the cause of their son Ion's death. Too bad for Kane it hadn't ended his life-long chain of taking her as a mate.

"No one needs to go on my behalf, Xander. This is my battle. I'll deal with it and answer for my actions."

"You wouldn't have to if fucking Viper hadn't been dicking that detective bitch."

Kaleb knew the truth to that, but he'd be damned if he'd blame his brother. Kane loved Cara, that much was obvious. And because of that, Kaleb would respect his decisions and therefore stand behind him. Even if that meant answering to the primordials for Alec's demise. If he had it to do all over again, he'd rip his head off with his bare hands instead of using the knife. Alec Funar had been a sick fuck and got his just end.

Kaleb bared his suddenly elongated fangs on Alexander, his ire held barely in check. "You won't refer to Viper's woman negatively. Regardless of how it came about, he loves her and we will respect that. Besides, Cara's one of us now. There's no changing that."

Alexander nodded, thankfully letting the topic of Kane and Cara drop. His brother needed to hightail his ass back to Pleasant and stop hiding from his actions. Surely once he's back in the day-to-day activities, the rest of the Sons will come to accept Cara. She may not be able to mate with Kane because of Rosalee, but in Kane's eyes Cara was his only. His mate was dead to him. As so, the Sons needed to see it as such, regardless of club rules. Kane had broken the rule to turn Cara without club permission. Because of his actions he had stepped down as club pres, Kaleb taking over the reins. He had paid the price and should be forgiven for his actions.

"I'm heading out."

Kaleb grit his teeth, knowing he should do the same. Staying here and drinking all the Jack in sight wouldn't make a damn bit of difference. Maybe it was time to head back to the clubhouse.

"Round up the brothers tomorrow. We'll need to deal with the bodies … give them a proper send-off."

"You going to be okay?"

"Yeah. I'll be heading out myself here in a few. I promised Draven I'd turn down the lights."

"Be safe, my friend."

"You as well."

Alexander placed his half-finished glass of tea on the bar, then turned and headed for the entrance. Kaleb heard the door open, then whoosh closed, followed by the soft click of the latch. Finally rising, he walked behind the bar and started tossing the empty Jack bottles into the trash. Taking his and Alexander's glass from the bar, he placed them next to the sink for tomorrow's bartender to clean. Footfalls caught his attention before his nose picked up the sweet scent of her return.

Fuck my life.

Why the hell did she pick this exact moment to walk back into his life? Not when his willpower had all but abandoned him. Damn her to hell and back for her lousy timing, and damn him for desiring to leap the short distance and take her into his arms. As he glanced up to see Suzi Stevens' standing before him, the bar the only barrier to keep him from doing what he hungered for, their gazes locked and held. His heart beat heavily, drowning out the industrial music. Jesus, his fangs still in their elongated state now ached for appeasement, while he watched her nervously stroke the vial dangling about her neck. The vial that gave him permission to take his fill.

A white billowy, button-down top dropped past her waist, unbuttoned to just above the rise of her breasts, hiding her pert tits from his view. A pair of black yoga pants completed the lower half, hugging her like a second skin. His gaze strayed and held on her long, lean legs. He could easily imagine picking her up and having her wrap those muscular thighs about his waist, her sweet center hugging the erection now plaguing him.

Hawk scrubbed his face with his palms as he tried like hell not to envision her sweet, plump lower lip that she drew between her teeth, or the crystalline blue eyes that held concern for him. He needed to get a handle on his emotions. Desire ruled his dick, which at the moment couldn't be trusted at making sound decisions.

"Hello, Hawk."

SIX MONTHS OF DENYING WHAT she felt for Kaleb Tepes and it sailed right out the window now that she stood before him in his vampire form. Beauty at its finest. Jesus, did they make them any hotter? One look and her libido decided to kick in from its dormant state. Not really what she needed at the moment, knowing full well Kaleb would be able to detect her rising desire from a mile away, let alone a few feet with only a bar separating them.

Not fair.

No man or vampire should be allowed to possess that amount of sex appeal. But she would be damned before she ever allowed him to use that to control her. He had caused her more mental anguish than any human being ever had the right to. She had lived this long without the likes of Kaleb Tepes, and she would continue to do so. Steeling her resolve and her shoulders, she raised her chin and faced him head on.

Remember, he only has the ability to hurt you if you allow him.

His dark black curls lay in soft disarray, brushing his shoulders, adding to his untamed presence. It had to have grown at least an inch since the last time she had laid eyes on him. His obsidian black eyes, fringed with impossibly long black lashes, held her in place, her image reflected in their mirror-like quality. His nostrils flared and the tips of his fangs protruded just below his upper lip as his red tongue darted out and moistened them. A shiver passed through her, already knowing what that tongue was capable of.

"I don't suppose you came here to fuck me."

Well, that kind of talk certainly wasn't going to help her rising desire situation. Not when her libido all but rose up and said, *"Yes, please."*

"Crude as ever I see."

His nostrils flared again. No denying she hungered for him and he knew it. Bastard. He could smell it. Pointless to refute what he already knew to be the truth.

"I came to see if you're okay."

He shrugged, bracing his hands on the bar top. The corded muscles in his arms tightened. She'd never get tired of looking at him. Kaleb looked as if he'd been carved of stone. Tattoos traveled his right shoulder to the wrist in a sleeve of color, while his left sported a black tribal cuff winding about the biceps in an intricate pattern.

"Why don't you bring your pretty little ass over here and I'll show you how okay I am."

Suzi closed the distance, leaving the bar as a separator, and laid her pocketbook on the surface. "You can joke away what happened all you want, Hawk, but I know you're hurting inside."

"You don't know shit about me."

"Look, Hawk—"

"No." He pointed a forefinger at her. "You're a cold-hearted bitch. You've already proven how much you care about another being. Why don't you take your righteous ass back out that door and go back to wherever you've been hiding the last six months. I don't need you."

Tears welled in her eyes. She knew Kaleb still held his nephew against her, and the fact that she didn't mourn his death as he thought she should. But he didn't know a thing about her and Ion's relationship. Kaleb had never given her a chance to explain, and in the end, it had been better to leave him with his beliefs.

"I loved Ion."

"You sure had a funny way of showing it when I told you about his death."

Suzi gritted her teeth. She would be damned if she'd allow him to guilt her into a confession. She would take her and Ion's secret to her grave. She owed Ion that much.

"I didn't come here to bring up old wounds."

"Then why are you here?"

"Because I fooled myself into thinking I cared..." She stopped herself from saying about you. "I heard about Wheezer and Red Dot. I had to come to see if you were all right. I'm sorry now that I did. I should've let you wallow in your self-hatred."

He stared hard at her, enough so she wished she could read what was going on behind those black hypnotic eyes. She wasn't sure if he wanted to leap the counter and strangle her, or kiss her senseless. Though she preferred the latter, Suzi knew the repercussions of those actions would crush her. Before she could stop him, he vaulted the bar effortlessly and now stood mere inches from her. She could smell Jack Daniel's on him, that and his intoxicating musk. Her heart nearly leapt from her chest.

Kaleb leaned in, his nose brushing the soft skin beneath her right ear, causing a flutter in her lower abdomen. His canines scraped across the delicate flesh, telling her he was a hairsbreadth away from biting her.

"I find I'm ravenous."

"Your problem, not mine." Suzi stiffened her spine, ready for him to do as he desired regardless of her wishes. "I didn't come here to offer you nourishment."

His right arm snaked around her, keeping her from fleeing. The fingers of his free hand toyed with the glass vial. "You're a donor. You offer me what I need."

"I can't stop you from feeding."

"I hear a *but* in there."

"I'm retired."

Kaleb stood back, releasing Suzi to stare down at her. Then he chuckled. His mirth misplaced given the situation.

"I don't find that funny."

"No?" He raised one black brow. "I find that rich. Suzi Stevens who offered her blood up to any Son who asked."

Her brows drew together. "It's what a donor does."

"Yes, their blood ... but not always do they spread their thighs."

"I am so done here. Go fuck yourself, Hawk."

When she turned to leave, Kaleb gripped her wrist and spun her back into his hold so that her back nestled against the erection he didn't try to conceal. She knew he might not like it, might even hate the idea, but he desired her.

"I told you, I'm hungry," he whispered. His warm breath passed over the shell of her ear. An ache settled between her thighs. She'd die first.

"And I told you I retired myself."

"Then I just un-retired you."

And with that, he sank his fangs into the soft spot just beneath her   ear.

CHAPTER THREE

H IS BALLS TIGHTENED AT THE FIRST TASTE OF HER SWEET blood as it flowed easily over his tongue like sweet ambrosia. He hadn't fed in a couple of nights, which wasn't extremely long by any standards, and not so much time that he had taken on the translucent death chill of not feeding. As long as he fed a half pint or so every two to three days, it was enough to sustain his kind. They didn't require much, and draining a human wasn't necessary. But damn if Suzi Stevens' blood didn't tempt him like heroine to an addict. One taste of her life's fluid and he was a goner.

A moan escaped her lips as the musk of her rising desire wafted to his nose. He inhaled deeply. His dick throbbed against the valley of her lower back, knowing that his feeding only intensified her craving. Kaleb bit back his need to strip her skin-tight leggings down to her thighs and bury himself to the hilt. He envisioned placing her hands on the bar and taking her from behind, his fingers digging into the soft flesh of her sweet ass until he had nothing left to give.

Suzi had always been his Achilles' heel. His entire reasoning at keeping her at arm's length for years. She was like a siren's call to his wounded soul. And tonight he had caved, given in to the need to feed from her and damn himself for longing for more. She reached down, squeezing his jean-clad thighs, her fingernails digging into

23

the material. Kaleb knew she fought the lust caused from his feeding sluicing through her body.

"Damn you, Kaleb Tepes," she cried out, pleading him to stop.

It wasn't her words that had him withdrawing his fangs though, but the tears he heard in her voice. Her disdain of him obviously ran so deep that she couldn't stomach the idea he could give her pleasure. He pushed her away, wiping his mouth with the back of his hand. Sucking in air through clenched teeth, Kaleb watched her closely. Her hand covered the wound on her neck, one that he should have licked to aid in healing. Instead, he chose to allow the sting of his bite to remain. For selfish reasons, he didn't want to spare her. Besides, without the healing qualities of his salvia, the angry wounds would last for days.

Kaleb wanted her to think of him every time she looked in the mirror. *Who the fuck was he kidding?* He wanted to erase Ion's memory from her. Every fiber of his being wanted to stake his claim. Good enough reason to keep her at bay. But now that she was back, no way in hell would he allow her to disappear again. He might not fuck her, but he sure as hell would feed from her.

Slowly turning, her eyes downcast, she reached for her pocketbook on the bar. Surprising him, her cheeks were dry ... not one wet trek from tears marred her pale cheeks. Just as she snatched her bag and meant to head for the exit again, Kaleb stopped her, this time with a tender hand on her shoulder. He heard her sniffle, knew that her bravado slipped and she was damn close to weeping.

"You will allow no one else to feed from you."

Her shoulders stiffened, her muscles tensed. When she turned to face him, he could tell his softly spoken demand pissed her off. *Good.* Her anger he could handle.

"I told you I was retired. No one feeds from me—and that includes you, Hawk."

He grit his teeth, his fangs now retracted. "As I said, I un-retired you."

"You can't do that. A donor has a right—"

"I can and I just did. My desire trumps yours. Or have you forgotten the oath you took when you became a donor? Unless I harm you in any way, you cannot refuse me."

"Why is it so important for you to claim me?"

"To claim you, sweetheart ... would mean I desire to fuck you."

A muscle ticked in her cheek. "Forgive me for misunderstanding then the pencil poking at my back."

Kaleb laughed, the sound cruel to even his ears. "Shall we test the size? I believe you already have and found it to your liking."

"I regret the day I allowed you anywhere near me."

"Just remember, sweetheart, you started this by seeking me out. I didn't come looking for you." He held her clear blues eyes captive. "If I say that I alone feed from you, then no one else shall take the pleasure in your blood."

"And if *I* allow every Son the right?"

Kaleb grinned. "No one would dare cross me."

A lone tear slipped down her cheek. "Why?"

"Because you hate me."

She nodded, then looked to the tiled floor.

"By being my personal donor, you will suffer every time I slake my thirst."

She visibly swallowed, then brought her gaze back up. Fire radiated from the depths. "You're a cruel bastard."

"That I am." He winked. "But I promise you, dear Suzi, by the time I'm done with you, you'll be begging me to fuck you. And when you do ask, I will and I won't stop until your last thought of your sweet Ion is erased."

Suzi's breath hitched. "You don't know anything about my relationship with your nephew."

"I know that you didn't care when I came to you, to tell you of his death," he said, gritting his teeth.

"I grieved in private. I didn't need every one of the Sons privy to my pain."

"So you say. Then you don't deny you loved him?"

She shook her head. "I loved Ion deeply."

"You slept with me before meeting Ion, yet you forgot me so easily."

"You slept with everyone, Hawk. Don't try to convince me that I was special."

"I wouldn't dream of it, sweetheart."

She rubbed the twin red puncture wounds on her neck. "If we're done here, I think it's time I headed back."

"To where?"

"None of your business."

"I just made you my business. Should I need to feed?"

"You'll find me here, in a club full of ravers. If you're serious about forcing this issue, then I prefer to meet you in public."

Kaleb mulled over her petition, knowing full well he could deny her again if he chose to. But instead he decided to allow her this one request ... for now. "Don't force me to come look for you."

"I wouldn't dream of it."

And with that she turned, her hips swaying as she headed for the exit. His dick stood up and took notice again. As she reached the door, one hand slammed into the lever opening it outward, while the other raised in a one-finger salute. Kaleb chuckled. She had just flipped him the bird. He did love her spunk. Too bad she had first belonged to his nephew, even admitted as much with her declaration of love for Ion.

Kaleb sat hard on the barstool, still gazing at the door she had exited through. Suzi had been correct. He had slept with everyone in sight following his sexual encounter with her. She had been young then ... much too young to handle the likes of him. And yet, even though he had tried to fuck her from his memory, he hadn't even come close. He ran a hand down his whiskered jaw, and sighed. Demanding that she be his personal donor? Yeah, he was pretty sure he'd be the one regretting that.

"HELLO," KALEB SAID INTO THE receiving end of the phone. Still groggy from a deep sleep, he had answered it blindly, having no idea what time of day it was or how many hours he had slept. His black drapes kept any light from filtering through since he normally preferred to sleep through the biggest part of the day. He was a late night man. Something about the moon and the stars that was preferable and calming compared to the bright afternoon sun, not to mention the sensitivity it caused his eyes.

Following Suzi's departure at the Rave, Kaleb had hopped on his bike and headed out in no particular direction. He needed the open road to clear his head and shake off his raging hormones. The cool wind caressing his skin and damp morning air clinging to him, he rode as if hell nipped at his heels. It wasn't until the first rays of dawn warmed the morning dew before he pulled into the gravel clubhouse parking lot. He had pulled up next to Grayson's candy apple red custom Sportster and a blue Nissan he didn't recognize. That was certainly nothing new for his roommate. Grayson rarely came home from the Rave alone.

"This better be fucking important," he grumbled, not giving the person on the other end a chance to speak. "Do you know what the hell time it is?"

"I don't honestly know, bro. Here in Italy it's just about time to hit the clubs. I guess that makes it about noon your time."

"Viper? What the hell are you doing in Italy?"

He heard a female voice speaking in the background before Kane said, "Cara says to tell you hello ... and before you say anything, it better be nice. I'd hate to have to come back to Pleasant just to kick your ass."

Kaleb closed his eyes and sighed. "I wouldn't dream of insulting your bit—woman."

Kane chuckled, the sound rich, making Kaleb realize how much he had missed his twin. "So what has you all so fired up you felt the need to call me four times in the last several hours?"

"If you would've answered your fucking phone, you'd know."

"You could've left a message. I wasn't at the flat where I forgot my cell. As soon as I saw the missed calls... Well, I'm talking to you now. So what the hell?"

"We got word from the Knights you called, informing them you needed their help."

"Why would I call them and not my own MC?"

Kaleb had asked himself the same question. Now, in hindsight, seemed pretty stupid to believe the other biker when he had called. But he hadn't been able to get a hold of Kane. He didn't want to take a chance that his twin might really need his help. He scratched his head, mussing his hair further and yawned.

"I don't know. Sounded urgent, they said you were in Seaside. We told him we take care of our own. I rounded up the guys and we hit the road."

"Why the hell would one of the Knights send out a bogus distress signal? You know the bastard's name?"

"No. I was more worried about answering your distress call."

"You get the phone number?"

"No. It came up *Unknown Caller*."

"I'll call Red and see what the fuck gives. Anything else?"

Kaleb sucked in a deep breath to calm his anger over losing his fellow bikers. Kane would be livid. But Kaleb needed him in Oregon, for crying out loud, not Italy. "Yeah. Wheezer and Red Dot are dead."

Kane let a stream of curses fly, before he inquired, "How?"

"It was a setup. A steel cable was stretched across the road ... took both their heads. They didn't have a chance."

"Jesus!"

Kaleb heard Cara's question and Kane reiterating the conversation to her before he came back on the line. "If you were all on the road on some bogus rescue mission for me, weren't you supposed to be out front, Pres?"

"You're getting the picture. It should have been Xander and me. I got a flat and we stopped. We sent Wheezer and Red Dot on ahead to get me a tire."

Kaleb lifted the cell from his ear as Kane let loose another stream of curses. When he finally finished, Kaleb said, "It had primordial scent all over it, Viper. I couldn't be one-hundred-percent positive because we were getting some pretty heavy storms, but I'd stake my life on it. Now answer my question. Why are you in Italy?"

Kane was silent for so long that at first Kaleb thought he meant to ignore his request. And in truth, it probably wasn't any of his business. But considering Kaleb's recent activities, he thought Kane owed him that much.

"I came here to see Mircea. Took me nearly five months to get an audience with him since I'm not really one of his favorite people at the moment," he finally said. "I wanted to wait to tell you in person. I needed to get this thing dissolved with Rosalee."

"And?"

"The bitch is dead to me. Mircea eventually granted my wish to mate with Cara. Let me tell you, he wasn't happy with the way it all transpired or with a primordial dead as a result. But because it all came about due to Rosalee's actions, he granted my petition."

"And what of Rosalee?"

"She's MIA. To me that just further proves her involvement with Alec Funar ... that and the text messages we found on his phone the night you took his head."

"You think she's here? That she might be responsible?"

"I really don't know. Doesn't make sense she'd go after you. Look, I'll pack my shit here and Cara and I will head out. I'm coming home, bro. We'll find this fuck responsible for Wheezer and Red Dot's death. One way or another."

"Viper? You might want to also find out if any of the other primordials are missing from Italy. This may be retaliation for me taking Alec's head and not a result of Rosalee going off the deep end after all. In any case, I doubt this ended with Wheezer and Red Dot. Whoever is responsible for this shit isn't going to stop until I'm dead. I'd like to get to them first."

"I'll ask around. You fucking stay safe, Hawk. I lost my son. I sure in the hell don't want to lose you. I'll be back as soon as I can get some answers here."

The cell went silent. Kaleb tossed it on the bed. Two damned hyped to sleep now, he swung his feet to the floor, stood and headed for the showers, not bothering with briefs. Just as he left his room, Grayson's door opened and a pretty petite blonde stepped out. She perused his body from head to toe. Not bothering to conceal her interest, then offered him a sexy smile.

"Aren't you just a sexy thing," she said as Kaleb noted the vial about her neck. She must've been fairly new to the society of donors as he didn't recognize her from the club.

"Hit the road, darlin'. I'm really not in the mood for company right now."

She approached Kaleb, her fingers trailing over his pecs and down his abs. "Are you sure? I could possibly assist you with your hunger ... be it blood or something a bit more intimate."

He gripped her fingers to keep them from sliding farther south. "Sorry, I'm not in the market for a donor."

"How about friends with benefits?"

"First, I'm not your friend. And second, I don't need a fuck buddy."

"That's too bad." She smiled. "I would've liked to have had a little fun with you. Maybe another time?"

Grayson emerged from his room with a yawn. She looked back at his MC brother and winked. "See you later, sweets. Call me?"

"Go home, Shel. If I need you, I know where the hell to find you."

Not in the least put off by his crude send-off, she walked to the door, then turned back and kissed the air. Kaleb shook his head. No ego issues that one.

Kaleb turned his attention to Grayson. "Where the hell do you find them?"

Grayson offered a sheepish grin, then headed for the bar and pulled down a bottle of Jack. "Shot?"

Kaleb shook his head. "Shower first, then you and I have a couple of bodies we need to prepare for a proper send-off." Just before he shut the door, he looked back at Grayson. "By the way, Viper will soon be heading home."

"Where the hell's he been?"

"Italy. Went to see Mircea."

"No shit?"

Kaleb shut the door, turned on the water and stepped beneath the steaming showerhead. He thought of the offer the little blonde had made. It's not that he couldn't have used the sexual release, but there was only one woman who had his attention at the moment, and he be damned if he knew what to do about it.

CHAPTER FOUR

UZI STARED AT HER REFLECTION IN THE MIRROR. SHE LOOKED like she had been run through hell and back. After returning from the Blood 'n' Rave following her confrontation with Kaleb, she hadn't been able to get much, if any, sleep. She had found herself tossing and turning until the first rays of dawn peeked through the white wooden slats of her blinds. She really hadn't thought about the light color before, but in hindsight, maybe she should've purchased room-darkening shades. So instead of sleeping until noon as she had desired, she crawled out of bed and started the coffee ... fully leaded.

That was six hours ago.

Nearly a full pot later and she had finally decided to step under the shower. Standing in a black lace, matching bra and panty ensemble, Suzi stared her reflection and the twin holes marring her otherwise unblemished skin of her neck. The bastard could've aided in the healing by simply licking the wounds following the retraction of his teeth, leaving nothing more than faint red marks today. But no, he had felt the need to mark her, and in turn, cause her to suffer the irritation. And far worse, she knew he wanted her to think of him every time she looked in the mirror or rubbed the aching twin holes. His ego governed his actions. She'd have to wear a scarf wrapped about her neck when she made a much needed trip to the store. Thankfully, she had the day off from work. Try explaining away the telltale sign of vampires to her coworkers.

Really, anaconda bite. You should have seen the size of that sucker.

Disgusted with Kaleb and herself for being foolish enough to track him down, she stepped into a pair of dark blue, straight-legged jeans and pulled them over her slim hips, fastening the button. Suzi grabbed a maroon pullover from the hanger and slipped it over her drying hair. The blouse hung loose past her waist to cover her back-side. Normally she preferred clothes with a bit more flash. Today, however, she preferred to grocery shop unnoticed. Had it not been for the lack of food in the house, she wouldn't even leave the town-house and sulk otherwise in private.

Hell, she had asked for this.

Whatever made her think she could go up against Kaleb Tepes and not get hurt in the process? Technically, other than the sting of the bite marks and her wounded pride, he hadn't exactly caused her real pain. Though eventually, the son of a bitch would hurt her and no doubt break her heart if she were ever foolish enough to drop her guard. Kaleb was a selfish bastard who loved no one other than his family and MC. He went through women like water through a sieve. And for that reason alone, she had worked damn hard over the years to ignore his existence. Well, other than her one night of weakness when she thought to proposition his twin, Kane. What better way to make Kaleb seethe than to sleep with his brother? But Suzi's plan hadn't worked and Kane had turned her down flat. The vampire had not been available to her, or anyone for that matter, because he had actually been in love with her best friend from high school, Cara Brahnam, though at the time he hadn't been aware of it.

When it came to Kaleb Tepes, Suzi was way out of her league. So keeping her distance had become a priority to protect her vulnerable heart. In the end, the one thing that had worked in her favor and earned her his scorn was his nephew Ion Tepes. Kaleb made it obvious he resented her affair with Ion and wanted nothing to do with her. And of course, she had never bothered to share what her true relationship with his brother's son had been. Certainly, she had loved Ion the way a sister loved a brother. They spent a great deal of time together, giving her many wonderful memories following his death. She had been a donor for Ion on several occasions when a lover hadn't been available to him, but the feeding had always been plutonic in nature. Suzi was of the wrong sex to entice Ion on any other level and Ion appreciated having Suzi as a buffer. As long as his father, mother, and uncle, not to mention the rest of the Sons thought that Suzi was his old lady, then no one would guess the real truth.

Suzi had taken his secret to the grave.

It had never been hers to tell in the first place.

The door to townhouse opened, then shut, indicating Tamera had probably finished her day at the *Florence Times*. Tamera started there as a journalist several months back, finally landing her dream job. Though now she spent her days covering social events about the city, and waiting for the day they actually gave her a juicy assignment worthy of the front page.

Grabbing her silk scarf from the bathroom doorknob, where she had hung it as she finished dressing, Suzi headed down the narrow staircase for the living area where she found Tamera putting on a new pot of coffee.

"Hey," Suzi said as she dropped her scarf by her pocketbook on an end table next to the worn, brown leather sofa.

Tamera turned and smiled, her green eyes turning up at the corners. "How did last night go?"

Suzi pulled out a stool next to the center island and sat, leaning her chin onto her palm. "I'll take one of those when you get the pot made."

"Bad night?"

"First clue?"

Tamera laughed. "Your mood. I take it things didn't go well with Hawk."

"You would be correct."

Her roommate's gaze landed on the red wounds on Suzi's neck. "Wow, I thought you'd given up on feeding those bloody vampires. Your words, not mine," she quickly added.

"Yeah, well apparently Hawk decided to change my mind."

"You okay with that?"

Suzi shook her head. "Not that he cares."

"You want to talk about it?" Tamera took a seat beside Suzi, the coffeepot beginning to gurgle.

Coffee always seemed to perk her up. But after the pot she had already consumed, if she didn't put something in her stomach, she'd wind up with caffeine shakes to rival all others. Suzi grabbed a banana from the basket on the island, peeled it and took a bite.

Finally she said, "Hawk decided I should be his personal donor."

"Are you serious? You told him to go fly a kite, right?"

"I tried. But according to him, his desires trump mine." Suzi took another bite of the banana.

"You think I should take this to Draven?"

Draven, the infamous owner of the Blood 'n' Rave, headed the donor society, put into place by the Sons themselves as someone who had their complete trust. It was his job to make sure all donors kept the rules without question, and his to hand out justice or discipline should he or the Sons see need. No one became a donor without Draven's approval.

"Absolutely not," Suzi said, tossing the banana peel into the trashcan behind her. "I'm not exactly on good terms with Draven. After I thought to retire myself six months ago, following the debacle with Viper, he's hardly spoken to me. I know darn well he'd side with Hawk. After all, he answers to him. What do you think?"

"I'd say you're right. Hawk wants you as a personal drinking fountain. You don't have much of a choice in the matter."

Tamera stood and walked back over to the coffeepot, pouring them each a cup. She carried them back to the island and placed Suzi's in front of her before adding a heavy dose of cream and bit of sugar into her own. She then retook her seat and patted Suzi's hand, noting the solitaire still present on Suzi's ring finger.

"I take it the ring didn't dissuade him?"

Suzi held out her left hand and looked at the sparkling carat, then groaned. "I completely forgot that I wore it and I don't think Hawk noticed either. At least he didn't mention it." Her lips turned down. "I'm sure it wouldn't have mattered much in his decision. But I'll keep it on for the time being. He's bound to notice it sooner or later. Maybe with luck on my side, it will have him recanting his demand."

"I'm here for you, Suzi. Anytime you need someone to talk to. You know that."

Suzi nodded, knowing the hopelessness of the situation. If the president of the Sons of Sangue wanted to feed from you, then you complied without question. She blew across the surface of the coffee, causing ripples to form before taking a sip.

"Excellent coffee."

"Of course." Tamera smiled again. "You make yours far too weak. So what's on the agenda for today? You look like you were on your way out."

"I was going to run to the store, stock up on some groceries. We're running pretty low. Otherwise, I'm staying in. Not like I want to run around town with this." Suzi indicated the twin marks on her neck.

Tamera grimaced. "So why did Hawk choose to leave them?"

"Undoubtedly his ego."

"They look sore."

"They hurt like hell ... the bastard."

"You want some salve?"

"No, unfortunately I'll live. But I *will* make him regret his decision to claim me as his personal donor. I'll make him so miserable he'll beg me back to retirement."

"That's my girl. Don't let him get away with being an ass." Tamera winked. "Now, about those groceries. How about I go change into something a little more casual and go with you? We'll buy some wine, rent a movie, and have a movie night. Spend the evening in with a huge bowl of popcorn. What do you say?"

"Sounds like an awesome idea."

"I'll only be a moment." Tamera placed her coffee cup into the sink, then headed for the second story of the townhouse.

Spending the night watching movies and getting her mind off Kaleb seemed like a perfect way to lift her spirits and get her mind off one pig-headed vampire.

"Let's rent *What's Your Number?*" she called out so Tamera could hear her on the second floor. "I could stand to watch Chris Evans run around half nude for about an hour and a half. That man tickles my libido."

And if she were perfectly honest with herself, so did Kaleb, but she'd be damned before she'd admit as much to him.

"Perfect." Tamera laughed as she descended the stairs, handbag in her hand. "Love that movie. Chris Evans is the perfect distraction to an otherwise crummy day."

Suzi wrapped her scarf about her neck and grabbed her own pocketbook. "Let's go get us that movie and a very big bottle of wine," she said with a smile as they headed out of the townhouse and down the front steps. Kaleb Tepes be damned.

KALEB SAT ALONE IN THE MEETING room of the clubhouse at one end of the long table, his finger absently tracing a scar on the wood as he awaited the rest of the MCs arrival, and contemplated the previous evening and his foolhardy demand. Suzi had stood twenty feet in front of him like a fallen angel, a healing balm to the gaping wound left by the death of his two MC brothers. The concern lacing her vivid-blue eyes had the power to undo him, to unravel the carefully thatched barrier he had constructed to guard his heart. He had made a promise to himself years ago that no woman would ever hold the reins to his happiness. Kaleb had watched what Rosalee had done to his twin, nearly destroying Kane when her actions had caused the death of his only son and vowed that he'd never allow any woman to have that kind of power over him ... ever.

His first instinct had been to leap across the bar, feed from her, taste the ambrosia of her blood, then fuck her until he no longer cared that she had once belonged to his late nephew. Kaleb had fought with every fiber of his being not to act on pure animal instinct. So instead of taking her against the bar as he desired, he set out to piss her off, to earn her scorn so that she would never again look upon him with pity, concern for his well-being. He needed her hatred to hold her at bay. Her anger he could handle in the worst of days, but her compassion and empathy were best left to someone else.

Oh, he detested Suzi all right, hated the space she took up in his universe. His nephew had died a horrible death and Kaleb had felt as if a part of him had died with Ion. He couldn't imagine the anguish his brother felt, nor did he want to. He wasn't even sure what he expected out of Suzi, but the blank, ice-filled stare wasn't it. Not a single tear had been shed, as if Ion's life had meant nothing to her. Kaleb had known then and there that Suzi Stevens' was a cold-hearted bitch.

And although he had slept with her once, long before Ion, his dick never failed to remind him how damn much he wanted another taste. She was like nectar to a honeybee. Suzi had been a mere eighteen years old at the time. Young, impressionable and provocative as sin. He'd never forgotten how they had laid in each other's arms, her dark hair bedridden and sexy as hell as she nipped his shoulder with her teeth and begged him to drink from her. Jesus, no woman had ever had that kind of affect on him. Suzi had a firm hold on his nuts and it scared the hell out of him. Women made you all stupid in the head. Kane and Cara lay proof to that. Kane broke all the rules because of the woman he loved. Hell no. He'd never give Suzi that kind of power over him. So instead, he'd set out to piss her off any chance he got.

His mind traveled back to the kiss they shared six months ago, the one that had him crawling on the back of his chopper and heading out in the middle of the night. Kane had promised to protect her and Cara from the primordial that had landed in Pleasant ... but Kaleb hadn't offered his services. And he'd be damned if he trusted himself enough to stay under the same roof with Suzi. So like the coward he was, Kaleb rode off into the night and prayed she'd be absent upon his return. Some higher power had been listening and granted him his wish. Suzi had been gone when he arrived back at the clubhouse long hours later. He hadn't laid eyes on her again until last night ... when he had been at his weakest. Now, he was strapped to her, forced to see her every few days because he was stupid enough to think that demanding she be his personal donor would be punishment for her. Kaleb ran a hand down his face. Punishment to her it might be ... but for him it'd be pure torture.

Grayson walked into the meeting room, saving him from further thought, and pulled out one of the fourteen chairs surrounding the table. His VP looked as if he hadn't had much sleep. He brushed his overlong bangs from his eyes and leaned back in his chair, his booted feet kicked out in front of him. He stretched his long arms overhead before crossing them behind his head. His white teeth flashed against his red lips as he yawned. "So what's with calling a church meeting so damn early?"

"It's after noon, Gypsy."

"Well, some of us prefer to sleep until dusk."

"We have two brothers who need a proper send-off."

"Which could've waited until nightfall. Not like they're going anywhere."

"You're such an ass, Gypsy."

The VP grinned at Kaleb, telling him that he only jested.

"Viper's on his way home."

"No, shit. That detective bitch take off her reins?"

Kaleb chuckled. "I'm betting those tethers are tighter than ever."

"How so?"

"I'll save that for when the rest of the guys get here to keep myself from having to repeat it. So who was the little blonde from this morning?"

Grayson shrugged. "Shel. Met her at the Rave last night. After what happened ... I needed a release. She followed me home."

One of Kaleb's brows tipped up. Grayson regularly had the company of two women. Kept them from getting all territorial, he had said. "Just one?"

His bright blue eyes twinkled in humor. "You ever have a cat fight in your bed?"

Kaleb chuckled. "No, can't say that I have."

"Last two bitches I brought home cut loose on each other. Fists were swinging, claws were out." Grayson shook his head. "I couldn't get them out of my bed quick enough. Seriously, who cares who gets the first ride? There's plenty of me to go around. Much less drama when only one bitch is involved anyway, and easier to send them on their way."

"So what're you saying? You turning a new leaf, Gypsy?"

"Hell no. I'm too much vampire for just one woman," he said with a wink and a large smile as the front door opened to the clubhouse and booted footfalls announced the arrival of more of their brothers.

Silence descended about the large open room as the remaining brothers filed in, taking their place at the table. Three chairs remained empty. That of one of their fallen brothers, along with Kane and Ion's. Kaleb knew it was time to bring some prospects onboard. They couldn't have their number dwindling. Problem was, their last prospect just lost his head. Time to make growing their numbers a priority.

The men sat about, sullen faces telling the nature of the called meeting. Not a one was happy about last night's events. Besides finding prospects, they had a primordial to hunt down. The sentence for taking two of his men's heads had yet to be determined. Kaleb raised the gravel and struck the wooden strike plate as all eyes trained on him.

"I called this meeting for a few reasons. First and foremost, to send-off our fallen brothers. We need to ash their remains and scatter them among the winds at midnight."

Kaleb laid both their cuts, the leather vests with arms cut off that sported their MC colors, on the table. He took out his hunting knife, flipped it open and proceeded to cut off the back rockers and remaining patches. The vests with the center death skull would remain on them as the bodies went into the pyre.

"I think it goes without saying that we are losing numbers. First Ion, now Wheezer. And of course Red Dot as a prospect. Viper's been MIA. I think it's time we bring up some of the hangarounds as prospects. We need strength in the Sons. Agreed?"

The vote traveled about the table, one aye at a time without a single nay. Kaleb slammed his gavel down again. "Then it's decreed. In a couple of weeks, we will return for another vote. For those of you who know and approve of a hangaround, bring their name to the table. If you agree to sponsor them, we'll put it to a vote. We've lost two members and a prospect, not to mention Viper losing his voting rights. I think we could add three or four new prospects at this time. Agreed?"

Again, the vote traveled the table without a single nay. Kaleb struck the plate with the gavel again. "Third order of business, we have another primordial running loose in the States. We have no idea of what their business is here, but I have an idea that they aren't done by a long shot. They missed when they took out Wheezer and Red Dot. I believe that their real target is me, and they won't stop until they accomplish what they've set out to do."

Anton "Blondy" Balan was the first to speak up. "You think it's because of Alec Funar, that you killed an ancient?"

Kaleb nodded. "We all know that killing a primordial is against vampire rules, Blondy. I'm not above that law."

"But the son of a bitch would have killed our Pres."

"I'm not entirely sure that's true," Kaleb said with a heavy sigh. "Yes, he was out to kill the detective, but killing Viper wasn't something we were positive of. I alone made the decision to take his head. I don't regret that choice. But no one should have to pay for my actions."

"I still think the son of a bitch deserved what he got. You don't come after one of the Sons or our families and not suffer the consequences," Alexander said. "We protect our own, the same way they do. No difference. I say we take this son of a bitch's head like you did Alec's."

"I happen to agree, Xander. But it deserves a vote. If you all don't concede, then I alone will answer for my actions." Kaleb glanced around the table, making eye contact with each of his brothers. "We take it to a vote."

Each man, keeping their focus on Kaleb, delivered an aye, leaving no doubt that their allegiance was with him. Kaleb was humbled by their decision. He slammed the gavel down again. "Then we have a unanimous decision to track down and eliminate this piece of shit."

Hollers, praise, and fist pounding rose about the room to a deafening level before Kaleb slammed the gavel to regain order. "I still have a couple of minor items to bring to the table and then we'll call the meeting adjourned and take care of our fallen."

Kaleb once again gained the attention of every man present. "Viper is coming home."

Murmurs arose again at the news, not every word positive. He knew some of his brothers held grudges with their former president for not only breaking sacred club rules and turning Cara when claiming her as a mate was out of the question, but for disappearing with nary a word following his light sentencing the club handed down as a result.

When all talking ceased, Kaleb said, "He's been in Italy the past six months."

"What the fuck is he doing in Italy?" Grigore "Wolf" Lupie asked.

"He went to speak to Mircea III, Vlad's brother, Wolf. Mircea's the only one who could put an end to his mating with Rosalee, if the vow could indeed be broken. My brother loves Cara, that much is obvious."

"And?" Grayson asked.

"He was granted the annulment. Viper is now mated to Cara."

Silence descended about the room. Kaleb ran a hand through his hair, further disheveling it. He couldn't make the men at the table forgive Kane. His brother needed to earn back their respect on his own. Alexander broke the silence first with a slow clap of his hands, followed by several others in unison, though not all followed suit.

Alexander said, "Rosalee didn't deserve our former pres. If Viper is mated to the detective, then I say Cara is now one of our own."

Kaleb nodded. "And as such, we will protect her and treat her with all due respect. Agreed?"

Kaleb grit his teeth, fearing the vote not going in Kane's favor. But instead the vote traveled the room without a single nay. He let out his breath, feeling the relief that came with Kane and Cara's acceptance. Kaleb had one last thing that needed voiced before he and his crew set about ashing his MC brothers' remains.

"Then the meeting is adjourned until we reconvene for a vote on potential prospects."

But before he allowed his brothers to stand and quit the room, Kaleb raised his hand and stayed their positions. "One final thing that I would ask of you, my brothers, before we set out to lay Wheezer and Red Dot to rest—Suzi Stevens."

"What of her?" Grigore asked.

"I'm sure most of you know her."

Several at the table nodded, some with sly grins that rankled Kaleb's ire. He shook off the little green-eyed monster that tried to take root. "She's my personal donor."

"You staking your claim, Hawk?" Anton asked.

"No, Blondy."

"Then what exactly are you saying?"

"She retired herself from being a donor six months ago. Let's just say I took her out of retirement."

"Then you're fucking her," Grayson said.

Kaleb glared at his VP, a muscle ticking in his cheek. "No."

"So what you're saying is she's still open game. We just have to keep our fangs to ourselves," Grayson continued.

Kaleb's nostrils flared in his rising ire. To hell with what his brothers thought of his actions or his demands. He was the president, and as such he was allowed to make such an outlandish request. Usually donors were only forbidden from other club members if a Sons claimed them as an old lady.

"Suzi Stevens is off limits. No one touches her, no one feeds from her. To do so means you're willing to suffer my wrath."

Without another word or waiting for further reaction, Kaleb turned and exited the meeting room, slamming the door behind him. He had made the decision not to share her. He didn't want any of his brothers feeding from his donor so that when he needed nourishment, she'd always be available to him. It had nothing to do with his messed up desire to fuck her. Hell no. If he ever gave into that desire, he'd need his own damn head examined.

CHAPTER FIVE

Suzi strolled through the DVD isle of the mom-and-pop grocery store that Tamera's parents owned in Pleasant, picking up videos and reading the jackets as she went. She held one up and smiled. "We have time for two tonight? Channing Tatum has all the right moves in this one."

Her roommate smiled. "You take Channing. I personally like Joe Manganiello."

"Was there really a bad dancer in the movie?"

Tamera laughed. "Yes, and I don't think I need to say who."

The sound of a Harley Davidson drew Suzi's attention away from the conversation as they both looked up from the *Magic Mike* jacket and peered out the large front window. A red and white sale poster, announcing ground beef at a bottom dollar low price, kept them hidden from view of the other side as they glanced around it. A bright red Sportster backed into an angled parking lot just outside the store. Suzi watched as Grayson kicked down the center stand, cut the engine, and swung a leather-clad leg over the bike's black leather seat. He unsnapped his skull cap, then hung it from the handlebar. Dark shades hid his eyes from view. The vampire took a quick glance around at his surroundings before turning and heading for the entrance to the store. A bell rang over the door as it opened. Grayson stepped into the cooler interior, pushing his rich brown hair back from his face and placing his sunglasses atop his head. The day had been unseasonably warm as they headed into the spring of the year, though Suzi wasn't one to complain. She hated the cold months of winter.

Clutching the Blu-Ray jacket to her chest, she watched the VP of the Sons make his way past them. With any luck, the biker would get what he came for and be on his way without noticing their presence. After last night with Kaleb, she wasn't in the mood to see any of the Sons today. But good fortune wasn't on her side as he turned his head and glanced in their direction.

"You think he knows we're donors?" Tamera whispered as the biker took a left and made his way through the aisles, heading toward them.

Suzi stifled a laugh. She had been a donor for far too many years for any of the Sons not to know of her, or at the very least recognize her. She'd probably fed nearly all of them at one point or another ... some of them several times in fact. This one, though, had been a rarity. She could only recall feeding him a time or two. But it was pretty likely that there were those who didn't yet know her roommate since Tamera was still young and fairly new to the society.

Grayson stopped just shy of them and gave a nod in greeting. His gaze went from Suzi's to the movie she clutched at her chest then to Tamera, where it held long enough to show interest. His gaze traveling back to the Blu-Ray, he plucked it from Suzi's clasp and turned it over, looking at the front. His full lips turned up in amusement before handing it back. Suzi quickly replaced on the shelf.

One dark brow lifted. "You two looking for entertainment?"

"What do you want, Gypsy?" Suzi asked, gritting her teeth. He certainly knew how to take the fun out of their evening. The last thing she had wanted was to be standing there having a conversation with any of Kaleb's MC brothers.

"I was commenting on your decision." His hand indicated the Blu-Ray she returned to the shelf. "I'm betting I have moves that will rival any of those in that movie."

"Seriously?" Suzi groaned, rolling her eyes. "You did not just say that."

His smile widened. "I'm just saying ... you could have the real thing."

"Not in this lifetime, Gypsy. Why not head for the Rave? I'm sure there are plenty of girls out there who would fall for your cheesy pickup."

He ignored her jibe, not offended in the least, and glanced at Tamera. "Who's the redhead?"

Tamera stepped eagerly forward, appearing way too happy to meet the one biker, in Suzi's opinion, she should stay away from. Suzi knew Grayson's reputation with the ladies. One woman never seemed to be enough for the vampire.

"Tamera Cantrell," she said, eagerly sticking out her hand which Grayson took to his lips. But instead of kissing the back, he turned her hand over and slowly licked a path up her palm.

"My pleasure. You—"

"Oh please, Gypsy." Suzi grumbled, not about to allow him to take advantage of her suddenly dumbstruck roommate. She definitely needed to have a conversation with Tamera on which Sons to avoid at all costs. The VP topped that list. "Move along already, Gypsy. It's obvious we have better things to do than entertain you."

The vampire flashed Suzi another heated smile, his fangs slightly extended. "Sweetheart, I'm talking to Ms. Cantrell. *You* are obviously spoken for."

What the hell did he mean by that? At first she thought he referred to the solitaire on her hand, but it hadn't been Suzi's hand that Grayson had just French kissed, giving him far too much credit that he would pay attention to detail.

"What do you mean?"

Grayson turned to Suzi. "I really don't have time to party, ladies. I have a couple of fallen brothers I need to help put to rest and the sun is starting to descend. So if you'll excuse me, I need to get the fifths of whisky I came for and be on my way."

Suzi grabbed his forearm, stopping Grayson from retreating. No way was she letting him off the hook that easy. He had brought up the part about her being spoken for, so he wasn't leaving without an explanation.

"What do you mean I'm spoken for?"

Grayson's smile reached his eyes, seemingly humored. "You don't know that the P's claimed you, sweetheart?"

"What the hell are you talking about? I belong to no one, leastwise Hawk."

"Then maybe it's Hawk you need to be having this conversation with. He's made it perfectly clear that you're off limits."

"Of all the—"

"Take that up with the pres, sweetheart," he said with a wink before turning back to Tamera. He reached out and trailed his forefinger down her jaw. "I'll catch up with you later, doll."

Tamera stared in Grayson's wake, her curiosity and attraction clearly written in her expression. She looked like a schoolgirl with a crush. Too bad Suzi had to be the one to let her roommate in on why Grayson "Gypsy" Gabor was so not the guy you crushed on. Grayson was far worse than Kaleb when it came to women. Oh, he loved them all right. Too much was his problem. Rarely was he seen with only one girl on his arm. Hell, he had a posse of women at any given time. She supposed his Hollywood good looks had a lot to do with it, that and his hundred-watt smile.

"He's—"

"Don't even start, Tamera." Suzi shoved the movie they came for into her roommate's arms. "I don't even know where to start with all the reasons Gypsy is all kinds of wrong for you."

"Why?" Her brows knit together over the bridge of her nose, clearly annoyed that Suzi would think to dictate who she should stay away from. "Who's he right for?"

"Let's just say no woman."

"Is he spoken for?"

"Well … no. Not that I know of anyway."

A smile returned to Tamera's lips. "Then that's good news for me. Maybe I'll head to the Rave—"

Suzi blew out a steady breath. "Fine. But don't say I didn't warn you."

"I hardly believe he can be that bad." Tamera headed for the checkout with two bottles of merlot and their movie.

Suzi tossed a large bag of popcorn into her cart along with several other items they were getting low on, then met Tamera at the checkout counter. She hugged her mom and thanked her as Suzi began placing the items on the conveyer belt.

"You taking good care of my daughter, Suzi?"

"Of course, Mrs. Cantrell."

She smiled widely, kissed Suzi on the cheek and said, "I'm glad she has you living in the townhouse with her. Otherwise, her father and I would worry something fierce."

Thanks to Tamera's parents owning the place, Suzi got a great price on the rent. Half the price of what it would cost her anywhere else. "Really, it's you and Mr. Cantrell that deserve my thanks."

"Nonsense, dear. Now you two have a great night. I have paperwork to get back to."

Tamera brushed her mom's cheek with a kiss before the older woman left the checkout area for the back of the store with a final wave. Suzi could see where Tamera got her stunning looks from. Her mother's bright red hair piled high on her head, and she didn't look a day over thirty-five even though the woman had just celebrated her forty-ninth birthday.

Items sacked and back in their cart, the two headed for Suzi's red Neon. By the position of the sun, it looked like they'd make it back to the townhouse just before it got dark. Suzi thought of Kaleb and Grayson's ridiculous statement that she belonged to Kaleb or that he had somehow claimed her. He had made himself perfectly clear the night he had fed from her. But if he thought for one minute that meant she was off limits to other men, he had a rude awakening coming. Maybe it was time to see if she could turn the tables and make the arrogant ass jealous.

"The movie and wine tonight are compliments of Mom," Tamera said as she helped load the groceries into the car.

"You'll have to thank her for me." Suzi shut the trunk, then walked around to the driver's side and climbed into the car.

Once they were both seated, Tamera looked at Suzi as she turned the key and started the engine. "Is Gypsy really all that bad?"

Suzi put the car into reverse and backed into the road, before sliding the gearshift into drive and heading toward home. "Let me just put it this way, Gypsy likes his women."

"That's not a bad thing, Suzi."

"It is if he likes them more than one at a time and you're not into that kind of thing. Are you?"

Tamera shook her head. "Not that I've ever tried it. But I'm not sure I'd want to share my man."

"Then Gypsy is definitely not the man for you."

She appeared to mull over what Suzi had to say as she stared out the front window for several long moments. Finally she said, "Then maybe he hasn't met the right woman yet."

"Maybe." Suzi chuckled. "But then again, I've known him for over ten years and the right woman hasn't come along yet. I just don't want to see you get hurt."

Tamera nodded, then focused on the road, remaining quiet the rest of the way home. Suzi felt bad for squashing the younger woman's crush. After all, what right did she have to comment on matters of the heart when her own love life couldn't be more screwed up? Suzi sighed. Two more days and Kaleb would come looking for her if she didn't show up at the Rave. That gave her two days to come up with a fake fiancé. Possibly one who would turn him green with envy.

"YOU SAID WHAT?" KALEB ASKED. A small chuckle erupted before turning into full-blown mirth.

His MC brother never failed to amuse him, even after something as gut wrenching as ashing their brothers. Nicolas and Steven wouldn't have wanted them to mourn their loss so much as celebrate their life, and the MC had been standing around the makeshift alter, turned pyre, in the back lot of the clubhouse. To all passersby, it looked like a rowdy bunch, passing a whiskey bottle around and sharing war stories. Those who saw and thought as much wouldn't have been far off in their thinking, except for the detail of their comrades' ashes scattering amongst the wind.

"It's a wonder you even get laid, Gypsy."

Grayson shrugged and joined in the humor. "You'd be surprised what bad pickup lines get you."

The two shared a twelve-pack as they now kicked back in the clubhouse's main living area, following the send-off. The rest of the MC brothers had retired hours earlier as the sun had long ago risen. But not before toasting to the brothers they would miss and vowing revenge on the guilty. The Sons had stood in the brisk night air knocking back the amber liquid, feeling the burn until the wee hours of the morning and every last drop of whiskey had been consumed.

Now, several hours later, still not yet ready to call it a day, Grayson and Kaleb sat on the worn sofas, feet propped on the scarred center table, rehashing the day over the last of the beers.

Grayson took a pull from his longneck, then looked at Kaleb thoughtfully. "So what's with Suzi Stevens' engagement ring? You didn't tell me she had a fiancé."

Kaleb's humor quickly died and the smile shed his face as anger began a slow burn in his gut. It irked him that Suzi had any affect on his mood at all. He was supposed to loathe the ground she stood on. He'd do well to remember how she had reacted to his nephew's death. Most women in her position would've fallen to pieces. But not her. Suzi had stood toe-to-toe with him, blue eyes locked on his without showing an ounce of compassion as if he had just told her nothing more significant than supper had been placed on the table. She had politely thanked him and walked away. No, Suzi Stevens was a cold-hearted bitch who had ice running through her veins, no matter how she claimed to have mourned in private. Kaleb would stake his reputation on his belief that she hadn't.

"What the fuck are you talking about, Gypsy? What ring?"

"The one she wears on her left hand, dude. Are you fucking blind? It has to be a carat at the very least."

Kaleb tipped back his bottle, finishing the last of his beer. His jaw ached as he clamped down on his teeth with rising fury, then launched the empty bottle across the room where it smashed against the rough-hewn, paneled wall, sending shards flying about the space.

Grayson held his palms facing out. "Whoa, I didn't mean to make you go all postal, dude. I was just making conversation. Besides, you were the one who said you weren't fucking her."

"I'm not." He all but growled, cursing the night she stepped back into the Rave.

Why did she have to be his one weakness? He should've tossed her out on her ass and found his nourishment elsewhere. But no. One bad decision and he would no doubt be left regretting it for a long time to come. He needed his head examined for claiming her as his personal donor. Jesus! Kaleb ran both hands down his tired face and blew out a steady stream of air toward the ceiling. Yep, it was official. He was a fucking idiot.

"What's got you all hell bent then? I'm sure whoever the unlucky bastard is, he isn't feeding off her. Ain't a vamp I know who follows that human tradition."

Kaleb had to agree with Grayson. None of his kind used rings of any sort to claim their mates. It was simple, when mated no vampire dared mess with another's mate. To do so meant certain death. He'd rip out the throat of the first man who tried to take what was his.

"She never mentioned she was engaged. And I was too focused on her carotid artery to notice. Not that I care. Like I said, I'm not fucking her. Regardless of her fiancé, she's still a donor. And as such, I have a right to claim her for nourishment."

Grayson chuckled. "Whatever you say, dude. Try as you might to convince yourself, but you've got a hard-on for that little donor."

"That little donor belongs to Ion."

"Past tense, dude. Ion's been gone for over ten years. You going to keep punishing her for not choosing you all those years ago?"

Kaleb grabbed the last longneck from the cardboard carrier and pulled the metal cap off with his teeth and spit it to the wooden floor. It tinged across the flooring and skidded to a stop next to the broken glass of his last bottle. He'd need to clean that mess later. Taking a healthy swig, he slammed the bottle on the wooden arm of the sofa. Foam bubbled up, nearly spilling over as Kaleb stared at the paneled wall in front of him. He certainly didn't want to admit that Grayson might be correct, that Kaleb had been trying to punish the young and impressionable girl all those years ago for choosing his nephew. Hell, he hadn't even wanted her. Sure, fucking her had been like an aphrodisiac. But one woman? There were far too many women willing to suck his cock to settle for just one.

So what the hell had him so bugged?

He glanced back at Grayson. The vampire looked at him unapologetically.

"You're full of shit, Gypsy."

"Am I, Pres? You just stood in a room full of MC brothers yesterday, forbidding them to touch your donor. You all but growled that demand. You might as well have stated right then and there that you claimed the little brunette for your mate."

"I have no need of a mate."

"Say what you will, but your actions speak otherwise."

Kaleb ran a hand over his lower jaw. "I need her to feed me when I desire communion. Nothing more."

"You keep telling yourself that, dude. If you have no intentions of tapping into that little piece of ass, then you won't mind if I do."

He knew Grayson was trying to get a rise out of him, and damned if it wasn't working. No one was going to fuck Suzi Stevens. Not even her fiancé, whoever the douche bag might be. He'd make sure of it. Then when he sank his fangs gum deep into her neck, he'd make sure she begged him to take her. And maybe, someday, he might be stupid enough to do just that.

"I'm going to bed."

One of Grayson's brows rose in challenge at his unanswered statement.

"Stay the hell away from her, Gypsy, or I'll rip your fucking head off," he said, hearing his VP's answering chuckle all the way to his room before he slammed the door and cut off the infuriating chortle.

CHAPTER SIX

"I WISH TO SPEAK WITH MIRCEA." KANE STOOD ON THE VERY stoop of the ancient castle he had two months prior when he had requested that his and Rosalee's mating be annulled. The elder vampire hadn't been happy with him then. Well, he sure as hell wouldn't be happy with him now.

Kane wasn't about to leave until he had his say.

His great uncle would either agree to see him or Kane would rip every door off its rustic hinges until he found the insufferable bastard. Kane was not a man to be denied. Not this time. He may have had patience when he and Cara first arrived in Italy, waiting four months to gain an audience with the one vampire who could grant him his desire to mate with Cara. Then he had all the time in the world. That was before someone had tried to take his twin's head. Now he'd be damned if Mircea would dictate when the inevitable meeting would take place.

"I'm sorry but Mircea doesn't wish to be disturbed."

Kane grabbed his uncle's "yes man" by the throat and backed him into the house. His normally tanned skin paled as his already bulging eyes damn near popped from their sockets.

"I didn't ask what the old bastard's wishes were. You tell me where to find him and I'll think about allowing you to live."

The balding man's mouth sucked in air like a beached fish. Kane easily tossed him aside. "Never mind, I'll find him myself."

The man's wheezes echoed down the hall after Kane as he gasped for air. Much more pressure and Kane could have easily collapsed his windpipe, killing the human. But his death would gain him nothing, other than Mircea's scorn. That, Kane was sure, he already had.

"Mircea, you arrogant bastard," Kane called out as he took the stone stairs to the second floor two at a time. "Where the hell are you?"

Just as he reached the landing, Mircea exited the sitting room adjacent to his apartment-sized bedroom. His white robe cloaked his body, dragging across the cold stone hallway floor beneath him. Leather thong sandals covered his bare feet. The pompous ass looked like an Egyptian pharaoh, for crying out loud.

"What's the meaning of this, nephew? Haven't I heard from you enough in one lifetime?"

"I'm just getting started," Kane said, his grin surely as evil as he felt inside. Rosalee would answer to his allegations if she had anything to do with Nicolas and Steven's demise. He'd see to it that she lost her own fucking head for her actions should she be guilty.

"So what is all hellfire important that you would think to disturb my siesta?"

"You can sleep any time, old man. Where the hell is that worthless stepdaughter of yours? And don't tell me you don't know this time."

Mircea rolled his eyes. "Back to that? If you must, then please join me in my sitting room. I already tire of this conversation. Please make it quick and be on your way, will you?"

Without waiting for a reply or to see if Kane cared to follow, he turned and reentered the large spacious room. Two large white, rounded sectional sofas faced each other in the center of the room. Several throw pillows littered the surface while a white cushioned ottoman completed the center. Mircea sat in the center of one of the sofas, arms stretched across the back, just as a servant appeared from another entrance with a bottle of wine and two glasses perched on a highly-polished silver tray. The tall lanky man glanced warily at Kane before pouring two glasses of the deep red wine.

"Merlot?" Mircea asked, as the servant held out a glass to Kane. "Please join me. I hate to drink alone."

Kane took the large glass from the man's long, delicate fingers, then took a seat across from his elder. His uncle may appear frail by all appearances with his thin frame and sunken cheeks, but Kane knew the man held the strength of many men and could easily take him out if he so chose. Kane twirled the deep red liquid in the glass, then took it to his nose and inhaled the rich woodsy scent before taking a healthy swallow.

"Good vintage."

"I should hope so." Mircea picked up the bottle and glanced at the aging label. "It's an '83. A very good year for merlot."

He placed the bottle back on the tray, took his own glass and looked Kane straight in the eyes. His silvery blue gaze cut right through him. "Now, what's this have to do with my tiresome stepdaughter, Rosalee?" he spat her name as if the word alone disgusted him.

"Do you even know if she is still in Italy?"

Mircea shrugged, then took his wide-mouthed glass to his lips and took a small sip. He didn't appear overly concerned with his stepdaughter's whereabouts. "I think I already answered this the last time we met. Either you're not listening or you're daft in the head, boy. What reason do I have to believe that she might've directly disobeyed my command and left the country?"

"You said yourself you haven't heard from or seen her. Have you talked to her since you allowed our mating to be dissolved? Does she even know?"

"No," he said, his tone casual as if he could care less what Rosalee might be up to. "Rosalee often goes off on her own. She's never once disobeyed me. Do you offer proof now that she might have? Isn't it enough I allowed you to mate with another? Why must you bother me with such bothersome drama?"

"I appreciate your kindness, Mircea. And I mean you no disrespect. Please do not mistake my reasoning for being here."

"Then out with it, boy. What the hell is all important that you would disturb my peace and threaten my *maggiordomo*?"

"I received a disturbing phone call from my twin yesterday."

"Kaleb? What trouble is my other nephew up to now?"

"Someone tried to take his head."

Mircea slowly nodded, but he didn't have the look of surprise that Kane hoped to see. Was it possible that Mircea had a hand in ordering Kaleb's beheading for daring to take the life of a primordial, whether his brother was justified in doing so or not?

"And naturally you think my stepdaughter is involved ... why?"

"As you already know Alec Funar tried to take my mate's life."

"Go on."

"It's still my belief that Rosalee had a hand in that."

"So you've said."

Mircea already knew about the events leading up to Alec Funar's beheading last fall. Kane had partially filled his great uncle in on the details when he had requested he be allowed to mate with Cara.

"All women that had been drained in Pleasant I knew or had relationships with. I don't think that it's a coincidence by any means."

"And I already told you last fall Rosalee was here with me. It's only been the last few months that I do not know where she's taken herself off to."

"I don't believe Rosalee drained anyone."

One of his black brows rose in challenge. "Then what's this have to do with her?"

Kane could tell the old man was quickly tiring of the whole conversation by his tone. He needed to get to the point before Mircea threw him out.

"Alec Funar acted on Rosalee's orders."

"You better have proof if you're yet again accusing my stepdaughter."

"I have proof. I didn't mention it before because you had granted my wish to annul my mating with Rosalee. No reason to drag the details out."

Mircea's gaze narrowed dangerously. "Yet you do now? Why?"

Kane all but squirmed in his seat. If Mircea desired, he could behead Kane with little effort. Kane wasn't a fool when it came to knowing how dangerous his adversary was. Accusing his step-daughter of conspiring against Kane would no doubt warrant the primordial's anger.

"Rosalee plotted against me, using Alec to do her dirty work. As you know, resulting in Kaleb taking that primordial's head."

The ancient's face reddened and his fangs lengthened. "Why are we rehashing this story? Is it your wish that I change my mind and demand restitution?"

"You already know that under the circumstance I feel my brother was justified."

"Where is this proof against Rosalee?" A muscle ticked in Mircea's cheek. He held his fury in check. "You accused my step-daughter of conspiring to kill all those who dare to get close to you. Yet, you have not offered proof. I already granted your wish to mate again, so why now do you feel the need to drag the unpleasantries back up?"

"Because I believe she's left the country and now is plotting to take my brother's head. We found Alec's phone. Rosalee had tried to call him following the—"

"The beheading."

"Yes. And although we didn't answer it or correspond with her, we were able to view the texts between them that proved our theory. She wanted to see me punished and miserable for her being banished to Italy. I assume now that's why she's missing. I believe she knows that I told you about her involvement at our last meeting. Not to mention you allowing our mating to be dissolved."

Mircea slowly nodded, then drained his wineglass. He set the empty on the silver tray so gently, Kane barely detected the sound of the glass clinking against the metal. He knew his great uncle's fury simmered beneath the surface, that much obvious in his obsidian gaze trained on Kane.

"Certainly, you can understand why now I would think your stepdaughter has her hands in the plot to behead my brother. Though whoever plotted against Kaleb, missed their target and took out two of my brethren in the Sons of Sangue instead. Forgive me if I'm not of a very permissive nature at the moment."

"That doesn't tell me why you think Rosalee is involved in this new supposed scheme. What reason would she have for going after Kaleb?"

Kane had asked himself the same question. By all accounts, Mircea could've ordered the hit, not Rosalee. "Kaleb smelled primordial scent all over the scene."

"So you naturally think of my stepdaughter?" His one brow tipped skyward in challenge. "How do you know that I didn't order the hit on your brother? After all, he broke a cardinal rule by killing a primordial. We both know the sentence that carries. Tell me, dear nephew, why should he be granted amnesty when to do so would show weakness on my part?"

"Because in our last conversation you told me you granted him immunity. Are you saying that you went back on your word and now you passed down the order?"

Mircea ran a hand through his slightly graying hair, attempting to tame the thick mass. "I did not. Though by all rights I should have. It appears someone else took it upon themselves to carry it out."

"And who would do that? You are the sole judge and jury as you are the eldest of the vampires. Who would act without your order?"

He shrugged, poured himself another merlot and sat back, his now obsidian gaze holding Kane's. "No primordial has ever acted without my expressed permission ... except that of Alec Funar. That's why your brother received absolution. Whoever tried to take your brother's life has done so by his, or her," he quickly amended, "own actions. You have my word that I had no hand in this."

"And if Rosalee is involved?"

"I will see she is punished as I see fit."

"By banning her from leaving Italy?" Kane failed to conceal the bitterness from his tone.

"Watch yourself, boy. Your sarcasm does not suit you well."

Kane grit his teeth. He hated to apologize to the old bastard, but he needed Mircea on his side. He ducked his head, looking into the bottom of his empty glass. "I meant no disrespect."

"You have your reasons for hating Rosalee more than anyone. She caused you the life of your son. So for that, I forgive your disdain against my stepdaughter." He sighed through thin lips. "Now go. I will dig into this matter and punish the individual guilty of acting on his own ... or her own desires, and for not first seeking counsel with me. Please send my regards to your pretty little mate. As for Kaleb, you tell him that I absolved him of his crime against Alec Funar. But should he take matters into his own hands again, I may not be so merciful."

———

"SUZI STEVENS... HAVE YOU SEEN her tonight?" Kaleb asked Draven, who stood with his back against the bar, drinking a shiraz from a stemless wineglass, surveying the patrons.

Red, blue, and yellow lights flashed about the room to the heavy beat of the industrial music. Ravers danced, hopped, and waved glow sticks to the pulsing heavy-laden bass beat. Normally Kaleb thrived on the energy coursing through the room. Some of the ravers were high on X, or ecstasy, a drug common to the Blood 'n' Rave and one Draven profited from.

The drug was useless to his kind as their blood regenerated too rapidly to feel the effects for more than a few moments. But should any of the donors be high on X at the time of feeding, ecstasy having tachycardia as a well-known side effect, it pushed the sexual experience for them over the top, resulting in too rapid of a heartbeat for the user. Something he and the Sons avoided due to the high risk of death for the donor. If a donor was high on X, then no one used them for communion.

Unfortunately, Kaleb had seen the fatal side-affect personally when one donor's heart went into SVT, or supraventricular tachycardia, while he had had her bent over the bathroom sink and fucked her from behind, his fangs buried deep in her shoulder. It was all fun and games until she face-planted the ceramic sink, leaving them a mess to contend with. The young donor became an unfortunate added number to missing persons. The woman had to have come by the Disco Biscuit via another route, since Draven never sold X to a known donor, the reason the Sons allowed him to profit off his drug sales without interference from the MC.

Wearing red, cat-eye contacts and rounded, blue sunglasses perched low on his nose, Draven glanced at Kaleb and shook his head. "Haven't seen her in months," he said. He held up his glass to the bartender for a refill. "What're you drinking?"

"I'm not." Kaleb grit his teeth. Hell, the only thing he had a thirst for at the moment was Suzi Stevens' blood. So where the hell was she?

Being a Monday, the Blood 'n' Rave wasn't exactly packed. If Suzi had been there, Draven would have seen her. It had been three days since she had sought him out, concern for his well-being clearly written in her blue gaze. Fuck her concern. Shoving his disdain for her aside in his moment of weakness, he had drank from her anyway. Not only that, but he had demanded that she feed him personally. And yet, knowing he would need to feed every three days to sustain himself, she had directly disobeyed him by not being here. Damn himself for agreeing to her terms that they meet in the public lounge.

If he had to, he'd break down every donor's door in Florence until he found her as he had no clue where the little bitch laid her head. If she thought to hide from him, then the state of Oregon was not nearly big enough. Kaleb would have every Son and Knight on a statewide search until she was found. And if she lived with her so called fiancé? Kaleb would love to go toe to toe with the bastard right about now. A one-carat solitaire wasn't a big enough deterrent to stop him from getting what he wanted. He'd see to it the bastard learned his place. Suzi Stevens may not belong to Kaleb, but he'd be damned if he'd allow someone else to stand in the way of his need.

"You needing a donor?" Draven broke into his murderous thoughts. "I could see one brought up to my office for you."

"What I need is a little brunette named Suzi. If you can't provide me that—then I'm not interested."

"Someone got you by the balls¬—"

Draven's question was cut short as Kaleb gripped him by the throat, lifting the tall man off the floor by a good four inches. Kaleb growled as his eyes blackened and his canines elongated. "Speak to me like that again and you'll be spitting blood."

"What the hell?" Draven wheezed, trying to catch a breath. The hand holding the glass of wine loosened, the glass crashed to their booted feet as he clawed the hand gripping his throat.

Kaleb sneered. "My reasons for wanting the little bitch is none of your concern."

"Point taken. Now," he croaked, "please let me down."

"Jesus, Hawk!"

Kaleb stifled a groan. Of course she would pick that moment to appear. How the hell had she slipped into the club without either of their notice? Kaleb released Draven, who dropped to his booted feet with a thump and staggered back against the bar, his hand going to his injured throat. The bar owner would likely sport a raspy voice for the next few days. Not that Kaleb cared.

"It's about time you decided to show up."

Lightning shot through Suzi's blue gaze in her anger. "I knew if I didn't show that you'd come looking for me."

"Why should that bother you, *piccolo diavolo?*"

"Because it does." Her gaze narrowed. A lesser man would've cowered from her piercing gaze. "What did you just call me?"

CHAPTER SEVEN

66 I CALLED YOU *LITTLE DEVIL*."

And why should that surprise her? Of course he did. "You manhandle Draven and you call me little devil? Seriously? That's like the pot calling the kettle black."

"Overused analogy."

"Bite me—" She stopped herself at the rise of his lips. "Strike that."

"¬If you would have been here, *piccolo diavolo*, then I wouldn't have had to manhandle Draven. That is on your conscience."

"Apologize to Draven. He isn't my keeper, nor does he know my whereabouts."

Draven shook his head, obviously not wanting to get involved in the middle of their pissing match. "There's no need."

She raised a brow. "Really? Hawk damn near crushed your windpipe for no reason." She turned her glare back on the object of her scorn. "I say he needs to apologize for acting like an ass."

A muscle ticked in Kaleb's cheek. "Be careful, *piccolo diavolo*. You need to know your place."

"And just what is my place, Hawk?"

Wisely, he kept his mouth shut for once. Instead he stood there looking all hot and sexy and way more delectable than any man had a right to. Damn him for kick-starting her libido in the middle of an argument. There certainly would be no hiding the truth from him, that much was apparent in the slight flaring of his nostrils and the knowing grin now full-blown on his lush lips. Men didn't have lush lips, did they? And yet there was no other way to describe them. She remembered all too well what those lips had felt like against hers, not to mention the many other places he had used them. Her memories of a young, innocent girl came to mind. Hell, she had been a virgin then. No wonder he hadn't ever wanted a round two. Now, she'd like to show him a thing or two.

But of course, she wouldn't.

A pair of worn Levi's hung low on his lean hips, hugging his muscular thighs before flaring slightly at the knees. A black Henley completed the top half, sleeves pushed to his elbows, showing off his one tattooed sleeve that alone made her heart trip over itself. She had a weakness for tattooed men, thanks to meeting Hawk in her impressionable years. A few buttons at his neck were left open, showing a spattering of hair that Suzi longed to run her fingers through, to feel the softness against her palms.

Yeah, she had it bad.

All the more reason to give him what she came for and get the hell out of Dodge. Yep, another overused analogy, but this time one he wouldn't hear.

"So where're we doing this? The ladies' room? Dark corner?"

"Draven's office." Kaleb glanced back at the bar owner, no doubt checking to see if it was available because no way would Kaleb seek permission for anyone.

The man saluted Kaleb with a fresh glass of wine as a bartender swept up the broken glass where he had last stood or rather hung from Kaleb's grip. "All yours."

Kaleb looked down at Suzi and held out a hand in the direction of the stairwell. "After you."

With a heavy sigh, Suzi marched past the insufferable bastard as he grabbed a full bottle of wine and two glasses, then followed behind. She took the stairs in front of him, feeling his gaze on her ass as thoroughly as if he had palmed each cheek and slowly caressed them. Suzi knew that feeding him wasn't going to be easy for her by a long shot. Keeping her hands to herself and her libido in check was going to be damn near impossible. But then she'd stake her life on the fact the jerk counted on it.

Suzi turned in the center of the room, not willing to get anywhere near that leather sofa. She wiped her sweaty palms on her tight, dark blue jeans. They rode low on her hips causing a bit of her midriff to show, the exact spot the damn vampire had focused on the minute the two of them were alone. Second-guessing her outfit was a little too late. Next time she'd wear whatever Omar the tentmaker was making this season.

"Well?" She drew his gaze upward. "Let's get this the hell over with."

"You have somewhere else you need to be, *piccolo diavolo?*"

"Maybe I do. But it sure in the hell does not include standing here having a tête-à-tête with you."

And the quicker she got him taking his fill, the sooner she could stop thinking of him in the horizontal with her straddling his lean hips. What the hell were those love handle things anyway that rode just above his jean line? Lord, those made her want to follow the muscle line with her tongue straight to his... Enough! At this rate, she'd never make it out of here unscathed.

Remember why you hate him.

Kaleb set the two wineglasses on a round table, uncorked the bottle and then poured them each a glass, before handing her one.

Suzi quickly shook her head. Too much wine and she'd be promising Kaleb her tomorrows. "None for me. I'm not here to fraternize. Take what you came here for and I'll be on my way. Don't make this harder than it has to be, Hawk."

"It's Kaleb to you."

"You will always be Hawk to me."

She caught a glimpse of his extended fangs as he took a swallow of the deep red wine then licked the remnants from his lips. His prominent brow only enhanced his dangerous look. And he called her little devil? He looked like the beast himself as his obsidian gaze seemed to swallow her whole.

"It's all the same, *piccolo diavolo.* But when I'm fucking you, I'd prefer you to call me by my given name."

"Well, then ... no worries there, Hawk." Suzi winked at him, then walked over to the end table and grabbed the other glass of wine, downing the contents in one swallow. If she were to endure his company, then she might as well do it with good wine. Tilting her head to the side, she asked, "Shall we?"

"You are one cold-hearted bitch."

"It takes a cold heart to know one."

Instead of taking her proffered artery, though, he grabbed her left hand and held the sparkling bauble up for his inspection. "So who is he?"

Suzi shrugged. "No one you'd know. Besides, he's irrelevant."

"I bet if you asked him, he'd beg to differ with you."

"Irrelevant to you."

"He's fucking you, isn't he?"

She looked up at his black eyes, seeing her own reflection in their mirror-like reflection. "Why would you think otherwise?"

"Then I'd say he's not irrelevant. How long?"

Suzi was quickly losing her train of thought this close to him. He smelled of the open road and musk, a scent unique to him and as heady as the wine she had just drunk. "How long?" she repeated his question.

"Since he's been fucking you?"

She pulled her hand from his grip, then grabbed the wine bottle and poured herself another glass. She downed it just as quickly. "I can see we're going to be here awhile."

Picking up the bottle, Suzi carried it over to the leather sofa and sank into its luxury. She poured herself a third glass, then set the bottle on the side table to her right. "Why are you doing this, Hawk?"

"What?"

"Don't play stupid with me."

"You're the one hiding a fiancé. I am nothing if not honest with you."

"So you just want me to be your personal donor ... nothing more?"

"No, *piccolo diavolo*, don't mistake my intentions. I also want to fuck you."

AND HE DID. IN THE WORST WAY. His cock strained against his Levi's, plaguing him something fierce. He needed to remind himself to wear looser fitting jeans around her. Much more and his intentions would be peeking out the top of the waistband, begging for attention. He quickly adjusted the front of his jeans, then grabbed his own glass of wine and stalked her to the sofa. He towered over her, the beast within barely leashed, and yet she simply looked back at him as if he stood before her in his human form. He had been full-fledged vampire since she had stormed into the club tonight like a dust devil, wreaking havoc on his emotions. And yet, not once had he seen her cower.

Maybe he needed to work on looking more menacing.

That or he needed to show the little slip of a woman her place, the thought alone nearly had him laughing. Kaleb sincerely doubted anyone could show Suzi her place. She might come in a small package, but her feistiness showed up in spades.

"You've already done that, Hawk." She leaned back, resting her head on the back of the sofa. The wine had softened the edge on her gaze. "I don't intend to allow you that privilege again."

"Oh you will. Count on it."

"You have a mountain-sized ego. No one could accuse you of self-effacement."

"There's a difference between ego and confidence, *piccolo diavolo*. But you would be correct. I have both."

"You won't get any arguments from me. Now if you've come to feed, have at it. If you've come to get laid, there's an entire club of Sons groupies out there that I am sure are more than willing."

The sound of the industrial music filtered through the room, the heavy beat thumping against his chest much like the cadence of his beating heart. And here he thought that forcing her to personally feed him would be perfect retribution for choosing Ion all those years ago, when in fact the comeuppance was his. Having her this close and not have the right to do as he wished was torture at its finest.

His nostrils flared as he caught the scent of her desire. Whether she chose to deny it or not, she couldn't hide her body's reaction to him. Suzi might not like him, though her libido sure in the hell did. Fucking her wasn't on tonight's agenda, but he would. Just not before she damn well begged for it. And he had every intention of getting her to do just that, her fiancé be damned.

Kaleb set his half-filled glass of wine next to the bottle and dropped to his knees in front of the sofa before her slightly-spread, slender thighs. Her gaze widened as he placed a palm on each of her inner thighs and spread them, making room for him to slip between. His hands slid up the muscular surface, causing her breath to intake just as his thumbs skimmed the sides of her center, yet not quite touching the soft folds concealed by her jeans. Here, the strong scent of her desire easily wafted to his nose. His balls tightened.

"Don't, Hawk," she said, the request weak at its best.

He had no intention on pushing the issue. No, he'd much rather leave her wanting, even if it meant his own groin plagued him. He ran his palms up to her hips to encompass her slim waist, contacting the bare flesh just above the line of her jeans. Kaleb pulled her forward so her thighs skimmed his ribs and his chest was just shy from touching hers. Her pebbled nipples didn't escape his notice, though at the moment he chose to ignore them. Kaleb bit back the desire to pull them between his teeth, nip them, then soothe the aching nubs with the pad of his tongue. His cock twitched at the idea of suckling her pert breasts, but he had no intention of appeasing that itch. He'd wait until she had gone, then take care of his aching groin himself.

"Please, Hawk."

Tears welled in her eyes. She no doubt hated herself for desiring him. Her pulse beat heavily at the base of her throat, telling him as much. He could hear her blood rushing through her veins. His fangs ached with the need to feed, which he wasn't about to deny himself a moment longer. Cupping the back of her neck, he drew her closer so that their chests aligned and her moist center straddled his abdomen, her backside still perched on the edge of the sofa.

Tilting her head to the side, just centimeters from the last bite, Kaleb drew his lips back and sank his fangs into the flesh. The soft pop of his teeth breaking through her skin and her slight gasp cut through the silence as the DJ below changed songs. Warm blood rushed over his tongue and down his throat. He could easily get lost in the potent flavor unique to her, and lose himself to the point of madness. Kaleb needed to keep a tight rein on himself in order to keep from yanking down her snug jeans and burying his cock in her balls-deep.

Suzi's hands released the grip she had on his shirt and slid up his chest to his nape where she tangled her fingers in the lengthy curls. Her arousal rose with the quickening of her heartbeat, telling him she wasn't far from an orgasm that he'd one day allow her. But that was not for today. Instead, he'd allow her to teeter on the edge.

Her breathing quickened and her fists tightened in his hair. Just scant seconds from her reaching the pinnacle, he withdrew his fangs and licked the twin holes closed. Her breath hitched, and her thighs trembled as he released her. Kaleb stood and wiped the back of his hand across his mouth. His fangs slowly retreated and his features returned to their normal state. Her gaze left his and traveled down his chest to the front of his jeans, still swelled with his heavy erection.

One of his brows raised. "See something you want, *piccolo diavolo?*"

Suzi clenched her teeth, her fiery gaze returning as she quickly stood and readjusted her shirt. "Go to hell, Hawk."

Her shoulder bumped into his arm as she brushed past, pushing him to the side.

"*Piccolo diavolo?*" Kaleb stopped her with his acquisition.

Hand on the door knob, her spine stiff, she kept her gaze on the door.

"That fiancé of yours?"

She glanced over her shoulder, her blue gaze so cold that a shiver passed down his spine.

"What of him?"

"He best not be fucking you."

Kaleb heard a colorful stream of curses and her hope to one day castrate him as she stormed from the room and descended the stairwell. Biting back a blaspheme of his own, Kaleb released his cock, wrapped his fist around it, and jerked it until he reached his own climax with the name *piccolo diavolo* roaring from his lips.

CHAPTER EIGHT

"LITTLE BROTHER."

Kaleb turned his head and caught his twin strolling into the clubhouse as if he hadn't been absent the last six months. His mate, Cara, followed him through the door, a khaki-colored backpack slung over her right shoulder. Her features had changed a bit, due to the changes in her DNA and becoming one of them. In truth, Kaleb thought she had never looked better.

"Only by minutes." Kaleb skirted the bar and walked over to his brother, capturing him in a one-armed hug, while the other hand clapped his shoulder. "About damn time you remembered where the hell you live. And speaking of..." He glanced at Cara, offering her a small apologetic smile. "No offense, but I do hope you two plan on getting a place of your own. I don't think I could possibly stomach the honeymoon noises coming from your room."

Kane laughed, the smile easily reaching his eyes. Kaleb hadn't seen his brother this truly happy in a very long time, not since Ion's loss some ten years back. It would do him well to remember that Kane's mate had everything to do with that. Kaleb would need to cut her some slack, no matter how rocky the beginning of their relationship was. If she made Kane happy, then who was he to get in the way of that?

"Duly noted, Hawk."

Kaleb rubbed his nape. "You bring news?"

"Mircea says he wasn't involved in Wheezer and Red Dot's beheading. He assures me that he has not put a hit out on you."

"And you believe him?"

"I do."

"And Rosalee?"

Kane sighed heavily, blowing air through pursed lips. "She's still missing, bro. Mircea hasn't seen her. If she's in the States, then she left without his permission and is acting on her own."

"I'm going to leave you two to talk," Cara interrupted. She rose on her tiptoes and briefly kissed Kane's lips. "Besides, I need a shower. That plane ride was hell."

Kane patted her on the backside as she turned and headed for his room. The door softly closed behind her before Kane turned back to Kaleb. "I'd stake my life on the fact she's here and behind this. But you and I both know Rosalee never acts on her own, case in point, Ion and then Alec. So the question is, who the hell did she recruit this time?"

Kaleb strode to the bar and pulled a bottle of Jack from the top cupboard and two highball glasses. After pouring two fingers of the amber liquid into each crystal cut glass, he carried them back over to Kane and handed him one. He held his glass up and touched the rim of his to Kane's.

"Salute," Kaleb said then downed his glass, the liquid warming his esophagus, then his gut. "Glad to have you back, Viper."

Kane wiped a palm over his lips. "Glad to be back. Good whiskey. Single Barrel?"

"Only the finest," Kaleb said, sitting heavily onto the leather chair in the living area and kicking his bare feet up onto the scarred center table. "Any ideas who she might've gotten involved in her schemes this time?"

Skirting the lone chair Kaleb sat in, Kane made himself comfortable on one of the sofas. He rested one arm along the back, giving Kaleb his full attention. "I called Mircea before we left Italy. The old man swore that all primordials other than his bitch of a stepdaughter were accounted for in Italy. No one knew of her whereabouts. The witch has definitely flown the coop."

"So she's most likely here in the States. But why come after me? Her beef is with you."

"Because she knows the easiest way to hurt me is through my family. You killed Alec, and because it's forbidden to kill an ancient, she probably feels justified, and that she'd have Mircea's blessing in coming after you. If she targeted me, then it would likely mean certain death for yet again disregarding Mircea's wishes. Rosalee's not stupid. She knows how to work the old man."

"How did Mircea handle the accusation?"

"How do you think? The old man pretty much demanded that we not take retribution, that he'd handle Rosalee if she indeed were the guilty party. He pretty much forbid us to act on our own."

"And what do you say?"

"I say fuck that. She entered our territory looking for a fight. Well, dear brother, I'll damn well give her one. Mircea better pray he gets to her first or I guarantee that I'll be taking her fucking head."

"You get a hold of Red? Find out what the Knights might have to do with all this?"

Kane nodded. "He knew nothing of the phone call made to you. As far as he knew, none of his men made that call. He assured me if he heard otherwise, he'd call. We have his and the club's support if we need them to help find this fuck who took Wheezer and Red Dot's head. He wasn't too happy to hear that someone had posed as a Knight when calling you. Both Red and I feel it's got to be someone close to the Sons or Knights who's helping her."

"Because they knew by calling me that I would set out to find you myself?"

"No, because they knew of our rapport with the Knights. Why else would the caller assume that you might believe I would call Red if I were in some kind of trouble?"

Kaleb scratched his nape. Damn, but he had acted the fool, even if he hadn't one hundred percent believed the caller. He had, though, organized a rescue mission due to that phone call. "But I didn't believe it without question, at least not fully."

"No, but you believed it enough so that you set out that night, organized a ride straight into the waiting trap. And whoever the caller was counted on you doing so."

TAMERA SAT AT THE WOODEN table of Murphy's Tavern looking much like a fish out of water, twirling a ringlet of red hair around her forefinger. She wore fishnet stockings under a tight, black leather skirt, with five-inch patent leather heals to compliment the outfit. On top she wore a white halter tank that dipped well into her cleavage. In truth, with her fiery-red hair, Suzi thought she looked smoking hot. Most the guys in the place were guilty of ogling her, and yet Tamera seemed completely oblivious to the attention. The large barkeep, who had to stand at least six-foot-eight, with shoulders like a linebacker, made his way toward them.

He seemed friendly enough as he stopped by several tables and talked to the various patrons who filled his bar on a Tuesday night before making it to their table in the back of the crowded room. A smile crawled up Tamera's cheeks. Obviously she knew the giant of a man by the warm look she bestowed him with upon his approach. Even dressed a bit more conservative, Suzi still felt a tad out of place as well where most patrons wore jeans, cowboy boots, and either T-shirts or flannels. Tamera and Suzi's attire was much more suited for the bar around the corner, the Blood 'n' Rave. Country music and the din of conversation made it difficult to carry on normal conversation. Murphy's Tavern had the reputation of being a rowdy bar at times with some guys having more braun than brains.

Tamera rose as the owner stopped at their table and leaned down to give her roommate a bear of a hug. "Hey, beautiful. How's my favorite niece?"

"I'm great, Uncle Lyle. You're handsome as ever."

"This ugly mug?" He chuckled. "Couple of beers on the house?"

Placing her hand on his large biceps, Tamera raised her voice to be heard. "A couple of pinot noirs and you have a deal."

Lyle turned toward the bartender, used his fingers to indicate a couple of glasses, then shouted, "Pinot noirs," over the loud hubbub.

Tamera's uncle had barely put his backside into a seat at their table when two long stemmed glasses, half-filled with the deep red wine, were set on the table in front of them. "You going to introduce us, Tamera? Or do I need to embarrass myself and make assumptions this lovely lady doesn't even know you and came here just to see me."

He winked, followed by a deep robust laugh that rumbled up from his chest. Suzi already liked the barkeep. Rounded cheekbones and deep set eyes, gave him that teddy bear appeal that made her want to wrap her arms around his waist and squeeze. In short, the big guy looked harmless, and a whole lot of fun. No wonder his bar was filled to capacity on a weekday night.

"I'm sorry. Suzi, this is my mother's little brother, Lyle Murphy. He owns this establishment."

"Little?" Suzi laughed, extending her hand, which he took to his lips and briefly kissed the back of. "I'm Suzi Stevens, your niece's roommate who can't seem to stay out of trouble. I'd say you are anything but little, Mr. Murphy."

"Oh, please don't call me mister. That's my dad's name. I'm Lyle. I don't answer to anything else accept maybe 'Hey, asshole,'" he said rubbing the bridge of a crooked nose.

Obviously he had been in a fight or two, resulting in a broken nose. By the size of Lyle, she had to wonder what broken bones the other guy received. Anyone would be a fool to call a man the size of Lyle an ass.

"I doubt anyone would call you that."

"You'd be surprised when it gets late and you have drunks not wanting to call it a night. I call them a cab, and I get called asshole." He looked from Suzi to Tamera. "What brings the two of you in tonight?"

Tamera held her glass to her lips and took a sip of the deep red liquid, before replying. "Do we need a reason?"

Tamera and Suzi, given the option, wouldn't normally have chosen Murphy's Tavern as a night out, and Lyle undoubtedly knew that. It was more of a known hang out for the Sheriff's Office and their ilk. Cara Brahnam would be more likely caught here knocking back a few than Suzi ever would. At least before meeting Kane anyway. Suzi couldn't help wonder what Kane and her childhood friend were up to. Suzi had heard from Cara at least a couple of times since they left town six months ago, their whereabouts unknown, but it had been at least three weeks since her last call. Cara's grandfather being a resident in the nursing home Suzi worked for, Cara had checked in frequently on his welfare.

She used the excuse she had wanted to make sure the old man behaved himself in her absence, when Suzi knew Cara worried about his health and well-being. The thought brought a smile to her face. Grandpa Brahnam had a way with the ladies at the nursing home and was way too ornery to die. Suzi had taken a job as the resident LPN at the Pleasant Care Nursing Home shortly after Cara and Kane had left town as her way of helping Cara, knowing that she would feel comfortable leaving her grandfather in her capable hands.

Suzi planned to go back to school to continue her education so that she could get her RN license, and open up her career opportunities now that she had put the Sons of Sangue behind her, or at least she had until Kaleb came crashing back into her life. She supposed she was partly at fault. But how could she have known her trip to the Rave, out of concern for his welfare, would end as it had?

"No, sweetheart, but I suspect you have one anyway. What can I do for you?"

"Suzi needs a pretend fiancé."

And she did, but Tamera could've at least forewarned her. Suzi damn near spit the wine she had just taken a sip from. Heat rose up her neck and warmed her cheeks. Tamera had said they were stopping by to have a drink with a family member. That family member now sat at their table scrutinizing her. Probably wondering what ailment she had that she couldn't get a boyfriend on her own. She had a disorder all right in the name of Kaleb Tepes. The corners of his lips lifted his cheeks as he slowly smiled, then guffawed, so much so that they now attracted the attention of several nearby tables. Suzi leaned forward, placing her chin on her palm. Sure it was all fun and games ... at her expense. She'd definitely kill Tamera when they got home, if they even made it that far.

Her uncle finally contained his mirth and smiled widely at Suzi. "So you're in need of a pretend boyfriend? Or are you looking to shack up, darlin'?"

Suzi knew he jested, trying to lighten her embarrassment, but it wasn't helping. She rolled her eyes, then placed her left hand out so the bauble on her ring finger reflected in the low lighting.

Lyle whistled. "That's some rock."

Suzi grimaced. "It's a fake."

He studied her for a moment, then said, "So why the pretend fiancé, and why now do you need to produce him?"

"I was hoping to dissuade someone's unwanted attention." Suzi leaned back in her chair. "I thought the ring alone would do it. I was wrong."

"So you need me to appear with you somewhere this man happens to be. He sees me with you and what? Backs off? " Lyle patted her ring hand that now lay flat on the table, then gave her fingers a warm squeeze. "You need me to rough him up too, darlin'?"

She looked at Tamera, giving her the stink eye. Telling Suzi about her little plan beforehand would have been preferable. But then again, maybe Tamera knew Suzi would've never agreed to such an outlandish scheme.

"I'm sorry, Lyle. Tamera shouldn't have brought you into my mess."

Lyle's warm blue eyes held her gaze. "Why not let me decide what I should get involved in? Tell me about this problem you have."

"I'm not even sure that I need someone to run interference." Suzi sighed, on the verge of tears. She quickly blinked away the wetness, before anyone commented on her misery. "I allowed someone to believe I had a fiancé."

"Because you didn't want his interest?"

She shook her head. "I'm pretty sure he doesn't want anything to do with me. He hates me and he makes sure I know just how much."

Lyle's forehead creased. "Why would he care if you had a fiancé then?"

"I used to date his nephew." Suzi looked to her lap, anywhere but into the caring eyes of Tamera's uncle. How would she ever explain her and Kaleb's complicated non-relationship? "I never really dated Ion. But this guy ... he believes I did. Thought I was all kinds of wrong for him, I'm sure. Then when his nephew died tragically, he thought I was the biggest bitch on the face of the earth for not reacting as he thought I should. I mourned his loss. I really did. But I missed my best friend. Not a lover. That's something Hawk will never understand."

"Hawk? As in the Sons of Sangue Hawk?" Lyle asked, one of his brows rose.

Great, he knew Kaleb. For all Suzi knew, Lyle wouldn't want anything to do with the president of the MC. Who in their right mind would? Even one of Lyle's size was no match for the biker, not to mention the Sons *take them all on* type mentality. No one went up against the MC in town.

"Yes, that Hawk."

He slowly nodded, probably trying to think of a polite way to get out of this scheme he had been unwittingly brought into. Instead, Lyle surprised her by saying, "So where do you want this meeting to take place?"

Suzi's gaze widened. "You'll do it?"

"Can't have the MC bullying my fiancée, now can I?"

She wanted to leap from her chair and give the big guy a hug. Hopefully, Kaleb would see her with Lyle and that would be the end of their ridiculous arrangement. After all, Lyle being easily six-foot-eight would intimidate most men. But then again, Kaleb wasn't anything like most men, and Lyle's sheer size wouldn't scare him off, not when he could easily take Lyle in a fight.

"Hopefully I don't look old enough to be your father. I'd hate to come across as some kind of pervert."

Suzi smiled. "You don't look anywhere old enough."

"Well, trust me, I am. So what's the plan?"

CHAPTER NINE

SUZI WALKED THE BLACK AND WHITE TILED CORRIDOR, HEADING down the long hall with a tray of meds balanced on the palm of one hand. Her soft soled shoes lightly squeaked off the freshly polished surface. The whirring noise of the machine could be overheard as the janitor polished the hallway of another wing. The previous night's events came to mind, more specifically Lyle Murphy and his acquiescence to help Suzi with her fake fiancé issue. Tamera, and her sincere desire to help, had not thought the scheme entirely through. Sure, her uncle towered over most men, but Kaleb and the MC were far from normal. Suzi knew if Kaleb wanted to he could easily hurt Lyle in an attempt to scare him off. The last thing Suzi wanted was to put Lyle in harm's way. Hopefully, Kaleb would see that her intended was indeed real, be a man about the whole ordeal, and release her from this ridiculous notion of being his personal feeding vein.

Too far into the game plan now to back out, Suzi knew she'd just have to carry through with their cockamamie plan and hope the barkeep didn't get harmed in the process. She'd never forgive Kaleb if he laid one finger on Tamera's uncle. Lyle had agreed to help Suzi out of the kindness of his heart, knowing full well what the MC and Kaleb were capable of. She certainly couldn't allow Lyle's mercy to be repaid by Kaleb's desire for revenge against her.

But for now, she had a job to do with patients who needed her attention on them and not her thoughts on tomorrow night's feeding of Kaleb and the many possible dire outcomes. Lyle had agreed to accompany her to the Blood 'n' Rave, where he would do nothing more than show up as her fiancé, proving to Kaleb that the man on the other side of the ring did exist. Suzi hoped he believed the ruse and would let her out of being his personal donor when there were so many others more than happy to step up and take her place. Suzi didn't think she'd survive many more feedings without desire muddying up the entire mess.

Dear Lord, deny it all she tried, but Kaleb had brought her to the precipice of what promised to be one hell of an orgasm, regardless of how she had fought against it, then denied her the culmination, pulling away just before she reached the brass rings. Storming from the club with any dignity on trembling thighs and weak knees was almost impossible. But somehow she had managed to square her shoulders and walk past Draven, though she dare not spare him a glance should he look at her with pity, and out of the club into the brisk night air which certainly helped to cool her ardor. Suzi didn't think she could withstand more nights of endless sexual torture. It was imperative that Kaleb believed her relationship with Lyle and release her from being his personal blood bank. If he didn't, then she would make him wish he never met her. If he thought her the biggest bitch when Ion died, then he had no idea what would be in store for him if he continued to tease her. She would turn the tables on his sorry ass and leave him begging her to fuck him.

Bless his black heart, but that would be a cold day in hell.

Turning the corner to her wing, Suzi heard a familiar laugh coming from Grandpa Brahnam's room. Thoughts of Kaleb quickly fled as she entered Cara's grandfather's room and found Cara Brahnam sitting on the edge of the bed, a large smile turning up her cheeks. Cara beamed, looking the definition of happy. It appeared that mated bliss had changed her life for the good. Kane must be treating her well. At least one of the twins was worth a damn. Suzi couldn't be happier for Cara and was glad that her childhood friend had found that once in a lifetime love. She placed the tray of meds on a side table, well away from Grandpa's reach, as Cara stood and walked over to Suzi and hugged her.

"It's so good to see you," Cara said.

"Well if it ain't my pretty little nurse," Grandpa said with a wink as he caught their attention.

Suzi smiled at the old man, squeezed his weathered hand and said, "You keep trying, Grandpa. Flattery will get you everywhere. Can I get you something? Are you hungry? It doesn't look like you ate much."

"Nope… and I don't think I need those pills you brought either."

"Sorry, but those you have to take."

"Always bossing me around," he grumbled, then turned to the television and aimed the remote at it. The chatter from the flat screen filled the silence.

Suzi turned to Cara. "When did you get back?"

"We just flew in this morning."

"I could've picked you up from the airport."

"We rented a car," Cara said. "We wanted to surprise everyone. We hadn't planned on coming home yet, but club business needed attended to. Have you heard about it?"

Moisture gathered in Suzi's eyes. "If you're referring to Wheezer and Red Dot, yes, I heard."

Cara blew out a stream of air. "So you've spoken to Hawk?"

"I wanted to make sure he was okay. Though nothing seems to faze him."

"I don't suppose," Cara said. "So tell me ... has Grandpa been behaving?"

"I'm sitting right here."

They both smiled at the older man, earning him a pat on the knee by Cara. "You love it when we talk about you, Grandpa. It reminds you how much you're loved."

"Then that would've meant someone brought me peanut butter pie." He pointed one gnarled finger at the dinner tray. "Do you see a piece of pie on that tray?"

"No," Suzi said. "That's because it isn't part of your diet."

"Bah! I'm ninety-two years old. I figure I can eat what I want and peanut butter pie is high on that list."

"I'll sneak you a piece next time I come by, Grandpa. That is if you treat your nurses like the saints they are," Cara said, patting the older man's shoulder. "Now, you finish your meal and quit being so damn stubborn."

"And take your meds," Suzi added, then handed him a small paper cup filled with four tablets. "You take these and I'll let Cara bring you that piece of pie."

"You heard her, Grandpa. You finish your meal and take those meds, and I'll make sure I bring you a treat tomorrow."

Suzi threw the empty paper cup into the gray receptacle, then looked back at Cara. "You seriously rented a car? I would have gladly picked you guys up."

"I know you would've. But it was all so sudden. We sort of just packed up, called the airport, and well ... here we are."

"Where'd you guys go?"

"Italy ... to see Mircea," Cara said, surprising Suzi. No wonder they kept their whereabouts a secret. "To see that Kane was available to me." She skirted the issue in front of her grandfather's ears.

"And?"

"He granted our wish." Cara's answering smile spoke volumes. "I wanted to tell you in person, that's why I never mentioned it in any of our phone conversations. Mircea granted Kane's wish to be mated with me."

"Mated?" Grandpa Brahnam asked, proving he was listening in on their conversation.

They'd have to be more careful what they said in front of the old man. His gaze honed in on his granddaughter.

"What the hell does that mean? Is it a new way of saying you got hitched?"

Cara winked at Suzi first before turning to her grandfather. "I was waiting for the right time, Grandpa. When Kane and I went to Italy, we applied for marriage so to speak. It's a bit different where he comes from. They call it mated."

"So what? Your name is now Cara...?"

"It's still Brahnam, Grandpa. The women don't take on their mate's name."

"That's crazy shit, you ask me," he grumbled. "Should've gotten married right here in the States and done it right."

Cara kissed his temple. "I know, Grandpa. It wasn't traditional."

"What makes him not want to just up and leave you then? You have no ties. Maybe I should have a talk with your husband."

Cara laughed. "Oh, no, you don't. That's why Kane's not here with me right now. I wanted to explain it to you first without you going all ape shit on him. In his beliefs, mating is for life. There is no such thing as divorce. As Kane would tell you, 'You work that shit out.'"

"Maybe he has more sense than I gave him credit for."

"So it's official then?" Suzi motioned for Cara to follow her into the hallway and out of Cara's grandfather's earshot. "What of Rosalee?"

Cara shrugged, leaning one shoulder against the cool hallway wall and crossing her arms over her chest. "Gone. After Kane and I were granted the wish to be mated, she up and disappeared."

"You think she's the one responsible for Wheezer and Red Dot then?"

"Kane believes she is. But I'm not sure. My gut tells me there's more to it. She's not acting on her own."

"Does she ever?"

Cara rolled her eyes. "She'll likely always be a thorn in my side. But I know what I signed up for."

"There's so much more I want to ask, but we can save that for another time."

"Good idea," Cara said. "I have to get going anyway. I need to stop by the Sheriff's Office."

"You asking for your old job back?"

Cara smiled. Suzi knew how much being a detective meant to her. Cara wasn't about to let a little thing like being a vampire stop her.

"I never left the job. Just took an extended leave. Sheriff Ducat already told me my job was waiting for me whenever I want to get back to the job of solving crimes. My only hope is that my partner will be happy to see me. Something tells me Joe Hernandez isn't going to be too happy with me. He hates the Tepes twins and the club. He'll undoubtedly hate my association. Speaking of the twins, what is it between you and Kaleb anyway?"

"There's nothing between us to talk about. If there was, you'd have been the first to know. Right now, he's just an ass who thinks he has ultimate power."

"Yeah?"

"And I plan to be the one to knock his sorry ass off that pedestal he's been standing on."

"What are you girls whispering about out there?" Grandpa Brahnam groused. "Ain't no cause for secrets."

Cara chuckled as she shook her head. Righting herself, she turned and headed back into her grandfather's room, saying over her shoulder, "Good luck with that, Suzi. In my experience, it's just better giving in to what they want." She lowered her voice, "And much more pleasurable, too."

"I heard that," Grandpa Brahnam said. Suzi and Cara grinned.

Cara gave her grandfather a hug and kissed his weathered cheek. "I have to be going anyway, Grandpa." Turning to Suzi, she briefly hugged her as well, then said, "Glad to be back, Suzi. I've missed you."

"Don't be a stranger. I live in Florence now. Pleasant was too small of a town to house both Hawk and I."

Cara chuckled. "I suppose so. As soon as I get settled, I'll come look you up for some girl time."

"Kane going to allow you out of his sight?"

Cara's eyes gleamed. She leaned in and whispered, "The man is insatiable, but we can't stay in bed all day."

"I heard that," came from Grandpa again, causing them both to burst into laughter.

KALEB PACED THE FLOOR, his booted heels striking the wooden flooring in his agitated state as he awaited the Knights' arrival. His skin crawled in restlessness. It had been two nights since he had last sought out Suzi Stevens. Keeping to his normal three-day feeding schedule meant he wouldn't see her for another night, which didn't sit well with him ... not at all. He needed to know where she stayed so he could keep eyes on her at all times, justifying his desire with the fear she might not hold up her end of the bargain and skip out on being his donor. Knowing her fiancé spent time with her ate away at him, reminding him of the days she spent in Ion's company. Christ, it all but killed him then to know she was in love with his brother's son, lying with him when the sun went down. Kaleb had fucked her only once, and yet in all the years following, he hadn't been able to forget her, the silkiness of her pale skin, the scent of her desire. Just thinking of her now stirred his groin.

Shit. He needed to get laid.

Maybe following their meeting with the Knights he'd head to the Rave and do just that. He had a lot of unspent energy he needed to get rid of. Nothing like a good piece of ass to take his mind off all his troubles. Kaleb stopped his pacing, let out a stream of curses, and flopped onto one of the sofas just as Kane exited his quarters and joined him. The coils groaned from the added extra weight.

Kane laid an arm across the back of the brown fabric. "What the hell is eating at you anyway, Hawk? You seem strung tighter than a violin."

Kaleb ground his teeth, not wanting to share his weakness for the little brunette who had occupied his every thought since she had walked back into his life six nights back. He especially didn't want to share his decade long obsession with Kane.

"What's taking the Knights so damn long?" he asked, opting to avoid the real reason for his shitty mood.

Red had been invited to the clubhouse for a little chat by Kane, hoping they might be able to discover who had made the bogus call to Kaleb. The pres of the MC had stood by his declaration that none of his men made the damning call. Kane might've been convinced, but Kaleb still had his suspicions. His cell number hadn't been public knowledge and the only other MC that had access to it had been the Knights. It seemed someone had a beef with the Sons ... more specifically him. Kaleb believed this all fell on Rosalee's doorstep. The entire incident had her scent all over it. But the question was, who the hell was helping her? She never acted alone, and Kaleb doubted she did now. Rosalee was a damn coward, always standing behind her stepfather's robe. She knew Mircea would always protect her, even if he had been the one to banish her to Italy for her last crimes against the MC.

The door banged off the inside wall as Grayson and Alexander made a grand entrance, robust laughter drawing both Kaleb and Kane's attention. Grayson pushed his ever-present sunglasses up on his head, pulling his overlong chestnut hair from his piercing blue eyes. The two MC brothers shared a private joke as Alexander shut the door and headed for the bar. Grayson joined Kaleb and Kane in the living area, sitting on the adjacent leather chair. His azure gaze turned up in merriment.

"You two seem far too serious for my liking. I say we grab a few fifths of whiskey and go looking for some tail. That is after our meet and greet with Red, of course. We haven't yet celebrated Kane's return. I say we gather the Sons and have a grandiose party."

Kaleb knew Grayson's desire to celebrate Kane's return had more to do with his desire for entertainment as he still hadn't quite gotten over Kane turning his back on the club, and all for the want of a woman. Grayson saw it as a sign of weakness. Maybe, Kaleb thought. But with his obsession over Suzi, he certainly couldn't condemn his twin for his actions. He'd like to think he'd let Suzi rot. But damn if he could say that for certain.

"Nice of you to show up, Gypsy," Kaleb said, at the late arrival of his VP. His heated gaze bore into Grayson.

"What the fuck?" Grayson's humor quickly fled. "Xander and I made it before the Knights got here, so I don't see what the hell you're being such a dick about. Dude, you need to get laid. I know some ladies from Florence who are always up for a party. I could call them."

Kaleb didn't know what pissed him off more. The fact that Grayson voiced his own thoughts just moments ago, or the fact that he felt the need to point out the obvious.

"We have business to attend, Gypsy. My sex life isn't up for discussion. Get your head in the fucking game."

"Jesus. Where the hell did the real Hawk go? And who replaced him with this asshole?"

Alexander wisely kept out of the spiraling conversation. Instead he pulled out a stool by the bar and straddled it, leaning back, elbows on the armrests. Apparently, he thought it best to sit on the sidelines for this one.

Smart man.

That, or he, too, still wrestled his own demons for surviving a near beheading. Only the two of them shared the survivors' guilt. Nicolas and Steven died in their place. Kaleb's foul mood stemmed from that, as well as the little sprite named Suzi Stevens. Grayson seemed bent on pushing the boundaries of Kaleb's self-control every chance he got, and at the moment those boundaries shouldn't be tested. He certainly couldn't argue with Grayson's logic that he needed a piece of ass since he had those same thoughts, though he didn't need a fellow brother to tell him as much. Regardless, their business with the Knights came first. Maybe then he'd take Grayson up on hitting the Rave, knowing he'd have several willing options for getting horizontal, because there were those biker groupies who made themselves available to the Sons. If Suzi meant to parade the fact she had a fiancé in front of him, then he'd make damn sure she knew his options were anything but limited.

The sound of approaching Harleys announced the arrival of their puppet club, saving an argument between the pres and VP. Gravel crunched beneath tires before the rumble of the V-twin engines cut short. Alexander walked to the door and opened it before the first knock came, showing Red and three of his men into the living area of the clubhouse. Kane and Kaleb stood while Gypsy stayed seated. The twins shook hands with each of the men, before offering them a seat on the sofa across from where they had been seated moments ago. Red and his VP sat while the other two men stood behind them, undoubtedly watching their backs. Trust no one seemed to be many MC's mantras since it was imperative to all their survival. The Knights, though, had nothing to fear from the Sons as long as they continued to be useful.

"You bring us news, Red?" Kane asked as he settled back onto the couch. He glanced back at Alexander. "Bring us some Single Barrel Jack and low ball glasses, Xander."

"I did some checking, Viper." He then looked at Kaleb and nodded in respect. "Hawk. No one admitted to making that call, nor did they know of Viper's absence from the States. I trust my men. If they say they didn't make that call of distress, then I believe them."

The man beside Red, wearing the VP patch, said, "I'm assuming whoever made that call had to have known that Viper had been MIA. Why else would Viper send out a distress call when he would be here among his brothers? Or why would the Sons be so willing to head out on a fool's mission if they knew Viper's whereabouts?"

"Bird and I interviewed every one of the Knights as well as our prospects," Red said, putting a name to the VP for Kaleb. "I won't vouch for our hangarounds. I don't think we've had enough time or interaction yet with any of them to swear they speak the truth or to trust them implicitly."

"Any new hangarounds within the last few months?" Kaleb asked.

"Not that I know of or that my men have spoken of. The Sons?" Red said.

"We haven't been open to a lot of hangarounds as we aren't a trusting bunch. This slaughter keeps up, we'll definitely be in the market for increasing our numbers."

Red narrowed his gaze. "You talking patching over?"

Kaleb looked at his twin, who sat quietly beside him. Kane's expression gave nothing away to his thoughts on the matter of adding new patch members, more specifically taking on the Knights' numbers. Since he had become a non-voting member, due to turning Cara into one of them, Kaleb supposed Kane probably felt he didn't have a voice in the matter. Kaleb would speak with him again once they were alone. He looked at Grayson, who up to this point sat quietly listening in. Kaleb would bet that his looking to Kane first for direction didn't sit well with his VP. Kaleb couldn't blame him. He needed to remember that even though Kane had returned, he still had no voice in MC matters.

"I'm not sure the Sons are ready to patch another MC," Grayson said, not taking his eyes from the pres. "It could be taken to a vote. But honestly, I don't think the Knights have proven themselves as a puppet club."

A muscle in Red's cheek ticked. "I think I made it clear when Kane asked for an alignment of clubs that the Knights were no one's puppet club."

Grayson raised a brow in challenge. "Then what're we even doing here? If you aren't with us ... you're against us."

"With ... you ... is what we are, Surfer Boy," Bird said with a sneer as he drew the words out.

Red gnawed on a toothpick that poked out from his beard. The toothpick switched sides as he said, "The Knights ... we're no one's patsies. I make that clear."

"Call it what you will, Red," Kane spoke up since he was the one who had made the original covenant. "You and I had an agreement that you would align yourself with the Sons. You prove yourselves, then maybe one day the Sons will patch you over and increase the Sons numbers. As Gypsy pointed out, you're either with us or against us. Against us and we cut off your avenue to the coast. It's because of our hospitality that you can run your guns through our state. Don't forget your place with the Sons, Red. It was you who needed our help. Not the other way around."

"May I remind you, I pay the Sons mighty well for that privilege? It's a very lucrative deal for you."

"Before this turns into a fucking pissing match, can we get back to the reason everyone is here?" Kaleb said, as Alexander placed the bottle of Jack in the center of the coffee table with eight glasses.

Kaleb felt the sooner they got the discussion over with, the quicker they got the Knights back on the road and out of Oregon. Grayson looked just shy of ripping someone's throat out for the Surfer Boy comment. Though with his overlong, shoulder length hair and the ever-present sunglasses, he couldn't say Bird was incorrect with his description of his MC brother.

Alexander poured two fingers of the whiskey in each glass, then handed them to each man.

"Look," Red continued, "we'll keep our ears out for someone who might have a beef with Hawk or the Sons."

"Does anyone besides us know of our alignment?" Kaleb asked.

"It's possible," Red said. "Not that we talk about it, but you allow us to ride through Oregon without repercussions. That speaks volumes in itself."

Kaleb certainly couldn't argue with that logic.

"We've had your back before, and we continue to do so," Bird said. "We hear anything, you'll be the first to know."

"Be sure that you do," Grayson said, obvious disdain rolling off him.

Kaleb wondered if there wasn't more to it than the reference to Grayson's pretty boy looks. Kaleb chose to ignore the underlying currents for now. After all, unless it was Sons' business, whatever issue lay between Bird and Grayson was no concern of his. Grayson could take care of his own.

Raising his glass in the air, he said, "Salute."

Each man followed suit and downed the amber-colored liquid. The burn to the esophagus warmed him almost as much as communion. Standing, Kaleb held out his hand to Red, which the man stood and shook. Bird got to his feet as well, staring down Grayson. Both men looked ready to battle. Kaleb planned to question his VP about it once the Knights made their exit. He followed the fellow MC to the door.

"We'll be in touch. You do the same."

Red nodded and the four bikers left the clubhouse. Kaleb shut the door behind them, then glanced at his own men.

Gone was the scorn from Grayson's face, now replaced with a large smile and a twinkle in his gaze. "Who's game for a trip to the Rave and getting a little ass? Not pointing any fingers, but, Hawk, I think you could use the release."

"You're certainly one to talk, Gypsy." Kaleb raised a brow in challenge. "Five minutes ago you looked ready to go to battle against Bird."

Grayson shrugged, with a devil-may-care look. "What can I say? The bastard rubs me the wrong way. Call it a sixth sense. Now, how about finding us some women to party with?"

"I'm all up for communion, but the partying with the ladies, I'll leave that to you three. I'm pretty sure Cara would rip some throats out if she caught another woman trying to get in my pants." Kane chuckled. "Now, let's go look up Draven and get us a party started."

CHAPTER TEN

CARA OPENED THE HEAVY GLASS DOOR TO THE SHERIFF'S OFfice, her shoulders stiff with unease, and walked over to the dispatch window. Sheriff Ducat had assured her that he would hold her position open for however long she needed to come to terms with her new lifestyle. Ducat knew the MC's secret. He had kept quiet about the den of vampires residing in Pleasant over the past decade in return for their protection should the S.O. need back up. Ducat liked having the Sons in his corner, not to mention taking care of society's degenerates. Cara supposed it was much better than the alternative of working against the law. No wonder Kane and his brothers had been so pissed when Cara and her partner tried to lay the murders of three women at their doorstep and why the sheriff hadn't pressured Cara and Joe to solve the case. The Sons had just as much interest in seeing the killer caught, if not more so, than the S.O. did.

Asking for her job back wasn't what had her more fidgety than a cock in a cock fight, though, nor the reason she had walked back through the door. Kane's pockets were deep enough to sustain them several lifetimes, so it wasn't as if Cara had returned for the promise of a steady paycheck. She had loved the job, plain and simple. Being an officer ran bone-deep, it was her identity. She missed the camaraderie of her fellow deputies. Hell, she missed Hernandez. Not that he'd be any too pleased to see her, which was the sole reason for her sudden case of the jitters. Like it or not, Joe Hernandez had been a good friend over the years, and her relationship with the Sons, more specifically Kane, was not going to sit well with him.

The dispatch looked up from her long row of monitors and smiled at Cara's approach. "Detective Brahnam ... I hadn't heard that you were back in town."

"Lisa," Cara acknowledged. "I sort of slipped in under the radar, no need for fan fair. Is Sheriff Ducat in?"

"Let me buzz you in. He's in his office on the phone, but I'm sure he'll be glad to see you."

The activation of the door buzzed and Cara grasped the handle, pulling open the heavy interior auto-locking door. "Thanks," she said, then walked past the dispatch office and started down the hall.

"Nice to see you again, Detective," Lisa called after her.

The sentiment made her smile. "Nice to be here," she said, and meant it. Cara had come home.

She supposed talking to Sheriff Ducat was the first order of business. Once they set a date for her to return to the job, then she'd talk to Joe ... alone. Cara had a feeling he wasn't going to make this easy for her. No matter how she presented it, Joe would look at it as a betrayal and he'd never accept her relationship with Kane or the Sons.

Sheriff Ducat replaced the phone in the cradle just as Cara walked through the opened doorway. A smile grew wide on his weathered face. Ducat looked as if he had aged several years over the past six months. She hoped like hell her tribulations and near death, followed by her lengthy absence, hadn't caused him grief.

"Well, I'll be damned," he said, beaming. The sheriff stood and rounded his desk, pulling Cara into a bear of a hug. "Dare I hope you came to beg for your old job back?"

Cara laughed. "I was sort of hoping you still had that spot for me."

"What would make you think any different?"

"Because ... I'm different." Her smile waned as she looked her old mentor in the eye, glad that she didn't see anything other than acceptance there. "You know what I am."

Ducat shrugged. "I've know what the twins were for years, and the rest of the Sons. The way I look at it, it's a bonus to the county. Pity the man who comes here looking for trouble. He'll definitely find it. As long as you can still do your job, you're welcome here. That side of your life, though, has no business here. I can't have your fellow deputies knowing about you or the Sons. I fear Lane County would become a modern day witch hunt."

"That part of my life will have no bearing on my job."

The sheriff smiled, stuck out his hand and shook hers. "Then welcome back."

She barely felt his tight grip, her strength growing every day, something she'd have to be careful using around her fellow deputies. Ducat circled his desk, opened the drawer on the lower right side, taking out her Glock and badge and placing it on the desk's surface.

"I've been saving this for you. I was hoping you'd be back. In truth, it will be like having someone with ... special skills on board if you will. You talk to Hernandez yet?"

"No. I wanted to speak with you first."

"You can start back officially Monday." He returned to his seat. "Hernandez is in his office. You two will still share the office."

"No new partner?"

He shook his head. "I was waiting for you. And truth be told, I'll bet he was hoping for your return as well."

Cara took a deep breath. "Not so sure about that. He's no fan of Kane or Kaleb. My being a part of their life won't sit well with him."

"If he has problems with your return, then you tell him to take it up with me."

Cara took in a deep breath then released it slowly. "Thank you, Sheriff. Your support means a lot."

"You're a good girl, Cara. That hasn't changed. Now go on, and prove that to Hernandez."

Cara slipped her Glock in the waistband at the small of her back, then picked up her badge.

"Monday will be soon enough to swear you in. See you at eight. I take it the hours won't be difficult?"

"Not at all, Sheriff. It's not like I sleep in a coffin."

Ducat smiled. "See that you don't."

She headed out of the office, just as the phone rang and the sheriff muttered something about election years and politics. Cara's feet grew leaden the closer she came to her old office. Florescent bulbs flickered in the hallway and the smell of freshly shined floors drifted to her nose. Funny how all her senses had heightened since becoming a vampire. The more blood she consumed, the stronger she became as well. Cara caught a waft of Joe's aftershave before she even entered the office, telling her he was in the room. She stopped in the doorway, leaning on the doorjamb. Hernandez's back muscles flexed as he combed through an open file on his desk, speaking with someone on the phone about the papers littering his desk, unaware of her arrival.

His dark hair cut short and curled softly about his ears, looking slightly longer and unkempt from the last time she had saw him. When he replaced the receiver onto the cradle, his spine stiffened as if he had detected her arrival. Joe slowly swiveled in his chair to see her standing there, his expression not one of welcome.

"What the hell do you want, Brahnam?"

"Nice to see you too, Joe." She offered him a weak smile.

Cara hated the mile-wide gulf between them. She had at one time felt like a little sister to the man. He would have given his life to protect her. Now? She wasn't so sure.

"No one said anything about it being nice to see you."

"Damn, Joe, why don't you really say what's on your mind? Get it off your chest so we can go back to being partners already."

"Oh, hell no!" Joe stood and faced off with her. "You're not coming back to the job and you're definitely not sharing this office with me."

Cara's ire rose. Where did he get off treating her like dirt beneath his Oxfords all of the sudden? "It's already been decided. I start Monday."

His gaze narrowed, dislike clearly evident in his brown eyes. "I see."

She stepped farther into the office and shut the door behind her. No sense allowing the rest of the office privy to their heated exchange. "No, Joseph Hernandez, you don't see." She planted her fists on her hips. "It wasn't that long ago you had my back. Nothing has changed. I have not changed." She thumped her fist against her chest for emphasis.

His anger seemed to rise off him. "I always had your back, Brahnam, that is until you started shacking up with that piece of—"

"Careful, Joe. Regardless what you think of Kane, or his brother for that matter, I do love the man."

Joe slowly nodded, though he wisely kept his mouth shut. He needed to hear her out.

"And he loves me unconditionally, regardless of what I do for a living. I owe him the same respect."

"You may, but I don't. Don't you think it's a conflict of interest you working here? He's an outlaw, for crying out loud, Cara. You're going to give him an inside to what goes on here. And what if he or any of the Sons are under investigation? You think about that?"

"Kane isn't breaking any laws."

"You're an idiot if you believe that. The Sons are all outlaws. I can't fucking believe the sheriff okayed you coming back."

Tears welled in her eyes, but she refused to allow them to fall. Not that she didn't think Joe would have a hard time with her relationship with Kane, but she hadn't realized how deep his dislike of them ran. Joe seriously didn't think he could force her to choose between him and Kane. He had to know that was one argument he couldn't possibly win.

"You know I love you, Joe. That's never changed. You've always been a big part of my life. But we don't always get to choose who we fall in love with. Kane Tepes is in my life. I can't and I won't give that up ... not for anyone or anything."

"I sure in the hell hope that doesn't come back to bite you in the ass, honey."

"Why not let me worry about that?" A tear slipped down her cheek unheeded. "I promise, Joe, that Kane or the Sons will not interfere with my job here. And if it comes to that, I'll resign."

Joe's stance softened. His anger lessened. He may not like Kane, or the idea of her in a relationship with the biker, but no one told her how to live her life ... including Kane. She may be mated to him, swore to love him until death, but Kane did not own her. He hadn't liked the idea of her working with Hernandez again, but he had also known how much the job meant to her. Kane would never stand in the way of her happiness.

Joe sighed, then stuck out his hand. "Welcome back, Brahnam."

But instead of taking his hand, Cara walked over to him and folded her arms about his waist. Joe paused but a moment before enfolding her within his embrace. "I do love you, Joe."

"Yeah, you just keep that biker out of my way." She heard the smile in his voice as she lay her cheek against his muscular chest. "And you tell him if he hurts you, he has to answer to me."

Cara smiled. Joe wouldn't stand a chance against Kane, but she'd let him think it a worthy threat anyway.

PULLING A BLACK TEE OVER HIS HEAD, Kaleb walked from his bedroom and into the living area of the clubhouse where the Sons gathered. The call from the Knights had come only a few hours prior, but Kaleb had been able to gather a crew at the last minute. The last gun run had been a mere two weeks ago, so they hadn't been exactly prepared. The caller had apologized to Kaleb, but apparently a deal had gone south and the Knights had been offered a lucrative deal. For the Sons, the money was easy—Kaleb wasn't about to complain about another forty percent coming their way this month. Kaleb had tried to get a hold of Kane, but his twin wasn't answering his phone. No matter, they had been doing these runs without him the past six months.

He took care of alerting the sheriff that the Knights would be skirting the town after midnight so that his deputies would be conveniently busy in other areas of the county. The runs had become routine enough that when the Knights rode through Lane County, the locals steered clear in case the state troopers might happen by. The Sheriff's Office could plead ignorance of the illegal transaction as long as they were on the opposite side of the county. This had been the monthly norm since his brother, Kane, had made the deal with Red six months back.

And a great money-making deal it had been.

The Sons made a good amount of money for little to no work. They did nothing more than usher their once rival MC through the state of Oregon and run interference should they attract attention from outside law enforcement. And the money helped when profits were down at the K&K, the twin's motorcycle shop, where most of the Sons worked, bringing them honest wages. Kaleb and Grayson had been regulars on every run, always making sure they protected their interest. But tonight, they elected to sit this one out due to prior plans to head to the Rave. He knew his men could handle the run without them, plus he offered each man a bonus on their next K&K paycheck for helping out on short notice.

Not a single man complained. On the contrary, they all stood in the clubhouse ready to go. Alexander, being the Sergeant at Arms, would lead the pack with Anton at his right. Kaleb hated leaving club business up to his men. After all, he was the president and should anything go wrong, he'd hold himself personally responsible.

Grayson had assured him the men were more than capable of playing babysitter to the Knights. He had pointed out that Suzi would probably be waiting dutifully at the Rave as requested. If Kaleb didn't show, she'd likely take that as a free pass and Kaleb would have to look for another donor or wait another three days to feed from Suzi, which to Kaleb wasn't acceptable. He needed to feed to keep his strength, so finding Suzi was on his high list of priorities. No other donor would do, not when he couldn't get the sassy little brunette from his mind. Hell, his dick hardened just at the thought of having her in his arms, whether it was to merely feed or not. He'd not give Suzi an excuse not to fulfill her duty as his personal donor for even a day.

"Everyone ready?" Kaleb asked as he walked up beside Grayson. "This should be an easy in and out for the Knights. Especially since this is so last minute. No time for the word to get out. Meet Red and his boys at the county line at twelve thirty, ride with them to Florence. Once the exchange has been made, escort them back to the county line. Xander, you and Blondy follow them to the state line. Any sign of trouble, get the fuck out of there. The Sons aren't going to take the heat for a puppet club. Questions?"

"What should we tell Red if he wants to know why you and Gypsy aren't there?" Anton asked.

"You tell him, Blondy, that it couldn't be helped. If he wants Gypsy and I there next time, give us more than a couple of hours heads-up." Kaleb glanced at the clock on the wall. The black hands read ten fifty. "VP and I are heading for Florence. You guys can hang out here until time to meet the Knights. Make sure you aren't late. Xander is in charge of this run. Don't give him reason to have to report back to me. See you don't fuck this up."

Kaleb grabbed his chaps off the back of the sofa and stepped into them, buckling them at the waist, before shrugging into his cut. He sat on the edge of the chair and slipped on his boots before standing and heading for the rack of keys by the door. Snatching his set of keys, he headed for the door, knowing Grayson followed. Once outside, he stepped over his chopper's seat, stuck the key in the ignition and turned it. The '79 Harley Davidson Ironhead chopper roared to life. He placed his skull cap on his head and buckled it beneath his chin. After kicking up the center stand, he looked back at Grayson. The VP gave a nod and the two pulled out of the gravel parking lot and onto the open road.

Pulling back on the gas, Kaleb opened it up and took off down the road, the wind whipping his cut behind him and beating against his leather chaps. Now that he had business behind him, hunger gnawed at his gut, and not just for communion. No, only one smart-mouthed brunette would do. If she wasn't at the Blood 'n' Rave tonight, he'd beat down every donor's door until someone gave her up. And after tonight, he'd make damn sure he knew where she lived. Keeping an eye on her and this fiancé had suddenly become a priority. If he wasn't sleeping with Suzi Stevens, he'd make damn sure that this piece of shit wasn't either.

CHAPTER ELEVEN

KALEB AND GRAYSON PARKED THEIR HARLEYS NEAR THE EN-trance to the Rave. Thursday being ladies' night, the parking lot was filled to overflowing. He was sure Murphy's Bar used some of the space. But by the noise spilling into the parking lot, he'd bet a big share of the vehicles belonged to those at the Blood 'n' Rave. Normally, the Sons were all regulars on ladies' night, with the exception of his brother, who had become a bit antisocial the last decade. Kane would show up every few days, find his donor, and head off to Draven's office for a private meet and eat, rarely sticking around to hang with his brothers. After Ion had been murdered, Kane changed, no longer much of a partier, preferring his life more low key.

Not Kaleb.

There weren't enough women in the world to satisfy him, the Rave never had a shortage. He'd take his pick of the ladies, find a back table, dark corner, bathroom, hallway—anywhere convenient—and fuck them like there was no tomorrow. Later, he'd hypnotize the non-donors into forgetting the change in his features, but not the sex. Kaleb was far too vain to allow them to forget the down and dirty. And he definitely liked the dirtier side of sex, dirty talk, dirty¬ fucking—no prim and proper missionary style for him. So why the hell did one little brunette have him by the balls and swearing off all others now that she had walked back into his life?

To hell with that!

Once he found Suzi and took his communion, he'd hunt up another lady or two—and get busy. He'd do Grayson proud if he for once decided to take on two. Kaleb had always been a one-at-a-time kind of man, where the VP often had two ladies on his arms at any given moment. No one liked the ladies more than Grayson. And he never seemed to have a shortage of them with his longish deep-brown hair, pulled back from his face with a pair of shades. He'd no doubt look just as at home on a surfboard as a Harley. Kaleb smiled. It wouldn't surprise him a bit to see Grayson on the beach, heading for the surf with a board tucked under his arm. He had that laid back-vibe going on that a lot of surfers did. Stepping over his bike, Kaleb hung his skull cap on the handle and looked at his VP.

Grayson pushed his sunglasses up on his mussed hair and grinned as big as the night. He rubbed his hands together. "You ready, P? Let's go find us some action," he said, grabbing his crotch.

"Communion first for me, Gypsy. Can't have my little donor getting cold feet and disappearing on me." Kaleb laughed. "But save me a lady or two, will you?"

"Then don't take all fucking night with a little bitch who doesn't deserve your time."

Kaleb grinned, slapped Grayson on the shoulder, then headed for the front of the club where a doorman nodded in greeting, opened the door and indicated for them to go ahead of those still standing in line waiting entrance. The line curled around the building. Packed house. He sure as hell hoped Suzi made it past that line.

Normally the doormen were trained to let the donors in before all other women, regardless of the length of the line. But the bald giant at the door seemed new as Kaleb hadn't recognized him on sight. If his donor hadn't made it inside, he'd make sure the man never worked another day at the Rave. Kaleb wasn't in the mood to be denied. That included his donor. After tonight, he planned to know the name of the man who thought to marry her and where the hell she laid her head. He had a vested interest in keeping an eye on her. If need be, he'd keep a prospect on her at all times, reminding him it was time to bring on new prospects now that they'd lost Steven.

The DJ spun records at near deafening levels, but with his acute hearing, Kaleb could still easily pick up the din of conversations. Gravers and ravers filled the dance floor, gravers being those with more of a Goth type appearance. Glow sticks swung about the floor as dancers waved them overhead and they hopped and swayed damn near chest to chest and chest to back. A good share of the them were probably already high on X and would be easy pickings once Suzi finished her obligation and fled into the night. Suzi had done her damnedest to convince Kaleb that she hated him, when in truth she wouldn't have sought him out once she had heard he'd almost been beheaded if she didn't care for him at least a little.

But what the hell did he care whether she did or not? Kaleb wasn't about to forget that she once belonged to his nephew, or what a cold-hearted bitch she had been when he had been murdered. When the rest of the family mourned the loss, she couldn't bother herself to approach Kane and give her condolences. She had simply stared coldly at Kaleb, after he had delivered the news, and turned and walked away. Not even a sorry for your loss had left her lips that had once kissed Ion in passion.

Kaleb planned to make her life a living hell for that alone.

He believed that karma came back to bite you in the ass, and Suzi was about to get bitten. Skirting the dance floor, Kaleb hung to the edge and out of the way of the tables surrounding it, filled with those trying to converse as they shouted at one another to be heard over the beat of the music. His gaze took in several hopeful donors, but he continued past them and headed for the main bar, hoping to find Suzi there. Grayson had long since left his side, already trolling the room for tail. With his dark good looks, Kaleb bet he'd have a woman on each arm before he even located Suzi.

A large man wearing a white sweater, stepped back from the bar and bumped into Kaleb. He glanced up at the easily six-foot-eight man who seemed to tower over him and outweigh Kaleb by several pounds. His brown hair cut short around his ears and he looked to be a little old for this crowd, making Kaleb wonder exactly why this man patronized the Rave when he seemed more suited for Murphy's Tavern next door.

"I'm sorry," the man quickly apologized. "I can be incredibly clumsy at times."

"No worries," Kaleb grumbled, skirting past the big guy's arm, holding a vodka and tonic. The scent of the vodka and lime gave way to what the glass held. At least the big ox had kept a firm hold on the glass and Kaleb wasn't now reeking of vodka.

Just as Kaleb cleared his way around the man, the short brunette on the barstool caught his attention. Suzi smiled up at him, one brow raised, making Kaleb immediately suspect her intentions. No way was she that happy to see him. His nostrils flared as he breathed in her unique scent. Blind, he still would have easily recognized her. His groin tightened, making him none-to-happy at his reaction to her. He'd prefer his body would cooperate with the hatred running through his brain. If that were the case, he wouldn't have gotten himself in this situation in the first place.

"Hawk," she greeted, her smile widening. "There is someone here I'd like you to meet. My fiancé who just nearly tripped over you. Lyle, meet an old friend of mine, Kaleb Tepes."

Lyle held out the beefy hand not holding his drink and smiled. Kaleb bet that hand would be great at knocking out most guys with a single punch. Fortunately, he wasn't most guys.

Kaleb ignored the outstretched hand. He tilted his head up and leveled the guy with his black gaze. "So you're Suzi's fiancé. Since when?"

Lyle cleared his throat. "Excuse me?" He shoved his ignored hand back in his pocket, not looking the least bit affronted by Kaleb's brush-off.

"How long have you and"—his hand indicated Suzi—"Miss Stevens known each other?"

"It's been—"

"A few months," Suzi quickly finished for him, capturing Kaleb's gaze.

"Really?" Her rescuing Lyle from having to answer the question didn't go unnoticed by Kaleb. "Six months ago when I kissed you, you and Lyle weren't yet an item?"

"Nope," she said with a big smile. "I didn't meet Lyle until after I left Pleasant."

Kaleb looked back up at Lyle. "You certainly work fast. I don't know if congratulations are in order, though. Do you also know she's a cold-hearted bitch?"

Lyle's face reddened as his large chest puffed out. "Now wait one damn minute."

Suzi quickly laid a hand on Lyle's forearm, wisely silencing the man but further pissing off Kaleb, saving the big guy a serious ass-beating, which at the moment Kaleb wouldn't mind handing out.

Lyle stood easily a foot and a half taller than Suzi. Hell, at six-foot-two Kaleb towered over her five-foot-two frame. They must look completely ridiculous walking down the street holding hands. Talk about a mismatched couple. But why that rankled his ire, he wasn't about to examine. No, that would give purchase to the green-eyed monster trying to take up residence in his gut.

"Must be awfully easy to get blow jobs."

Suzi jumped from her barstool, coming between both men, probably hoping to diffuse a likely all-out war. Kaleb almost laughed at the thought. Hell, he'd welcome a good fight right about now. Unfortunately, Lyle wouldn't be it. Where was the fun in whipping someone's ass who didn't stand a chance in the fight in the first place?

Suzi poked her pointy index finger against his sternum. "You're out of line, Hawk."

He raised one of his brows. "You brought the fiancé to the soiree, piccolo diavolo. This is on your shoulders."

"What did he just call you?" Lyle's deep voice rumbled up from his gut, which probably cowered most men. "I've had about enough of your foul remarks and attitude, buddy."

Kaleb ignored Suzi and instead focused on the man behind her. Funny, she thought to shield him from Kaleb. It was like bringing a Chihuahua to a dog fight. "And what exactly do you plan to do about it?"

"I'll take your ass out—"

"Hawk," came from behind the bar. Draven stood, back ramrod straight, glaring at him. "The last time you came to blows in my bar it cost a fortune."

Not even glancing at the barkeep, he said, "And the Sons paid for it."

"It took a month to repair the damages. Damn it, take it outside!"

Suzi shoved at Kaleb's unmoving chest. He barely felt her nudge. "No one here is throwing a punch, Draven. Got that, Hawk?"

He ground his teeth. The ache in his gums spoke of his lengthening fangs. If he didn't control his anger, her fiancé would witness something he had no intention of trying to explain. Kaleb took a deep breath and tamped down his rising ire.

"Let's get this over with, *piccolo diavolo.*" His heated gaze landed on her. "Then you and Romeo here can be on your way. I don't give a fuck what you do, or with whom you do it, once we're finished."

Kaleb turned, passed the bar, and swung the curtained covering over the doorway to the side, then took the stairs two at a time. Once in Draven's office, he walked over the cut glass whiskey decanter and poured himself two fingers, then took the crystal rock glass to his lips and downed the amber liquid in one swallow. Jesus, his emotions had gotten out of control. He normally prided himself at having unbreakable composure when it came to humans. He ought to send her packing, forget about his ridiculous request, and find one of the willing donors downstairs. But instead, bullheaded as ever, he'd rather piss her off instead.

Suzi walked into the room as if on cue and slammed the door so hard that the picture frames bounced off the adjoining wall. Guess he accomplished what he had set out to do with his little tirade downstairs. Good enough for her ass. She should've known how he'd react if she brought her fiancé to the bar when she was supposed to be here to feed him. The big ox fit in with this crowd about as well as a cop at a biker rally.

"What the hell was that about, Hawk? Explain yourself."

"Fuck you," he said, his voice rising as his teeth elongated.

Suzi took a step back in reaction to his features becoming more prominent, his heated gaze becoming black as coals. He allowed himself to fully turn. To Suzi's credit, she didn't run from the vampire now standing before her, nor did it soften her mood. Only she wouldn't be threatened by his animalistic side.

"Could you have been more rude?"

"Could you have been more stupid? You knew I would be here to feed."

"Yes, and I am here fulfilling that duty."

"So why the hell bring lover boy?"

Suzi rolled her eyes. "It's what engaged couples do. We spend time together."

"Does he know about me?" Kaleb poured himself another couple of fingers and downed it as quickly as the first, trying to stave off his gnawing gut. "Why you're up here?"

Her mouth gaped. Kaleb knew she would tell no one of their existence. It was the number one rule of the donor society. To do so could mean her death.

"Of course not."

"Then what do you think you'll tell him we're doing up here, *piccolo diavolo*? Fucking?"

She sucked in breath. "Absolutely not."

Kaleb slowly approached her, gripping her wrist and pulling her flush against him. She couldn't mistake his erection, hot and heavy against her abdomen. "Are you so sure about that?"

Before she could utter a protest, he gripped her short bob and tilted her head to the side, sinking his fangs into her carotid artery. The sweet tang of her blood flowed over his tongue as her slight gasp filled the room. She shuddered within his embrace. He could smell the scent of her desire. Hell, he caught the scent long before she followed him up the stairs. Suzi could deny her desire for him all she wanted, but Kaleb knew better. She was just as hot for him as he was her. He may not like her much, but that didn't mean he didn't want to bury himself to the hilt. His balls tightened at the thought of it. It was no secret he wanted her in a bad way.

Suzi's heart beat heavy against his chest as he held her tightly against him, the sound barely detectable over the heavy bass of the dance music filtering through the club. Draven's walls had been sound-proofed, but nothing seemed to filter out the sound of bass played at deafening levels. The sound beat against his sternum along with that of her heart. Suzi leaned into him, aligning them from hip to chest as he continued to feed. Her hips arched into him ever so slightly, telling him of her own weakening resolve.

Kaleb palmed her sweet ass and lifted her off the floor so that her center rested intimately against his cock as she wrapped her legs about his waist. His jeans became incredibly uncomfortable as his erection strained against the zipper fly. He resisted the urge to reach between them and unbuckle the front of his chaps and slip the button free of his Levis. The more barriers between them, the least likely he'd be to do something he'd no doubt regret in the light of day. Kaleb refused to allow his desire to rule his actions. One side of his brain said there would be no harm in taking his due, the other reminded him whose dick had already been there. He'd do well to remember who she had first belonged to.

"Hawk," she whispered, her breath feathering over his ear. "Please."

Had his fangs not been artery deep in her neck, he might have chuckled at the idea she pleaded for him to take what his own body begged for. Her blood was like an aphrodisiac. Feeding was in itself sexual. Couple that with someone you coveted, and the combination could be explosive. Kaleb wanted his fill. He neared the stopping point of feeding, much more and it could put her at risk of anemia. Even as much as he disliked the woman in his arms, he'd never dream of putting a donor in peril. Kaleb's lust teetered excruciatingly close to giving her exactly what she had pleaded for. His cock pained him as she rode the length of him, trying damn hard to reach the pinnacle she desperately sought. He gripped her hips, undoubtedly hard enough to cause bruises, to still her actions before she caused them both to climax prematurely. He'd much rather be buried, her walls milking the pleasure from him.

Should he give into that hunger they both longed for, he feared not getting her out of his system, but desiring her that much more. And the last thing he needed at the moment was to think with his dick. He needed his head on MC business and finding the asshole who had tried unsuccessfully to take his head. Women ... this woman ... was a distraction at the moment he couldn't afford. He'd much rather save himself the frustration and drama.

Her fiancé was barely out of hearing distance and yet she clung to him as if her next breath depended on him. Maybe, he ought to throw caution to the wind and take another taste of what he had had all those years ago, and brag to the bastard on his way out the door. It would serve Suzi right for bringing the poor schmuck into his territory. His willpower wavered at the breaking point. If he didn't stop now, there would be no turning back.

Kaleb withdrew his fangs and licked the wounds closed, then trailed his tongue up her neck to the fleshy part of her ear where he nipped the tender skin. Her breath caught and he stifled a groan. How much could one vampire take? Kaleb was used to finding pleasure in the opposite sex damn near nightly. Now that Suzi had walked back into his life, he had hit a dry spell, one he desperately wanted, needed to end.

Suzi whispered his name again as he backed her against the closed door, anchoring her against the solid surface. His black gaze held her bright blue ones, waiting for the denial sure to come to her lips.

Her breath hitched. "God, help me. Either let me go, Hawk, or end my torture."

He pressed his steely erection against her center. He didn't have to touch her to know she was wet. The scent of her damn near finished what the taking of her blood had nearly accomplished.

"Is this what you want, *piccolo diavolo*? Tell me you want me to fuck you and I will." Kaleb leaned in, breathing in her scent, his lips grazing hers. "Tell me how bad you want my cock inside of you," he whispered against her lips.

"You know I want it, Hawk. God help me, I always have."

"Kaleb," he corrected. Her admission momentarily stunned him. Surely, she meant after Ion's death. "Know that it is Kaleb who fucks you against this door with your fiancé a hairbreadth away. Not Hawk."

He licked the crease of her lips. She gasped, opening for him. But before he kissed her, he needed to hear her say what very few called him. "Say my given name, piccolo diavolo."

Instead, she gripped the hair at his nape and pulled him forward and kissed him, shoving her tongue into his mouth and taking control. And just that easily his willpower snapped like an over strung guitar string. He lowered her to her feet and flicked open the button of her black pleather pants with his thumb and forefinger, then slid the zipper down. Sliding his hand inside, his palm cupped her sex, feeling how incredibly wet she was. A moan escaped her lips as he slipped one finger across her slick clit and into her heat. Her walls gripped him and her breathing quickened. Kaleb knew much more and she'd tumble over the peak, but he wanted to be inside her when that happened. He needed to feel her walls tighten around his cock like a silken glove, squeeze his own climax from him. He knew they were both at the point it would take neither but a matter of seconds to reach the common goal.

Kaleb withdrew his hand, hearing a whimpered protest. But he had no intention of stopping now. His hand found the buckle to his chaps when she stopped him, placing her hand atop his.

"Allow me."

Without waiting for his compliance, she slid to her knees, her small fingers deftly undoing the buckle to his leather chaps. The tip of her pink tongue slipped to the corner of her lips as she then worked the fastening of his jeans and slid her palm inside, her small hand fisting him. Kaleb was none too quiet with the growl that followed. His hooded gaze watched her with enthusiasm as she withdrew his rock-hard erection and looked at it with heated interest. Her tongue darted out, capturing the drop of pre-cum from the tip. And before he could stop her, she wrapped her pink lips around him, taking him into her mouth. Another growl escaped his lips as he bared his teeth and continued to watch the erotic scene. Jesus, where had she learned to give head with such fucking skill? Her lips and tongue worshiped him, giving him pleasure like never before.

Kaleb arched his hips toward her mouth, wanting ... needing to finish. He wouldn't be able to hold out much longer and if he didn't stop her now, he'd lose his chance to get inside her. Just as he grabbed the sides of her head to pull her to her feet, a knock sounded on the door that startled them both. Kaleb cursed a blue streak as her wide gaze swung to the closed door. He knew his window of opportunity had closed at the sound of her fiancé's voice.

"Suzi? Are you all right in there?"

Kaleb grit his teeth. When he left this room, he'd find Draven and beat the stupid bastard to a bloody pulp with his bare hands for allowing Lyle anywhere near the office door for Christ's sake. Suzi stood, righting herself and smoothing down the wrinkles now in her blouse. Kaleb tucked his penis back into his jeans, leaving them hanging open as he stood glaring at her, hands on his hips.

"I'm fine, Lyle," she said. "I'll be right down, sweetie."

"Are you sure?"

"Absolutely. Give me a minute."

Kaleb wasn't sure what kept him from opening the door and throwing the ox down the stairs. But at the moment, nothing would give him more pleasure. He heard the heavy footfalls as they retreated down the steps. The only thing that kept him from murdering the bastard was the look on her face as she refastened her pants. The same look she had when he had seen her a few nights back, the one that made him think she might care he had almost lost his head.

"Go," Kaleb groused. "Before I change my mind and fuck you anyway."

A slight smile played at the corner of her lips. "My loss, Kaleb Tepes. Something tells me I'm the one who's going to regret missing out. I may not like you much, but you look fucking hot in those chaps. Any woman would be a fool to deny you."

Hand on the doorknob, she turned back to look at him, raising one of her delicate brows. "See you in three days?"

Not waiting for an answer, she opened the door and left the room, leaving him with another hard-on to contend with. The bright side? It wouldn't take near as long to finish the job this time. He was already on the verge of exploding.

"Motherfu—" he let hang, letting out an ear-piercing growl instead.

CHAPTER TWELVE

"WHAT THE HELL HAPPENED?" KANE ASKED FROM HIS SEAT on the sofa in the living area of the clubhouse, where he and Cara lounged with her tucked beneath his arm.

Cara sat up quickly pulling a T-shirt over her head, hiding her leopard-skin brassiere Kane was just seconds away from divesting her of. Being that both Kaleb and Grayson were out for the night chasing tail, he hadn't thought they'd have company for hours. Kane stood, pulled his own shirt back over his head and fastened his jeans, not bothering to hide the erection paining him. Had he not been so perturbed, he might have chuckled at Cara's reddened cheeks. Only a woman would be embarrassed by being caught in a compromising position. Men were just annoyed.

His gaze landed on Alexander's healing wounds. He must've laid his bike down to cause the road rash that marred the right side of his face and arm. His chaps likely saved him from further damage.

"Run into trouble?"

"More likely some bitch with an ax to grind," Alexander grumbled. Anton standing to his right remained untouched. "Thankfully Blondy saw the steel cable before I did and brought my attention to it not a moment too late. I had to lay my bike down to keep from getting beheaded. I'm starting to think I have nine lives and two are now gone."

"You see Rosalee?" Kane's blood simmered just beneath the surface at the thought of his ex being behind the recent targets on the Sons. He'd kill the bitch with his bare hands.

"I smelled primordial blood. If you say they are all accounted for in Italy besides your bitch ex-mate." Alexander's gaze flitted to Cara. "Sorry."

"No need," Cara commented. "She is a bitch. I'd take her out myself if she presented me the opportunity."

Kane glared down at Cara, who wrapped one arm around his back. "You'll do no such thing, *mia bella*. You aren't near strong enough to take out an ancient and I'm not about to lose you."

"No." She smiled at his concerned gaze. "But my Glock pointed straight at her cold heart would work wonders. I'm a good shot. She wouldn't stand a chance."

"You best be if you think to pull that trigger on Rosalee. As much as I like your spunk, I think I prefer your head attached to your shoulders." Kane leaned down and placed a kiss on her forehead. "You leave Rosalee to us."

He turned back to Alexander and Anton. "Give me the play-by-play. What the hell happened? Anyone else get hurt?"

"No. It happened after Anton and I followed the Knights to the border. Once they crossed over, we turned back. About twenty-five miles back down the road, Blondy saw something shine off the headlights. He managed to shout over the sound of the engines," Alexander said. "He slowed his bike. By the time I glanced from him back to the road, the only chance I had was to lay it down. I have to have my bike hauled back to K&K. It's not drivable, so I'll need to borrow the covered trailer tomorrow to go back out there and pick it up."

"You ride back with Blondy?"

Anton chuckled. "Xander wasn't too happy to have to ride bitch. I kept reminding him that at least he still had his head. Still didn't keep him from complaining the whole way back though."

"Someone had to know about the run," Kane said. He looked at Cara, "Why don't you start us some coffee, *mia bella*? I think a call is in order to Red. No one could've known about the run other than the Sons and the Knights. It was too last minute. Hell, I didn't even have time to get back here after receiving Hawk's call. I'll insist Red make a trip here with his VP tomorrow—no one else. At this point, I don't trust anyone in his MC. Someone with an inside track is working with Rosalee."

Cara walked over to the bar area, the only kitchen the clubhouse had. She pulled out the coffeemaker, and began prepping to do as Kane had asked. Damn he loved her. Unlike Rosalee, she had no problem being there for him, or helping out where she could. He sure as hell would miss her when she went back to work on Monday. He'd much rather have her next to him. He supposed, though, it would give her something to do rather than hanging at K&K, he and Kaleb's motorcycle shop.

Kane pulled out his cell and found Red's number and hit the number to dial. He placed the phone by his ear as he started pacing the scarred wood flooring. After several rings, Red's hoarse voice came across his answering machine, indicating the caller to leave a message. Kane supposed he wasn't back yet from the run.

"Red," Kane said. "This is Viper. We have a situation that needs your complete confidence. You aren't to speak about this to anyone. Stop by the clubhouse tomorrow after lunch and only bring your VP. See you tomorrow."

Punching END with his index finger, he gave Alexander and Anton his attention again. The smell of coffee filled the room as Cara returned to the living area. Kane leaned down and briefly kissed her lips, though he'd prefer to take up where they'd left off before the interruption. There would be plenty of time for that later. Cara pulled her blonde hair off her shoulders, and wound it in a knot at her nape as she headed for the sofa. Just the sight of her pale throat had his cock standing to attention again. Damn, he couldn't get enough of her.

"Thanks, Cara," Alexander said as he headed for the bar to get a cup of the fresh brew, drawing Kane's gaze back to his brothers. The wounds on the side of his face were barely visible anymore.

"Pour me a cup too, will you, Xander?"

"Sure thing, Viper. Blondy?"

"Ah, hell ... wasn't planning on sticking around, but maybe we should wait it out until the Pres and VP gets here."

Cara barely got situated under Kane's arm again before the door banged off the inside wall of the clubhouse and Kaleb stormed into the room, slamming the door behind him. His twin looked ready to do battle, and he had yet to hear the latest club news. Kane couldn't help wonder what had him in a mood. No matter, Kane was about to make it worse.

KALEB RAN BOTH HANDS THROUGH his hair as he stared at all the extra bodies in his house. He sure as fuck wasn't in the mood to entertain. Not after leaving the Rave with a raging hard-on. He hadn't felt like jerking one off, not after having Suzi's sweet lips wrapped around his cock. So instead, he had stormed from the club, past Draven and ignoring his impulse to beat the bastard, and out the exit. He hadn't even bothered looking for Grayson. He undoubtedly had already gotten busy with no less than two ladies and Kaleb wasn't in the mood for his antics. So instead, he crawled on the back of his chopper and headed for the clubhouse hoping to find solitude.

No such fucking luck.

"Someone want to tell me what the hell is going on?" Kaleb's gaze landed first on his twin, then on Kane's mate.

"I had nothing to do with this." Cara raised her hands up, palms out. "But it is something you need to hear, Kaleb."

"Someone tried to take Xander's head, bro," Kane supplied, gaining Kaleb's attention. "And I am pretty sure they were hoping it was you."

Kaleb glanced at Alexander, seeing the healing road rash for the first time on the right side of his face. "You okay?"

"Just a bad rash, P. No biggie. Thankfully Blondy saw the steel cable or you guys might be ashing a couple more brothers tonight. We need to catch this son of a bitch before she accomplishes what she's setting out to do."

"She? Rosalee?" Kaleb asked. "You see her? Know for sure it's her?"

Alexander shook his head. "Just the scent in the air laying proof to a primordial. But who the fuck else is that hungry for our blood?

Jesus, P. I don't know how many more lives I have left. I'm in no hurry to lose my head."

Cara jumped up and headed for the counter, her sudden movement cutting through the tension in the room. She pulled a couple of stoneware mugs from the cupboard and started pouring the hot liquid.

Kane walked over to her, placed his hand on the base of her spine and placed a kiss at the crook of her neck. "Thanks, *mia bella*," he said, grabbing a cup.

Alexander inclined his head, and said softly to Cara as she reentered the room, " I'm sorry to have interrupted your evening."

She waved a hand at him. "Please, the Sons have much more important business at the moment. I don't want to see any of you guys hurt."

A smile turned up the corner of one side of his lips. "Sure is different now than when Kane first met you."

Cara laughed. "That's because I was trying to pin a crime on him that he didn't do. Trust me ... he never fails to remind me of it," she said with a wink.

"Only when I'm trying to get in your pants, Cara." Kane wrapped his arm around her waist and led her back to the sofa.

Kaleb growled. His gut churned with the consumed whiskey from the club. He was in no mood to watch his twin fawn all over his mate. It wasn't that fucking long ago she hated all their guts. He clenched his teeth as he headed for the cupboard and pulled down a fifth of Jack. He'd be damned if he was going to sit around and shoot the shit with the likes of this group. If need be, he'd set out on his own and find Rosalee, separating her head from her shoulders just as he had Alec Furner. Mircea be damned. Kaleb didn't give a rat's ass what the patriarch would have to say about it. This landed on Mircea's doorstep. It was his stepdaughter he hadn't been able to control.

After knocking back a couple of fingers of the amber liquid, his gaze landed on Kane. "So what the hell is being done about this?"

"I left a message on Red's answering machine, told him to stop by tomorrow and only bring his VP. I think there's a rat in his club and we need to flush him out like yesterday."

"What happened that you no longer trust the Knights?"

"Think about it, Hawk. No one knew about tonight's run ... including me. It was so last minute. No one knew that you wouldn't be at the head of the run as you and Gypsy normally are. Instead, you both headed for the Rave. The only ones who knew you and Gypsy wouldn't be there were the Sons." He paused, his stare holding Kaleb's. "It was your head they were gunning for again."

"We need to set a trap. Find out who the hell the rat is. He needs to answer for his crimes."

"My thoughts exactly," Kane said. "I trust Red. And since Red trusts his VP to be his right-hand, I think the rat is further down the line. Let's get Red here tomorrow and see what he has to say about all this. Not much more we can do tonight."

"No there isn't, bro." He looked at Alexander and Anton reclining on the sofa across from Cara and Kane, sipping from their mugs of coffee.

What the hell was this? A book club?

Kaleb raised his voice. "So why the hell is everyone still here?"

Cara looked at Kaleb, unfazed by his outburst. "You go to the Rave tonight?"

"Your first clue?"

"Your color ... you've fed. So why so cranky, Hawk? Suzi have anything to do with your foul mood?"

"Seriously? You can't be that stupid. She has everything to do with it."

Kane's gaze darkened. "Watch yourself, Hawk."

"Hawk's made us all promise to keep our hands off," Anton added. "Suzi is to be his personal blood bank."

"Shut the hell up, Blondy."

He certainly didn't need Cara privy to his self-inflicted drama. If Cara knew how he treated his donor, more specifically her close friend, she'd be all over him like a hellcat.

"So you've seen her. And you're using her as your personal donor, Hawk?"

"None of your damn business, Brahnam."

Kaleb growled again, feeling his fangs lengthen. Just the thought of his little pain in the ass donor had the animal coming out in him. Problem was he wasn't sure if he wanted to wring her pretty little neck or fuck her into tomorrow. He was pretty sure he wanted to do both, which aggravated him further. Cara's intuition kicking in wasn't helping.

"Well, I'll be damned." Cara smiled. "You got a thing for Suzi."

Kaleb's eyes heated as they blackened. "You don't know shit, Brahnam. Why don't you two go back to playing house and leave me the hell alone. And you two," he glared at the other two Sons on the opposite sofa, "hit the road. I'd like to brood in fucking silence if you don't mind."

Kane stood, and approached Kaleb. *Just fucking great. Big bro to the rescue.*

He placed a hand on his shoulder. "Sounds like you need to get laid, Hawk."

Whatever he expected Kane to say, it sure in the hell wasn't that. Pouring a quick finger of whiskey, Kaleb downed it, then slammed the cup so hard on the bar surface it shattered. He didn't bother cleaning up the mess. Instead, he headed for his room, hoping to hell he'd get some peace yet this evening. But as soon as he stripped naked and crawled into bed, visions of Suzi Stevens' mouth wrapped around his cock danced behind his closed eyelids. Every inch of him hardened in remembrance.

Shit!

He wasn't about to get any peace this night ... or any night for that matter. Not until he either gave into his desire to fuck her or let her out of his ridiculous demand that she be his personal blood bank. He had thought to punish to her, when in reality it was he who was being tortured and left unappeased.

Cara Brahnam had just hit the nail on the head. He did have a thing for Suzi and damn if he didn't have it bad.

THE LITTLE BASTARD HUNG BY his throat, his feet dangling as he gasped for much needed life-giving oxygen. Rosalee allowed him to hang there, her hand tightening around his throat ever-so-slightly as she contemplated whether or not she'd allow him to live. His brown eyes nearly popped from their sockets and his fingers clawed at her hand. His incompetence had cost her sweet revenge yet again. Kaleb Tepes should be ashes by now and yet he still breathed air.

Had she seriously misjudged the little ass-kissing biker hanging by his neck?

Rosalee had zeroed in on him the moment she spotted him in a tavern next door to the Knight's clubhouse alone, bitching nonstop over his lack of love for the leadership within his MC ranks to the bartender or anyone near who would listen. He hated the fact the Knights were in bed with the Sons. *They were no one's puppet club, by god. He'd teach them sons of a bitches a lesson himself if need be.*

His cocky attitude appealed to her, that and his desire to please. He had been all over her the minute she pulled out the stool next to him, promising sexual favors that he had unfortunately fell short of. Hell, she should've taken his sorry ass out then and there had she not needed eyes and ears within the club. Unfortunately most humans had trouble matching the stamina of a vampire ... and no vampire alive today could match the thrill of fucking Kane Tepes. That vamp certainly knew his way around the bedroom, the kitchen, and every damn room in the house. She still hadn't gotten over his dismissal of her, or the fact her bastard of a stepfather had allowed their union dissolved. Once she finished with Kaleb, she'd personally take out Kane's newly acquired, supposed mate. Cara Brahnam would beg Rosalee for death by the time she finished with her.

No one crossed a primordial and slept with their mate.

Kane belonged to her ... always would. They had been mated and mating was for life, regardless of whether her stupid-as-fuck stepfather had granted Kane's wish to annul it. Cara's days were numbered. Then she'd take out the rest of the Sons, one by one, until Kane agreed to take her back and forgive her for her involvement in their son's death. They should've suffered their loss together. Instead, he had sent her to Italy, banished her for a misjudgment that had unfortunately caused Ion's death.

Didn't he know that she suffered too?

Rosalee would be damned if she'd ever allow the little detective to carry his next child and spend an eternity with him. She'd behead the bitch. Of course, she'd allow someone else to do the dirty work or Kane would never forgive her for such a deed. Then she'd be there to help him pick up the pieces. Remind him that she was his one true love, that Cara had been just a passing fancy. Who wouldn't rather mate with a primordial than a newly turned vamp? Kane should feel lucky that she, Rosalee, had chosen him over all the primordials, for crying out loud. Any vampire would be honored to walk by her side. For that alone, Kane needed to be taught a little respect.

The biker kicked feebly and gasped, drawing her attention back to his dangling form. The fight seemed to drain slowly from him as he started to run out of oxygen. Rosalee sighed. Hell, she still needed the pain in the ass. Letting go of his windpipe, he dropped to a heap of tangled arms and legs, his hands surrounding his neck as he took in large gulps of air. He'd undoubtedly be hoarse for a couple of days, but no real damage done ... yet.

"Now, are we ready to get serious?" She glared down on his form as he scrambled backward from her, stopped only by his back hitting the wall again. She raised one of her brows. "I will not allow your incompetence a third time. Is that clear?"

Hand still at his throat, he looked at her through bugged eyes. "How was I to know that Hawk and Gypsy had left the run to their Sergeant at Arms? They didn't even tell Red. No one knew the Pres and VP weren't there to help escort the Knights through Oregon."

Rosalee advanced on him, flashing him her fangs. His limbs trembled as he cowardly placed a palm out as if to stop her. She'd show him pity because she was not yet done with him. But should he fail her a third time...

"You still live because I have use of you. Don't fail me another time or you won't live to see another day, biker."

"How could I have possibly known?"

"You eat and sleep club business. You make it your job to know everything that goes on behind the clubhouse walls. Your president has gotten into bed with the Sons. And you ... you are his right-hand, for fuck's sake. As VP, you should know everything that the president does. He should be confiding in you all things Sons. You make that clear with him. I don't care what you say, or how you do it. There will be no more excuses."

The man quickly nodded. "I promise. If Red knows what's going down, I'll see to it that I am in the loop."

"See that you do, Bird. I won't show you mercy a third time. Cross me and the Knights will be looking for a new VP and you'll be fitted for a casket. Do I make myself clear?"

"Absolutely. You'll see. I'll deliver Hawk to you on a platter next time."

Rosalee gripped the front of his tee and pulled him to his feet, their gazes mere inches apart. "You do, and I will see your wish come true. I'll turn you and you can live your days out as a vampire. Cross me and you're a corpse. Got that?"

He quickly nodded again.

"Good. Now I find that I'm hungry."

Without waiting for consent, Rosalee tipped his head to the side and sank her fangs into his flesh and began to take her fill. Bird's gasp filled the air and his penis hardened. She could easily drain the bastard and probably would once he outlived his worth. Stupid human. Did he seriously think she went around turning humans into vampires?

CHAPTER THIRTEEN

SUZI HADN'T SLEPT MORE THAN A FEW HOURS. HER EYES STUNG, dry as dirt, from shedding more than a few tears over the course of the long night. What the hell had she done? She could blame the endorphins racing through her caused by the act of feeding, but she knew better. Nourishing a vampire was most definitely a sexual act, but she had done so over the years without acting on the raging hormones surging through her. No, she had wanted to get Hawk off, wanted him to know that she was no longer the naive eighteen-year-old who hadn't a clue what to do with a man, let alone one sexy-as-hell vampire. And had it not been for Lyle's untimely arrival, she would've managed to finish what she started.

She may not like Kaleb much, but that didn't stop her from desiring him. Only a cold corpse would be immune to his deadly charm. Damn, but she acted no better than a nymphomaniac on a dry streak. Insert Kaleb's fangs and she went weak at the knees, batshit crazy, and all but begging him to take her.

Hiding the fact she wanted in his chaps in the worst way wasn't an option either.

Hell no, his nostrils flared whenever she got wet. He knew damn well the effect he had on her. Just the thought of last night's activities involving her on her knees and her mouth wrapping his velvety, hard-as-steel cock and she was crossing her legs. Her night had

151

been dream-filled with unrequited desire, needs she had no intention of giving purchase to. She deserved to suffer after the way she
left Kaleb standing in Draven's office, moments away from comple-
tion.

Talk about a tease.

After tossing and turning for the hundredth time, she finally
gave up the hope of getting any sleep and put in a phone call to the
one person who might understand, Cara Brahnam. They had been
friends going way back, and even though they had lost touch for
several years, when she came back into Suzi's life, they had taken up
right where they'd left off. No one understood her better than her
best friend from school. Thankfully, she had been more than willing
to drop any plans she might have had and promised to come by for
coffee.

Tamera had left for the newspaper about a half hour prior, starting the pot before she left. Suzi had filled the redhead in about her
disastrous night upon arriving home, and how Kaleb had wanted to
kill her Uncle Lyle. Maybe involving him hadn't been such a good
idea. The ever-optimistic Tamera thought Lyle could take care of
himself. One look at the large man and Tamera figured Kaleb would
concede to defeat. Her roommate had no idea how determined
Kaleb could be when he wanted something. He might think her a
cold-hearted bitch, but Suzi knew his desire for her ran thick
through his veins. Kaleb Tepes was but a hairsbreadth away from
giving into what they both tried so hard to deny.

Following her rapid descent down the stairs the previous night,
Lyle met her at the bar and had been the gentleman, taking her
home without question. He'd been concerned about her well-being,

but Suzi assured him that Kaleb would never hurt her ... at least not physically, though she had kept that little nugget of information to herself. Kaleb may not raise a hand in harm, but he had the power to stomp all over her heart as just he had in the past.

Never again.

His growl following her down the steps and fleeing into the night, had haunted her throughout the night. She had callously left him on the verge of an orgasm. Suzi smiled weakly as she took a sip of her coffee. Kaleb no doubt finished the job, calling her all sorts of colorful words as he reached gratification. A knock sounded on the front door, drawing her attention and disrupting her from her reflections. Rising, she walked across the polished wooden floors and opened the door.

Cara handed her a coffee-shop cup with a cardboard sleeve, then gave her a one-armed hug. "Caramel latte, two shots of espresso."

"Tamera made coffee," Suzi said matter-of-factly, taking the offered cup. "But this is so much better."

"I thought you might think so. You sent me the SOS and I was worried. I thought the treat might cheer you up. So what the hell has Kaleb done this time?"

Cara kicked off her shoes and strode over to the sitting room, dropping into the large, cushioned chair facing the picture window, curling her legs beneath her. She took a sip of her own coffee and sighed.

"Delicious. I'm so glad you called. It gave me a reason to run out for real coffee. Not that rot-gut stuff the guys call coffee at the clubhouse."

Suzi sat in the adjacent brown, worn-leather recliner, placing her paper cup on the leather and wood trunk that acted as a coffee table in the center of the room. Leaning back, she pulled her knees to her chest and wrapped her arms around them. Tears filled Suzi's eyes. She swatted away the lone tear that passed her lashes and cleared her throat.

"You're going to think I'm an idiot, Cara."

"What happened?" She leaned forward and laid a hand on Suzi's knee. "I'm sure whatever it is, Kaleb is likely at fault. He wouldn't know how to treat a woman even if she came with an instruction book. You want to tell me about it?"

Suzi took a deep breath. Where to start? She knew Cara wouldn't judge her. Cara likely felt that Kaleb deserved everything he got. He was far from innocent in what had transpired. After all, he had been the one who demanded they see each other every three days so that he could feed, when there were plenty of willing donors to take her place.

Finishing with her tale of the evening, omitting the part about voluntarily giving Kaleb head and leaving him with a full-blown hard-on as she raced into the night with her fake fiancé, she waited for a reaction from Cara, who sat tight-lipped. Suddenly, she cracked a wide smile, then burst into laughter. *Great.* Not exactly the reaction she had hoped for. Shouldn't she be pissed at her brother-in-law for being so rude to Lyle?

Heat rose up Suzi's neck and centered in her cheeks as she waited for Cara's mirth to subside. She wasn't sure if she should be mad at Cara for her reaction, or maybe join her, realizing the ridiculousness of the situation. Besides, Kaleb had been the one left to suffer.

Not that she hadn't left the club horny herself, but by the time she had arrived home and humiliation had set in, her ardor had cooled ... at least until the erotic dreams began.

"I'm not laughing at you, Suzi," Cara finally said, containing herself. "Really ... it's Kaleb who's the butt of this joke."

"How do you figure?"

"You should have seen him last night when he got back to the clubhouse. He was ready to murder someone. I know now, you were the cause of his sour mood." Cara sat back and took another sip from her coffee and sighed. "Though, I'm not quite sure why Lyle Murphy, or his arrival up the top of the stairs, would cause such an outlandish reaction from Kaleb. Lyle is as gentle as a giant teddy bear. The man is beyond nice."

Suzi had a hard time looking Cara in the eyes, knowing full well why Kaleb had been so angry. But how does one admit to being so turned on you couldn't control yourself, then not bothering to finish what you started?

"So you know Lyle?"

"Of course, I do," Cara said. "He owns Murphy Bar's next door to the Blood 'n' Rave. I used to hang there occasionally with the guys from work. Now? I'm not so sure I'd be welcome. My coworkers aren't too happy with my choice of mate."

"I don't suppose" Suzi toyed with her fingernails.

Cara leaned forward and laid a hand over Suzi's, stilling her actions and forcing Suzi to look at her. "What aren't you telling me?"

"I don't know what you mean. I've told you about Hawk and how he reacted to Lyle."

One of her brows rose. "Yes, but you obviously left an important detail out. What is it?"

Suzi looked out the window. "I have no idea what you are talking about."

"Come on, Suzi." She drew her attention back. "What kind of a detective would I be if I didn't detect that you're nervous about something that happened. You can't even look me in the eye. What is it? You have to know I'll take your side in this. Kaleb deserves everything you dish out and then some."

Suzi stared at Cara, another tear slipping past her lashes, feeling the need to confess the entire story. She hadn't even told Tamera about her naughty desire to get Kaleb off.

"I won't judge you, Suzi. Surely, you know that."

Suzi nodded, then took a deep breath before letting Cara in on the other of part of her tale. She sure hoped her good friend wouldn't judge her. Suzi had openly cursed the ground Kaleb walked on. What would Cara think when she found out how Suzi truly felt?

"I left Hawk with a hard-on."

Cara chuckled. "I'm sure it wasn't the first time he fed and didn't get laid. It's really not a big deal, Suzi. Don't beat yourself up over it."

"No, it wasn't just excitement from communion." Suzi shifted in her chair. "I fed him, and I should've stopped there. But I didn't."

"Did Kaleb take advantage of you? If so, I will knock his block clean off his shoulders when I get back to the clubhouse."

"More like the other way around."

Cara's gaze rounded, but she patiently waited for Suzi to elaborate.

"I took advantage of him, Cara ... and then I didn't have the decency to finish him off."

"You had sex?"

"No. I was giving him a blow job when Lyle knocked on the office door to check on me, to make sure that I was okay." Suzi winced, rubbing the back of her neck. "Hawk was probably damn near on the edge when I stopped. I was so humiliated. So instead of being an adult about it, I just turned tail and left."

Cara sat perfectly still, not saying a word until a bubble of laughter burst forth. Suddenly, she was laughing so hard she was mopping up tears from her eyes. Suzi couldn't help but chuckle herself. She supposed if the shoe were on the other foot, she would've found the situation damn near hysterical. After all, she would bet that Kaleb wasn't used to being denied.

"I'm sorry, Suzi." Cara tried hard to contain her humor. "But surely you have to find this hilarious."

"Well, maybe not exactly hilarious. You remember I have to deal with him in two days again when he's ready to feed. I'm not so sure he will be amicable company."

Cara winced. "That or you'll be dealing with a vampire bent on seducing the pants off you. You best be careful, Suzi. I think you might be playing with fire."

Suzi shrugged, unwound her arms from her knees, then leaned forward and grabbed her coffee. "Hawk probably just found another willing female after I left."

"Would that bother you?"

She pondered the question when she came up with the one an-swer that disturbed her most. Tears sprang back to her eyes as she looked at Cara. "I don't think I want to know if he did."

"So it would."

Suzi nodded. "I've been trying hard to deny that I want Hawk. I always have. But I also knew I would be just setting myself up for hurt. So it's been easier to hide behind the hate I've carried around in my heart these past ten years."

"Suzi," Cara leaned forward and placed a hand on Suzi's knee again. "You have to go after what you want. If you want Kaleb, as I think you do, then I'll help you. He won't know what hit him."

Suzi swatted at a tear. "You're forgetting he hates me."

"Does he think you hate him?"

"With every fiber of my being."

Her lips turned up. "He thinks you hate him, when you really don't. Maybe he doesn't hate you either, Suzi. What if he's denying what he feels? Self-preservation can be a bitch."

"You're forgetting about Ion."

Cara leaned back, settling into the deep cushions of the chair. "Why don't you fill me in on that part of the story. The most you've told me is that after Kaleb acted like you no longer existed, you dat-ed Ion."

"Hung with," Suzi corrected. She had never shared Ion's secret with anyone ... until now. She trusted Cara, and if she were to get her understanding, then she needed to know what had really hap-pened. "Ion and I were good friends. We were there for each other, told each other secrets no one else knew."

"That was before I left town, right?" Cara asked.

Suzi nodded.

"You couldn't share it with me?"

"You wouldn't have understood. I was a donor. You would have freaked knowing I was feeding vampires. As you recall, I took you to the Rave. You left town rather quickly following that night ... without saying goodbye."

Care winced. "Guilty."

"I had my reason for keeping it all a secret, Cara. I thought by taking you there, maybe you could see for yourself, maybe even join the donors. But it didn't work that way. Instead, I frightened you into leaving town. You stayed away ten years."

"I left because of Kane."

"But you would've never known about Kane and the vampirism if I hadn't taken you there."

Cara narrowed her gaze. "You think I blamed you?"

"I didn't know what to think, Cara. All I knew was I took my best friend to a den of vampires and then you left me."

"I'm so sorry, Suzi. I had no idea what you were thinking, or into for that matter. I didn't leave because of you. I left because I feared the monster I saw that night."

"And now?"

"I was so wrong. Had it not been for you, I would've never met Kane." Cara smiled, a wicked gleam in her eye. "And I plan to pay you back. I'm going to help you get Kaleb. After what I witnessed last night, you had him tied in knots. I am positive he didn't hook up with some willing club raver. You definitely pushed his buttons. Now, tell me about you and Ion."

Toying with the cardboard sleeve on her cup, Suzi knew it was time to let the past go. "Ion was gay, Cara."

"So? I'm not sure what that has to do with anything other than answer the question of whether the two of you dated."

"Kane and Kaleb didn't know. None of the Sons did. He didn't want them to. He feared what they might think."

"He didn't even try to tell his father?"

"No. And he thought by hanging with me, then his secret would be safe."

"What did Kane think about you dating Ion?"

"I'm not even sure he knew. To be honest, I don't think Kane really knew I existed at all until the day at the Rave when I tried to sleep with him, the night we saw you when we came out of the Rave."

Cara grimaced. "I remember. I was pretty jealous of you being with Kane."

Suzi laughed. "Well, that was certainly unfounded. By then, Kane was already yours. He just didn't know it."

"He needed a little convincing." She chuckled.

"Anyway, Kaleb did know I was with Ion. Only he thought I was Ion's girlfriend. I never bothered correcting him because Ion wanted his secret kept. So when Ion went off to see his boyfriend, he probably just told his uncle he was going to see me. When Ion died, Kaleb took it upon himself to give me the bad news."

"How'd that go?"

"That's when he figured me to be a cold-hearted bitch. I didn't cry, and he's held that against me. Hell, I was so stunned I didn't know how to react, so I just left. I had to be the one to tell Ion's boyfriend. It killed me to have to deliver that kind of news. Kaleb never talked to me again and avoided me when we happened to be at the Blood 'n' Rave at the same time."

Suzi took a shuttering breath. "I had to watch him parade woman after woman in front of me. I learned the easiest way to protect myself from the hurt was to hate him."

"And now?"

A tear slipped past her lash. "I realize how much of a liar I've been."

"You like him?"

"I think it's much worse than that, Cara." She smiled weakly, her lower lip trembling. "God help me, I think I'm in love with him. I'm afraid I always have been."

Cara sat forward, holding her cup between her hands as her elbows rested on her knees. "Then, girlfriend, we're about to teach Kaleb a lesson in Love 101. Besides, I still owe him for the way he's treated me in the past. This should be fun watching him squirm. When we're through, he'll be begging for mercy."

CHAPTER FOURTEEN

T HE SOUND OF A COUPLE OF V-TWIN ENGINES CUT SHORT, JUST before a knock sounded on the door. Cara had left the clubhouse a few hours earlier, giving them the privacy they needed to meet with the Knights' president and vice president. Kane had messaged Cara, telling her to take the day out, not to return too soon as they had important club business to attend to. Not that women didn't have their place with the Sons, but the MC was comprised of only men. When it came to club politics, then the women were to make themselves scarce. Besides, he had heard that Cara took her job back at the Sheriff's Office. He knew because of her love for Kane that she would never jeopardize the MC, but he wasn't about to take a chance that something might accidentally slip from her lips or put her in a situation where her ethics would be compromised.

Kaleb walked over to the old oak door and swung it inward. Red and Bird stood alone, as requested, on the stoop. He stepped back and invited them in. Grayson sat on the sofa, booted feet kicked up on the scarred coffee table, long arms outstretched along the back of the fabric sofa. His sunglasses perched on his head, holding back his overlong rich brown hair, his bright blue eyes undoubtedly not missing a thing. After their last meeting, Kaleb got the idea that there was no love lost between the once rival VPs. He couldn't help wonder about the story behind it, or if Grayson simply did not like the man for any other reason than a conflict of personalities.

No matter, they had a deal with the Knights, and as such, Grayson would have to learn to tolerate the VP of their puppet club. There might come a day when the Sons would need to rely on their fellow bikers and Kaleb couldn't allow the fragile bond to be broken over some personal shit Grayson had with Bird.

"Have a seat." Kaleb indicated the unoccupied sofa.

As they did so, Kane skirted the bar and met them in the living area, taking his seat next to Grayson, who kept his icy-blue glare on Bird. To his credit, the man actually squirmed. He'd do well to remember Grayson would be a dangerous opponent, one who shouldn't be fucked with. Though Grayson had an outward cavalier attitude, when provoked, he was one of the more dangerous Sons. The man was daring and feared no one. Grayson would never back down from a good fight. And as a matter of fact, Grayson always seemed to pick the biggest man in the fight, even if he wasn't the largest of the Sons at his six-foot height.

"Thank you for coming by on such short notice, Red," Kane said. "We certainly appreciate you keeping the rest of your men in the dark about this … due to the delicate subject."

Red nodded. His beady-eyed gaze swept the room, stopping briefly on Grayson. He glanced back up at Kaleb. "According to Kane's phone call, you somehow think the Knights are involved in a plot to take your life."

Kaleb walked around the leather chair and sat on one of the arms, bracing his hands on his knees. "We have our suspicions."

The pres looked at Kaleb, narrowing his gaze. "Care to elaborate why you think our word is not good enough, that we wouldn't take this unification seriously?"

"There is no union, Red. You agreed to be our ally. That's it."

Kaleb paused, waiting for Red to respond. Other than his cheeks mottling red above the roughness of his beard, the Knights' pres said nothing.

"You know that I was almost beheaded along with one of my men on a bogus run just over a week ago. Instead of it being me, we had two other fallen brothers to bury."

"I'm aware of that." He stroked the length of his red beard. "I thought we agreed that wasn't the Knights' doing."

Kaleb's gaze heated as he bit back his rising ire. His anger would gain them nothing. He knew the Knights were somehow involved. He felt it clear to his marrow. But that didn't mean Red was aware of a rat within his MC as a member could easily have acted on his own. Rosalee always seemed to involve others in her machinations. First she had caused the death of Ion, followed by Alec Funar falling victim to her scheming. So the question was which of the Knights was guilty of helping Kane's bitch of an ex and who would fall next due to her wrongdoing?

"We had another incident last night on this latest run. One that nearly cost me a couple more of my men. Luckily, Blondy saw the steel cable stretched across the back road beforehand and was able to warn Xander, who laid down his bike to avoid decapitation." Kaleb steeled his jaw and grit his teeth to stave off the lengthening of his canines. "To say I'm pissed is putting it mildly."

"What evidence do you have that it points to the Knights? What would we gain by taking your life?"

"Last night's run was last minute, Red. No one else knew about it. We barely had time to contact the law to keep them across town," Kaleb said. "Kane wasn't even made aware of the run until later that evening when Xander and Blondy returned to the clubhouse, Xander sporting the rash from the road."

"We have reason to believe the target is Hawk, Red," Kane added. "No one knew that Hawk and Gypsy wouldn't be riding out front ... not even you. Only the Sons were informed right before they left the clubhouse to meet up with you. So whoever had the knowledge of the run, wouldn't have known about the pres not being out front."

Kaleb glanced to his right at Grayson, who still sat unmoving on the sofa, his eyes on Bird. To the Knights' VP's credit, he completely ignored Grayson's antagonistic behavior. Kaleb meant to ask Grayson about it once the clubhouse cleared.

"Are you sure it isn't one of your own?" Red looked to Kaleb, the slit in his beard inching up on the sides, the only indication that Red smiled and mocked Kaleb's accusations.

Kaleb suddenly understood Grayson's feelings toward the VP. He wasn't liking the president of the rival group at the moment and wanted nothing more than to place his fist in the center of that bushy-ass beard of his and knock his smug block clean off his shoulders. No one ridiculed him. If the Knights' president continued to scoff at Kaleb's authority, then all of Kane's work to get into bed with the MC would be for nothing. Although lucrative, they didn't need the money from the guns or the puppet club in his opinion.

For that matter, Kaleb could take over the guns and cut the Knights out completely if he so chose to. He didn't need the Knights and wasn't a fan of the pres or the VP at this point, no matter what Kane had to say about it.

"My men, aside from Kane, knew I wasn't going to be there before the run even started, asshole," Kaleb said, barely keeping his anger in check.

Kane cleared his throat, a good indication he didn't like Kaleb's behavior. Screw him. He may still be part of the Sons, but he had no voting rights. He loved his twin, trusted his opinion, but in this, he wasn't so sure he agreed with Kane.

"The steel cable appeared after your boys crossed the state line and my two men had turned back. Who of your men were missing from the run, Red?"

He shook his head. "No one. All of them were accounted for that night. No one missed that run."

"Then who left your side once you left Oregon and crossed the state line?" Kane asked.

Red looked at Kane. "Once we hit Washington, we spread out. My men, those without the guns, are instructed to fan out and keep the law off our backs."

"So you would have no idea if all of your men followed instructions. In fact, it would be easy for any one of them to double back?" Kaleb asked.

"I suppose." A muscle in Red's cheek ticked. "But if your men turned at the border, how does my man get back down the road before your guys and find time to string steel cable across the road before they arrive?"

Kaleb supposed Red battled not wanting to believe his men could be capable of betraying the Sons, and in turn breaking his trust. It certainly was possible that someone within their ranks might not be happy going to bed with their one-time rival MC.

"We don't believe your man is acting alone," Kaleb said. "He has a partner. That person was waiting at a designated point. If your man drove faster than my men, it was easy enough for him to arrive before my men got there."

"Again," Red asked, "what proof do you offer? If I'm to accuse one of my men, then I need solid proof. So far you haven't shown me anything but your assumptions."

"If you ask me, I say this is bullshit." Bird spoke up for the first time. "It's also possible that you arrogant asses are too fucking blind to see the deception within your own ranks."

Grayson sat forward, baring his teeth. Thankfully his fangs were retracted. "Why the hell would we want to see any of our own men dead, you son of a bitch? You best be careful with your accusations, asshole, or I might be affronted."

Bird actually smiled, undoubtedly knowing he baited Grayson. "I don't know, Gypsy. You not happy with Viper's decision to bring the Knights on as a fucking puppet club? You want to take the hierarchy out of the equation? Chase the Knights back across the border? I don't recall your neck ever being at jeopardy. Aren't you supposed to have Hawk's back?"

Grayson leapt over the coffee table effortlessly and wrapped the fingers of one hand around Bird's scrawny neck, pinning him against the far wall. Red turned to see Bird hanging by his neck, the toes of his boots not quite touching the floor, gasping for air. Kaleb was damn close to allowing Grayson the pleasure. At the moment, though, Bird's death wouldn't do them well while wanting Red's cooperation.

"Gypsy, release Bird," Kaleb said.

The muscles in Grayson's arms tightened. "No."

"It wasn't a suggestion, Gypsy. Release. Bird. Now."

His broad back expanded with his deep intake of breath before he finally did as ordered. Bird dropped to the floor, his hand covering his throat as he wheezed for air. Kaleb figured he'd be hoarse for a few days, but otherwise unharmed.

Red's eyes became angry slits as he turned back to Kaleb and Kane. "You get me proof that one of my men is a rat and I'll personally take him out. In the meantime, I'll feel out my men. See if any of them may have an ax to grind with the Sons."

"Fuck," Bird started before Red interrupted.

"Shut the hell up, Bird.." He didn't once take his eyes from Kaleb's. "If this turns out to be nothing more than empty accusations, you owe me."

"I'll owe you nothing, Red. You work for us, not the other way around."

Kane stood and approached Red as the man stood. "If the shoe was on the other foot, Red, I'd personally take a look at my men. That's all we're asking. But if one of your men disrespects mine again, I'll let him rip your man's fucking head off. Now get the fuck out and call me when you have information."

Red glared at him. "This isn't over, Viper."

"No, Red, not by a long shot."

Red turned, collected Bird from his position by the wall, then slapped him behind the head as they left the clubhouse. "Show some fucking respect," he grumbled at his VP, just before Kaleb shut the door on them.

He turned to Kane, anger radiating from him in waves. "Your men? Did you forget you're no longer the president, brother?"

"Oh for crying out loud, Hawk, I meant nothing by it. Don't let your ego outshine what's important here."

"And what's that, Viper? Care to enlighten me?"

"We're on very shaky ground here with the Knights."

Kaleb's brow furrowed. "You think I care? This gun run was your idea because you thought you might need help keeping an eye on your—"

"Careful, brother," his twin warned. "She's my mate."

"So fucking sensitive." He rolled his eyes. "When you thought Cara might be in danger. The threat is dead. The Knights are no longer needed."

Kane pointed a forefinger at the floor. "The money is lucrative."

"We make plenty at K&K with motorcycle sales and repairs."

Grayson stood, walked over to the two brothers and smiled. They turned their heated gazes on the shorter man. "What?" they asked in unison.

"Why don't you both shut the fuck up and let's go get some tail?"

Kane smiled at Grayson's well-timed interruption. "Cara would have your head, Gypsy, for even suggesting as much."

He shrugged, unscathed. "Fine, you wait here for your little mate. Kaleb?"

He rubbed his brow. Hell, he hadn't been laid in over a week. And after last night's fiasco with Suzi, he certainly could use a good piece of ass. The problem? He wasn't sure just any old bitch would do when all he could think about was getting inside a pretty little brunette. He best be careful, or he'd wind up exactly in the same position as his twin ... whipped.

Kaleb sighed heavily. "What the hell, Gypsy. Let's get out of here. I could use a good fucking."

Grayson's smile widened, his hand indicating the front of the clubhouse. "After you, brother."

Kaleb grabbed his skull cap from a hook by the door and headed into the parking lot. Kane's laughter followed him to his bike until he turned the key and started the engine, thankfully cutting off his brother's mockery. Yeah, he needed to get laid in a bad way. Not waiting for Grayson, he kicked up his center stand and headed off down the road, the wind whipping his motorcycle cut behind him.

CHAPTER FIFTEEN

KALEB STOOD BY THE BAR, HIS BACK TO THE CLUB RAVERS. NINE Inch Nails blared through the speakers, the heavy music fueling his dark mood. The night sure as shit hadn't turned out how he had envisioned. He had wanted to let off steam, get away from the MC, let loose, party with some women.

Jesus! What the hell was wrong with him?

Grayson had no troubles at all getting busy. They had arrived at the club a few hours earlier. His VP spent little time finding a woman for each of them, not that Kaleb needed help. But Grayson knew Kaleb all too well, and the fact that a little brunette had him all tangled up inside. He couldn't think straight with his dick pointing in one direction. The problem wasn't that Grayson couldn't find a passel of gorgeous women. Hell no—the two that Grayson had brought around were model material. But after about five minutes, Kaleb found himself uninterested and unmoved in the nether regions.

What was Suzi? Some sort of witch?

She certainly had cast a spell on him, no doubt about it. Kaleb had one of two choices, just as he had all those years ago after the first time he had fucked her. He knew then if he didn't forget about her, act as if the night they shared had not happened, then he'd fall ... and fall hard. Something about her tripped his every trigger. Kaleb knew what Kane must certainly feel for Cara, because he imagined it being the same for him if he ever allowed himself to care for Suzi. The way he looked at it, he had one of two choices. He either gave in, fucked her, and no doubt ruin his desire for any other woman. Or turn her loose and attempt to fuck her memory away between the thighs of any other willing woman.

Kaleb couldn't keep feeding from her and keep his head about him.

It was that simple. Kaleb knew what he had to do. He wasn't about to wind up like Kane. Not that Cara was that bad, if he were truly being honest. She worked well with his twin, complimented him even. She was his perfect other half. But he'd be damned if he ever told her that. He'd rather let her think he hated the ground she walked on, though at one point he certainly did. But times had changed and Kaleb was starting to warm up to her brassiness. After all, she was his brother's mate and he could respect that. Kane deserved happiness, especially considering all he had gone through with Rosalee and losing Ion. One day he'd kill that bitch. He knew Kane wanted the honors. Nevertheless, his brother had too much to lose, now that he had the love of a good woman ... and though he hated to admit as much, Cara was. He, on the other hand, had nothing to lose.

Kaleb tipped back his drink, draining the contents. Just as he set the glass back on the bar's surface, Draven exited the storage room, skirted his bartender, and headed for Kaleb. He took off his top hat and set it on the bar.

"You need another drink?" Without waiting for an answer, he waved the bartender down, who quickly handed Kaleb another tumbler of Gentleman Jack. "You look like you could use it. Why aren't you using the office upstairs instead of Gypsy?"

Kaleb's gaze traveled to the curtained doorway that hid the stairwell. "I wasn't in the mood."

Draven toyed with the brim of his hat. "You weren't in the mood," he repeated, then looked up. "Since when? That damn office has been a revolving door between you and Kane for years. Now that Kane no longer needs it, seems Gypsy's making himself at home up there."

Kaleb chuckled. "I hope we aren't cramping your style. You ever get to use your own office?"

The barkeep laughed with him. "When is it ever free to use? You guys seem like a permanent fixture. But no, it's not a problem."

Kaleb grinned. "Sorry, man. Didn't mean to be a cock block."

"Not at all. I have another office back in the storeroom."

"Seriously?"

Draven shrugged. "Once Kane started using my office for his personal fuck space, I knew I needed my own place to … relax. So, I built another office off the backroom. That's where I take my ladies."

"Anyone special?" Kaleb couldn't remember a time he had seen Draven with anyone.

"Oh, hell no. Variety's my thing."

Kaleb looked down at his glass and swirled the amber liquid. "Yeah. I used to think that myself."

"What the hell happened to you, man?"

Scratching his nape, Kaleb winced. "I'm afraid it's a little brunette I need to distance myself from."

"Suzi Stevens?"

"You know her?" Kaleb's heated gaze went to the barkeep. "How well?"

Draven laughed, holding up his hands. "Down, fang boy. I know all of the donors. But she is a cute little thing."

His grip tightened on the glass, not acknowledging how incredibly hot he really thought she was. But since Draven brought her up, he'd bet the barkeep already knew his feelings on the matter. Not much seemed to slip by Draven.

"I take it you aren't too happy about having a hard-on for her. She's got you acting all out of character. I think you got more than your dick involved with this one."

"No feelings involved, man," Kaleb said, knowing full-well it was a lie.

He was in way too deep. He should be the one upstairs right now, relieving some tension. Instead, he stood here with the long-haired, brown-eyed barkeep who wore round, blue-tinted sunglasses perched on his nose and a soul-patch just beneath his lower lip, playing Dracula for heaven's sake. Tonight, he must have decided to forgo the creepy red contacts.

Kaleb looked back to his whiskey. "I want to fuck her. No secret there."

"If that was all there was to it, then you would. Why abstain? I'm thinking you have feelings for her. You know she'll give you a run for your money, Hawk."

"How so?" Kaleb asked, his chin coming back up.

"I've known Suzi for many years, my friend. Where a lot of these donors give you boys everything you're looking for, Suzi doesn't.

Most of the Sons know that if they want to be fed, Suzi's more than willing. Anything else ... they look up another donor."

His gaze narrowed. "Other club goers?"

Draven shrugged again. "I can't be sure what happens outside of here, but Suzi... She's a good girl."

"You?"

"I don't normally fraternize with the donors."

Kaleb let the fact slide that Draven hadn't actually answered his question. "What about Ion?"

One of Draven's brows rose. "Kane's son? They hung together."

"She fuck him?"

Draven shook his head, then chuckled. "Jesus, Hawk. You got it bad. Why not ask her yourself? I've already said too much. I need to protect my donors' right to privacy as well."

Kaleb motioned for the bartender to pour him a couple more fingers of the whiskey.

"All I'm saying, Hawk, is if you want that pretty little brunette, you best snatch her up before someone else does."

"She already has a fiancé." He sipped from his glass. "I'd say that's pretty taken to me."

"Lyle?" Draven laughed. "You aren't too bright now are you?"

Kaleb's gums ached as his fangs started to elongate. He tamped down his growing anger, knowing it wouldn't do him any good to harm the barkeep for his insult. Draven was only calling them as he saw them, and at the moment Kaleb wasn't exactly firing on all cylinders. Suzi Stevens had him so messed up, he couldn't even keep his head on club business. He should be out there looking for the son of a bitch helping Rosalee, who was trying her damnedest to take his head. If he didn't rid himself of the bitch soon, he might as well hand Rosalee his fucking head on a silver platter.

Draven picked up his hat from the bar. "Look, you do what you want, Hawk. No disrespect meant, but Lyle Murphy ain't that girl's type. She's yours already. Anyone can see it in the way she looks at you. All you have to do is open up that stubborn heart of yours and take her."

"What if I don't want her?"

"Then let her go, man. Don't string her along. She's too sweet of a girl for that."

Kaleb took another swallow from his glass. "She's a cold-hearted bitch," he mumbled more in an effort to convince himself.

"Says you." Draven placed the hat on his head. "Enjoy your evening, Hawk."

The barkeep disappeared through the backroom swinging doors, leaving Kaleb to his misery. He tapped the bar for another drink. When the bartender brought the Gentleman Jack over to pour him another half glass, Kaleb took the bottle from him.

"Leave it, man. I'm going to need it."

KALEB DRAGGED HIS TIRED ASS BACK to the clubhouse. He had left a message with the bartender to let Grayson know that he had called it a night. It probably wasn't smart to be traveling by himself knowing that not only did Rosalee want his head separated from his shoulders, but a good possibility that one of the Knights did too. He pulled his chopper into the gravel parking lot, kicked down the center stand and sat on his bike, staring at the clubhouse entrance.

Hanging his skull cap on the handle bars of his bike, he dragged a hand through his hair and expelled the breath he held. What the hell was he waiting for? Hoping no doubt that Cara and Kane had made themselves scarce so he could have a moment's peace and quiet. Christ, he didn't think he could handle listening to those two going at it until the wee hours of the morning. Truth be told, he was still horny as fuck and hearing their pleasure would only heighten what he felt. Kaleb stepped over the seat of his bike, suddenly wishing he had taken Grayson up on the model material he had presented. Hell, he could've just closed his eyes.

A flash of red caught his eye. Kaleb turned to see a small red Neon parked adjacent to the building. "Ah hell!" he exclaimed.

His night had just taken a turn for the worse, if that were indeed possible. If he got through the remainder of his night without having Suzi Stevens horizontal beneath him, while he pumped into her like a crazed vampire, it would be nothing short of a miracle. Kane and Cara needed to get their own digs. If listening to their nightly screwing wasn't enough, bringing her best friend into his home certainly proved they needed to move. He had half a mind to turn his bike back around and head the hell for the hills. He needed to clear his thoughts before seeing Suzi, no doubt about it. But the threat of losing his head had him moving toward the clubhouse instead. Maybe, with any luck, they'd ignore him. He could take an ice cold shower and hit his bed with a pair of Bose headphones and his music cranked to drown out the sound of her voice.

That would certainly work, but how the hell was he going to stop her scent from driving him to the brink of insanity?

Kaleb took in a deep breath and continued toward the entrance, his boots crunching across the gravel. He could hear the muted conversation through the door, and if he really tried, he could actually pick up every word. The fear of not liking what might be said behind his back had him swinging the door inward and ceasing all conversation as he stepped into the room.

A large smile he did not feel curved his cheeks, though he'd much rather go postal on Cara for bringing Suzi into his home. What the hell was she thinking?

"Waiting on me?" Kaleb asked. "I could use a couple more fifths of whiskey. Who's with me?"

"Hawk," Kane warned, from his position beside Cara on the sofa.

Suzi sat across from them, her feet tucked beneath her, making her appear even smaller than her five-foot-two self. Her fingers toyed with a strand of dark hair by her ear, twirling it around her index finger, looking as nervous as a whore in church. Rather than approach the three of them, Kaleb walked behind the bar and grabbed a fifth of whiskey. Having his blood regenerate at such a rapid rate that he couldn't feel more than a slight buzz at any given time normally served him well. This wasn't one of those times. How he wished he could drink himself into a stupor.

"Where's Gypsy?" Kane asked.

Kaleb knocked back two fingers, then wiped the back of his hand across his mouth. "I left him at the Rave. Last I saw he was headed up to Draven's office with a blonde on one arm and a brunette on the other."

Kane baited him. "And you came home?"

Kaleb's gaze went to Suzi's, pinning her to the sofa. He could hear her slight intake of air. "I wasn't interested."

"Really? Going soft, little brother?"

"Not a chance, Viper. Just wasn't anyone there I was interested in fucking," he said, not taking his eyes off Suzi's. To her credit, she held his stare.

If Suzi intended on visiting her high school classmate here, then she better develop thick skin because he wasn't about to go easy on her. The last vision he had of her was on her knees. By the look on her face, he'd bet her own thoughts traveled to the previous night and how she left him in a very high state of arousal. His nostrils flared. In fact, he knew damn well the thoughts running through her mind, if her scent was any indication. Kane and Cara no doubt picked up on the fact that Kaleb easily affected the little brunette as well. If Cara was smart, she'd get her friend the hell out of the club-house and as far away from him as possible.

CARA'S PLAN WAS WORKING IN SPADES if Kaleb's obsidian gaze was any indication. But then again, getting him to desire Suzi had never been the issue. Breaking down the walls of hate surrounding his heart was. Other than telling him the truth about Ion, she didn't see how that would be possible. She'd always be the cold-hearted bitch who hadn't mourned the loss of his nephew ... *her lover.* Suzi couldn't betray Ion's memory. He had been the only Son who truly treated her as a person, and not just someone needed for survival. Ion had loved her, just as thoroughly as Cara had.

Moisture sprang to her eyes, but Suzi blinked back the tears. She'd be damned if she'd allow Kaleb that kind of power over her.

What the hell had she been thinking? She couldn't do this. Maybe she should just beg him to release her from being a donor and walk away for good, move to the east coast and start a new life. Forget about the vampire whose sex-appeal was off the charts. Sure she craved Kaleb like crack to a junkie, but if she weren't careful that desire would be her downfall. If she walked away now, then she did so with dignity and without allowing him to destroy her completely.

Suzi stood, smoothed her hands down her dark-blue, super-straight jeans. She had worn them, knowing they fit her like a glove and would capture Kaleb's attention—at least that had been her hope. His gaze zeroing in on her ass as she turned slightly to the side, told her the outfit had worked. Not only had his eyes changed, his face was starting to take the shape of the vampire in him.

Most would be frightened by the transformation, but to her it was one hell of a turn-on.

Time to make excuses and quit the clubhouse before she did something stupid like grab his biceps and pull him in the direction of his quarters and beg him to make love to her. She doubted she'd get much of an argument from him. His nostrils flared, obviously detecting the scent of her arousal. Her gaze left his to land on first Kane, then Cara, who probably detected her reaction to Kaleb as well. Both tried unsuccessfully to look indifferent to protect her from further embarrassment. Great … now they were all aware of the affect Kaleb had on her. Suzi rolled her eyes and grabbed her keys from the center table.

Cara leaned forward, laying her hand on hers, and stopped her from her hasty exit. "Kane and I were just about to go for a ride."

Kane glanced at Cara. "Seriously? Shit is just getting good," he said with a humor-laced smile.

Cara swatted his arm. "Let's take that bike of yours for a ride, vamp boy. I promise to make it worth your while."

Kane gripped the front of Cara's shirt and pulled her in for a deep kiss, leaving Cara damn near panting.

"Get a room, for God's sake," Kaleb growled. "And please ... not here. I don't think I could bear another night of you two tearing up the sheets."

Suzi wasn't sure allowing Cara and Kane to leave at this exact moment was the wisest choice for her. She suddenly wished she hadn't gone for Cara's idea to gain Kaleb's notice by hanging at the clubhouse, wearing clothes sure to peak his interest. Playing games with an angry vampire was one thing, tempting fate with a highly sexually charged one was another. The minute Kane dropped his hold on Cara, Suzi grabbed her arm and pulled her toward the back of the clubhouse, hoping it was far enough out of vampire earshot.

"What the hell are you doing?" she whispered.

Cara smiled. "Giving you time to talk to Kaleb."

"Does he *look* like he wants to talk?"

Biting back a laugh, Cara said, "No. No, he doesn't. But he does look like he's ready for some hot, sweaty makeup sex."

"Makeup sex, Cara, is what you have when there is something to make up for. Hawk hates me."

"So change his mind, sweetie." She gripped Suzi's face between her palms. "Sex can help mend a lot of fences and show Kaleb what he's missing out on."

A tremor slipped down her spine. "I'm not sure I can do this."

"Sure you can." Cara released her, gave her a wink, and headed for the front of the clubhouse. Kane grumbled as he followed his mate out the door, something about missing all the fireworks.

Suzi stood stock-still, staring at the back of the closed door, weighing her options. She could try to make it out of the clubhouse before Kaleb stopped her, that is if he even bothered himself to prevent her from leaving. Or she could walk over to the bar, swallow her dignity, and actually try to be cordial.

"You just going to stand back there all night or are you going to come join me for a drink?" Kaleb groused.

Suzi's gaze went to his heated one. *Yep, his desire hadn't been squashed one iota.* She was in deep shit if she stayed. She'd make sure to pay Cara back big time for leaving her alone when Kaleb was clearly in one of his black moods. Her friend might've meant well, but Suzi felt more like a sacrificial lamb at the moment.

Taking a deep breath, Suzi headed for the bar and slapped her palm on the wooden surface. She was already in this far, she might as well carry it through and pray her heart didn't get slaughtered in the process. "Hit me."

Kaleb's grin widened, his fangs showing white against his lush red lips. He quickly poured her a shot, then held up the amber liquid in his glass. "Salute."

Suzi couldn't help but return his smile as she touched glasses with his, then took the small shot to her lips and downed the fiery liquid, the whiskey warming her clear to her toes. Liquid courage. Maybe if she had enough shots she could later blame the alcohol for her inhibitions.

Slamming her shot glass on the bar, she said, "Hit me," again.

Kaleb chuckled. "Easy there, *piccolo diavolo*. If we're going to do this, I don't want you in a drunken stupor. I'd rather have you fully functioning."

"Do what, Kaleb?"

Suzi didn't think it possible, but his fangy smile went even larger.

"You called me Kaleb."

"I did."

"Does that mean I'll be fucking you in a few minutes?"

Lust, pure and simple, arrowed straight to the juncture between her thighs. Suzi should be slapping his face for all his crudeness, instead she had an extreme desire to rip off his clothes and lick every square inch of his pale skin, starting at the wrist and working her way up his tattoo sleeve. She had always found his tattoos incredibly hot. Now was no exception.

She took a steadying breath. "No, Kaleb, it means I find myself in an amicable mood. One where I can tolerate being in the same room with you. Don't push it."

One of his brows arched. "I've told you in the past, *piccolo diavolo*, I'm always up for a challenge."

"So you did."

"And speaking of up..." He ran a palm down the steely erection, unmistakable beneath his jeans. "I believe we have unfinished business from last night."

Suzi licked her suddenly dry lips as her gaze took in his hand running the length of him. Jesus, he had no idea what that did to her. *Or maybe he did.* She could easily imagine him pulling out his cock and fisting it, putting on a show just for her. Her entire body hummed with unrequited desire, causing her to shift in her stance.

Would it be so bad?

"Hit me," she said again.

Kaleb stopped running his palm down the front of his pants, his gaze traveling her length. Heat spread through her limbs. Hell, she was already on fire. She certainly didn't need the help of more whiskey.

His obsidian gaze landed back on hers. "No more alcohol."

Kaleb's nostrils flared as he took in a deep breath, then stepped forward, leaning in so close that his lips almost touched hers. Her knees damn near gave out. Where she sucked at the art of seduction, he more than made up for. Dear Lord, he could have written the damn book.

"About fucking..."

Screw what he thought of her. She needed Kaleb and wasn't about to deny herself again. Fisting his black T-shirt, she closed the gap, her lips meeting his and shoving her tongue into his mouth, earning her a low growl before he palmed her ass and lifted her from the floor. Her legs wrapped his trim waist as Kaleb deepened the kiss. He tasted of all things illicit. Everything her father had warned her to stay away from. And deliciously, like the whiskey they had both just consumed.

Kaleb's rock-hard erection rested hot against her center. The clothes separating them had become a damned nuisance. As he backed her against the closest wall, one of his hands left her ass to slide beneath her tight, black sweater to palm her breast. Her nipple instantly pebbled. He took little time pulling down the cup and freeing her breast. He pinched the small pink tip between thumb and forefinger. She gasped against his mouth.

"Please, Kaleb," she whimpered.

"Say it, *piccolo diavolo,* and I'll be happy to oblige." Kaleb now licked a path up her neck, his fangs grazing her artery before nipping the fleshy part of her ear. "Fuck, I think I might just die if I don't slide inside you soon."

Suzi shivered from the warm breath spanning her flesh. "Take me, I'm—"

Stopping her from saying stupidly, "I'm yours," the door to the clubhouse banged inward, Grayson strolling in with a redhead on his arm, and by the looks of it a very inebriated one. But just as she was about to suggest they find Kaleb's capable bed, the woman raised her head with a drunken stupor smile plastered on her face.

"Suzi!" she slurred.

Jesus! Suzi swatted Kaleb, getting him to put her down. Once her shaken legs hit the floor and she righted her sweater, her fists went to her hips as she faced Grayson head on. Her anger skyrocketed at the other vampire standing before her, just as an unknown blonde and brunette followed the guilty two in the door.

"I brought the party home," Grayson happily announced.

Suzi marched over to the cavalier biker, grabbed Tamera from his grasp and hissed, "Stay the hell away from her, Gypsy!"

He held up both palms and backed into the waiting arms of the other two women. "Suit yourself, woman. I have all I need here." He winked at her, then looked from the blonde to the brunette. "Ladies?"

Grayson set off for his quarters, before calling back, "You really do know how to spoil a party, doll."

"Asshole," she spat after him, holding Tamera up.

She looked at Kaleb in apology. "I'm sorry," was all she could think to say before grabbing her keys and heading out of the clubhouse with her roommate's arm slung over her shoulder, leaning a good share of her weight on Suzi. No way could she allow Grayson to corrupt the young donor. Tamera needed a quick history lesson on Grayson Gabor.

Just before the door swung shut behind Suzi and Tamera, she heard Kaleb's growl. "You really are an asshole, Gypsy." Followed by a, "Fuck!" and the sound of breaking wood as if something had struck the bar top with extreme force.

Suzi winced as she helped her drunken roommate into the Neon. If Kaleb didn't hate her before, he sure as hell did now. Suzi hurried around her car and quickly slid behind the driver's seat and started the engine. She needed to get away from the clubhouse before she changed her mind and left Tamera to sleep her drunk off on the sofa while she and Kaleb... What the hell was she thinking? Had it not been for Grayson's untimely arrival, she'd no doubt be waking up with a boatload of regret come morning.

"Let's get you home," she said, looking at a frowning Tamera.

"What did you do with my Gypsy Wipsy?" she whispered, already half asleep as she settled more fully into the car's cloth seat.

A chuckle escaped Suzi's lips before turning into full-blown mirth. She couldn't help wonder what the bad-ass vampire would think of his new nickname. With more peals of laughter, Suzi tucked that bit of information away for another time, and headed for Florence, back to their shared apartment.

CHAPTER SIXTEEN

"GOOD MORNING, JOE." CARA WALKED INTO THE OFFICE AS if every morning had started much in the same way over the past six months.

She shrugged out of her light jacket and hung it on the coat tree by the door. Keeping her return to little or no fanfare seemed to be the best bet. *Pick the path of least resistance.* Her singular goal was to make Joe feel as if nothing had changed between them, when in actuality everything had. She resided with known outlaws, in her partner's opinion, ones they had tried to put behind bars. How could he ever understand her relationship with them ... with Kane? It wasn't like she could tell Joe that she was now one of them, that she grew fangs and drank blood to stay alive.

Protect your neck, human.

Cara didn't expect Joe would take it easy on her, nor did she think she deserved special treatment. She'd need to earn his trust again as partner if she hoped to one day have the camaraderie they once shared. She needed to prove to Joe and herself that she could still do the job. So for now, she planned to ease back into her role and let him keep the reins for awhile. She had more years on the job, but he hadn't been the one who disappeared for six months.

She placed a box of Tim Horton's donuts on his desk. "I brought breakfast."

Joe looked up from his desk, fighting the smile trying to inch up on his cheeks. "You brought donuts, Brahnam. Seriously?"

"What's a cop without donuts and coffee?" She laughed. "I hope you started the coffee."

He pointed to the shelf in the corner of the office. Cara walked over to the maker and grabbed the carafe, looking for her mug that was no longer there. She supposed Joe wouldn't hang on to it for memento's sake.

"I threw it out, about two weeks after your departure," he said, not looking up from his paperwork, nor sounding apologetic in the least. "Use Styrofoam, Brahnam. Guess you'll need to bring a new one from home. I didn't want the reminder that you traded your partner in for a gang of outlaws."

"They aren't exactly a bunch of outlaws." Cara grabbed a white cup and poured herself a cup of the java.

"Whatever." Joe glanced up at her. "You call them how you see them, and I'll call them how I do. Don't expect me to cut them any slack because you're shacking up with one of them."

"I'm not shacking up."

"You and Kane get married and didn't send me an invite?"

Cara blew out a breath. How could she possibly explain being mated to Kane? It wasn't like they had a marriage certificate, and yet mating with a vampire was much more permanent than any human marriage. There was no such thing as vampire divorces. Kane's had been a special case, getting the okay of Mircea to dissolve his mating because, let's face it, his stepdaughter was a first-class bitch.

"No. We didn't get married. But make no mistake, I do love him."

"Then he's free to dump you as soon as he's bored?"

Cara took a seat in her old desk chair across from her partner, grabbed the box of donuts and pulled one from the carton. She took a bite of the sugary delicacy, then washed it down with a sip of her coffee, giving her time to think about how she wanted to answer Joe's question.

Licking the sugar from her lips first, she then said, "I know you don't understand, Joe. But I don't need a certificate to tell me Kane is faithful to me. We may not be married in what you believe to be the perfect union, but we are together. Kane loves me and would never do anything to hurt me. That includes jeopardizing my job here."

"I hope you're right, Brahnam, because I'm about to test that theory."

Cara's gaze narrowed as they landed on the folder Joe slid across their back-to-back desks. The bar's name caught her attention. Her heart skipped a beat. She looked up at her partner. "What's this about?"

"The case I've been working on for the past few month's involves your new love's favorite haunt, the Blood 'n' Rave."

"What about the place?" Cara picked up a pen and toyed with it, tapping it on the desk surface.

"You can't even hide the fact that I already made you uncomfortable, Brahnam." Joe grabbed a donut from the box and sat back, pointing at her with his free hand. "Are you going to sit there and tell me this won't be personal to you? If it is, I'll bring up a uniform to help me with the case."

"No, I can handle this," Cara said quickly, knowing full well she couldn't breathe a word of this to Kane. This would be the perfect opportunity to prove herself to Joe that she could separate her personal life from her work.

She couldn't allow herself to think how Kane might react to the fact their feeding grounds was under investigation. Kane would flip a switch. Kaleb would go back to hating her, and whatever truce they had managed to date would be forever severed—not to mention how the rest of the Sons would view her. No way would Kane allow Draven or the club to go down for anything illegal. And if she didn't say something? Talk about a conflict of interest. There was no way Joe hadn't thought this through when he decided to invite her in on his case. He was testing her—a test she couldn't fail if she meant to keep her job. Cara nearly groaned. Maybe coming back to the job had been a bad idea after all.

"You want to tell me what's involved?"

"That's your case file. I made you a copy to look over. But no taking it home, Brahnam. Sorry, I don't trust your roommates not to tip off Draven. He's going down." Joe took a bite from his donut and then smiled at her as he chewed. His Adam's apple bobbed as he swallowed, then he said, "These things are awesome. Thanks, partner."

Cara smiled uneasily. "I thought you might like them."

"It really is good to have you back, partner. I hope we can work through our differences." Joe winked at her, making her doubt the sincerity of his statement.

Trust went both ways, making her wonder if she could truly trust him now that he called out one of Kane's friends. Cara had been correct in her earlier assessment, everything between them had changed. There would be no going back.

"I'm sure we can." Cara offered him a smile of her own. "So, about the Rave. What's going on there?"

"The club owner?" Joe's face sobered as he sat forward, excitement lighting his dark brown gaze. "He goes by the name Draven. Not his real name as you see there under the property's ownership name. Anyway, looks like the man has been dealing ecstasy to the club goers. I think he's bringing his drugs up from California."

"And you have proof?"

"We don't have enough to make a case yet. But we will." Joe leaned back in his chair. "The cartel smuggles drugs across the Mexican border from what we can tell. There's an OMC called the Devils. Heard of them?"

One of Kane's rival clubs. The same MC partly responsible for Ion's death. "Yes."

"They're known dealers in California. Big distributors for the cartel. As far as we can tell, they stay south of the Oregon border."

"So then what's this have to do with Draven at the Blood 'n' Rave?"

"We think he's driving south to get his product."

"Is it a big surprise that a club such as his has ecstasy? After all, it is a rave."

Joe took a sip from his coffee, then leaned forward. "It's not Draven that we're ultimately after, Cara. I'm working with the feds here. This is no small time dealer we're going after. Draven isn't the target. It's his supplier they want."

Cara didn't like where this was going. Now that the feds were also involved, it complicated matters even worse.

"I figure if we can get someone close to Draven, someone he trusts to find out where he's getting his drugs from—"

"No fucking way, Joe! I'll not use the Sons' relationship with me against them. They won't go for this. None of them would betray Draven. He may not be in the Sons, but he's like a brother to them. Besides, most of Kane's MC brothers barely tolerate me as it is because I'm a cop."

"I don't expect any of the Sons to cooperate, Brahnam."

Her mouth rounded. "Oh, hell no, Joe. I won't do it either. You can't ask me to betray Kane."

"Who better? You already have an inside track. We just need a little information from Draven is all."

"Information that could wind up costing Draven his club and possibly cause him jail time. You think he's just going to tell me who he gets his supplies from?"

Joe laughed. "If you believe that, then you must seriously think I doubt your detective skills, Brahnam. On the contrary, I do expect you to get the information, but by using your head. I trust you'll find a way to help us with this case."

How the hell could she possibly do that without damaging her relationship to the Sons, let alone Kane? If she were smart, she'd walk away now, pack up her things and leave the job behind. Her love for Kane far out-trumped her love of the job. She had foolishly thought she could have the best of both worlds. And she could, had it not been for Joe's desire to test her loyalty. Cara took a deep breath. She could do this. She'd find a way to keep Draven from falling into the hands of the feds, and help Joe solve this case. She didn't yet know if she'd accomplish the impossible task put before her. But if there was a will, then there was a way. Cara would show Joe that she could manage both her career and her loyalty to Kane and his brethren.

KALEB WALKED INTO THE RAVE, his mood blacker than it had been in a long time. He knew what had to be done, but he sure as fuck didn't like it. He had damn near did the one thing he had sworn off of, and had it not been for Grayson's untimely arrival, he would have been kicking himself to hell and back come morning. He should have kissed Grayson upon his return instead of cursing the ground he walked on. If nothing else, Cara and Suzi had taught him a lesson. He could not be trusted around that woman.

The way Kaleb saw it, he was left with one option—to cut Suzi Stevens loose.

When he had forced her hand out of retirement to become his personal donor, he hadn't been thinking with the right head. He had wanted to torment her, when in truth, he had successfully caused himself great agony in the process. Seeing her every three days, let alone on nights when he wasn't required to feed, proved to him that he couldn't do so without his libido getting in the way ... or his emotions. Sure, he wanted to fuck the little brunette in the worst way. But with Suzi, he wanted so much more. He wanted to feed from her, wanted to bury himself in her, surround himself with her. Hell, he wanted to wake up next to her and start all over again. *Fuck* ... when had he become so pussy whipped? He gritted his teeth.

How the hell was that even possible when he wasn't even getting any?

Kaleb wasn't a one woman kind of man.

He loved variety, he thrived on not being tied to one woman for all eternity. No way in hell was he cut out to be anyone's mate. Brunettes and blondes turned his head, he wasn't discriminatory ... he loved black haired and redheaded females, too ... and of course there were the brunettes. Kaleb shook his head and growled low. Damn, he had it bad. He wanted Suzi, regardless that she had loved Ion first, regardless of how she reacted to his nephew's death. He had wanted her from the time she had taken a hold of his dick all those years ago. Avoiding her had become a necessity to keep from admitting, even to himself, that he had fallen hard for the brunette, which is why it had stung so much when she had turned to Ion. Not that he could blame her after the way he had crassly tossed her aside for the next available female. Kaleb had used his nephew as an excuse to keep her at bay and fuel his anger. It may have seemed like a viable rationalization at the time, but now that so much time had passed, his enmity seemed to diminish. Kaleb knew the true reason he avoided her. It was because he no longer trusted himself to be around her.

Last night lay proof to that in spades.

He had known that if he ever allowed himself to have sex with Suzi again, he'd be incurable. A mess of emotions. Kaleb couldn't think straight around her. On one hand he wanted to hate her, be mad as hell, wanting to throttle her. On the other, he wanted nothing more than to walk over to her and kiss her senseless. All he had to do was walk into a room, lay eyes on her, and he was sporting an instant hard-on. Desire raged precariously close to the surface, demanding appeasement. If Grayson hadn't come home with the inebriated roommate of Suzi's the night before, he would've taken her against the clubhouse wall, regardless of her fiancé. Kaleb had been mere seconds from doing just that, knowing full-well he wouldn't have gotten an argument from her. Her lips may spout her disdain, but her body told an entirely different tale. Grayson had no doubt done them both a favor.

Tonight, Kaleb would do one for her.

Following his feeding, he'd tell her that he was retiring her once again. No way in hell could he stomach the idea of any of his brothers feeding from her. If he wasn't using her for communion, then neither were the Sons. He may not claim her, but he'd be damned if he allowed anyone else to. Her fiancé came to mind, causing him to curse beneath his breath. A frown turned down his lips. Kaleb couldn't stomach the idea that she went home to the bastard night after night, giving to him the one thing he so desperately craved. He ran a hand down his face as he approached the bar. How could he think to dictate her life when he didn't want to be a part of it? Kaleb faced a no-win situation. If he kept feeding from her, he'd be fucking her in less than a week. If he released her, he'd likely never see her again, in which he'd have to allow her a life outside of being a donor. He'd bet if asked, Suzi would no doubt prefer the latter.

"Who the fuck died?" Draven combed his fingers through his long curls and brushed the stray strands from his face. His top hat was nowhere in sight tonight.

The man's overlong hair brushed his shoulders as a heavy five o'clock shadow dusted his cheeks. Kaleb bet the barkeep got nearly as much tail as the Sons. It seemed there were always a bevy of women who hung near the bar, vying for his attention. Draven never seemed to pay them any mind. The barkeep made sure the Sons were well-taken care of and had his undivided attention. His personal life, if he allowed himself one, came after making sure the Sons were well-attended. Draven had been a great and much trusted friend to the Sons of Sangue. And as such, the Sons would always have his back.

Kaleb ignored the reference to his sour mood. "You see Suzi?"

"She's waiting upstairs for you." His thumb indicated the curtained staircase. "She's been up there for about a half hour. Said she didn't feel like hanging at the bar tonight and asked if it was okay to wait for you in my office. I told her she was more than welcome to the space. I didn't think you'd mind. By the way, she looks fucking hot tonight. Be careful, bro."

"Great," Kaleb mumbled.

He thanked Draven and headed for the stairs, in no mood to carry on a conversation with the barkeep at the moment. He took the stairs one step at a time, feeling the weight of what he was about to do heavy on his shoulders. Absolving Suzi of her duty as his donor wasn't exactly making him a happy camper. Hell, no. He truly wanted to throw her over his shoulder, take her home and bed her. But that wasn't going to happen, not without losing a part of himself. Reason enough to cut his ties. Allowing her beneath his skin had been a bad idea from the moment she walked back into his life a little over a week ago. If he were smart, he'd take the coward's way out and about-face, tell Draven to make an excuse for him and find himself a new donor. He didn't need a reason to do so. He was the

President of the Sons of Sangue and could do as he pleased. Instead, hand on knob, he forced himself to open the door and face her one last time. He owed her that much after forcing her to endure his company.

Stepping into the dimly lit room, his gaze landed on her. His breath stopped. She sat on the Italian leather sofa, thigh-high boots hugging her shapely legs, stopping just shy of a very short, black-leather mini-skirt. The five-inch heels on those things could certainly be used as weapons. He'd do well to remember that. But damn if they didn't have his balls tightening and his cock standing at attention at the thought of them digging into his bare ass as he fucked her. On the top half, she wore a red halter, cut damn near to her belly button, barely containing her small, pert breasts. Her nipples pebbled against the silky material. He could easily imagine drawing them between his teeth. It was a most-definite "fuck me" outfit, which nearly had him forgoing his reasoning to cut her loose out the window. Damn her for knowing full-well the reaction that outfit would have on him and wearing it anyway. He could easily envision bending her over the arm of the sofa and tearing her panties from her, shoving into her in one fluid motion.

Kaleb cursed, his mouth suddenly dry as dirt. A half-empty glass of wine set next to her on the end table. Walking over to it, he grabbed the glass and tossed back the rest of the contents before turning his heated gaze on her. His change wasn't far off, as it never seemed to be in her company. Kaleb was either wanting to throttle her or fuck her whenever she was in his company. He sure in the hell wished he could just give in and take the latter. His groin tightened at the idea, begging Kaleb to do just that. Strengthening his resolve, he clenched his jaw and bridled the lengthening of his fangs. Conversation first. Then he'd feed.

"Kaleb," she acknowledged, using his given name and causing his heart to skip a beat.

He needed her anger back. This seductive side to Suzi was knocking down the barrier to his resolve. Much more time spent in that holy-hell outfit and he'd forget about sending her packing. He'd take what he craved, to hell with her fiancé, and worry about tomorrow later.

Jesus! He certainly couldn't take much more.

"We need to talk."

Her gaze took in his as her pink tongue moistened her lips. Good, he made her nervous, never mind the desire he detected coming off her in waves. He knew her panties were already wet. He didn't need to touch her to know how he affected her. *Down boy!*

"You need to feed, Kaleb. I can see it in your pallor. We can talk after."

His groin plagued him. No way could he feed from her and walk away. He was an idiot to think he might be able to. "Look, Suzi ... this isn't such a good idea—"

She stood from the sofa and approached him, stopping him in mid-sentence. It was as if his tongue had become glued to his mouth. The sexy sway of her hips drew his heated gaze. His eyes burned in their transformation and his gums ached as his fangs lengthened.

So much for talking.

Suzi lay her hand on his chest and tilted her head to the side, giving him easy access to her artery. He'd need every ounce of willpower to stop at communion. Kaleb wanted so much more and here she stood very willing and eager to give into all his desires. But rather than deny himself the pleasure of nourishment, he fisted her hair at her nape and sank his fangs gum deep into her artery. The sweet tang of her blood flowed easily over his tongue, hardening his dick damn near painfully. Much more and he feared splitting his jeans.

Suzi's one hand fisted his tee as she melded against him, moaning his given name. The scent of her desire wafted to his nose. He knew he had to quickly finish and cut her loose if he had any chance at all of walking out of here without caving, and completely messing up both of their lives. *She has a fiancé* played through his brain like a mantra. Not that it would stop him from taking what he wanted. He just needed a good deterrent.

Her free hand slid down his abs to the front of his jeans, sliding across his rigid cock. All sane thought flew from his brain as she quickly released the button and slipped her hand inside to encompass him. The shock of her touch had him withdrawing his fangs with a growl. Quickly licking the twin holes closed, he disengaged himself and stepped back from her. Tears sprung to her eyes. Kaleb felt like a complete shit, even if he knew what he was about to do was best for both of them.

Suzi held a trembling hand over her lips as the tears slipped down her cheeks unheeded. "Am I not good enough?"

Why the hell would she want to be? He hadn't once given her a reason to think of him in a positive light. On the contrary, he had tried his best to earn her scorn. Kaleb's heart beat arduously. Full-blown panic settled in his chest at the desire to soothe her. He couldn't be the man that she needed in her life. It was time to give her back to her fiancé, even if he'd rather suck the man dry than allow him to touch Suzi again. Kaleb needed to get the hell out of Draven's office, and stop thinking that she somehow belonged with him.

"You're released," he said, repositioning his cock and buttoning his jeans.

Her brows knit together. "What?" came her watery question.

Kaleb took another deep breath. He needed a drink. Something much stiffer than wine. But right now, he chose to get back on his chopper and get the hell away from the vision before him, not allowing his self-discipline to fail him now.

"You're permanently retired, Suzi." He approached her, grabbed the small vial around her neck and yanked the leather cord free. "You will no longer feed me or any of my brothers."

Suzi sucked in a sob. Her hand went to the hollow of her neck. "How could you?"

"Consider it me doing you a favor," Kaleb said as he turned and quit the room, her blood vial gripped tightly in his fist.

Her sobs followed him down the stairwell, causing his heart to pang. He was most definitely a bastard. Kaleb didn't pause as he passed the bar, catching Draven out of the corner of his eye, his look damning him. What the hell did he care? He had just done the little brunette a favor by cutting her free. Kaleb needed fresh air and the road before his selfish side kicked in and he took what Suzi offered anyway. Using both hands, he pushed through the exit and into the parking lot of the Rave, the cool air on his face much welcomed. Just as he reached his chopper, he caught sight of a large man to his right, staring at him. Kaleb stopped just short of swinging his leg over the seat of his bike. Turning, he looked up into the brown eyes of Lyle Murphy.

The big man glared at him, hatred evident in his gaze. "If you hurt her, dirt bag, I'll wipe the cement with you."

It was all the provocation Kaleb needed. Gritting his teeth, he walked over to Lyle and easily lifted the man off the ground by his throat. His fingers dug into the chorded muscles of Lyle's neck. Flashing the man his fangs, he growled. Lyle gasped for air, his eyes wide in fear seeing the vampire … monster before him. But before Kaleb had a chance to rip out the man's esophagus from his throat, he heard Suzi's approach, detected her scent.

"Let him down, Kaleb," she warned. "You hurt him and I will see that you pay for your sins the rest of your life. I promise I will make your life miserable, you ass."

Kaleb growled again, causing Lyle to blaspheme, his hands grappling at Kaleb's hand about his throat. With one final squeeze, he slowly lowered the man to his feet and released him.

"What the hell are you?" Lyle croaked.

His throat would no doubt plague him a few days, Kaleb having come just shy of crushing his windpipe.

He looked Lyle square in the eye, his obsidian gaze mirroring back at him. "You'll forget what you saw, asshole. You won't remember seeing the monster before you or the biker you have come to hate. Now go and be lucky I don't hypnotize you into despising the woman before you."

He turned to Suzi, who stood with fists perched on her hips, hatred shining clearly in the depths of her eyes. *Good.* She could now move forward with her life. Kaleb had club business to deal with.

He surely didn't need this little slip of a woman throwing him off course. No way in hell was he about to follow in his brother's footsteps. Cara had been all sorts of bad for Kane and his twin had damn near turned his back on the brotherhood because of her.

"Goodbye, Suzi," Kaleb said, then headed for his chopper without so much as a glance back.

"Kaleb Tepes ... I hope you rot in hell, you son of a bitch!"

Her following sobs would likely haunt him for days. But he had done them both a favor, regardless of the misery now worming its way through him. Turning the key to his chopper, he hit the ignition and started the engine. Kaleb kicked up the center stand with his booted heal, pushed off the bike, and headed out of the parking lot and down the road.

CHAPTER SEVENTEEN

SUZI CURLED HERSELF INTO THE CORNER OF THE SOFA, TUCKING her legs beneath her, miserable and dejected. Her hand went to her naked throat, her fingertips resting in the now-vacant jugular notch. How could Kaleb be so cruel? That vial and lifestyle had become a part of her, defined who she had become. Taking the donor necklace from her was akin to removing a part of her soul. Kaleb took the one thing from her that would ensure her hatred for him ... and the bastard knew it. He had been deliberately cruel. The question was why?

Her leather boots lay in a heap by the door, long forgotten as she stared into the dark interior of the room, wrapping her arms about her center in an attempt to keep herself warm. A shiver ran down her spine. She supposed she could start a fire in the hearth, but the room temperature had little to do with the chill invading her body that Kaleb had started at the club. Her heart panged. Lord, she wanted to despise him with every fiber of her being, turn her back on him and never set eyes on the bastard again.

Instead, here she sat in the quiet interior of the clubhouse, waiting for his return. He had to come home sooner or later, and when he did, he best be prepared for her wrath. The only way she was leaving was with her necklace in hand and an apology. It would be her decision to walk away from being a donor, not his. He said that he no longer lay claim to her as a donor or otherwise, so if she opted to feed one of the other Sons, then that should be her choice. She'd be damned before allowing him to make decisions on her behalf. Whether or not she loved Kaleb was beside the point, she'd die before giving him the opportunity to hurt her any longer.

Suzi rubbed her dry and itchy eyes, knowing she must be a sight. *So much for making the vampire realize what he was missing.* One look at her now and he'd likely thank his lucky stars to have dodged her attempt at seduction earlier. Though Cara may have had good intentions in helping her turn Kaleb's head, Suzi's delivery had sucked. Sure his erection had shown his interest, but any woman could have gotten a rise out of him. In the end, he had turned his back on her, and walked away without a care. He hadn't wanted her. Plain and simple. And that had stung, hurt her as thoroughly as if he had caused her physical harm.

Suzi's chest ached, the pain nearly debilitating her. God, she was a mess. She stood and walked to the bathroom, flipping on the light and staring at her pathetic reflection in the mirror. She couldn't allow Kaleb to see her as she stood before the sink. Turning on the water, she splashed her puffy face with cold water, hoping to wash away all traces of her sorrow. She needed to be strong, show him that she too could walk away without a care, even if it truly was killing her inside. Grabbing one of Cara's kohl pencils, she relined her eyes, then used some of her friend's mascara. She'd not give Kaleb the satisfaction of knowing he had that kind of influence over her happiness. Finished, she dusted her red nose with facial powder, then stood back and studied the reflection.

Satisfied, Suzi flipped the light switch off and padded back to the living area where she resumed her vigil, hoping that he'd make his return soon. Kane and Cara had promised to busy themselves elsewhere, both feeling Kaleb deserved Suzi's retribution after hearing how heartlessly he had treated her. Suzi hadn't missed the sound of Kane's humor though, as he and Cara closed the door behind them more than an hour ago. She supposed that humor was aimed at the shit-storm of fury Suzi planned to release on his twin. Grayson hopefully heeded Kane's text to spend the evening out. She didn't think she could stomach the egotistical ass if he decided to return with a couple of bimbos on his arms.

Suzi blew out a breath as her thoughts returned to Lyle, standing in the parking lot of the Rave, not far from his own tavern, confused as to what might've caused his throat such discomfort. The taillights to Kaleb's bike had not long faded before she turned to Tamera's uncle and thanked him for all he had done.

An apology spilled from her lips, as she tried to explain how truly sorry she was to have involved him in the mess that was her life. The fake engagement ring glinted on her finger, drawing her attention to the bauble that had already caused her so much trouble. Pulling it from her finger, Suzi tossed the fake solitaire into the bushes and walked off. Now she sat alone, waiting on Kaleb's return and hoping she hadn't caused Lyle any more trouble when his intentions had been pure. The good-hearted Irishman had tried to help her dodge the one person Suzi quickly realized was unavoidable.

The sound of an approaching Harley kicked up her already rapid heartbeat. The simple black and white wall clock told her dawn was yet a few hours away. With any luck, she'd get her vial back from

Kaleb and be home and in her bed by daybreak. She had the afternoon shift at the nursing home and would need to catch a few hours of sleep if that were even possible.

The engine cut short, further jangling her nerves. The time to change her mind had now passed, Suzi hugged her knees tightly to her chest and watched the back of the door.

KALEB STEPPED OVER THE SEAT of his bike, unsnapped his helmet and hung it on the handlebar of his chopper. Reaching into his pocket, he pulled out the simple black leather cord and looked at the red vial dangling from it. The red jewel glimmered in the florescent lighting of the parking lot security light.

He really was an ass.

What the hell had he been thinking when he had yanked it from Suzi's neck? He had no right telling Suzi what she could or couldn't do with her life. Jealousy had spurred his actions and the thought of her with another man had him nearly ripping out the throat of someone who had done nothing to earn his scorn. Kaleb didn't even want to think what might've happened if Suzi hadn't followed him out of the club and saw Lyle hanging from Kaleb's iron grip, his toes barely scraping the cement of the sidewalk.

Not that he had hurt the man. But he easily could have. Kaleb fisted the necklace and headed for the dark clubhouse. He wouldn't apologize for his actions. Right or wrong, he couldn't allow Suzi to remain a donor without more similar outbursts. Suzi Stevens could no longer be used as a donor, it was that simple. If he wasn't feeding from her, then certainly no one else would be.

She undoubtedly hated him now anyway. He hadn't missed the look on her face when he had cruelly yanked the leather cord from her neck. If she hadn't despised him before, he had just insured that she did. Kaleb couldn't blame her, and in fact welcomed her hostility. Better for him and the club if he got his head out of his dick and started concentrating on club business and who the hell wanted him dead. Not to mention the mess they now had with the Knights. Kane and he sat in opposition as to whether to continue the gun runs. Fact was, someone in the Knights had betrayed them, and until Kaleb discovered the identity, no way in hell would he trust any of them, Red included. Kane no longer had a voice in the matter. Kaleb was club pres, and as so, his twin had no choice but to abide by Kaleb's decision to put their tenuous truce with the Knights to a vote. He'd call a church meeting and place his concerns on the table. He'd bet that his men would rule in favor of cutting their losses. Most hadn't been happy with Kane's decision to work with the Knights in the first place and the fact he had done so without polling the rest of the MC. The bottom line was the Sons of Sangue didn't need the Knights, never would.

Grasping the knob and pocketing the necklace, Kaleb pushed the door inward and strode into the darkened interior, telling him everyone was either in bed or still out. He hadn't noted any vehicles in the parking lot, but then deep in thought, he hadn't really paid attention. The sweet scent of Suzi Stevens' damn near knocked the air from his chest the minute he cleared the doorway, long before his enhanced sight caught a glimpse of her sitting in the corner of his sofa, looking far too wounded for his peace of mind.

Jesus! Was he responsible for that?

"What are you doing here, Stevens?" he asked, his tone brusque. He needed her anger back because he sure as fuck couldn't handle the delicate woman now before him.

She unfolded her arms from her lean muscled legs and stood. Her "fuck me" skirt rode high on her thighs. Kaleb caught a glimpse of her boots lying in a heap by his feet. Thank goodness she had the foresight to remove them. Those spiked heels called to mind all sorts of erotic images, visions that were getting harder to ignore by the minute.

"You have something of mine and I want it back," she said as she headed in his direction.

His eyes damn near fell out of his head watching her approach. Her pert tits swayed gently beneath the red silk halter. Kaleb shoved both hands into the pockets of his jeans, no longer trusting himself not to touch. His hands itched to palm each breast and test their light weight. Shit, he wanted to draw the pert tips into his mouth, soak the red material before tearing it away. Suzi had never been large breasted, but man did she have a nice set of tits.

"Looks like you wasted your time then, Stevens." Pulling his hands from his pockets, he used one thumb to indicate behind him. "I threw the necklace alongside the road."

"You prick!"

She raised her hand to strike his chest, but he easily caught her wrist and yanked it high, tucking it behind her nape. She struggled in his grasp. Kaleb's heated gaze dropped to her breasts again as they thrust forward, not sure if he wanted them to slip from the fabric, or praying they'd stay put. His mouth parched. Thankfully he had fed earlier, the only thing fueling his willpower at the moment not to carry her off to his bed at the back of the clubhouse. His cock lengthened, tightening his jeans uncomfortably. He needed to get laid ... bad.

"I hate you!"

Her words caused him to smile, his fangs now fully extended. Suzi may despise him, but she could no more deny the fact they hungered for the same end. If she were smart she'd run like hell, because he was but a fraction away from losing control and taking his fill. And damn if he couldn't come up with one good reason at the moment not to fuck her. His earlier argument quickly took a back seat.

"No, you don't, sweetheart. Though I wish to hell you did."

"I swear to all that's holy I do, Hawk. I loathe you and curse the day I ever allowed you to touch me."

Kaleb chuckled, though not one of humor, before pinning her with his black gaze. "Why, Suzi? Because you can't rid yourself of the remembrance of my dick inside you? I'll be all too happy to refresh your memory."

"As I recall, I told you once before that would never happen."

Kaleb grinned, raising one of his brows heavenward. "And I believe my exact response was that I'm always up for the challenge. You know as well as I do we want the same thing. You forget... I can smell your desire, sweetheart."

"You're a pig."

"That may very well be, but it didn't stop you from giving me a blow job the other night now did it?"

Suzi gasped, tears springing to her eyes as she yanked unsuccessfully on her wrist. He'd let her go all right, but not until he was damn good and ready.

"If not for your fiancé, I would've already been inside you."

Her lower lip trembled, the fight seeming to drain from her and she sagged against the wall. "Let go of me, Kaleb."

"No."

He growled, baring his teeth, and grabbed her other wrist, pinning them both overhead as he backed her against the wall by the outside door. He used his booted foot to slam it closed. His breathing labored as he leaned in, her scent fueling the savage in him. Kaleb walked a fine line of self-restraint.

"You don't want me," she whispered so quietly that had it not been for his keen hearing he might not have heard her accusation.

"That's where you're wrong, *piccolo diavolo*. I want you so badly that every part of my being aches to be inside of you right now." Kaleb leaned in, his lips grazing the shell of her ear, his knee splitting her legs so that her hot center rested on his thigh. "Are you ready to walk away from that fiancé?"

A tremor passed town her spine. "He was never my fiancé, Hawk."

Kaleb stepped back, still holding tight to her wrists with one hand and looked down on her. His forehead furrowed. "What the hell did you just say?"

Suzi looked up, her gaze still watery with unshed tears. "I lied."

Kaleb clenched his jaw, reining in his temper, hoping she had a damn good reason. "Why?"

"Because…"

He waited for her to finish, when she didn't, he asked again, "Why, *piccolo diavolo?*"

"I was afraid," she said, looking to the floor.

"Afraid?" He ran his free hand through his overlong loose curls at the top of his head, brushing the hair from his eyes in frustration. "I would never strike you, Suzi. I'd rip the throat out of anyone who tried."

"I'm not afraid of you, Kaleb." Suzi worried her lower lip between her teeth. Her cerulean blue gaze looked back at him. "It's me. I fear the feelings you cause in me. I'm afraid I won't have the sense to resist you."

"Then don't." Kaleb leaned down and tasted her lips.

He sure in the hell hadn't thought to end the night this way, not after taking her necklace and attempting to destroy any feelings she might have had for him. But he had misjudged her. Suzi's resolve was more resilient than even he had speculated. After treating her so callously the years following Ion's death, she had returned to the Rave a little over a week ago ... to see for herself how he fared after nearly losing his head. Instead of embracing her benevolence, he did his damnedest to push her away and punish her for all her goodness. But Suzi's spirit couldn't be beaten, no matter how hard he'd tried, and for that he owed her his reverence.

His free hand rested on her waist, his fingers skimming the bare flesh of her back as he deepened the kiss, his tongue sliding into her mouth. She tasted of cinnamon and whiskey, telling him that she had probably been looking for some liquid courage and gotten into his Jack while she waited for his return. No longer did he care about his absurd prejudices or the fact that at one time she had chosen his nephew over him. How could he hold that against her when he had all but pranced every willing floozy from the Rave in front of her? The fact that she stood here now, choosing to be with him rather than turn her back on him, spoke volumes.

Shit, he really was a goner.

He slid his hand up her slender side, brushing the side of her small breast, her answering moan spurring his craze to have her. Palming her through the soft silk, her pebbled nipple brushed against his flesh. His groin tightened. Suzi arched into his hand, as she gently yanked on her still captured wrists. She gasped for air as his mouth left hers and trailed wet kisses across her cheek to the sensitive spot, just beneath the fleshy part of her ear. Her heart pounded, causing blood to roar through her veins. Kaleb's gums ached with the desire to sink his fangs into her artery and drink from her, though he had done so mere hours earlier. To take communion from her again so soon could put her at risk of anemia and Kaleb would never put her life in jeopardy to satisfy his own selfish needs.

He trailed the tip of his nose along the artery, inhaling her unique scent, knowing it would have to be enough. Licking the same path his nose had taken had Suzi tilting her head to the side, giving him permission to drink, a license he could not take no matter how much the vampire in him demanded more.

Kaleb ran a forefinger down her sternum, teasing the flesh between her breasts, before slipping beneath the silky material and brushing across one of her hardened nipples. Suzi's breath hitched as she pushed the tip more fully into his hand, her body begging for his touch. Only too willing to comply, he rolled the taut bud between forefinger and thumb, eliciting a moan from her, laying proof that she desired him and not just the vampire capable of drawing a sexual response by the simple act of feeding. He'd be lying if he didn't say the thought of her wanting the man in him didn't please him.

His nostrils flared, his cock hardened, and if he didn't slide inside her soon, he feared he might just die from want. Kaleb couldn't remember the last time he had been this crazed with desire.

Not since her.

Damn it all to hell!

He was tired of trying to outrun, and outfuck the one thing he had always coveted. He had it bad for Suzi Stevens and, like it or not, he no longer wanted to live without her. Better to be fucking her, than walking away from her.

"I lied." Her admission had caught him off guard, sent him spiraling into the company of goners. He competed with no one. Suzi Stevens was his for the taking, and he'd kill anyone who thought to challenge him for her. Kaleb wasn't about to fuck up a second time. She didn't belong to Ion. And whether Suzi liked it or not, she belonged to him. Pity the fool who tried to tell him otherwise. She may not be his mate ... no, never that. But his nonetheless.

CHAPTER EIGHTEEN

SUZI HAD PASSED THE POINT OF STOPPING, NOR DID SHE WANT to. Foolish as it may seem, she wanted Kaleb more in this moment than she could ever remember in the years following the first time she had given herself fully to him. Now it seemed such a distant past and all the hurt and anger in the years that followed easily melted away. She was here, with him, and that's all that really mattered. She loved this man, always had, even if at times her hate and anger had overshadowed the feelings she tried desperately to deny.

Her center rested on his muscular, jeans-clad thigh, nothing more than a sheer thong separating her from him. Kaleb anchored her to the wall, and a good thing too, or she'd have slipped down the rough-paneled wood to pool at his feet. Suzi tried to draw a breath as his one hand toyed with her highly sensitive nipples, while the other held her wrists trapped overhead. She couldn't help but wonder if it were indeed possible to pass out from sheer pleasure. If that were the case, she'd never make it through the foreplay.

In the years following their first joining, Kaleb had become a more attentive lover. That or he had at some point decided pleasuring her was more important than taking his own. Ten years ago she had been barely out of high school when he had carelessly taken her virginity, fucked her and walked away without a backward glance.

Now? She sucked in another breath as his fingers skimmed her stomach and headed south. Lord, he had been practicing. Suzi arched into him, wanting more ... needing to feel him inside her.

Hell, she wanted the orgasm she teetered on the brink of.

Suzi hadn't exactly been celibate, but most of her attempts at relationships ended with her comparing them to Kaleb. Even though he hadn't been an overly considerate lover at the time, no one had compared to her brief coupling with him. Kaleb had become her obsession. Her reason for remaining a donor, befriending Ion, and her last attempt to sleep with Kane over six months ago. All had been aimed at getting Kaleb's notice.

And now that she had it, he would forever ruin her for any other man. If he walked away after this night, she might as well enter a convent. Two of his fingers smoothed over the sheer material covering her. Suzi moaned, her head tilting into the wall, reveling in the moment. She never wanted it to end.

Kaleb leaned down and suckled one of her nipples through the silk top, pulling on it gently, before using the pad of his tongue to soothe the bud through the material. Arching into him, she urged his fingers forward. Hell, she needed him to rip the material from her, unbutton his pants and shove into her. Nothing short of feeling his cock inside her would do. But just as the thought materialized, he instead slipped two of his fingers past the line of her panties and into her, causing her to cry out.

Much more....

His thumb caressed the tight knot of nerves of her clit as his two fingers worked in and out of her, the friction sending tremors throughout her body. Two seconds, three ... and just like that her world shattered as his given named tumbled from her lips. Her orgasm tore through her, shaking her foundation to the core, telling her in that moment that she was most certainly his and always would be. No living person could ever take his place. And unfortunately, if she for once forgot her head and told him her true feelings … she would no doubt lose him forever.

Biting her lower lip, she stilled the voice inside her and instead concentrated on freeing her hands. She needed to touch him, to run her hands over his rigid muscles, to tell him with physical contact what her mouth in no way ever could.

Kaleb relented, released her hands, as he also withdrew his fingers. Suzi looked into his heated gaze, saw herself mirrored in the depths. No way would she allow him to back out now as he looked at her in uncertainty. If he had ruined her for all eternity for any other male, then she meant to make damn sure she left her stamp on him too. By the sound of his ragged breathing, she knew that he still wanted her, warred with the idea of seizing what was already his.

Suzi needed to lighten the mood before he changed his mind. If she were to ever win him over, then she'd need to do so with baby steps. Anything that looked like commitment and Kaleb would no doubt turn tail and run. She had never seen him with one woman for any period of time. He changed women as often as he changed his briefs. If Suzi wanted to be that one woman who outlasted all others, then she needed to convince him he couldn't live without her.

Right! She had a better chance of tightrope walking across Niagara Falls.

Kaleb leaned forward, his forehead resting on her shoulder as though he warred with his decision of what to do next. Suzi needed to keep him from retreating.

"Wow." She chuckled, in her attempt to keep it light. "Where did you learn that trick?"

He joined in her humor, his breath teasing the flesh of her shoulder. Score one for her. He wasn't running yet.

He kissed the crook of her neck, then whispered, "You haven't seen anything yet, *piccolo diavolo.*" His breath fanned feather-light across her flesh. A shiver passed down her spine.

"Then what the hell are you waiting on, vampire? I could die of old age waiting on you to give me a proper orgasm."

Kaleb leaned back, his smile wide as his fangs flashed in the low lighting. "You sure about that, sweetheart? Oh … I am so up for that challenge."

Not allowing her to catch a breath, he gripped her about the waist and easily lifted her off the floor, sitting her on the bar top and ripping her panties from her. Palming the inside of her thighs, he gently spread them, his obsidian gaze taking her in. Jesus, her heart pummeled her sternum. Had it not been for the hold on her thighs, she would have closed them, feeling incredibly exposed and suddenly self-conscious. Kaleb's nostrils flared just before leaning in and touching the tip of his tongue on her moist flesh. Suzi sucked her lower lip between her teeth and bit it to keep from crying out. Fisting the dark curls of his head, holding his mouth flush to her, she watched as he sucked her fevered flesh between his teeth. As he gazed up for just the briefest of moments, Suzi thought she detected a deeper emotion in the depths of his eyes ... one she feared could only be a product of her longing.

His mouth damn near brought her to another blinding orgasm, but just before she reached the pinnacle, she yanked on his curls and pulled him away. "Kaleb Tepes, if you don't fuck me now, I swear I'll make you pay."

The corners of his eyes turned up as an impish grin split his face. "What are you saying, *piccolo diavolo?* That I was right? Never say never?"

"Get over yourself already, Hawk." She smacked his shoulder. "Take what I'm offering while I'm still willing to eat crow."

Slowly backing from her reach, he slid a hand to the front of his jeans, running his palm over the ridge that rested beneath. *Oh damn!*

"This what you want, sweetheart?"

Suzi had the insane urge to cross her legs to assuage the ache Kaleb started there. If he so much as stroked himself she might just climax seated on the bar without any help from him. Her gaze centered on his hand leisurely moving over the fabric, his answering chuckle telling her he enjoyed torturing her.

Thanks to all things holy, his fingers finally traveled to his fly and slipped the button from its mooring. Suzi licked her parched lips as he deliberately took his time pulling down the zipper. His hand disappeared behind the fabric, stroking what her eyes could not yet see. If Kaleb didn't do something soon, Suzi might just join him in the self-gratification department.

"Kaleb Tepes," she warned.

His response was a wink before he pulled his large cock from his pants. Her breath stuck in her chest as he fisted his erection and slowly ran his hand from balls to tip and back with practiced precision. "You see something you want, sweetheart?"

Suzi jumped from the bar, strode toward him and pushed his teasing, sorry ass over the arm of the sofa and onto the cushions, earning her another chuckle. "You're damn right I do."

Without so much as another word, she walked around the sofa and straddled his lean hips, using her hand to guide him. She paused, allowing herself to adjust to the size of him, before slowly sinking onto his cock. Damn, she didn't remember him being so big their first time. He stretched and filled her completely as if nothing ever felt more right in her life. Suzi undulated her hips, slowly rocking on his shaft, reveling in the feel of his hard, hot silky flesh within her.

"Ah, Jesus," he blasphemed. "Mother in heaven ... so fucking good."

She wouldn't last long, already on the edge of another mind-blowing orgasm. The walls surrounding her heart collapsed, taking Kaleb in, where he took up ownership. She'd be damned before she'd allow him to walk away from her again.

If any woman even thought to touch her man, she'd personally see they regretted their actions. Suzi meant to let it be known that she had just staked her claim on Kaleb Tepes around the Rave. She had officially taken him off the market. Now she needed to prove to him that no one could take her place in his heart ... if he indeed had one.

Just as she was about to reach release, Kaleb flipped their position, his arms now bracing on either side of her head as he pumped into her, fast and hard. The cords of his neck stood out, tightened in his exertion. His black gaze held hers hostage. Her breath quickened as the love in her chest blossomed and tears sprang to her eyes.

"Kaleb … oh … god¬—"

"That's it, sweetheart." He growled. "Let go for me."

Tilting her head back, she cried out as every muscle in Kaleb tightened and he joined her in their mutual release. Several seconds went by before he collapsed on top of her, giving her just enough room to move and breathe, his head resting in the crook of her neck.

"Did you just refer me as a supreme being?" He chuckled against her neck, his breath spanning the soft skin. "Damn. That good?"

Suzi tasted his salty flesh with her tongue, then nipped at his shoulder, drawing the smallest amount of blood to the surface.

Before she could taste the sanguine fluid, he pulled out of her and sat back, his gaze pinning her, nearly scaring her in their intensity. "What the fuck?"

"What's the matter?"

Kaleb jumped from the couch, pulled his pants up from about his knees and tucked himself inside. Suzi quickly followed suit, attempting to right her own mussed clothing. She must look a fright. He ran a hand through his long curls, brushing the hair from his face and looked back at her.

"Don't ever do that again, sweetheart."

"What?" Her brow furrowed. "Make love to you?"

Suzi was rewarded with a small grin, making her feel a tiny bit better about what just happened. Hell, she thought Kaleb was already regretting what had taken place. She never would. In fact….

"No, please—that I'd like a repeat performance of." His smile grew. "And I plan to continue in that big empty bed of mine in a matter of minutes. But, what I was referring to," his face sobered, "is drawing my blood. You can never drink from me ... not even a taste. Is that clear?"

"I'm sorry, I didn't mean anything by it."

Kaleb approached the sofa where she sat, kneeling in front of her and framing her face between his palms. "To do so would mean your damnation. By drinking of my blood, your DNA would begin to change and you would become a monster like me."

Suzi placed her hands over his. "You not a monster, Kaleb. I don't see you that way."

He took a deep breath. "Suzi, it's forbidden. I cannot allow you to become like me."

"Cara—"

"Kane did so to save her life and he had to pay the penance for it. I'm the president of the Sons, sweetheart. I cannot go about breaking the rules. Promise me you'll keep those teeth to yourself." He paused, a devilish gleam twinkling in his gaze. "At least don't use them to draw blood. Agreed?"

Suzi nodded, not trusting herself to speak should she break down into tears. Not taking his blood, also meant not mating with him. She refused to allow Kaleb to see the hurt his words had caused.

"Now," one of his brows rose heavenward, "you have someplace else you need to be?"

She shook her head.

"Good." He chuckled, stood and tossed her across his shoulder as he headed for the rear of the clubhouse, slapping one bare ass cheek. "Because I have someplace I need you to be ... in my bed and beneath me."

"Rosalee."

The voice on the other end of the line caught her off guard and kicked up her heartbeat a notch. She hated it when he used that tone with her. She knew whatever was about to come next she wasn't going to like. She'd best tread lightly, for she had no idea if the old vampire even knew she'd left Italy. Due to the untimely call, she'd bet he at least suspected.

"Yes, Stepfather?"

"I'm surprised you finally decided to answer your phone."

The exasperation in his voice told her he was extremely annoyed with her. The ass no doubt knew by now she had skipped the country and was on a one-woman mission to no good, at least not for Kane and Kaleb Tepes. But nothing he said would change her mind. Kaleb would soon lose his head, an eye for an eye.

"Where have you taken yourself off to?" The old man had actually tsk, tsked her. "And don't think to lie to me, Stepchild."

So much for the false truth she was looking to save her ass from his wrath. Mircea knew damn well where Rosalee stood, or he wouldn't have bothered himself to call her.

"If I find out you withheld the truth, I will see you punished for going against my wishes." He paused, no doubt more for dramatic effect than to catch his breath. The old bastard was healthy as a horse. "Even your mother won't be allowed to speak on your behalf this time. Do I make myself clear?"

Rosalee sighed. "All right. It's not as if you don't already know. I'm in the States."

She heard his deep sigh through the speaker of the phone. She could very well imagine the disapproval on his face. "For what purpose?"

Rosalee grit her teeth. Her ire skyrocketed. The man was such a politician at times. He should have taken care of this six months ago. If he had, she would still be in Italy, being coddled by his staff and drinking the finest of wines. Instead she was running around the back woods of Oregon, chasing down a vampire that refused to die.

"To do what you neglected to, Mircea."

If her stepfather had had any balls at all, Kaleb would have been tried, found guilty for his actions, and been beheaded long ago. Kane would have lost the one thing more precious to him than that damn detective he thinks to call mate ... his twin. And Rosalee would have had her revenge, even if it cost her to be exiled from Italy for all eternity. Sometimes she really hated her stepfather. He could be such a pompous ass. But had it not been for him, she and her mother wouldn't have had the chance at eternity. So for that alone she was indebted to him.

"You allowed Kane and Kaleb Tepes to make you look weak. Someone needs to rectify that."

"So you make yourself judge and jury, thereby thinking to take Kaleb Tepes' head as his penance?"

"Yes."

She bit back the not-so-nice names she reserved for her stepfather. At the moment, her anger would gain her nothing. Now that Mircea knew where she was and her plan to kill Kaleb, she needed to assure the fact he didn't send someone after her and try to stop her from seeking her revenge.

"And if I order you back to Italy ... to stop this foolhardy mission you're on?"

"I won't return home, Mircea ... until it's finished," Rosalee said. "You would be wasting your breath, old man."

"You know that I cannot give you my blessing. Kane already suspects that it's you who's behind these attempts at his brother's life."

"Think I care?"

"If you kill Kaleb," Mircea's tone rose, "Kane won't stop until he finds and kills you."

Rosalee laughed, not feeling the humor. "You wouldn't allow that."

"And what reason would I have to stop him." Again he paused. "Or care for that matter?"

"It's written that to take a primordial's life, is to bring certain death unto yourself." Her jaw ached. The bastard had a way with bringing the worst out in her. She'd never understand what her mother saw in the pompous ass. "Have you forgotten your one cardinal rule? You put it into place so that you of all people could live out eternity without threat. If you allow Alec's death to go unanswered, then what's to say someday, someone might decide to end your existence?"

Mircea stayed silent for so long, that at first she thought he might not answer her, then he said, "Alec acted on your behalf, not mine. He was on a fool's mission, and as such, got what he deserved."

"So what are you saying, Stepfather?"

"That if you decide to follow through with this asinine plan, then you will have to suffer the consequences should Kane decide to take your head as restitution for his brother's. In truth, my wayward stepdaughter, he would've been in his right to do so following your son's death. And yet, he returned you to me unharmed."

"His mistake," she growled in response. "Are you sending someone to stop me?"

"No."

"You realize then, that is as much giving me the okay."

"I'm telling you, dear stepdaughter, that should you accomplish your goal, I will not come to your rescue, neither will I allow your mother to. You're acting on your own, and as such, you will face the consequences alone. I will not get involved in your petty revenge against my brother's great grandchildren." He paused. "Should Vlad ever surface and know that I sentenced his offspring to death, it would be an all-out war."

"He's not shown himself in well over four centuries."

"His tomb was found empty."

Rosalee rolled her eyes. "If his ego is anything like yours, dear Stepfather, then he most certainly is dead. No way could the arrogant ruler not show his face in over four hundred and seventy years."

"If you do this, Rosalee," she could hear the warning in his tone, "you will no longer be allowed to return to Italy."

"Then so be it." Her smile grew. "Kaleb Tepes will die. I cannot allow Kane a moment of peace."

"Then be prepared to start a war with the Sons, of which I cannot be part of."

A true leader would stand with her. "You're a coward, Mircea."

"Wise, my dear, never a coward. You're a fool to think you can best a Tepes. You forget Vlad was my little brother, and he was feared for good reason. His offspring should not be underestimated."

"Duly noted, old man," she said and hit the END on her cell.

Rosalee smiled, knowing now that she would get no interference from her stepfather. The coward would never leave Italy to raise a hand against his brother's offspring, for fear of retaliation from the feared ruler. She laughed. Vlad Tepes hadn't surfaced or been heard from in centuries. The Impaler had died in 1476 at the tender age of thirty-five. He wasn't about to just show up in Oregon to save his great grandson, far removed, from being beheaded.

CHAPTER NINETEEN

CARA AND JOE HERNANDEZ LEANED AGAINST HER BLACK Charger in the parking lot of the Rave, waiting for their mark to arrive. The clubs doors opened promptly at eight every evening, even on Sundays. A quick glance at her watch told her that someone should be arriving soon. Hernandez stood beside her, arms crossed over his chest, looking pretty damned pleased with himself. Her partner had to know exactly what this interrogation would cost her.

Kane would no doubt have her head. Cara had made a brief call to him, informing him that she would be working late. At the time, she had no idea that the person Joe had in mind was Draven, the Blood 'n' Rave's elusive owner.

Yep, she would be dead meat.

The minute they left the club Draven would no doubt put a call in to Kane, asking him what the hell gives. Cara and Kane both used the Rave for donors. It was what Draven had given them, a place of anonymity to feed, women to provide that nourishment. Cara hoped to put in a request for male donors one day. *Why should the men have all the enjoyment?* Her sly smile at the thought was hard to contain. She doubted Kane would ever allow the petition. The look on his face, knowing she had asked, would be worth the trouble though. Cara needed to keep Kane on his toes, keep him from getting complacent in their relationship.

Now? She'd be lucky to live through the night. Figuratively of course. Cara knew Kane would never raise a hand to her in harm. But she'd certainly consider herself lucky if he spoke to her at all. Not to mention what the rest of the Sons would think.

Yep, dead meat.

The rumble of a Harley's V-twin caught her attention, telling her of someone's arrival, long before she caught sight of the black bike, red flames gracing the gas tank, pulling into the paved parking area. Cara recognized the barkeep, even before he removed his helmet. They hadn't escaped his notice as his gaze swung to them briefly. Stepping over the bike, he tucked his skullcap under his arm as he removed a set of keys from his pocket and headed toward the side door of the building. Joe pushed off the car first, and walked at a clipped pace, no doubt hoping to head Draven off before he entered the building and forced them to knock, and possibly not gain an audience with him.

"Draven," he said, securing the man's attention.

Draven paused, booted foot between the door and the frame to keep it from closing. He barely gave her partner a glance before his gaze landed on Cara. "What the hell you want, copper?" he addressed Joe.

As Cara came to stand beside her partner, Draven's lips turned down, obviously pissed to see her in the company of the Sheriff's Office. Cara hadn't exactly advertised the fact she was back on the job. Word would soon spread.

Joe broke the tension by clearing his throat and gaining Draven's attention. "Just a few questions for you, if you have time."

Draven shrugged, opened the door wide and indicated with his
hand for them to proceed him into the backroom. The barkeep followed them through the side door and flipped the switch, flooding
the room with light. Running his hand through his longish dark
hair, he then set the skull cap on an old vinyl and steel high top
chair sitting beside the exit.

Cara had never been in this part of the club before, never really
had a reason to. Since Kane and some of the other Sons frequently
used Draven's upstairs office, she supposed he needed his own place
to hang. The office upstairs was far more plush. A plaid orange and
brown sofa bed sat along the back wall with a matching ottoman in
the center of the small room. A tweed, brown chair that looked as if
it had seen better days, graced the other wall. A scarred end table sat
to one side with what looked like last night's empty glasses.

A dark walnut, pantry-style cabinet took up the entire wall
across from the sofa bed, possibly containing extra bottles of liquor,
or whatever might spill over from the storeroom behind the bar
that Cara knew to be on the other side of the interior door facing
them. The only other piece of furniture gracing the tiny backroom
was a rolltop desk, with a worn black leather desk chair. The top
had been left in the up position, papers and whatnot strewn in a
haphazard fashion. If this was Draven's private space, it didn't appear as if he concerned himself with neatness.

Draven placed one black booted foot on the steel round of the
yellow vinyl chair by the door and crossed his arms over his knee as

he leaned in and gave them his attention. "What sort of questions? Ones that I might need a lawyer for?"

"You have a reason to need one, Draven?" Joe didn't hide the smirk on his face. He baited the barkeep.

"Why don't you ask your questions, copper ... then be on your way. I have a business to open."

Draven's gaze went back to Cara, making her uneasy. She was pretty sure Draven was angry with her for not giving him a heads-up about their little visit, when in truth, she hadn't known herself.

"You know anything about drugs being dealt from your night-club?"

Draven's expression remained unchanged, even though Cara knew for a fact Draven personally sold X to some of his customers. "Nope."

"You sure about that?" Joe rubbed his chin between forefinger and thumb. "I have it on pretty good word that you might."

Again, Draven's gaze went to Cara before landing back on Joe. "I say your source is fucking lying. You got no proof. And unless you provide it, hit the door."

Great, now Draven thought she was the snitch. This couldn't be going worse for her at the moment. And yet, she had no clue how to fix it. If she didn't say something soon, she'd be lucky if Kane ever talked to her again.

"Draven," Cara said, hoping her eyes conveyed what her mouth could not, "no one mentioned your name. We need you to keep an eye on things, and if you see anything, promise you'll call one of us."

Cara handed Draven her business card, which he took. Joe, on the other hand, nearly murdered her with his dark look. No doubt unhappy that she had all but excused the barkeep's involvement. The "damned if you do and damned if you don't phrase" stared her in the face. No doubt about it, either way she'd be damned for her association with the case.

Draven looked at her business card, then tapped it on his raised knee. "I'll be sure to do that. Now if you don't mind—"

"Look," Joe said, "my partner may excuse away your part in this, but I don't. Honestly, Draven, I think you're in this up to your neck. I won't go as far as saying that you are personally dealing the X from your club, but someone is and I think you know who that person is."

"As I said earlier, show me the proof. Now unless you have a warrant to search the place, I'd say it's time for you to get the fuck off my property."

"We'll be back. I'm far from done." Joe squared his shoulders. "But just so you know, it's not you I want to take down. You're small time, Draven. I could care less what you do. I want the name of your supplier. You provide me with that, and I'll cut you a break."

"Are you done?"

Joe smiled. "Think about what I said. We'll show ourselves out."

"You do that. Come back again and you best have a warrant."

"You call that number on Brahnam's card if you have a change of heart and want to talk." He winked at Draven, whose scowl blackened. "But until you do, know that we're watching your every step."

Draven didn't move a muscle as Cara exited the door behind Joe. Thanks to her partner's closing statement, she'd be lucky if she were ever allowed in the front door of the Rave to feed. Cara shook her head as she followed Joe to her car. Shit just got complicated and

Kane would no doubt let loose on her the moment she walked through the clubhouse door.

KANE PACED THE CLUBHOUSE. His gums ached with the need to unleash his checked anger. He wasn't used to holding back. But where his mate was concerned, he needed all the self-control he could get at the moment.

What the hell was she thinking?

He knew her job meant nearly as much to her as he did, but she had just crossed the line. Maybe allowing her to go back to work had been a mistake from the beginning. Kane would have to tell the rest of the Sons, and certainly didn't relish the idea, but first he needed to talk to his mate and see where the fuck her head was.

A car door slammed and her scent hit him long before the door opened. Kane thanked his good luck that the rest of his brethren weren't in residence at the moment. He needed some alone time, and not for his usual reasons. If Cara didn't quit her job following this major fuck-up, he'd walk into Sheriff Ducat's office himself and hand the bastard his mate's badge. If she stayed, no way in hell the rest of the Sons would forgive her. Cara messed with their lives. They couldn't very well live without their donors, and Draven had the power to take that all away.

The door opened, and Cara walked through. His heart panged. He wanted nothing more than to go to her, wrap her in his protective arms to shield her from the oncoming shit-storm. If Kane knew about her actions, it wouldn't be long before Kaleb did. His twin hadn't liked Cara from the beginning, but seemed to be slowly softening where his mate was concerned. What a fucking mess she had just created.

Cara paused inside the doorway, her blue gaze landing on his. He saw genuine fear in the ocean-blue depths. At least she had the decency to feel bad for her ultimate betrayal to the club. They'd never trust her again and this time Kane couldn't say that he blamed them.

Tears immediately spilled from her lashes. Kane opened his arms and she walked into his embrace. "I'm so sorry," she said into the front of his tee.

Kane smoothed his hand down her back. Hell, he couldn't even get rightly pissed at her when she turned on the waterworks. He kissed the top of her blonde head, then inhaled the scent he loved so much. He needed to figure out how best to handle this situation, with the least amount of damage for everyone. His biggest obstacle in this mess would be Kaleb, no two ways about it.

He gripped the sides of her head and tilted her gaze up. "You want to tell me what the hell happened so I can possibly help?"

Her lower lip quivered. She pulled it between her teeth as though trying to hold back more tears. "I never meant for this to happen. I thought I could handle it."

"You should have come to me, *mia bella*."

"I couldn't, don't you see?" Another tear fell from her lashes to mix with the others already wetting her cheeks "Joe would've spotted the fact I told you the minute we questioned Draven. It's probably why he never told me who he wanted to question tonight until we were already there. And by then, I couldn't so much as warn you."

"Draven called."

"I knew he would."

"Look, I don't approve of the drugs he deals from the nightclub. I'm not a big fan of the club drug. But other than the fact Draven provides us cover and manages all donors, I don't give a rat's ass what the man does in his spare time. You do understand, he can't get busted for this, correct?"

She gave him a quick nod.

"If his club is closed down due to the drugs he runs through there, we're all fucked. I supposed we could find another place, someone else to watch over the donors ... but it would be damn inconvenient and take more time than we have to spare. I'll make sure the drugs disappear from the club. You get the heat off Draven's back. Is that understood?"

Again she nodded. Kane leaned down and kissed her lips briefly, tasting the salt of her tears. When he pulled away, her pink tongue darted out and licked her full bottom lip. Damn if the sight didn't stir his groin. It didn't take much when it came to his mate. But right now wasn't the time to get side-tracked. They needed a plan to placate Kaleb or they'd be looking for new digs before the sun rose. Kane had already lost too much when it came to the MC and being stripped of his pres patch. He didn't think he could stand losing the rockers off the back of his cut as well.

"The first you got wind of this was tonight? When you went to question Draven?"

She shook her head, her lower lip quivering again.

"Jesus, Cara. When the hell did you hear about this and why didn't you come to me?" Kane worked his jaw, trying to ease the tension. "You only started back to the Sheriff's Office yesterday."

She took a deep shuddering breath. "Yesterday Joe presented me with the case. Apparently the feds are looking into Draven because they think he can provide them with the bigger picture."

"They want his supplier."

Again, she nodded. "Draven isn't the target, Kane. Maybe if we can get him to roll over, I can convince the feds to leave him out of it."

"What if I bring you the supplier?"

"How?"

"You may not be able to get Draven talking, but I can."

Her gaze widened. "Kane, these aren't small time dealers. They think this leads back to the cartel."

"The same cartel, no doubt, responsible for Ion's death. I know. They run drugs up the west coast. I'm betting Draven gets his supplies from the Devils MC, who in turn gets it from the cartel."

Cara swallowed, her tongue wetting her lips again. "I can't let you do this. Those men killed your son. I can't chance losing you too."

"You aren't going—"

"What the fuck do you think you're doing, Brahnam?" came from the direction of the door as it bounced off the interior wall. Kaleb stormed in, his vampire features unleashed in his anger. "I ought to have your fucking head for this."

"Hawk," Kane warned.

"You stay the hell out of this, Viper. If you can't control your mate, then someone else needs to."

Kane placed himself between Cara and his pissed-off twin. His reflection mirrored in his brother's obsidian gaze spoke of his own rising ire.

"Your anger will solve nothing, Hawk," he said, barely holding himself in check. He needed Kaleb's understanding, resorting to fists would gain them nothing.

"You knew about this?" Kaleb asked, one of his brow's arching upward.

"No." Kane let out a deep sigh. "I just found out moments ago the same way you did—Draven called me."

Kaleb nodded in Cara's direction. "And what do you plan to do to her?"

Kane growled. "I don't plan to do anything to her, dear brother. And you will likewise keep your hands off my mate."

"Then control her, damn it!" Kaleb bared his teeth. "Before she brings this fucking club down on all of our heads."

Cara poked her head from around Kane's biceps. "You're an ass, Hawk. I'd never do anything to harm this club."

Kaleb tilted his head back and laughed, one that didn't reach his eyes. "You could have fooled me, bit—"

"Hawk," he warned. "Watch yourself."

Kane clenched his jaw and his hands. Nothing would give him more pleasure than making his brother eat his fist at the moment. But he needed Kaleb's understanding and cooperation if they were to help both his mate and Draven. They needed a solid plan and he needed every member of the Sons with him if they were going to take on the cartel. Kane never got restitution for Ion. Maybe Cara had just handed him the perfect opportunity.

"Hear me out."

"Yeah?" Kaleb scoffed. "Give me one good reason why I need to listen to anything your mate or you have to say when she is jeopardizing our way of nutrition? Even you aren't that pussy-whipped, are you?"

"Do you seriously want me to beat your ass?" Kane had reached his breaking point. One more fucking comment...

"You let that bitch—" was all Kaleb got out of his mouth before his head snapped back from Kane's fist connecting with it. Cara squealed as she jumped from around Kane and put herself between them.

Kaleb wiped the blood from his nose with the back of his hand, a grin splitting his face. "Glad to know you still have it in you, Viper. Now what the hell is this plan you're talking about?"

Grayson and Anton walked into the clubhouse, both bikers looking at the stream of blood coming from Kaleb's nose that had already started to slow.

"Looks like I'm always missing out on the fun," Grayson chuckled. "What the hell? Hawk can't watch his mouth around the ladies?"

"There has to be a lady—"

"I'm going to give you a serious beating, Hawk," Kane growled.

"Okay, okay," Kaleb raised his hands in surrender. "Not that I seriously think you can best me, brother, but I do think we have more serious issues to deal with."

"Somebody want to fill me in?" Anton asked, pulling out a barstool.

Kaleb turned to Anton. "Call a church meeting, Blondy. Tomorrow night, here. Mandatory. I believe we have a couple of issues that need tabled."

"You want to give me a heads-up?" Anton asked.

"Nope," Kaleb replied. "You just get everyone here."

CHAPTER TWENTY

UZI STEPPED UP TO THE DOOR, A MIXED BAG OF EMOTIONS, HESI-
tant on whether to knock, walk in, or run like hell ... having
no idea where her and Kaleb stood after one night of mind-blowing
sex. Crawling out of Kaleb's massive bed, Suzi had left the clubhouse
in the pre-dawn hours before any of the other residents came home.
She had returned to her townhouse in Florence, slept for a few
hours, then worked her twelve-hour shift at the Pleasant Care
Nursing Home. Kaleb hadn't so much as called, leaving her unsure if
he'd welcome her presence or resent her for showing up unannounced. But Suzi needed to see him, the uncertainty was eating her
alive.

Cara's black Charger sat to the left of the entrance in the large
gravel parking lot, alongside several of the members' Harleys.
Knowing Cara's whereabouts gave Suzi an added excuse for her
arrival should Kaleb be unhappy that she had taken it upon herself
to show up on his stoop. The fact that several members of the Sons
were also in attendance kicked her jitters into overdrive. Maybe it
had been wrong to show up here or to even think that Kaleb might
want to see her. She should do an about-face and return when there
was a lesser chance of making a complete fool of herself. But before
she had an opportunity to make a speedy exit, the door opened with
Kaleb standing on the other side. She offered him a weak smile, not

sure by his impassive expression if he welcomed the fact she made the trip, or was bothered by her unannounced return.

"Suzi." His even tone masked his disposition.

"I—" She wet her lips. "Maybe I should come back at a better time."

Kaleb looked briefly behind him, before returning his gaze to her. "Calling might have been better."

She nodded, attempting to swallow the sudden lump that took up residence in her throat, her heart plummeting to her stomach. Suzi had known full well going in that she had possibly set herself up for another rejection. Having got what he wanted, maybe he was already inclined to move forward. It was no secret that Kaleb liked the ladies. So why did she think he'd change his ways just because he had taken what she had readily offered? Suzi sucked in an unsteady breath as she took one step back, ready to bolt. Best to cut her losses. Before she turned and found her feet, Kaleb gripped the fingers of her left hand, staying her. His dark gaze held hers, the corners turning up in humor, then swept the length of her, touching her as thoroughly as if he ran his hands over her flesh. Suzi drew her lower lip between her teeth. Kaleb's eyes darkened just before he lowered his head and covered her lips with his.

Suzi gasped and he took the opportunity to slip his tongue between her lips. She melded into his frame, all her apprehensions about showing up unannounced slipping away. Sliding her hands up his chest to his nape, she tangled her fingers in the silky black curls she found there. She doubted she'd protest if he chose to pick her up and carry her past the clubhouse occupants to his big comfy bed. But instead, Kaleb ended the kiss and stepped back, holding her upper arms in his hands. Good thing. Her footing was precarious at best.

"Just bad timing, *piccolo diavolo.* I meant nothing else."

Her tongue swiped her lower lip, tasting him. Damn, she wanted a repeat performance of the night before last. "I wasn't sure you'd want to see me again."

Kaleb laughed, took her hand and placed it over the obvious bulge in his jeans. Suzi sucked in her breath. "Does that feel like I don't want to see you again?"

"Too bad there are far too many vampires in residence," Suzi said, leaning in and hoping the acute hearing of others couldn't overhear. "Or I'd take care of this little—"

His brow furrowed. "Little?"

"Figure of speech, Hawk. *Very* large problem." She laughed. "So what's going on? Want me to come back at another time?"

"No, stay. It will save me the trouble of having to look you up later." He winked before leaning down and claiming her lips once more for a quick kiss. "We have some business on the table. A church meeting was called. Maybe you and Cara can find something to do—go shopping, do girl stuff."

"She can't be here during the meetings? But she's a mate and a vampire."

"She's also a woman. Why not come in, go chat with Cara, then make yourselves scarce in about fifteen minutes. We're still waiting on Xander."

Before allowing her entrance, Kaleb pulled her back against his hard frame and whispered, "Make sure you come back. Because as soon as the Sons are done with their business, I have some private matters I'd like to address with you ... naked and in my bed."

"Keep talking like that, Hawk, and I'll see to it you never have reason to leave it."

He growled in response, nipping her ear, before stepping back and opening the door wider for her to enter. Walking in the door, her knees damn near quivered, this time having little to do with Kaleb and everything to do with the other vamps in occupancy. She had no idea how the others might perceive her having a relationship, if indeed there was one, between their president and her. With whatever was going on, she bet they needed his focus on the matter at hand and not on her.

Thankfully, most of them barely gave her a curious glance, then went back to talking among themselves. Kane was the first to speak up from his seat on the sofa, where Cara was tucked comfortably beneath his arm.

He stood, winked at her, then said, "Why don't you take my beautiful mate and go have a girls' afternoon out? I think she's been dying for the gossip."

Suzi smiled, her eyes going from Kane's to Cara's. She thought she heard Kaleb mutter something about it being none of the damn detective's business, behind her back. The look on Kane's face proved she had heard correctly. And here she thought Cara and Kaleb had come to a truce, making her wonder what happened to break that tenuous reprieve. She most definitely planned to ask Cara once they were away from the club.

Cara looked briefly at Kaleb, before grabbing her bag and heading for the door. Her expression seemed more of anguish than anger. "Let's go get some coffee and pastries," she said to Suzi on her way out the exit. "I'll drive."

Suzi looked back at Kaleb, whose expression was back to one of indifference. When she paused by the door, he offered her a wink in reassurance. Following Cara out of the clubhouse, she knew at least one of them was in good standing with the club pres. Thank goodness it was her. Now to find out why Kaleb seemed so hostile toward his twin's mate.

ALEXANDER STROLLED INTO THE meeting room after everyone else had already been seated. Kaleb couldn't help wonder what the unobtrusive biker had been up to … that is until he took one look at the top of his head. His long black hair had been chopped, cut around his ears and looking all GQ. Not that the man didn't look good, but what the hell? He looked more ready for a New York runway than an MC church meeting. Since when had Alexander worried about what he looked like?

He took his seat at the table, not a word yet said about the man's newly shorn locks. And true to his more quiet nature, he didn't bother commenting on why he felt the need to clean himself up. Instead he looked directly at Kaleb and said, "So what's on the table, P?"

Kaleb shook his head, meant to leave it go but he just couldn't. A smile grew on his face. "We keeping you from a hot date, Xander?"

"No. Why?"

The puzzled look on Alexander's face nearly had Kaleb laughing. Surely, the man didn't think walking in here with a college-boy cut would go unnoticed.

"What the fuck?" Grayson piped up. Brushing his own overlong hair back from his face, he said with a chuckle, "You realize church meeting is just a slang term, right, Xander?"

"Ha ha ha," Xander quipped. "Go on and get it over with if you must, but I'm sure we have more important matters at hand than the top of my head."

Joseph "Kinky" Sala, the Sergeant in Arms and the quietest of the Sons, was the first one to laugh, then followed by several of the others. Running his hand through his own, very curly, overlong hair, he finally said, "What the fuck, Xander?"

"Go to hell, Kinky. You look like you could have used the sharp end of a pair of scissors a long time ago."

"Can't fix perfection," Joseph said, followed with a wink.

"So?" Kaleb couldn't let it go without an explanation. "What's got you looking all prim and proper all of the sudden?"

Alexander rolled his eyes. "I see we aren't going to move forward. Fine. One of my donors just opened a salon. She begged me to come by for a demonstration. Shit, I had no idea she meant to cut it this fucking short. Last time I volunteer for anything. Now? Can we move on? What's the agenda?"

Kaleb laughed but decided to let it pass without further comment, though he couldn't help wonder if Alexander had his eye on the salon owner. He never seemed to stay with women for long periods of time, but then again you had to date in order to have a relationship. He couldn't remember in the last ten or so years when Alexander had actually done the dating thing. He seemed to show up at the Rave, feed, and be gone.

"Blondy, you taking notes?" Kaleb looked at the club secretary.

"Got you covered, boss."

"Then let's get started." Kaleb struck his wooden mallet against the strike plate and took his seat.

The two empty seats of the fourteen stared back at him—Nicolas "Wheezer" Basil and Ion. He still needed to address bringing on prospects, add to the Sons numbers. That wouldn't be today.

"First order of business is the Knights."

Kaleb glanced at his twin who sat at the table but wisely kept his mouth shut. He loved his brother more than anyone in this room, but the man had fucked up, costing him his P patch and his voting rights. Maybe one day he'd see about getting him his voting rights back. That wouldn't be today either.

"We're all aware of what went down at the last two attempts of helping the Knights run their guns. Two of our men lost their heads, and if it hadn't been for Blondy paying close attention, we would've been ashing his and Xander's remains as well. I'm not keen on the idea of losing any more brothers to this fuck."

A "hear, hear," went about the room as fists bumped the table.

"Viper, Gypsy and I had a little meeting with Red and his VP, Bird. Red assured me he would look into the matter of his men, and the possibility one of them might be responsible. I think someone from the Knights is either helping Rosalee in her revenge or feeding her information. At any rate, I no longer trust them."

"Fuck Bird." Animosity dripped from Grayson's tone.

"I'm proposing that we cut our losses. The Knights are no longer allowed to run their guns through Oregon. That is until we find out who wants my fucking head so badly. Let's take it to a vote."

"Yay," Grayson was the first to agree.

Each member consecutively returned a "yay" with not one of them in disagreement. Kane's face remained impassive, but Kaleb knew his brother seethed inside. This had been his baby from the beginning and his money-maker. Fuck that! The Sons made enough money off their motorcycle shop, K&K, to more than sustain themselves. Kaleb never agreed with Kane over the idea the Sons needed the puppet club.

"One order of business down. I will speak with Red—"

"I'll do the honors," Kane interrupted. "This was my decision from the beginning. I'll be the one to let him know."

Kaleb nodded. "I'll concede to that, Viper."

"And if he wants to know if we will reinstate the agreement should we find this mole?"

"You tell him I'll take it under advisement at that time," Kaleb said. "I'll not make him any promises. You tell him that if we find this fuck and take him down, I'll reintroduce the topic to the table."

Viper leaned back in his chair. "I'll let him know."

"You do that, Viper, and you let him know this is far from over. He won't be able to convince me that someone in the Knights doesn't have it out for me. And until we find the son of a bitch, I better not catch one Knight rocker in my state." He glanced around the table. "Does anyone have anything to add?"

When Kaleb didn't get any argument, he said, "Then we move onto the next order of business, Viper's mate, Cara."

Viper sat forward. "Back up, bro. My mate is not an order of business. You bring this to the table and I'll personally kick your ass."

Kaleb smiled. "You'll have fun trying. Sit back, Viper, and calm the fuck down. As much as I relish the idea of you trying to kick my ass ... which by the way, ain't happening ... I'm not here to ostracize Cara. On the contrary, she and I have had our differences, but this time I'm actually on her side. The rest of the Sons need to be aware of what's going down, though. Because if I'm right, we could be in for a shit-storm before this is over."

All eyes at the table turned to Kane, who still looked as if he wanted to beat Kaleb's ass. *Let him try,* Kaleb thought with a chuckle. It certainly wouldn't be the first time the two had resorted to fists. Hell, his nose still hurt.

Kaleb cleared his throat and gained the room's attention back. "We all know Cara returned to her job at the Sheriff's Office. We allowed it because, let's face it ... she's eyes and ears on the inside. We can use her to our benefit just as the sheriff helps keep us informed."

Going into detail, Kaleb shared the events of Cara's visit to the Blood 'n' Rave to question Draven. When he finished, the men began talking amongst themselves. Kaleb banged the gavel to get their focus back where it needed to be—off the fact Cara had betrayed Draven and the club, to what the Sons planned to do about it.

"Cara's still got an inside. I say that's a non-issue right now. I'm positive that the fucker Hernandez made sure to put her in a position we'd go ballistic over." Kaleb glanced back around the room, getting no argument where Cara's partner was concerned. "We need to figure a way to keep Draven the fuck out of this and the Rave not involved. First and foremost, Draven needs to get rid of the X he deals out of there, without the Devils any wiser to the fact we're protecting our interest. They need to think Draven is still working his club. Regardless as to what happens with Hernandez, or how we keep him out of the loop, we need to get the feds aiming in the right direction."

"And just how do you propose that, P?" Grigore Lupei asked.

"It's simple, Wolf. As I said, we have an inside. We get Cara to pretend she now has Draven's cooperation in the matter. Screw Hernandez. We'll make sure she looks good in the end, thus solidifying her place at the Sheriff's Office. They won't question her loyalty again. It will be a win-win."

"And how do we get Draven's cooperation?" Joseph asked. "I'm sure dealing X has been a pretty lucrative deal for Draven."

"That and we benefit as well, lots of party girls on X," Grayson piped up. "I can't say I haven't enjoyed the spoils."

"We won't give Draven a choice, Kinky," Kaleb said before looking at his VP. "I highly doubt you'll have trouble attracting women who aren't high, Gypsy, so let's just call that a non-issue as well. Besides, you know as well as I do the dangers of having sex with a human high on X. No more waiting for the high to start to diminish."

Grayson smiled, kicked out his booted feet, and leaned back with a smile on his face, obviously not about to argue with Kaleb on that point.

He looked at his twin. Kane didn't look too happy at using his mate in this game of cat and mouse. "You remember, Viper, it was Cara who insisted on going back to the job. Now she needs to prove her worth to the club."

"What do you want out of her?" A muscle ticked in his cheek.

Kaleb grinned. "I'll take care of Draven. He'll be more than willing to work with her."

In truth, Cara wouldn't need to do a whole lot, just make sure she arrived where Kaleb needed her and to have the appropriate authorities where they were needed. In the end, he'd help her cement her loyalty to the Sheriff's Office, and the Sons would have a permanent man ... woman on the inside. They had always had Sheriff Ducat's cooperation for the most part, now they'd have the S.O. in their back pocket.

Kane narrowed his gaze on Kaleb. "You want to share the plan with us, bro?"

"I haven't worked out all the details yet, Viper. Once I talk to Draven, I'll call another church meeting. The plan will be to have Draven lure the Devils into a trap, one that includes the cartel. It won't be easy, but I want to see the bastards responsible for Ion's death to finally pay. The way I see it? This will go down one of two ways. Either those at the head of the cartel will spend their days rotting behind bars if the fucking cops can do their job ... or they'll be rotting for all eternity when I unleash the Sons on them. They'll be wishing for life behind bars, right before we send them all to hell."

Kaleb glanced around the room, getting no argument from his men. Instead, he saw interest and excitement in their eyes. The Sons looked ready to take the cartel on. They had waited ten long years for retribution and the time had just presented itself.

"Shall we take it to a vote?"

One by one the men all returned a "yay" vote. Kaleb smacked the gavel against the strike plate. "Then our job here is done. Viper? Will we get Cara's cooperation in this?"

He nodded. "One hundred percent."

"Good ... let's go get us some whiskey. This meeting is adjourned."

CHAPTER TWENTY-ONE

KALEB SMELLED HER THE MOMENT THE DOOR TO THE CLUB-house opened, kicking up the beat of his heart. Cara strode in first, followed closely by the one person he couldn't seem to get enough of lately. Suzi looked like sex on a stick with her tight, black pleather pants and pink fuzzy sweater that ended just beneath her small, pert tits, showing a fair amount of tanned skin. His mouth dried up like the Sahara desert, just aching to draw her nipples between his teeth. Kaleb groaned, he really couldn't be within ten feet of Suzi and not think about sliding into her. He might as well admit defeat and get it over with.

In her hands, Suzi carried what looked to be a big box of donuts and a container with a spout, filled with liquid caffeine in the form of coffee from the corner bakery on Main Street. Damn the owner for being open around-the-clock. His men would certainly devour the treat, but at the moment he wanted them using the exit, not staying for coffee and donuts. Leave it to the cop to think about the sugary pastry.

Kaleb hoped the Sons took their fill then got the fuck out, because he didn't think he could sit around shooting the breeze when what he really wanted was Suzi naked and in his bed. There were far too many vampires present for him to throw her over his shoulder and carry her off to his king-sized bed. He didn't need the whole lot

257

of them privy to his sex life. Not that most of them hadn't already guessed. But he'd be damned before he'd advertise it.

What he did with Suzi Stevens was his own business.

His twin opened his arms and accepted Cara into his beefy hold. She leaned up and kissed his lips. Kaleb growled beneath his breath. He still wasn't too happy with Kane's mate. She should've forewarned them about the case on Draven. That she couldn't excuse away and, in itself, was a betrayal to the MC. Kaleb would give her a chance to make up for the omission. They needed her onboard, and manipulating her partner, if they were to set up the Devils and the cartel. Fuck the drugs. Kaleb didn't give a rat's ass about what the rival MC or cartel did to make money. Business was business. But he did want them to pay for their part in Ion's death. Handing them to the feds and the Sheriff's Office would go a long way in getting Kane's revenge.

Toying with his glass of Jack, Kaleb glanced at Suzi, who set the two containers on the bar surface. His men crowded in, thanking her for the treat and helping themselves. Kaleb curbed his need to growl again. His gums ached. When the hell had he gone all territorial over any female? *Fuck!* Grayson even went so far as draping his long arm over Suzi's slender shoulders and kissed her upon the cheek. He ought to slug the arrogant ass. Knowing Grayson, though, he'd taken advantage and bussed her cheek just to get a rise out of Kaleb. He wasn't about to give the bastard the satisfaction.

Several minutes later, Suzi extracted herself from the throng of greedy vamps and made her way over to the wall where Kaleb leaned, one booted foot against the baseboard. Her hips swayed gently, making his hands itch to reach out and pull her flush against him. He already knew his hands easily spanned her tiny waist. But instead of touching her, he simply looked down and grinned.

"Enjoying yourself, *piccolo diavolo?*"

"Don't ruin the moment, Hawk," she said, taking the whiskey from his hand and downing the remains of the glass. "I came here to see you. No need for me to wear a neon sign proclaiming it. I think they all know who I'm here for."

"Good." Kaleb leaned down, close to the shell of her ear, and whispered, "That means they'll be taking the fucking hint and leave."

Suzi placed her hand on his sternum, searing his flesh. "Practice patience, Hawk, and I'll promise to finish that blow job I started a few nights back."

Kaleb hissed. His dick hardened. Practice patience? Hell, he needed restraints. "I'm a vampire, sweetheart. I'm not known for my patience."

"Well, then, I suggest you become creative because 'Get the fuck out' doesn't work for me." She winked at him. "I'd prefer a much more subtle way of ridding the clubhouse of its inhabitants."

"Like? I'm up for suggestions."

"Last I knew, Draven could use a morale boost, or so Cara told me. Why not get the Sons to show their support? If he's going to get out of the drug business, he's going to need to make up the sales in alcohol."

"Sweetheart, you're not only right on the money ... you're brilliant." Kaleb leaned in and covered her lips, kissing her far too quickly for his liking. But right now, he needed to get some alone time. "Gypsy?"

His VP's dark head swung in his direction. "Boss?"

"Take the party over to the Rave. Show Draven we got his back."

Grayson strode over to Kaleb. "You have a message you want me to deliver?"

"Yeah." Kaleb's lips turned down in a scowl. "You tell him to get the X out of the club. I find it there and I'll personally kick his ass."

"You got it, P," Gypsy said as he turned to do Kaleb's bidding.

"And Gypsy?" Kaleb gained his attention again. "Tell him Kane and I will be by in the afternoon. He better be there."

Within a matter of minutes, his twin and his mate, lounging on one of the sofas, were the only ones left in house. Kaleb didn't suppose kicking them out as well would work. They had been more than generous by making themselves scarce in the past and Kaleb presumed Kane wanted some alone time as well. He'd just have to deal. It wasn't like Cara wasn't already privy to the relationship he had with Suzi. Kane's frustrating mate had probably already heard everything from Suzi's lips. Women couldn't keep secrets when it came to the men in their life, not even if their life depended on it.

Kaleb looked down on Suzi. When had he started thinking of himself as Suzi's man? He ran a hand through his hair as she looked up at him expectantly. The petite brunette was most definitely growing on him. Christ, he suddenly felt like a schoolboy. Truth be told, he wasn't sure whether to pick her up and carry her to his bed or let her make the first move. Feelings had never entered the equation of sex before. For the first time, Kaleb, like it or not, actually cared about what a woman wanted, and damn he didn't want to disappoint this one.

"You might as well admit it, Hawk." Suzi looked up at him as though she had read his very thoughts.

"Admit what, *piccolo diavolo?*"

A smile of satisfaction grew on her face. "That you kind of like me."

"Oh, I more than kind of like you, sweetheart." He reached down and grabbed a handful of her ass and brought her against his steel-hard erection. "Get in that big bed of mine and I'll show you just how much."

With a laugh, she backed from his hold and dashed off to his room, leaving him stare in her wake. That was his little *piccolo diavolo* ... as insatiable as him.

KALEB'S SIX-FOOT-FOUR FRAME filled the doorway, blocking out most of the light from the hallway, illuminating his impossibly large shoulders. His acute vision seemed to have no problem zeroing in, finding her in the darkness where she stood at the foot of his bed, rooting her to the floor. Even with his face in the shadows, she had memorized every nuance and curve, knew how impossibly handsome he was, stealing her breath from her chest. She had done the one thing she had told herself not to. She had fallen hopelessly in love with the man and set herself up for eventual heartache.

She knew Kaleb hadn't wanted a mate, had said that very thing to her. And yet Suzi had been willing to risk her heart, and take whatever he was willing to give. When he turned his back, and she knew he eventually would, she'd pick herself up again just as she had so many years ago. Suzi had been immediately taken with the bad boy biker then and far too young to know the difference between infatuation and love. Now? She was definitely foolishly in love. This time when he decided he'd had his fill, he'd no doubt crush her. But Suzi wasn't about to live with regrets. The idea of not spending time with Kaleb out of fear of rejection was far worse than not having had him at all.

With trembling fingers, Suzi gripped the edge of her sweater and slowly pulled it over her head, earning her a low growl as she then let it fall from her fingers to pool at her feet. Not that she was nervous about having sex with Kaleb. Hell, no ... that part would be fantastic. But the fact that she'd be making love to him and not just fucking him scared the shit out of her. Especially knowing the vampire didn't feel the same way, which made her heart ache.

There was no doubt that Kaleb liked her tenacity when it came to taking what she wanted. And she wanted Kaleb all right, all of him, his heart, his mind and his body. So she wasn't about to admit defeat. No, Suzi planned to make it damn hard for him to walk away. Kaleb desired her, that much was evident every time she came near. She just needed to prove to him that she was the one thing he couldn't live without.

Suzi flipped the button of her pants free from its mooring, slid down the zipper, kicked her shoes off and shimmied out of her pleathers, adding to the pile started by her sweater. Wearing nothing other than her white lace bra and thong ensemble, Suzi crooked a finger at Kaleb to beckon him forward. His sharp intake of air was her reward as he had yet to move a muscle. With the hallway florescent lighting his back, she couldn't see if his vampire self had yet taken over. Just the thought of it sent a shiver down her spine. What might cause some people nightmares, to her was a total turn on. Just seeing his fangs, prominent brow and sunken cheeks, not to mention his black obsidian gaze, made her go all molten inside. Her now wet thong proof of her desire.

"You going to stand there all day, vampire?" Suzi hiked one of her brows. "Or are you going to let me catch a cold standing over here all but naked?"

Kaleb stepped into the room and slammed the door closed in his haste. It took him less than a millisecond to cross the room and grip her upper arms, hauling her against his hard frame and claiming her mouth with his. His tongue slipped past her lips to tangle with hers, to possess her mouth thoroughly like she wanted his body to do. Suzi slipped her hands up his stern chest, feeling his muscles bunch beneath her touch and gripped the curls at his nape. Holding onto him like a lifeline, she returned his kiss with fervor, matching his intensity, feeling his total possession. This was no chaste kiss. No, this was a promise of what was to come.

Suzi's knees weakened and the muscles in her legs damn near liquefied. His mouth left hers to smooth across her jaw to the soft spot beneath her ear. His fangs dragged across her flesh. Her breath hitched. Tilting her head, she all but gave him permission to feed, knowing how much more heightened her desire would be. But instead, he soothed the area with his tongue, then traveled to the hallow where her vial would normally rest. His tongue darted out a second time and licked the pulse point as his hands went from her biceps to her lace-covered breasts.

"I love your tits," Kaleb whispered, just before pulling the lace cups down and covering one with his mouth, sucking the nipple sharply between his teeth.

His left hand toyed with the other, pinching it between forefinger and thumb. The brief, sharp pain quickly dissipated to pleasure. She squirmed in his grasp. Damn, but she needed him inside her. Fuck foreplay. She needed his cock filling her, stretching her and making her feel whole.

"Damn, Hawk—"

"Kaleb," he said as he released her nipple and covered her mouth once more.

Suzi was a whisper away from climaxing and he had yet to really touch her. Her body all but screamed for his. He ravished her mouth, further heightening her hunger to have him filling her.

Tearing her mouth from his, she said, "I can't take it, Kaleb. Please."

"Please what, sweetheart?" His smile told her that he teased.

Make love to me. Words she knew that could never leave her lips for fear of losing him forever. "Fuck me."

Kaleb growled, turned her around in his hold so that her ass nestled his erection. He placed a hand in the small of her back and urged her forward. Suzi gripped the quilt covering his large bed in her fists, her breath coming out in shallow pants. She felt his hands caress the globes of her ass.

"I love your ass almost as much as your tits."

One hand left her as she heard the whisper of his zipper, just before she felt the warmth of his silky hot cock lying against the cleft of her ass. Kaleb pulled aside her thong and ran his fingers between her legs, spreading her juices up her slit before she felt the head of his cock at her entrance.

"Dear Lord," she said on an expelled breath. "Now, Kaleb."

And with that, he shoved inside, filling her completely. He paused once seated, giving her time to adjust to his size. Suzi gasped, moved against him, urging him forward. She didn't want nice and slow. She wanted him hard and fast. As if he had read her mind, he pulled out damn near fully, before slamming back into her, his hands now gripping tightly to her waist.

"Is that what you want, *piccolo diavolo*? My cock?"

"For once shut up, Kaleb, and just fuck me."

She heard his answering chuckle, just before he started moving in and out of her swiftly. Her orgasm built within. Words failed her as she reached for the blinding lights and weightlessness she knew awaited her. Kaleb leaned forward, taking one of her breasts in his hand, pinching the nipple, just before she felt the tips of his fangs at the flesh of her shoulders. And just as swiftly as he had entered her, he sank his fangs deeply into the meaty flesh, drawing from her.

Her orgasm began ripping through her, stealing her very breath. Damn, but she didn't think she'd ever had one so intense as he continued to pound into her, the slapping sound of flesh on flesh carrying to her ears. Seconds seemed like minutes as she tilted her head back and cried out his name. His hand at her waist now wrapped across her abdomen as if knowing her legs would no longer hold her. He continued to hammer against her until he reached his own climax, his muscles tightening his hold on her. With a sharp indrawn breath, Kaleb withdrew his fangs and licked the twin holes closed. Releasing her, she tumbled to the bed in a pool of languid muscles.

"Round two?" he asked, hearing the smile in his tone. The sound of rustling cloth told her he stripped his body before the mattress dipped and he joined her on the bed.

Suzi scooted closer to Kaleb's heat. He wrapped his arm about her shoulder and nestled her against his side. Resting her cheek against his solid chest, she did her damnedest to calm her racing heart. Rank that right up there with the best sex ever. Kaleb certainly knew his way with women. Hopefully, for now and all her eternity, he reserved that for just her. Otherwise, she might be forced to take out every woman Kaleb showed interest in. Which might get her in trouble with her best friend the cop. She smiled.

"Can we have the lights on for that?" she asked, looking up at him, barely making out his features.

Her answer was the sound of his laughter rumbling up from his gut.

CHAPTER TWENTY-TWO

KALEB RAN A HAND THROUGH HIS HAIR AND BLEW OUT A steady stream of air. Damn, he needed to catch his breath before heading into round two. And he would. He was far from done with Suzi. Not that what just happened wasn't hot as hell, but he wanted to take his time and enjoy her ... make love to her. The animal had certainly come out at her suggestion to skip the foreplay. Not that he minded. Hell no, he had been so fucking horny that he thought he might just split his jeans as he stood in the doorway and watched her remove each article of clothing, leaving her in white lace.

Now? He wanted to watch her face as he brought her to another orgasm. Her suggestion at putting a light on, definitely worked for him, even though he could see well enough in the dark. The fact she didn't seem to mind the way his face changed from its human form certainly pleased him. Hell, in truth, Suzi seemed turned on by his vampire side ... and that he really liked. Most donors seemed unable to look him in the eyes once the change begun, as though they desired his human side and only tolerated his true nature. Not Suzi. Anytime she spotted the change in him, he could smell her desire rising. A smile came to his lips. Yeah, he really liked that.

Kaleb reached over and switched on the bedside table lamp, the soft glow filling the room. "Better?"

Her smile reached her eyes. "Better."

He had put that grin in place, which charmed him more than he'd care to admit. Never had he seen anything more beautiful than when his little *piccolo diavolo* beamed at him. Damn, it cut straight to his heart. First order of business though, he needed to confess. She had to know he would never be so cruel as to toss her necklace carelessly along the side of the road. Time to stop trying to piss her off just to hold her at bay. He'd much prefer to have her sated, and lying naked in his bed.

"I have something of yours," he said, drawing her attention from tracing the tribal art on his arm with her forefinger.

She looked up at him. "What's that?"

Kaleb eased her to the mattress and rolled to his side, opened the drawer of the bedside table and withdrew the leather cord. "I believe this belongs to you. I never threw it along the road as I said."

Suzi gasped. "You lied? Why?"

He tightened his hold on her, tucking her firmly against him, not wanting her to dash off because of his mean-heartedness. "Honestly? I didn't want you to have it. I couldn't stomach the thought of any one of the Sons having their mouth on you, to feed or otherwise."

"What changed your mind?"

"You need to be the one to make that decision. I don't own you, *piccolo diavolo.* That choice needs to be yours."

Suzi slipped the necklace from his hand and dangled it above her before fisting it and looking back at him. "I don't want to feed any of your brothers, Kaleb. Only you."

"Seriously?" he said with a smile. "Does that mean you're back to being my personal donor?"

Why the fact she chose to only feed him didn't really matter, but it thrilled him nonetheless. Kaleb looked at the ceiling, more content than he had been in years. And although he accepted the fact that he enjoyed having her in his bed and his life, there still lay so much between them. Too much hate darkened their past. If he were going to keep her in his life, then he needed to come to terms with what happened ... even if the pain of it killed him. It was time to let old hurts go.

"Can I ask you a question?" he asked.

"Sure." Suzi hooked the necklace around her nape, the vial falling back to the hollow of her throat before giving him her full attention. "I have no secrets, Kaleb. I never have. You just never bothered to ask the right questions."

Kaleb thought about what she said. He hadn't bothered to question her at all and had only been too quick to accuse. "Ion ... why didn't you mourn his passing?"

Suzi sat up beside him, brought her knees to her chest and hugged them. "If we're going to go there, then you need to know the truth, Kaleb. I'll no longer lie or hold back anything from you. You have to promise me you won't now accuse me of being untruthful and realize I have no reason to be. Deal?"

He nodded, too confused by her statement to comment anyway.

"I loved Ion. And Ion truly loved me. I know that. I also know that he told you he wanted to take me as his mate."

Kaleb's heart panged at the reminder, but he remained silent. What the fuck could he say? He couldn't blame his nephew for wanting her.

Suzi swallowed before continuing. "It was never that kind of love, Kaleb. I never chose Ion over you. You were too busy parading women in front of me and breaking my heart that Ion became my rock. He was there for me when you weren't."

"I'm sorry ... I never meant—"

"You did, Kaleb. You made it clear you didn't want one woman. Or for that matter ever wanted to mate. And honestly, I couldn't even fault you for that. Not when there were always so many women throwing themselves at you and vying for your attention. Ion kept me sane, treated me like I mattered."

Kaleb growled, but said nothing in his defense. He had been an ass.

"As a friend, Kaleb. He never loved me the way you're thinking. And I never had that kind of love for him either."

"But you slept with him."

"I won't sit here and say that I've been celibate. I wasn't going to wait around for you to come to your senses. You were usually too busy to notice me anyway. But no, to answer your question, I never slept with Ion."

"Why not? He was a good-looking man."

Another smile graced her face as though the mention of his nephew brought back good memories for her. "Ion was handsome. But he wasn't you."

"Me?"

Suzi laughed uneasily. "You can be pretty thick-headed at times, Hawk. It's always been you. No man could ever live up to the damn pedestal I tried to keep you on. Even if you did fall off the thing more times than I care to count. But I did try to move on. I even propositioned your brother once."

"Kane?" his voice raised. "I'll kill him if he so much as touched you."

"Down, boy." She smiled, doubtlessly pleased by his show of jealousy. "He turned me down. At the time, I looked at it as just another failure. But in reality, it wasn't Kane I wanted. I wanted to hurt you. I thought I could use Kane to do that. My plan backfired. He didn't want me either."

"Oh, I wanted you, sweetheart. Don't mistake that." Kaleb reached out, wrapped his hand about her calf, then ran it along the smooth flesh, just wanting to touch her. "So you used Ion to hurt me as well?"

"No, not Ion. It was the other way around, Kaleb. Ion used me."

His brow furrowed.

"Ion helped me through a tough time. I was dying inside watching you with all your women. I could barely stand it." Suzi drew her lower lip between her teeth, as though studying his reaction before continuing on. "He showed me how to survive without you and love myself because of the strong man he was. Ion lived with a dark secret, knowing his father, uncle, and all the Sons might very well turn their backs on him if they knew. And yet, he couldn't change that part of his life, nor did he want to. In truth, Ion needed me as a cover, which was his reason for wanting to take me as his mate.

Because I understood him, knew who he was inside and out, and loved him anyway."

Part of Kaleb wasn't sure he wanted to Suzi to continue. "What could be so fucking bad that Ion would feel the need to hide it from Kane or me?"

Tears welled in her eyes and slipped down her face. "Kaleb ... Ion was gay. He had a boyfriend, significant other, who he loved with all of his heart."

Shock tore through Kaleb, making him dumbstruck. Not that Ion being gay would have made him love his nephew any less, just that Ion had hid it so well.

"When you told me Ion had died, I was numb. All I could think about was breaking the news to his lover, the one person Ion couldn't live without. The real person he wanted as a mate ... not me. I couldn't break Ion's confidence, especially in his death. I had to let you believe what you would because I couldn't allow your memory of him to be tarnished. I lived with his secret to protect you and Kane. It was never my secret to tell."

Suzi placed a hand over her trembling lips as she tried to hold back her sorrow. Her shoulders shook and tears wet her cheeks. *Oh, for fuck's sake!* He really had been an ass. Kaleb sat and gathered Suzi into his arms, smoothing his hand down her back as her tears continued to fall, wetting his chest. How the hell had he been so blind? He had made Suzi suffer his anger and wrath for ten long years when she had deserved none of it.

In truth, he had been so fucking jealous of Ion. He had wanted to be the kind of man his nephew had been, and offer Suzi the one thing he never thought he'd offer to anyone ... to be his mate. Even now he wasn't sure he could be that man for her. His heart broke in two at the sound of her sobs, to know that she carried this grief and Ion's secret for far too many years. Damn his nephew for being a coward and not trusting him or his father, and instead laying all that guilt on a young, innocent woman. No one should've had to carry his secret in life, let alone death. He should have manned up and trusted in his family that they would have loved him regardless.

Kaleb gripped her shoulders and sat her back from him. She used the heels of her palms to wipe away the wetness, her lower lip quivering adorably. Leaning down, he kissed her gently, not one of passion, but one of adoration. If he were honest, then yes, he loved this woman who had shown nothing but bravado and courage over the past ten years. The one person who had put her prejudiced aside to come see if he were indeed all right after nearly being beheaded. And he had accused her of being a cold-hearted bitch. What a selfish bastard he had been. He didn't deserve this woman in his arms. His heart swelled and he knew how his twin must have felt when given the choice to save Cara's life.

"I am so sorry, *piccolo diavolo*. You deserved better ... you certainly didn't deserve my wrath."

"No." She smiled through her tears. "I didn't. And I wanted to hate you for it, only I couldn't."

"Thank the good Lord you didn't," he whispered, before covering her mouth once more and following her down to the mattress.

His dick hardened, needing to be inside her again. But this time, he'd make love to her and show her what his lips could not yet say. Maybe it was time to start thinking about a lifetime with her. Because suddenly an eternity without her scared the hell out of him.

———

BLINDING WHITE STROBES FLASHED about the club, while rays of red, blue and green lights sliced like a saber sword through the fog-filled room. Ravers gyrated in what appeared to be slow motion from the strobes on the dance floor, most likely high on X. Grayson's conversation with Draven had ended with allowing the bar-keep to sell his stash over the course of the evening and to not peddle another pill or suffer the wrath of the Sons. In truth, due to Cara and Detective Hernandez's little surprise Q&A the day before, Draven had been more than amendable. The Blood 'n' Rave had just gotten out of the pill pushing racket.

With the MC business now behind him, the real party had just begun. The Prodigy blared through the giant speakers hanging from the corners of the large dance floor, the bass drumming against his chest. He lived for this shit. Loud music, wild women and great whiskey. Let Kane and Kaleb fuck up their eternity saddling themselves to one woman. Of course, Kaleb had yet to take Suzi as a mate … but he would. He was as much of a fool as his twin.

Variety was the spice of life.

That Cowper dude knew what the fuck he was talking about when he coined that phrase. Grayson tossed back another shot of Jack, leaned against the polished bar and studied the small group of women dancing just for him. He'd always been popular with the ladies. Not that he was arrogant about it. Hell, no. He didn't figure he was any different than any of his MC brothers, but the number of women surrounding him at any given time spoke for itself.

The ache in his gums told him he'd need to decide which of them would follow him upstairs to Draven's private quarters and soon. He didn't need his vampire self coming to light in front of the women when all of them weren't wearing donor necklaces. His thirst wasn't even his biggest issue at the moment, his lust was off the charts, largely due to the curvy redhead dancing at the front of the pack. Damn, but her dark blue, skinny jeans fit her ass like a glove. She was the same redhead Suzi had all but had a conniption fit over and swept her from his embrace and took her home before Grayson could sample a taste. Lucky for him, Kaleb kept Suzi's ass busy tonight, because the redhead was number one on his list of contenders.

With her fiery red hair, she definitely stood out. Maybe he'd veer from his norm and enjoy a little one-on-one action tonight. He certainly wouldn't mind spending some time getting to know this one. Not about to waste another minute, he crooked a finger at her, beckoning her forward. She smiled wide and sauntered in his direction, her hips swaying nicely in her tight jeans. He all but swallowed the piece of gum he chewed. Damn, but she was a hot piece of ass. Yeah, he definitely didn't need any other woman fucking up his chance to get inside this one.

The redhead stopped just shy of touching him, looked up and grabbed the aviator style sunglasses perched on the top of his head, placed them on her cute little nose and smiled.

"What can I do for you?" she asked, just above the loud din of the music.

Her smile told him she knew exactly what she could do for him. He meant to take her up on it.

One of his brows inched upward. "I don't know, doll. What can you do for me?"

Pushing the glasses up her nose using her middle finger, her grin widened. Damn, if he didn't take that as a clear invitation. The small gesture hardened his dick as thoroughly as if she had gotten on her knees and licked the sudden ridge lining in his leathers.

"Truth of it? I've probably had way too much to drink." She giggled. "I'm not sure I could answer that question without you thinking poorly of me."

"*Il mio dolce rossa,* my sweet red, what's your name?"

"Tamera." She leaned in and nipped his chin with her even white teeth. "You can call me Tam."

"Well, Tam"—he liked the way her nickname felt on his tongue, probably a bit too much—"how about you follow me up those stairs behind the bar so I can spend a little time getting to know you better? It's far too noisy and crowded down here if you get my meaning."

She leaned in, her breath fanning his ear. "Do you want to fuck me?"

This time, he did swallow his gum. Damn near choked on it. His dick hardened painfully. If he didn't get her out of those super tight jeans and straddling his lap pronto, he might wind up not needing her at all.

Grayson leaned down, ran his tongue across the shell of her ear and said, "I do."

She stepped back, fisted his black tee and pulled him in for a quick, but deep kiss. Her tongue shoved into his mouth and he tasted the sweet liquor she had consumed. Just as quickly, it ended, causing him to growl.

"Good. Because I *really* want to fuck you."

Grayson picked Tamera up, and slung her over his shoulder, slapping the ass that was now at his shoulder level, earning him a giggle. Not wasting a moment more of time, he left the pack of women to stare in their direction as he ducked between the curtains and carried her up the stairs, taking them two at a time. Once inside the room, he deposited her back on her feet. Hell, her ballet flats had barely hit the floor before she pulled her dark green top over her head, leaving her standing in front of him in a black lace bra that left nothing to the imagination. Dusky rose colored nipples poked against the material vying for his attention.

Normally, Gypsy had always been the aggressor, but this woman... *Wow!* She took his breath away and more. He loved her boldness, reveled in it. Less he had to work for. Before he could even compliment her, she kicked off her shoes and pulled down her skinny jeans, stepping out of them. In nothing but a black lace brassiere and matching boyshort panties, her vivid green eyes looked at him expectantly.

She wasn't tiny and slender like a lot of the women he slept with. No, this one stood at least five-foot-ten to his six-foot height. She had nice curves, not reed thin like some women. Man, she had a killer body. For the first time he felt rooted to the floor and unsure what the hell to do next. Well, he knew what to do, it's just that this woman stole all reasonable thought from his lust induced brain.

"You going to stand there all day, handsome? Or you going to come over here and take advantage of what I'm offering up?"

His gaze traveled her long legs, up to the lace covered center, past her belly button, onto her D-cup breasts and landing on her donor necklace. Thank his lucky stars. His vampire self all but begged to be unleashed. Tamera was obviously aware of what he was and his change wouldn't send her fleeing, nor would he have to hypnotize her into forgetting him. Not that he wanted more than one night. But he damn well wanted her to remember it.

He yanked his black tee over his head and sauntered toward her, her green gaze going to the ridge in his leathers. *Had she actually licked her lips?* If there were ever a woman his equal, this woman was it in spades. Before he could even so much as revel in the smoothness of her flesh, her hands had gone to his belt buckle and slid the leather free from the pant loops. Grayson chuckled. *Hot damn!*

"What's the hurry, *il mio dolce rossa*? We have all night."

Tamera leaned in, nipped the fleshy part of his ear, then soothed it with her tongue. "I don't want the X to wear off."

Shit! "What the hell did you just say?"

Grayson set her away from him and scowled at her. "How much have you had?"

"Just one pill."

"You ever take X before?" If he fed from her it could cause her pulse to skyrocket dangerously.

"Only one other time."

"Let me guess, the night you came back to the clubhouse and Suzi took you home."

She nodded, her smile going wide. "Let me tell you. That sucked big time. Self-gratification isn't near as good—"

Grayson gripped her shoulders. "And how much have you had to drink?"

She looked at him queerly. "Just two drinks."

"What were they?"

"Long Island Iced Teas."

Double shit! He knew Draven loaded those with shots. Had it not been for her size, she'd likely be flat on her back and comatose right about now. He grabbed her pants from the floor and handed them to her. "Get dressed, *il mio dolce rossa.*"

"Why?" Her brow furrowed. "I don't understand."

"I'm not about to take advantage of you. I like you ... a lot. If you were anyone else..."

She placed her hands on her delectable hips. "I thought you liked your women wild."

"Is that why you took the X? Because you thought I might prefer it?"

Tamera gritted her teeth. Grayson could tell she was trying to be brave, failing miserably. Finally, she said, "I can't compete with the gorgeous women draped on your arms. My only way to get your attention was to lower my inhibitions and take what I wanted. Make you think—"

"You're something you're not?" he finished for her, his tone rising. "Get dressed, *il mio dolce rossa.* I'll take you home."

She ran her hands up his chest. His muscles screamed for her attention. But here he was, being a dumb ass and turning down what she offered. He had to be a fucking idiot. "Get dressed," he repeated.

Grayson turned, strode to the sidebar and poured himself two fingers of whiskey. He quickly downed the shots, then poured two more. Just as he turned to see if she had done as he asked, he ran smack dab into her naked form. Instead of doing as he had asked, she instead rid herself of the lacy lingerie. Yep, she was most definitely a natural redhead. His hold on the crystal rocks glass slipped and the tumbler fell to his feet, breaking into large shards.

Tamera knelt quickly to help him pick up the glass, nearly falling over in her drunken and drugged state. Grayson reached out to right her at the same time she meant to steady herself, the glass shard in her hand forgotten, laying his forearm wide open. Blood pooled to the surface from the deep gash and ran down his arm in dark red tracks.

A curse left her lips. "I am so sorry."

She held his arm up as though inspecting the deepness of the wound. But before he had a chance to tell her not to worry about it, he'd heal before they ever hit the club exit, she leaned down and latched on like a babe to a teat. Grayson gripped a fist full of red hair and pulled her free from his arm, his blood smearing her gorgeous plump lips. *Oh, for fuck's sake.* His heart hammered heavily.

"Do you have any idea what the hell you just did?" he damn near roared.

Tears swelled in her eyes. "What's the big deal? It was just a taste."

Grayson slapped his forehead with his palm. *Fuck me!* The silly twit didn't even know she had just saddled herself to him for all of eternity. He tipped his head back and growled, nearly taking the rafters from the building and no doubt heard above the music played below. How the hell would he ever explain this one to the MC? Tamera's days as a human were now numbered, as was his bachelor status. She may have just mated herself to Grayson, but he'd be damned before he ever pledged her his fidelity.

Standing, he walked back over to her clothes, and threw them at her. "Get dressed, *il mio dolce rossa.* Looks like you're coming with me to the clubhouse ... and not for the reason you think. Because, now ... you'd be the last person I'd ever want to fuck."

CHAPTER TWENTY-THREE

KALEB LEFT HIS ROOM, FEELING MORE CONTENT THAN HE PROBably had a right to, and headed for the dimly lit living area. He had Suzi to thank for his sudden high spirits. Could he possibly live his eternity with the love of just one woman? His twin and his first mate came to mind as he padded barefoot over to the bar, scratching his nape. Truth be told, Rosalee and Kane's volatile relationship had discolored his idea of claiming a mate early on. In the beginning they had seemed a good match, until Rosalee had started acting out and making poor decisions on her own, without consulting Kane or the MC. It was as if she had been determined to destroy her relationship with Kane. In the end they had spent more and more time apart, until both their worlds came crashing down due to her foolish actions, resulting in their son's death.

Now, regardless of his feelings toward the detective, his twin had never seemed happier. And for that alone, he had Cara to thank, even if there were times she got under his skin. His brother's happiness trumped his prejudices.

A corner, floor lamp had been left burning, illuminating the front room of the clubhouse. Walking over to the bar area, he flipped on the switch and flooded the room with even more light. Kaleb grabbed the box of leftover pastries from the back counter, placed them on the center bar and started a pot of coffee. The aroma filled the air. After freshening up, he thought his *piccolo diavolo* might be hungry. The caffeine would aid in keeping her awake as he was far from finished. That thought brought out a smile.

His Levis' hung low on his hips, but he hadn't bothered with a shirt. He had only donned the jeans in case Cara ventured out of his twin and her room. Opening the cardboard box, Kaleb took one of the yeast glazed donuts and took a bite. He seldom abided human food because it held no nutritional value, so he rarely felt the need to bother with it. The pastry melted over his tongue and the sweet goodness filled his mouth. He supposed there were times like this he missed partaking in normal foods.

The sound of a Harley drew his attention. He placed the half-eaten pastry back into the box and licked his fingers as he waited for Grayson to walk through the door. He had recognized the sound of the VP's motorcycle engine. What he hadn't heard was the sound of other tires. Grayson rarely came home alone. A quick glance at the clock told Kaleb that it was barely past two in the morning. The engine cut short and brief seconds later the front door opened. Grayson stormed into the clubhouse, a deep scowl lining his face. Something or someone had seriously pissed off the VP.

Just as Kaleb was about to ask him what the hell had him so bugged, he detected the scent of a woman. Grayson wasn't alone as Kaleb had originally thought. The same redhead Suzi had rescued from Grayson earlier in the week, followed him through the opened door. Poor woman's makeup ran down her cheeks, making her appear as if someone had kicked ... worse yet, *killed* her puppy. His VP didn't bother with an introduction. Instead he continued straight to his quarters without an explanation and slammed the door, rattling the windows.

Suzi exited the bathroom, her gaze swinging in the direction of Grayson's room. But before she could question Kaleb, her dark eyes landed on the distressed redhead.

"Tamera?" she asked.

The woman took in a shuddering breath and did her best to offer Suzi a faint smile.

"What's wrong, sweetheart? What's Gypsy done?"

Tears slipped down her face. Her lower lip trembled. "It's not Gypsy, Suzi. I fucked up."

Suzi grasped her cheeks and forced her friend to look down on her. "Tell me."

"It was an accident," Tamera said on a sob.

"What, sweetie?"

The redhead swiped the back of her hand beneath her nose, wiping away the wetness. "I was on X."

"What? Why the hell would you do that?"

"I don't know. I experimented with it a time or two. I liked how it made me feel." She wobbled a bit on her feet. "I think I had too much to drink too."

"This isn't just about the X, is it?" Suzi gripped her upper arms to help steady her. "Want to tell me about it?"

"I accidentally cut Grayson."

"It's okay. He'll heal."

"I wish it were that simple. I was so turned on by him I didn't think about my actions ... that is until Grayson pulled my head back."

Suzi's gaze widened and her breath hitched. "What did you do?"

"I grabbed his arm and drank some of his blood."

"What?" Kaleb nearly roared, not caring if he woke the entire neighborhood. "Grayson Gabor, get your sorry ass out here. Now!"

Kane's door swung open. His twin entered into the fray, pulling on a pair of his jeans as Cara followed behind, wearing one of Kane's over-large black T-shirts where it fell about her knees.

"What the hell is going on?" Kane asked as Grayson exited his room and came back into the living area, refusing to look at the redhead, clearly irate.

"You want to introduce us to your mate, Gypsy?" Kaleb asked, one of his brows arching upward. "Jesus! You really are a fuck up!"

Grayson bared his fangs. "She"—he pointed a finger at Tamera—"is not my mate."

"Are you denying that she ingested some of your blood?"

"No!" He ran a hand through his hair, knocking his sunglasses to the floor. He didn't bother picking them up. "I broke a glass, and when I went to pick up the broken pieces, little miss drunk and high stumbled with a piece in her hand and laid my arm wide open. Before I could stop her, she latched on like a frickin' vampire."

"You know you can't take a mate without first taking it to a vote." Kaleb choked back the humor of his own idiotic statement. Obviously, Grayson wasn't at fault, nor did he have time to take it to a vote. "She's your responsibility, VP. And as such, you'll see her through her change."

"She is not my responsibility, Hawk."

The look on his face could only be explained as pained. Sure Grayson's eyes shot daggers when he took in the redhead, now standing just behind Suzi, as if her five-foot-two inch frame could protect her from the furious vampire. Grayson's anger shouldn't be taken lightly and could definitely be thought of as lethal, Kaleb had seen the vampire at his worst. But never had he seen the man raise a hand to a woman. On the contrary, Grayson seemed to adore all women ... no matter the shape or size. And in return, they seemed to love him as well.

Kaleb might've laughed if the situation wasn't so fucked up. "She drank your blood, Gypsy. I'm sorry, but that marks her as your mate."

Grayson growled, his fangs fully extending in his rage. "There has to be something that can be done. I didn't ask for this."

"I'm sorry," Tamera said, gaining all their attention. She ran a shaken hand beneath one eye, swiping at the tears. "I really wasn't thinking. This is all my fault."

"You wear a fucking donor necklace." Grayson turned his fury back on her. "You know drinking from a vampire is not allowed. You set me up, you fucki—"

"Gypsy!" Cara spoke up. "The woman is clearly upset by what's happened. There is no need for name calling."

"Stay out of this, bitch."

Kane strode over to Grayson and shoved the angry vampire against the bar. "First, you will fucking apologize to my mate, or I'll take you out back now and kick your sorry ass. Then, you'll apologize to Tamera."

"I'll apologize to Cara, because I was out of line ... but *il mio dolce rossa* ... never!" Grayson glanced at Kane's mate who now stood beside Tamera. "I'm sorry, Cara. I meant you no disrespect."

His eyes damn near blazed as they lit on Tamera. "But you ... you would do best to stay out of my fucking way."

"Female vampires are only allowed as mates," Kaleb warned.

"Then let her hang with Rosalee, who has found herself recently unmated," he growled.

"Gypsy," Kane said, still standing close enough to restrain Grayson if need be, "clearly this was a huge mistake and I'm sure Tamera hadn't thought her actions through. It is what it is. Maybe in time, you'll even come to accept her."

"Never."

"If you take this to Mircea, he'll not rule in your favor. Someone needs to be responsible for this woman. Rules are put in place to protect women from being abused by our kind."

"As I recall, you broke rules, Viper."

"I had no choice and I paid the price for it."

"And I'm not given a choice either."

"Jesus, Gypsy," Suzi spoke up, drawing everyone's attention. "It's not like you saddled yourself with an ogre, for crying out loud. Why not suck it up? We'll try to find a way out of this for both of you."

"Suzi," Kaleb all but laughed at her reason, "*piccolo diavolo,* there is no way out. Why do you think Gypsy is so pissed? By drinking his blood, Tamera has become Gypsy's mate, willingly or not. She will become one of us."

"Then she'll be club responsibility," Grayson said. "She can stay here in my quarters, and I'll sleep on the sofa or find a new place to live. But don't expect me to be or act as a mate to her."

With that, Grayson stormed from the room, slamming the door to his quarters again. Suzi placed an arm around Tamera, who looked back at Kaleb. He could tell the redhead regretted her grave error. Unfortunately, there would be no turning back and the damage had been done. He doubted Grayson would be there for her, which meant he'd need Cara to help the poor woman through. The sound of a feather hitting the floor could've been heard in the room. Not a single vampire spoke up after Grayson's parting. Poor Tamera appeared on the verge of a breakdown. Being a male, Kaleb had no idea how to help the poor woman. Women were better at handling these type of situations.

"Suzi, make sure Tamera has several days of clothes," Kaleb said. "She won't be going anywhere for a few days. The change won't be a walk in the park. I'm sure Cara can attest to that, though she had her mate to help her through. You two will have to do it. It doesn't look like we'll get any help from Gypsy on this."

Grayson's growl in response, indicating his acute hearing picked up on Kaleb's directives, echoed through the clubhouse. Kaleb reached down and picked up the VP's sunglasses and laid them on the bar next to the forgotten box of donuts. Damn, he couldn't help but feel sorry for his VP. This certainly wasn't of Grayson's doing … and yet as Kane had said, *"It is what it is."* Kaleb scratched his nape and grimaced as he looked at Tamera being comforted by the women. Poor fucking Grayson.

KALEB REVELED IN THE COOL SPRING drizzle washing over him, dampening his chaps as he headed down Highway 126 for the Blood 'n' Rave. Kane and Grayson followed closely behind, taking the curves at nearly ninety-miles-per-hour. Nothing like the open road to clear one's mind. Sitka spruces and Douglas-firs lined the road, the rich evergreen scenting the air. He had been only too happy to have a reason to venture outside the clubhouse. There were far too many women in attendance for his liking. He'd bet, if asked, his two MC brothers felt much in the same way. How could six months' time change everything? First Cara had Kane breaking rules and compromising Kane's position as club pres, then Suzi came crashing back into his life and turning it upside down, and now ... Tamera.

Damn, he felt bad for Grayson.

He'd take Kane or his own troubles over his VP's any day. If there was ever a list of unsuitable vampire mates, Grayson topped the chart. He hadn't done anything to deserve the circumstances of the night before, but fate could sometimes be a bitch. He didn't blame the vampire for not wanting to be in the same room with the redhead. Given the same fucked up happenstance, he'd probably want to take her pretty little head. Mircea had listened to his twin once. Maybe Kane, being the eldest of Vlad's kin, could appeal to the primordial again. If there were ever a reason for a mating to be annulled, this one surely took the cake.

Unfortunately, other than his brother's annulment to Rosalee, Kaleb had never heard of it in all his years. Once a mate was taken, you pledged your life to that female, helped her through her change, and stayed by her side for all eternity. The exact reason Kaleb had never wanted to enter the ridiculous union. Now, he wasn't sure he could live that forever and a day without Suzi in it.

Kane gassed his engine, coming alongside Kaleb and signaled for him to pull over, breaking into his reflections. Kaleb left off his throttle and pulled his chopper to the side of the road, his tires crunching over the small pebbles and pine needles. Placing his booted feet down, he cut short the Ironhead, looking back at Kane as he unsnapped his helmet.

"What's up, bro?" Kaleb asked.

Kane nodded toward the right side of the road, up the hill and into the dense foliage of the Siuslaw National Forest. "There's a primordial in the area. I can smell the bastard."

Kaleb's nostrils flared. "Fuck. You think it's Rosalee?"

"It might very well be," Kane said. "Damn weather is keeping me from getting a clear scent. But I'm suspecting whoever it is has been following us on foot. I detected the scent miles back."

"What do you want to do?" Grayson chimed in. "I am in the mood to kick some primordial ass. Just say the word, P."

"Stay put, Gypsy. We have another reason for being on the road today," Kaleb said. "You think we need to worry about a trap, Viper?"

"It's a definite possibility. We need to keep aware. You want to take the rest of the trek on foot?"

"I'm willing to ride out front," Grayson volunteered.

"No fucking way, Gypsy. We aren't on a suicide mission. I agree with Viper. We only have about five miles left, let's take it on foot. There's a rest stop just around the bend. We can park our bikes there and hoof it the rest of the way, stay to the forest and off the main road."

"If she's here, she'll follow us." Grayson voiced Kaleb's exact thoughts. "Better to be on foot, I guess, than worry about another steel cable stretched across the road."

"She won't have the guts to face the three of us at once. That's why she's using cowardly tactics." Kane started his engine, then pointed down the road.

They followed him down the highway about a half mile to a stone alcove where they parked their bikes, just out of the line of sight from anyone happening to travel along the same path. Kaleb hung his skull cap on the handle grip, pocketed his keys, then looked at his brothers.

"I'm no longer catching the scent of a primordial, but in this weather that doesn't mean much," Kaleb said.

"She's still out there." A muscle in Kane's cheek ticked. "I can feel it in my bones. She knows we're aware she's here. Let's take the opposite side of the road. If we head straight up that hill and then take a right, we should be in Florence in about five minutes time."

Grayson was the first to cross the road and head into the foliage. He wasted no time as he took off on a dead run. Kaleb and Kane followed Grayson into the thick of trees, jumping effortlessly over downed logs and ducking low hanging branches. Forest critters scurried out of their way, giving them a wide berth as the trees became but a blur. Grayson's long legs kept him easily ahead of Kaleb and Kane. The vampire ran like a gazelle, easily running and leaping over the rough terrain, while Kane and Kaleb's larger build made the trek a bit more treacherous. Grayson may have been shorter than their six-foot-four frame, but his more lean body allowed him the faster speed.

The first to clear the woods, Grayson took the steep hike down the path and into the back parking lot of the Blood 'n' Rave. Draven's bike sat near the back door, telling the trio that he had already arrived. The rest of the parking lot sat empty, as the club was hours away from opening its doors. They'd have plenty of time to talk to the barkeep without interruptions. Kane had wanted to bring along Cara, since she would play a major part of the scheme, but Suzi needed her more at the moment. Tamera's change had started and Suzi had no idea how to help the woman through the excruciating pain. Of course, in the end, there really wasn't much that could be done, but offer comfort. At least Cara knew what Tamera was going through firsthand. Kaleb couldn't help but think that by the time the three of them returned, Suzi might ruminate long and hard about wanting to mate with him and going through the pain herself. Even childbirth couldn't compare to the agony.

Kaleb and Kane came to stand beside Grayson.

"What the hell took you boys so long," Grayson asked, a cock-sure smile on his face.

"No problem with your ego, Gypsy," Kane said as he walked past the shorter vampire, the twins having a good two inches on him, and headed for the back of the club. "Let's get this over with. I still have a meeting with Red later today."

Kaleb glanced at his twin. "He won't be happy."

"No, he won't. But club voted to stop the gun runs."

"Not our problem. He's the one with a mole."

Kane turned and looked at Kaleb. "We have yet to prove that, so Red won't see it that way."

Truth be told, Red would likely be livid. Kane would be the best person to diffuse the situation and smooth things over. After they found the son of a bitch helping Rosalee, then maybe they could revisit the Sons relationship with the rival club.

"You get with Red and Bird, tell them the gun deal is off. Later we can revisit the issue of running guns again."

"Fuck that," Grayson said. "I'll go with Kane. I'd love to visit with Bird."

"What is it between you two, Gypsy? You have a hard-on for that biker?" Kaleb asked.

"Something about him doesn't sit well with me. I'd just as soon rip his throat out than sit down and have a chat with him."

"I'll go alone." Kane shot down Grayson's offer. "You two can take care of the women."

"Jesus, Viper … suddenly I regret that decision allowing you to tell Red. You stay with the women."

Kane laughed. "Not on your life, Hawk."

Grayson grumbled beneath his breath and headed for the back of the nightclub, telling Kaleb his thoughts on the matter of babysitting the women. He had a strong feeling Grayson would use every excuse not to be at the clubhouse. Moments later, Kaleb rapped his knuckles on the steel backdoor. Within minutes Draven opened it and motioned them into the club. The three followed the barkeep through the backroom and into the bar area.

"Whiskey?" Draven took down four highball glasses from the shelf above the bar. "On the rocks?"

"Straight up," Kaleb said.

Draven poured two fingers into all four glasses, then slid one across the bar to each vampire. All four of them quickly downed the tumblers' contents and Draven refilled them.

"So, what's up with the impromptu meeting today?" Draven asked.

"Gypsy told us you're officially out of the drug selling business," Kaleb said.

Draven nodded. "As of last night."

"Good. We need you to keep it that way. Heat is coming down from not only the locals but the feds. Word is, they want your supplier." Kaleb twirled the amber liquid around in his glass. "We don't need the Blood 'n' Rave getting caught up in the mess. We're here to make sure that doesn't happen."

"Detectives Hernandez and Brahnam were pretty clear on wanting my supplier's name—"

"And you're going to give it," Kaleb finished for him.

"That would be a death wish and you know it, Hawk," Draven said, the anger evident in his tone. "It's not just the Devils I have to worry about. Those fuckers get their drugs from the cartel."

"Which is why we're involved," Kane spoke up. "That same cartel is responsible for the death of my son. It's payback time. And you're going to help us."

"And why should I do that, Viper?"

"Because if you don't, I'll give Cara full license to come after you. The Blood 'n' Rave will be shut down and you'll go to jail. Don't think we can't find a new haunt. Our donors go where we go, you ass."

"You going to give me around-the-clock muscle?"

"If we have to."

Draven nodded again, no doubt weighing what little options he had. Finally, after taking another shot of whiskey, he said, "Tell me what I have to do."

CHAPTER TWENTY-FOUR

ROSALEE TRAILED BIRD FROM THE SMALL ALCOVE AS HE PUSHED Kaleb's chopper to the center of the highway. Kane, the son of a bitch, had managed to catch her scent even in the spring drizzle, masked by the smell of wet dirt, pine and animals. She had hoped the weather would camouflage it. His power had undoubtedly gained strength. Had they ridden another half mile down the road at the speeds they were traveling, Kaleb would've encountered the steel cable that strung across the highway and nothing short of a miracle would have kept his head attached to his broad shoulders. While eavesdropping at the clubhouse, Rosalee had heard their plans to head for the Blood 'n' Rave. She quickly contacted Bird and set the plan into motion.

So fucking close.

She was beginning to think Kaleb had more lives than a damn cat. Curse his good luck. Sooner or later it was bound to run out. But Rosalee wasn't about to be dissuaded from her goal. On the contrary, she would see Kaleb dead and then Bird would outlive his usefulness. She watched as he slowly moved the chopper to the center of the highway. The fool! Once her mission here was completed, she'd take the dirtbag's head herself. Rosalee couldn't afford to leave loose ends. And Bird was definitely a threat to her exposure. She fed from him, fucked his brains out, and promised to turn him for his help in taking down the president of the Sons of Sangue. Stupid man. She'd not saddle herself with him for all eternity, even if women had the ability to turn humans into vampires. She couldn't turn Bird if she wanted to. That right belonged to the men of her species, only their DNA could cause the change in a human. *Talk about an archaic race.* Hell, their damn DNA made women inferior to them.

In the end, Kaleb would die and Kane would pay the ultimate price. He had not only banished her to Italy but acted as though she no longer existed, easily replacing her with that blond detective bitch. She was a primordial, for fuck's sake, and as such she should be revered. Instead, Kane, the ungrateful ass, thought he could take another in her role as his mate … even went so far as getting Mircea's blessing. When she was done with Kaleb, she'd take out the little detective next with great pleasure.

Cara Brahnam would be no match for someone of her age. And now that she'd returned to her role as detective, she'd no longer be hiding in Kane's shadow, making her an easy target. Rosalee would get Kane Tepes' attention one person at a time until she beat him down and forced him to turn to her in penitence … or death. The choice would be his.

If Kane Tepes did not belong to her, then no one would have him.

"Light it," Rosalee said.

"With pleasure," the biker said, a slick smile on his weathered face.

Bird took a small can of lighter fluid from the satchel he carried and squirted the liquid liberally over Kaleb's beloved bike. Bird took a few steps back, took out a pack of matches, pulled one free, and slid it across the strike plate. The match flitted to life, flickering in the damp wet air. He took the match to the rest in the pack, watching it as the fire began to burn bright, then flicked it toward the motorcycle. The bike burst into flames, quickly engulfing it due to the accelerant. Bird's face glowed from the light of the fire as he watched it grow in intensity.

Rosalee wished she could stick around to see the look on the younger Tepes' face when he saw his prized bike blackened and charred. But she couldn't risk being caught ... not today. Soon, she would capture Kaleb unaware and when she did, she'd take his head personally. No more fucking around.

"Time to cut our losses, Bird. Kaleb will live to see another day."

And with that, the two of them disappeared into the foliage and headed for Bird's bike, left hidden about a half mile down the road. The quicker she got him away from the scene, the less chance the three Sons would have of catching them. Not that she cared what happened to Bird, but she wanted to be the one to drain his sorry ass dry.

KALEB LED MOST OF THE TREK BACK through the dense Siuslaw National Forest, heading for the small alcove where the bikes were parked. Draven had given them his word to work with them on laying a trap for the rival MC, the Devils, and the cartel that fed them their stash of drugs. With Cara's help and feeding the feds the right leads, they'd be able to take down those responsible for his nephew's death ... and give Kane the much needed closure. Hell, he needed to avenge Ion's murder for Suzi as well, not to mention the man Ion had loved. Why the hell hadn't he seen the signs? Because

Ion hadn't wanted him to and because he used Suzi to hide behind. All these years he had hated Suzi for choosing Ion over him, when in fact she hadn't.

Pissed? Damn right.

Ion should have taken the blunt of that anger. He should've trusted in both him and his father, should've known they would have never judged Ion for his preference. Damn! It galled him to think that Ion went to his death thinking so little of them. Kane had a right to know. But for now, he'd keep Ion's secret and allow Suzi to tell his twin in her own time. He owed her that much.

As they drew nearer to the rest area, the strong stench of lighter fluid, gasoline, and smoke clogged his sinuses, long before the forest provided him a view of the orange glow. The fire crackled, sizzled and popped. Had it not been for the smell of gasoline, Kaleb might be tempted to believe the forest was ablaze.

"What the hell?" Kaleb ducked under a couple of branches and leapt over a large fallen tree as if it were nothing, advancing on whatever had gone up in flames.

A quick glance back showed Kane and Grayson quickly on his trail, obviously detecting the conflagration as well. Dread sat in the pit of his stomach the closer he came to the cause. And just as he cleared the woods, his chopper tank blew. The explosion knocked him off his feet and onto his ass about twenty feet back into the forest covering.

"Jesus," he blasphemed, his mouth left agape.

Kane pulled him to his feet. "You all right, bro?"

Kaleb stepped back out of the woods and stared at the fire licking the remains of his chopper. Parts littered the tarmac. "Well, if
that isn't a pisser. I will so kill that bitch of yours—"

"Not mine." Kane followed Kaleb onto the road. "I got rid of that
long ago. Looks like she's made herself your best friend, though."

"She's gotten my attention, all right. And the next time I see her,
I'll rip her fucking head off." Kaleb walked an arc around the charred
remains of his chopper as it continued to smolder, his stomach stuck
somewhere mid-chest. "I have to hand it to you, Viper. You really
know how to pick them."

Kane smirked. "At least it was your ride."

"Seriously, Viper?" Kaleb turned and glared at him. "You did not
just say that to me? All this anger that bitch is harboring should be
aimed at your sorry ass."

"You killed Alec."

"You sent the bitch back to her stepfather and then annulled
your mating. I think that trumps taking Alec's head."

Kane shrugged, not doing a very good job of hiding his humor.
He ought to cold-cock the son of a bitch. All this shit should be
aimed at Kane. But no, instead she wanted his head. What the hell
had he ever done to the spoiled brat to earn her scorn? Alec Funar
might have been a primordial, but he was most definitely a douche.
She should have thanked him for getting rid of the pompous saddle
bag. Instead, here he stood staring at the remains of his beloved
chopper.

"So what are we going to do, Hawk?" Grayson asked, chuckling.
"You riding bitch with Viper back to the clubhouse? He's got the
extra seat."

402 | PATRICIA A. RASEY

"Fuck you, Gypsy."

Kaleb was certainly in no mood for his wise ass either as he listened to Grayson chortle at his own joke. He pulled out his cell and called K&K Motorcycle's land line. After a few rings the phone was picked up.

"K&K," came Alexander's deep voice. "What can we do you for?"

"Bring the box truck." Kaleb damn near growled. "Highway 126, about fifteen minutes out, heading for Florence."

"What you need with the truck?"

"Just do what you're told, Xander. Don't leave me standing here all day either."

He heard the dark-haired vampire take a deep breath. What the hell did he do? Interrupt his fucking nap?

"Give me a few minutes, got a customer here—"

"You the only one there?" Kaleb's voice rose in irritation.

"No. Blondy, Wolf and Kinky are in back."

"Then get one of those losers to take over. Bring me that fucking truck ... now!"

Kaleb hit the END of his smartphone, glared at a smiling Kane and Grayson and curbed the urge to chuck the cell phone at them. Fifteen minutes later, the box truck rounded the corner, then rolled to a stop just a few feet away from what was left of his chopper. Not very damn much. He'd kill the bitch for that alone.

Alexander stepped down from the cab of the truck, his dark gaze fixated on the charred cycle. "What the hell happened?"

"Rosalee," Kaleb grumbled. "Grab the leather gloves from the glove box and let's get this thing loaded."

Alexander walked around the cab, opened the door and grabbed the gloves along with the fire extinguisher. Walking over to the center of the road, he aimed the spray nozzle from the canister, pulled the safety pin, then squeezed the lever and dowsed the bike, extinguishing what might be left of heat and flames. Kaleb's heart sank to the pit of his stomach as he stared at the mess. Gone was the seat, gas tank and damn near everything else. He had the blackened frame, motor... Hell, even the tires had melted to the rims, making them unusable. Part of him wanted to pitch the whole sorry excuse for a chopper and start over. The other part needed to rebuild it, piece by piece because he loved that bike. He'd not allow Rosalee to win this round.

Damn that bitch for drawing breath.

He made a promise right then ... he'd see her dead by his own hand or die trying.

THE LARGE, WHITE BOX TRUCK PULLED onto the paved lot of K&K Motorcycles, the wipers on delay swiping at the continuing drizzle. Much the way Kaleb felt. Gloomy and dismal. He supposed he needed to snap out of his present mood. It wasn't as if he couldn't rebuild his chopper. Or better yet, create a whole new radical design, but he'd had that Ironhead chopper since 1979. He had made a few restorations over the years, but for the most part, it had remained intact. He hated losing the old girl. Kaleb jumped from the cab after it rolled to a stop, then headed for the back of the motorcycle shop.

Alexander alighted behind him, but went around back of the truck to retrieve the frame and what else was left of it. Kane and

Grayson had beaten them back to the shop, their motorcycles parked in the front lot. Using the keypad, Kaleb punched in a series of numbers, waited for the beep, then swung open the back door and waltzed into the parts room, florescent lights illuminating the room. He heard the laughter, long before he saw the five vampires standing in a semi-circle, no doubt sharing humor over the demise of his chopper. Asses. Every single one of them.

"Nobody has anything better to do?" Kaleb rounded the corner of a row of silver racks containing parts and accessories. "Now we pay you to stand around and bullshit?"

"My, aren't we in a snit." Grigore flashed him a smile filled with humor. "You don't pay us enough to begin with, Hawk."

"There's the door, Wolf, if you have a better opportunity."

"Fuck you, Hawk. Viper would just hire me right back."

"So why not ride your Ironhead chopper back?" Joseph asked, not bothering to contain his humor either. Along with Alexander, he was also one of the quiet ones, never speaking unless he had an opinion on something.

Comedians, all of them.

"Maybe you'd like to rebuild it for me, Kinky?"

"I'll be glad to detail it out for you, but you know as well as I do, no one would build one to suit your picky ass."

"What do we have on the floor in the meantime?" Kaleb would need a ride while he rebuilt his chopper.

"Ask Xander. He was the last one in the showroom," Joseph said.

The back door to the parts room opened and slammed shut, indicating Alexander had brought the frame in. The smell of the burnt parts hung heavy in the room. He needed to take care of this issue with Rosalee. No more fucking around.

Anton walked over to where Alexander set the charred remains and whistled. "Not much left, Hawk. I would've had Xander deposit this shit in the Dumpster out back. Ain't worth saving, if you ask me."

"No one did, Blondy. Xander, we have anything decent out there? Or did you sell the best bike on the floor to whomever was occupying your time when I called?"

Alexander pulled off the leather gloves and tossed them on one of the stainless steel counters. "Go take your pick. You interrupted a sure sale. We have a showroom full of sweet rides."

"We going to get that sale back?"

He shrugged. "I suppose she might be back."

Kaleb's gaze swung from his chopper's frame to Alexander. "She?"

Grigore slapped Alexander on the shoulder and laughed. "Xander's beautician thinks she needs a sweet ride. Right, GQ?"

"Go to hell, Wolf."

"The lady that gave you that"—Kaleb gestured to Alexander's newly shorn locks—"now wants to buy a motorcycle?"

"Yeah." He scratched his nape. "Said she'd like a Sportster."

"It's a great bike for a girl, right, Gypsy?" Kaleb asked, looking at Grayson who seemed deep in a conversation with Kane.

"What's that?"

"I said Xander's girlfriend is looking for a girly bike. Why not sell her your custom Forty-Eight Sportster?"

"Go to hell, Hawk. I like the smaller bike. I don't need a big piece of machinery between my legs to compensate for a small dick. I don't have any complaints in that department, unlike you—"

"I didn't get any complaints..." Kaleb stopped himself from bringing up Suzi's name.

He wasn't sure it was the right time to broach the subject of what the two were or were not doing. He needed to spend more time with her before he started thinking in the long-term, though part of him knew damn well he was being a stubborn ass because he most certainly did not want a future without her. Regardless, that was a conversation he'd reserve at a later time.

"So that's why the little brunette's been hanging at the house lately? She's sniffing at that dick of yours?"

Kaleb crossed the large backroom in very few strides and stuck his finger in Grayson's chest hard enough to knock him back a few feet. "Suzi Stevens is not up for discussion, Gypsy. Unlike Tamera, whom you've found yourself mated to."

Grayson growled as three pair of eyes trained on the shorter man. Anton, being the Secretary, was the first to speak up. "You hold a church meeting without us, Gypsy?"

"Fuck no. "

"Then what's this about a mate?"

"The fucking bitch was high as a kite. Not my fault."

Kaleb said, "You call the clubhouse? See how she's faring?"

"Why the hell would I care again?"

"I talked to Cara," Kane spoke up. "She said she's doing fine, all things considered."

"Someone want to fill the rest of us in on what the hell is going on?" Anton asked. "Or am I the only one in the dark?"

Kaleb quickly filled the rest of the members of the Sons on what had taken place the night before. Grayson paced the parts room like a caged animal, fidgety and unsettled. Kaleb couldn't help but feel sorry for him, but it wasn't like he had gotten saddled with someone like Rosalee. No, Kane had taken that honor. Although to his credit, she wasn't the crazy bitch she is today until after Kane had scorned her.

Joseph scratched his ear as he tried to fight the rising smirk. But once Anton started laughing, the others followed suit. Aside from Grayson. No, he wasn't finding humor in his situation at all.

He walked over to Anton and smacked him behind the head. "I wouldn't laugh, Blondy, seeing as how I'm moving in with you."

"The hell you are." His humor shed his face. "Why my house?"

"Because you live in that big old farmhouse all by yourself. You have plenty of room."

"And your mate?"

Grayson growled low again. "She's staying at the clubhouse. There's far too many women there for me these days, let them keep her out of trouble."

"You know you're responsible for her," Kaleb said. "It's not my job to make sure she makes it through the change and learns the life."

"No, it's not. But since you're the pres, you figure it out." He turned back to Anton. "Which room is mine?"

"You can have the top floor, bro. I haven't used it in years."

"Good. Now if we're done here, I'll go grab my things. Anyone needs me, I'll be at Blondy's."

Grayson walked through the swinging doors leading to the showroom and out the front of the shop. The bell to the front door sounded, just before the door slammed closed, signifying the vampire had left the building.

"Damn!" Kaleb broke the silence. "Poor Gypsy."

Grigore was the first to laugh again, which started a round of guffaws. Once the humor died away, he said, "I can safely say it couldn't have happened to a better man. Maybe now the rest of us will get some action and he'll stop hogging all the women to himself."

"Who said he'll remain faithful to his mate, Wolf?" Alexander asked. "If it were me, I'd sure as hell wouldn't. Viper never stayed faithful to his."

"That's because Rosalee stopped being my mate when Ion was killed," Kane said. "I didn't owe her shit. Cara, on the other hand, has nothing to worry about. I'd never think to break my vow to her."

"If there was ever a reason to break that vow, Gypsy certainly has one." Kaleb grimaced. "I'll not say a word about what he does with his evenings, and I expect the same from all of you. We're going to cut Gypsy some slack because he didn't ask for this."

"So who will be responsible for her?" Joseph asked.

Kane sighed. "Cara will no doubt insist since she's living under our roof. I suppose that will make Tamera my responsibility as well."

Kaleb nodded, satisfied with his twin's answer. "That settles it. Kane and Cara will finish seeing Tamera through her change and she'll be their responsibility for now. That is until we can figure out what to do with this fucked up messed. Now, I have a bone to pick with a primordial bitch ... and for that I need a ride."

"Go take your pick, boss," Alexander said. "Just don't touch the new Seventy-Two Sportster with the Hard Candy Chrome Flake that came in last week."

Kaleb raised a brow. "You seriously think I'd be caught dead driving a bike with fucking sparkles, Xander?"

His cheeks mottled red. "No, I just wanted to make sure it was still here tomorrow."

"Don't worry, GQ ... your girlfriend's bike will still be in the showroom. I doubt any of the Sons would be caught dead on that bike."

CHAPTER TWENTY-FIVE

SUZI LEANED A SHOULDER AGAINST THE DOORFRAME, NOT DAR-
ing to step a foot closer, surveying Grayson's room where her
roommate thrashed about on his king-sized bed. Sweat beaded
Tamera's forehead and upper lip as she bared her teeth to pain that
only Suzi could imagine. The small, bedside lamp, fitted with a bur-
gundy shade, lent a dim illumination to the room. Suzi was thankful
for the low lighting, even if Cara had said it was for Tamera's benefit. Anything brighter would have been like shards of glass shooting
through her roommate's pupils. Suzi stopped asking questions,
thinking she might be better off if she were spared further details of
what to expect when going through the change. As it was, Suzi was
a fraction away from bolting.

Deep red satin sheets spilled to the floor, reminding her of
spilled blood. How ironic that she'd be reminded by the color of
Grayson's sheets of the very thing that now caused Tamera excruciating agony. She could barely stand to watch as Cara mopped her
roommate's brow, sitting on the edge of the bed and keeping vigil,
when it should be Suzi offering Tamera comfort. After all, she had
been the one to fail her.

Hadn't her warnings to steer clear of the vampire been clear?

Yet Tamera still fell for Grayson's deadly charm. Sure, he was
probably the most appealing of the Sons when you threw in his

311

carefree personality and insouciant attitude toward life. But in truth, Grayson was the last vampire you wanted to get caught up with. His love of life and women meant that he didn't know the meaning of the word faithful, even if always having a woman on each arm wasn't enough of an indicator. And why should he when he had so many women competing for his attention?

Alexander, on the other hand, with his newly shorn locks could easily be thought of as the more handsome one of the MC. Even Suzi had been surprised by what he successfully hid under all that hair. Being one of the more quiet ones of the bunch, he had a tendency to stay out of the limelight. He'd probably be the most mateable one of the motley bunch. And yet Suzi had to fall for the one with a stubborn streak a mile wide with a healthy ego to match.

She wanted to fault Grayson for what she now witnessed, but in all honesty, she couldn't. He hadn't supplied Tamera with the X. Draven had. The Sons knew it was far too risky for a human to be high on X when they fed from them. Donors also knew the dangers, and for that reason never touched the stuff if they planned to provide communion. So why the hell had Tamera?

Suzi had been too preoccupied with her own selfish desires to see what was going on with her roommate right under her nose. As the elder donor, she should've made sure Tamera knew and followed the rules. Suzi drew her lower lip between her teeth, knowing she had failed Tamera. If she hadn't been so occupied by Kaleb and her desire to make him suffer, she might've seen the signs that her roommate had been on a course to self-destruction. She'd bet that Grayson hadn't expected the outcome of his night either, now strapped with a mate he didn't want.

Where the hell was he anyway?

A scream rent the air, bringing her attention back to her room-mate. Moisture gathered in her eyes and a shiver passed down her spine. Tamera's back arched from the bed, her hands fisting the red sheets and whitening her knuckles. Suzi clenched her own teeth in imagined pain. The coward in her wanted to make an excuse, to flee the clubhouse and skip out on the rest of the show. But her loyalty kept her rooted in place. Tamera had pleaded with her to stay, say-ing it would help knowing Suzi was near.

Not able to watch a moment longer, Suzi's gaze drifted about the room, focusing on Grayson's chosen furnishings. Somehow it didn't surprise her that Grayson's bed had been fitted in the soft, silky fab-ric, topped with a a rich black comforter. Matching black material hung from the corners of the four posters, tied midway by deep red scarves. Suzi didn't want to guess what those scarves might've been used for. Black lacquered furniture finished off the look. Other than the splash of red, the room was devoid of any other color. It fit Grayson. Funny how she could easily imagine him lounging in the center of that big bed with a woman on either side. She supposed if the situation were different, it would be him there with Tamera and not Kane's mate.

Mate.

Cara sat by Tamera's side ... Grayson's mate, and continued to mop her brow with the cool cloth. She held Tamera's hand with her free one, even though it looked as though Tamera's grip might just crush Cara's smaller hand. But Cara hadn't so much as flinched. A half hour had passed since retrieving Tamera's change of clothes and

Suzi had yet to enter the room. Truth be told, watching the change and the pain that it inflicted scared the bejesus out of her.

Becoming Kaleb's mate was quickly losing its appeal. Not because she didn't desire to be with him for all eternity, or love him with all her heart, but because there was no way in hell she could endure the kind of agony she had been a witness to.

Tears leaked from the corners of Tamera's eyes, eyes that now seemed closer to the obsidian black of the vampire than the bright green of her natural gaze. Tears wet Suzi's cheeks as she hugged her middle. She couldn't help her thoughts retuning to Kaleb and how she had wanted this ... to be his mate. Now, the coward in her had her wanting to tuck her tail and run. To leave this crazy life behind and opt for a more normal one.

Suzi feared she wasn't cut of a strong enough cloth to cross over. Good thing for her, Kaleb had already expressed his desire to remain unmated. He had always been upfront with the women he slept with. Word traveled amongst the donors that he had no desire to date exclusively. No doubt as Suzi grew older, he'd want to replace her with a younger, more energetic donor—if she lasted outside of a year. The thought of Kaleb lying with any another woman gripped her gut and panged her heart. Maybe she'd be better off ending things now before she invested any more of herself. For surely, more time spent in his company would make it that much more painful to walk away.

"Is she going to be okay?" Suzi asked, drawing Cara's attention.

The blonde smiled, her own eyes hovering between the normal vibrant blue and the glass-like obsidian. Great, she'd be the only human left in the room. Not that she wasn't used to seeing the Sons as their vampire selves, but it was an entire different thing to see her best friends become one of them.

"She'll be fine, Suzi. Tamera will get through it." Cara smiled. "I did."

"You had Viper to help you," Suzi pointed out. "Shouldn't Gypsy be here?"

"Normally, yes. The mate helps the woman through their change. He has the ability to make it more bearable."

Tamera screamed again, ending on a sob, drawing both their attention. Suzi finally dared to enter the darkened room and cross to the opposite side of the bed. She reached out for Tamera's hand, but Cara stopped her.

"She'd crush the small bones of your hand and not even realize she had."

Suzi's gaze went to Cara's hand still held within Tamera's grip. "What about yours?"

"My bones get stronger every day, and the more blood I ingest the more powerful I'll become. It's part of the change. Some things take longer."

"How long has it been since you had communion?"

Cara smiled, the light from the lone lamp twinkling in the glassy surface of her gaze. "Why? Are you offering?"

Suzi's face heated. "If it would help you."

"Tamera may need it before this is over. She'll need to learn to feed. But I'm fine."

"How long does this last?" Suzi scratched her nape, wanting to be anywhere but in Grayson's bedroom.

"A few days."

Suzi looked at Tamera. "I'm so sorry." More tears slipped down her cheeks.

"Not. You're. Fault." She gritted between her teeth through what looked to be another wave of pain. "But I may just kill the bastard..."

Tamera tilted her head back and let out an inhuman-like growl. The changes were becoming more in-human. It probably wouldn't be long before she sprouted fangs.

"How soon before she needs to feed?"

"A day or two," Cara said. "The process is different for each person from what I'm told. I lost track of time, but from what Kane told me, it was three days before I finally fed and completed the change. Do you need to be somewhere?"

"I feel like a coward."

"Suzi, go. I've got this. Tamera will be fine in my care."

Suzi placed a hand against her trembling lips. "I'm so sorry, Cara. You shouldn't be the one."

"No." She chuckled. "It should be Gypsy, the rat bastard. But I'm much more equipped to help. Go, take some time. Call me later and let me know you're okay."

Suzi couldn't utter another word without falling to pieces. So she nodded briefly, then exited the room. Walking to the table by the sofa, she grabbed her set of keys. Just before she opened the door, she gripped the necklace around her neck as an afterthought. Taking it off, she walked over to the bar and laid it on the surface, then turned and left the building.

KALEB ROLLED UP TO THE FRONT OF clubhouse on his new ride. He had chosen a Harley Davidson new edition Night Rod Special with a black denim paint job and orange striping. It wasn't his chopper, but it was a sweet ride nonetheless. As he unsnapped his skull cap, he noticed Suzi's red Neon wasn't in the parking lot. Hanging the half helmet on the handle grip, he stepped over the seat of the bike, thinking that she possibly hadn't returned with Tamera's clothing.

Gravel crunched beneath his boots as he headed for the front door, knowing Cara would be inside. Her black Charger sat to the right of the stoop, telling him as much, but her scent gave her away along with that of Grayson's mate. He couldn't help wonder how the poor woman fared. The process of the change was grueling and could take a few days. Going through it without a mate at your side had to suck. At least then, she'd have known Grayson would be there for her in the end. Unfortunately with the fucked up circumstances, she'd have no one, making her future foreign and likely a bit scary. By process alone, she'd be considered Grayson's mate. After all it was his blood that ran through her veins. But Kaleb knew there was no way in hell his VP would honor that. And given the same situation, he probably would have reacted much in the same way as Grayson … maybe even more so.

Thankfully Cara had been there to aid her through the process.

Suzi came to mind. He couldn't help thinking of her, lying on the bed between his spread thighs as he helped her through the process and agony. Kaleb shook his head and sighed as he opened the door and stepped into the clubhouse. Damn, he had it bad. Suzi must have seized the heart he feared he didn't possess to even entertain the idea of taking on a lifelong partner. But now that she was back in his life, he couldn't imagine a life without her. No more fucking around. He wouldn't chance losing her a second time. Even though the idea damn near stole the breath from his body and went against everything he thought to once believe, he knew what he wanted... needed.

"Back here, Hawk," Cara called out.

Not that she'd needed to inform him. He could smell the pain and fear of the young donor. His sympathy went out to the redhead and he suddenly felt like kicking Grayson's ass. Even though he couldn't have been faulted, he should have been more aware. This should have never happened in the first place. Kaleb walked the short distance to the back of the clubhouse and peered in the dim room.

"How's she doing?"

"Pretty well, considering. You talk to Gypsy?"

Kaleb rubbed the stubble on his chin as he took in a deep breath. "Sorry to say, but I don't think you're going to get any help from him."

"Can't you do something? You're the club president. You could order him to be here."

"I could, but..." He stopped himself, not wanting to speak his mind in front of the young redhead.

"But what, Hawk? You don't think he should be? It's his job as her mate to help her through this."

"Look, Cara..." Kaleb scratched the spot behind his left ear. Cara would undoubtedly be livid with him. But this sure in the hell wasn't Grayson's fault. "Call it what you want, but Gypsy didn't ask for this. I can't hardly fault him. Give him time."

"Where's he at?"

"Blondy's. Said he was going to live there for the time being," he said. "Hell, I'm betting he'll even send Blondy after his clothes."

"Are you kidding? And you're okay with this? Who's responsible for Tamera then?"

Kaleb grimaced. "Blame your mate, Cara. Viper volunteered the two of you."

"Oh, that's rich!" Cara rose from the bed, her cheeks mottled with color from her rising anger. "You guys all band together, and in the meantime, Gypsy skirts his responsibility."

"It's okay," Tamera said, sucking in air as she did so. "Gypsy isn't at fault. This is my doing." She bit back another rush of pain, if her face was any indication. "I don't want to be anyone's burden."

Cara sat back on the bed and smoothed Tamera's bangs from her forehead. "Sweetie, you are not a burden. I'm angry with Gypsy is all."

"Where's Suzi?" Kaleb asked, in a sudden hurry to be anywhere but in this room. Not that he didn't have compassion for the woman, but every second spent there made him seriously want to beat his VP to a pulp for being such an insensitive ass.

"I told her to take a break, Hawk. She doesn't seem to be handling this well. You may want to see if she's okay."

"Her car is gone."

"I don't know where she went. Maybe home to freshen up. She's been gone about an hour." Cara glanced back at him, telling Kaleb she worried about her friend. "Call her, Hawk."

He pulled his phone from his pocket, thumbed through his contacts then hit her name and placed the phone next to his ear. After ringing several times, her answering system picked up. Kaleb hit the END and re-pocketed the phone.

"She's not answering."

"Maybe she's in the shower."

Kaleb bit back the rising panic. Something wasn't sitting right with him. He supposed a shower could be a likely explanation. Quitting the room, he headed for the bar, needing a shot or two of Jack. After the day he had, he certainly could use one. Kaleb skirted the bar, pulled down a short highball glass, and placed it on the counter when his gaze landed on a donor necklace.

"Cara?" he called out. "Does Tamera still have her donor necklace on?"

"Yes, why?"

"Son of a bitch." He growled loud enough to raise the rafters. "Where the fuck does Suzi live?"

Cara came trotting from Grayson's room, wide eyed. "What is it?"

He lifted the donor necklace from the counter, allowing it to dangle from his fingers. Just hours ago he had thought asking Suzi to be his mate was completely out of the question. Now, faced with losing her. He'd rather die than not have her by his side for all eternity.

"Suzi's?"

"Who else would it belong to? What the hell happened here?"

Cara wet her lips, her gaze thoughtful. "I knew she was having a hard time watching Tamera go through the pain. For awhile she was so pale I thought she might get sick. I told her to take a break."

"Where the fuck does she live, Cara?"

"Not far from the Rave in Florence." She rattled off the directions and the street address. "What are you going to do?"

"Go get her ... what the fuck does it look like?"

"Anything I can do?"

"Try calling her. If she's at the house, get her to stay put. But for heaven's sake, do not tell her I'm on my way." He shoved the donor necklace in his jeans pocket. "She has any inkling of what I'm about to do, she may just run and then I'll never see her again."

Cara's brow furrowed. "What are you going to do, Hawk?"

"I'm going to ask her to be my mate."

Cara's mouth rounded as Kaleb pulled his bike keys from his other pants' pocket. "If she calls you, find out where the hell she is, then call me. I can't lose her a second time."

Heading for the door, he yanked it open and headed for his bike. He sure as fuck hoped she had gone home. Otherwise, he didn't have a clue where to begin looking. Last time she ran it had cost him six months. And Kaleb wasn't about to lose another day.

CHAPTER TWENTY-SIX

THE RED COLOR OF HER CAR WAS THE FIRST THING THAT caught his eye as Kaleb brought his bike to a halt at the stop sign, placing his booted feet on the pavement for balance. The townhouse with the beige brick facade and white flower boxes adorning each window Cara had described sat across the road and down two houses from the corner. A large wreath graced the center of the burnt orange door. Thankfully, Suzi's Neon sat in the driveway, along with another car he didn't recognize. The midnight-blue Chevy Camaro looked fairly new with its thirty-day plates. Maybe a friend of hers or Tamera's had stopped by ... or possibly a family member. In truth, he hadn't bothered to get to know anything about Suzi, if she had parents or siblings, her likes or dislikes. Kaleb had been a self-centered son of a bitch and he didn't deserve her. Hell, it was a miracle Suzi even bothered to stick around all these years. Kaleb needed to rectify that.

Pushing off with the soles of his boots and pulling back on the rubber handle grip to gas the engine, Kaleb rounded the corner and pulled up alongside the second car, then killed the engine. He stepped over his black seat, hung the skull cap from the handlebar, and peered into the tinted windows of the Camaro. Someone had good taste in cars, if one didn't mind riding in a cage. He admired the sleek, black leather interior, proving the owner had spared no

323

expense. Flat-black, wide stripes finished off the exterior paint job, giving it the mean look of the modern-day muscle car. Well, if he were to ride in a cage then this was certainly the type of car he'd choose.

Kaleb looked back up at the townhouse, then headed for the entrance. Just before he reached the door, it swung inward and Draven stepped out. Kaleb's ire skyrocketed. Not seeing Kaleb, the barkeep leaned in, kissed Suzi on the cheek, then turned and ran straight into Kaleb's fist, snapping his head back as he crumbled to the floor. What the hell was the bar owner doing here? And why the fuck was he kissing his woman?

Draven's hand rose to the lump already swelling over his quickly purpling jaw. Kaleb reached out and helped the man to his feet. About that time all hell broke loose and Suzi started going ape shit on his ass, jamming her tiny fingers into his sternum and forcing him back toward the steps. Finally having had enough, he gripped the tiny brunette beneath her arms and set her away from him and smiled. Damn, he loved her spunk.

"What the hell, man?" Draven worked the kink from his jaw, drawing both their gazes.

Kaleb turned and faced the barkeep head on. "What the fuck are you doing here, Draven?"

"She called me ... not the other way around, man. Don't go all postal on me. Take it up with your little donor. I'm here as a friend."

"You're leaving." It wasn't a question.

Draven placed his hands up, palms out. "I am. No need to get violent."

"Stay the fuck away from my woman, or next time I'll break that jaw."

"Since when has anyone been yours?" Draven asked. "Last I knew, Hawk didn't lay claim to any one woman."

"That's none of your fucking business, Draven."

"Jesus, Hawk," Suzi piped up. "Stop being a fucking bully! Why not head back to the clubhouse where you're needed. Last I checked, I wasn't anyone's woman, yours or otherwise."

Dismissing him, just that easy, Suzi walked into the entrance and meant to slam the door in his face. Kaleb stuck the toe of his boot into the jamb, stopping her from shutting him out. He could tell by the puffiness of her eyes that she'd been crying before he had arrived. Not acknowledging that Draven still stood behind him, Kaleb easily nudged aside the door with his shoulder, then closed it, giving Draven no choice but to leave. Kaleb sure in the hell wasn't about to worry about manners, not when he had more important matters at hand ... namely, Suzi.

He pulled her necklace from his pocket and hung it from his forefinger in front of her. "Yours?"

Her bloodshot gaze locked with his. "Not anymore. That's why I called Draven. I'm done, Hawk."

"You're damn right you are." No one was going to feed off his woman. And soon, neither would he if everything went as he hoped ... not for nourishment anyway.

"You can't tell me what to do," she crossed her arms beneath her breasts in a self-protective manner.

"I can ... and I will."

She rolled her eyes and walked away from him, leaving him standing by the door. Kaleb heard the soft rumble of the Camaro as it started, and backed out of the driveway. He'd deal with Draven later. He'd not be making anymore more house calls to Suzi, whether invited or not.

"Is that all Draven was here for?"

Suzi spun on her heel, and straightened her spine. All five-foot-two of her stiffened like a board. "What are you suggesting, Hawk?"

"That you fucked him."

"Seriously?"

"Answer the question, Suzi. Have you fucked him?"

"If you are asking, in rude-like manner, if that's what we were just up to, then no." She perched her fists on her hips and glared at him. "I called him over to give him the news. I'm done donating."

"That's only part of the question, Suzi." Kaleb wasn't sure he was going to like the answer, but he had to know. "Answer me."

Why it should matter, he didn't know. It wasn't fair of him to expect that she had remained celibate while he fucked anything with a skirt. "Did you ever fuck Draven?"

"Yes."

His heart squeezed. "When?"

"On occasion, Hawk. Why now does that matter?"

"How long ago?"

"Oh, for crying out loud. It doesn't matter, Hawk." She flopped down into the large cushioned chair. "I'm not having sex with him now."

"When?"

"The last time was six months ago."

"Before or after I kissed you at the clubhouse."

Suzi took in a deep breath of air, then let it out slowly. "That night. I had nowhere else to go, so I went to see Draven."

His heart panged. "And he took advantage of you."

She rolled her eyes. "No, I took advantage of him, Hawk. I was pissed at you. I thought he could help me forget."

"Did it work?"

She shook her head. "If it had, I wouldn't be here. I'd still be with him."

"How many times since?"

"That was the last time. Afterward, he introduced me to Tamera so I would have a place to stay and the rest is history."

"Did you love him?"

"What the hell, Hawk?" Her voice raised. "What is this? Twenty questions?"

"Please." He knew if he demanded, she might not answer. "I need to know."

"No." Tears slipped down his cheeks. "I never loved Draven."

It was time for truths. He'd not lose her to the barkeep. "Do you love me?"

Her lower lip trembled. She was damn near close to breaking down. His intention was not to hurt her, but to prove to her that she belonged with him.

"Answer me, *piccolo diavolo*. Do. You. Love. Me?"

Her gaze left his, darting everywhere but at him. More tears fell, and she angrily swiped them away. Her chest rose and fell with exertion as if she had just ran a marathon. A sob escaped her as she finally looked back at him. His heart ached at the pain he saw within their depths. Suddenly, he feared what her answer might be. Maybe he shouldn't have come, shouldn't have slugged her ex-lover, and sure in the hell not pushed her into an answer.

What if the answer was no?

"Please, *piccolo diavolo*," he whispered.

"Why is it so important to you?"

"Again, I need to know, Suzi."

"I left the clubhouse because I was scared. I left the lifestyle because I'm not strong enough to do this anymore. I thought I could. But I can't Kaleb."

"None of that matters if you love me."

She chuckled non-humorously. "It all hinges on me being a complete coward. It doesn't matter if I love you or not. What I saw today ... what Tamera was going through. I'm not strong enough to ever endure what I witnessed."

"What you saw today was a woman without a mate."

Suzi nodded, looking to the floor. "How could that make a difference? The pain and torture Tamera was going through was excruciating."

"Cara survived it."

"She's stronger than I am." Suzi glanced back at him. "So is Tamera, for that matter. I've never been good at pain. I damn near pass out at the sight of my own blood."

Kaleb walked to where she sat and knelt down in front of her, her knees touching his ribs. Running his hands up her calves, he whispered, "Do you love me, Suzi?"

Her brown gaze held his, and he saw his answer clearly within the depths before she ever uttered the words. "With all my heart."

Kaleb smiled, his hands leaving her calves to wipe away the tears from her cheeks, then trailing his thumb over her swollen lower lip. "How much?"

"You're impossible." Her eyes turned up in the corners as she bit her lower lip. "Do I need to show you?"

"Not in the way you're thinking, *piccolo diavolo*." He palmed her face and brought her in for a deep kiss, one of possession. He hoped she could feel his desperation in that moment to claim her as his. Then, letting her go, he leaned back on his haunches.

Something told him that if he asked her now to be his mate she'd refuse him outright after what she had witnessed. He needed to keep her away from the clubhouse a few days, just until Tamera completed the change. Kaleb didn't want to chance giving Suzi any more reasons to deny him. But in the end, she'd be his ... in every way. He never thought to ever claim a mate. Now he wouldn't be denied.

He leaned in and kissed her again, though just a brief meeting of their lips. "Do me a favor?"

A shiver shook her shoulders. He could smell the fear on her, scared of what he might ask of her, undoubtedly afraid he would request that she go through the agony her dear friend had endured.

A smile crossed his lips. "Don't ever fuck Draven again."

Suzi's eye twinkled as the corners turned up. "I have no desire to."

"Good." Kaleb flashed her just a hint of his fangs, causing her to take in a slight breath of air. "I plan to keep you too busy to even think about fucking another man."

"Promise?"

He chuckled. "Most definitely."

"Kaleb?"

His gaze traveled to her tits, before landing back on her face. Damn, he was suddenly horny as hell. He wanted to sink his fangs into her flesh, draw an orgasm from her, then slide into her balls-deep until he took her to the edge again.

"Yes?"

"What about me?"

He raised a brow, somehow in his carnal thoughts he had lost the train of the conversation. "What about you?"

"I answered your question." Her gaze wavered. "Isn't it customary to let me know how you feel in return? Don't leave me hanging here."

Grasping her behind the knees, he pulled her forward so that her heat laid against his lower abdomen. "I don't think you said anything yet, *piccolo diavolo*. As I recall, you said, 'With all my heart.'"

"Technicalities." She used her thumb to trace his lower lip. He sucked it into his mouth and nipped at the tip, drawing the tiniest bit of blood. "Do you love me, Kaleb?"

He growled.

"With all my heart." Standing, he slid one arm beneath her knees and one behind her back, easily lifting her. "Your bedroom?"

"Up the stairs to the left."

"You have any plans the rest of the day?"

She shook her head.

"Good, because I'm about to show you how much my cock loves you too."

Suzi laughed, the sorrow and fear in her eyes now replaced by desire. "You're incorrigible."

"No, my dear, I'm insatiable." Then he deeply kissed her once more before heading for the stairs.

THE BACON SIZZLED AND POPPED in the skillet on her glass stove top as Suzi turned it to brown the second side. The smell of cooking pork wafted to her nose, setting her stomach to growling. After hours of sex and very little sleep, not that she was complaining, she was suddenly starved. Moving the two pieces of bacon to the side, she then dropped in an egg. She used the spatula to spread the grease from the bacon, then flipped the egg. Suzi walked over to the bread basket, grabbed two slices, then placed them in the toaster and pushed the lever down.

As Kaleb lie sleeping, Suzi tip toed down the stairs and made her way to the kitchen twenty minutes prior. She hadn't wanted to wake him. He looked so peaceful as he lay on his back, tattooed arm slung over his eyes, his mouth parted slightly. He wore nothing, aside from the sheet covering his groin. The vampire had a magnificent body. Suzi smiled thinking about how well she had explored his flesh from head to toe, pausing on his arm tattoos, those on his calves and thighs, and the large, full back piece that matched Kane's Sons of Sangue death head with two fangs dripping blood. Kaleb sported more tattoos than his twin, and Suzi loved every inch of them.

Reaching on the tips of her toes to the overhead cupboard, she stretched to retrieve a plate when a warm body pinned her to the granite countertop. His large hands caged her in as he nestled his erection in the small of her back. The only thing that separated them was the oversized sleep shirt she had pulled over her head before leaving the bedroom. Obviously, Kaleb hadn't bothered with clothes.

He leaned down, trailing his fangs along the crook of her neck and nipped at her shoulder, sending a shiver racing down her spine. Her desire kicked up a notch, making her more than ready for another round. Kaleb hadn't been lying that he was insatiable. But if he didn't give her time to nourish her body, he'd plumb wear her out. After all, she didn't have his vampire DNA and couldn't hope to ever keep up.

"I'm hungry, Hawk," Suzi said, glancing at him.

His wicked gleam and black obsidian gaze told her he was hungry for an entirely different thing. Slipping one hand from the counter, he trailed it down the front of her sleep shirt, over her abdomen and between her thighs, where he cupped her sex, no doubt feeling her readiness all over again.

He growled low, the sound feathering over the flesh of her neck. "I'm famished."

She sucked in a sharp breath as his fingers slipped past the cotton and ran along her slick flesh, dipping just the tip of one finger inside. "I ... I didn't make you breakfast."

Kaleb withdrew his hand, flipped her in his hold so that now she faced him and his erection lay intimately between them. Leaning in, he nipped at her ear, then trailed the points of his fangs along her neck, his tongue then soothing the path. "Trust me, it's not bacon and eggs that has me ravenous."

Her breathing quickened, her desire trumping what popped and sizzled in the frying pan. Suzi reached over and shut off the burner about the time the toast popped up. Kaleb gripped her by the waist and set her on the counter, spreading her thighs. His nostrils flared.

"The scent of your desire is driving me beyond sane thought."

"I have to go to work in a few hours. I need food. I need a shower."

"Food is overrated." His gaze went to the V of her thighs. "But this ... damn, I can't get enough of."

Suzi placed a few fingers beneath his chin and tilted his gaze back to hers. "Promise?"

"Seriously? You doubt how much I want you after the night I just spent showing you?" His face sobered. "What has you worried, *piccolo diavolo*? I've told you that I love you. I've never said that to another woman."

"What happens when you tire of me?" She inched her legs back together and pulled down on her sleep shirt. "You've never been with one woman for longer than a few months, Kaleb. How do I know I'm not just another notch on your belt? The idea of you walking away..."

He ran a finger across her lower lip before she sucked the digit into her mouth briefly, earning her another growl. "I'm not going anywhere."

"I'll grow old," Suzi said, not able to look him in the eye as she laid her fears bare.

She toyed with the snake-like pattern running down the length of his right arm, afraid to bring up the subject of mating. After what she had witnessed, Suzi feared the change, that she couldn't possibly survive the agony. Though the thought of losing Kaleb terrified her enough to actually consider it should he desire to ask her.

"Suzi," Kaleb said, "Look at me."

When she did as instructed, her heart skipped a beat. She had never seen a more handsome man, even in his vampire state. She supposed the depths of her feelings had a lot to do with how she viewed him. Suzi ran trembling fingers across his more prominent brow, down his hollow cheeks and across his full lips that hid his fangs from view. She had never loved him more than she did in this moment.

"There is something I need."

Her brow creased. "What?"

"Do you trust me?"

"I'm here." She smiled. "I've given you everything I have to give."

Her admission had him leaning forward and placing a quick kiss on her lips. "I treasure you and the fact you didn't give up on me, even though you rightfully should have. You must know that I would never wish you harm."

Her fingers fiddled with the edge of her sleep shirt, but she said nothing.

Kaleb cupped her cheek. "I want you with me."

"I want that too, Kaleb."

"No, *piccolo diavolo* ... I want you with me for all eternity."

He gripped her waist and pulled her flush so that her thighs parted and hugged his sides. Her center rested against the heat of his abdomen, eliciting a moan from her. Suzi couldn't help envisioning him taking her here on the countertop.

"I want what Kane has with Cara," he said, then followed it with a chuckle. "Never thought I'd say those words. But I can't lose you a second time."

"Are"—her gaze fastened on his—"you asking me to be your mate?"

"I'd demand that you be my mate if I knew you'd listen." He smiled, the white tips of his fangs peeking beneath his upper lip. "You need to get to work and I need to call a church meeting. I wanted you to know that I plan to ask for the MC's blessing. If their vote is unanimous, then you can name the day and time. I will be there every step of the way."

"I'm scared, Kaleb. What I saw—"

"Suzi." He pressed his lips to hers. "You saw a woman without a mate."

"Are you telling me I won't go through that kind of pain?"

He shook his head. "You'll feel pain like never before. But I can make it bearable for you."

Her breath hitched. "I'm not so sure—"

"I want you to be my mate, Suzi, to love me until the end of time. You can do this for me ... for us."

She worried her lower lip between her teeth. "I want to, but I'm afraid."

He smiled, knowing he was breaking through her fear. "I promise you that you can endure it. Do you think you can put up with me? I know I'm not the easiest of vampires—"

"Kaleb..."

"There can be times I'm down right impossible—"

"Kaleb." She framed his face with her hands. "Shut up and kiss me."

His smile widened. "Is that a yes?"

"I swear, Hawk. I must be some sort of a fool to put up with your sorry ass some days, but I wouldn't have you any other way. If you so much as think to abandon me while I go through the change—"

His possessive kiss stopped her from completing her requirement that he stay with her. Kaleb wouldn't think of leaving her on her own as Grayson had Tamera. Before she had a chance to say another word, he stepped back, spread her thighs then pulled her forward, and onto his thick erection. She tilted her head back and moaned as he gripped her ass cheeks, sliding in and out of her. Her breath hitched, and damn if she wasn't already on the edge of another orgasm as he took her slowly, her ass sliding on the granite.

"Look at me, *piccolo diavolo.*"

And she did, seeing him for the first time as the man ... vampire she'd spend the rest of her days loving.

CHAPTER TWENTY-SEVEN

C HANGE OF PLAN, BIRD," ROSALEE SPOKE INTO HER CELL AS SHE walked from the back of the townhouse and headed for the little corner market where she had left the biker waiting for her. "I know how we can finally get to Hawk."

Several minutes later, she met up with the scrawny, long legged VP of the Knights. She was quickly losing her patience with the man. There wasn't much that she liked about him, other than his loyalty to her. Hell, Rosalee was even beginning to tire of fucking the man. Time to get her work here done so she could rid herself of the annoyance. Bird leaned against his bike, his booted feet crossed at the ankle, hands shoved into his jeans' pockets. He wore a tattered tee under his motorcycle cut, and a pair of oil-stained jeans. The man utterly repulsed her.

He scratched the back of his neck as he looked at her. "So what's this new plan? Hopefully, better than the last. This fucker just won't go down."

"Never thought I'd see the day, but apparently the fool has found himself in love."

"Hawk? Seriously? That fuck chases everything in a skirt from what I hear. Has quite the reputation."

"Seems the little brunette, who lives in that townhouse, has caught his attention in a big way."

"So what's the plan? Wait until he leaves ... follow him—"

"Don't be an idiot. That's the plan we've been working, dipshit. And he always seems to be one step ahead of us." A smile rose on her lips. "No, we wait until he leaves and follow the girl. I overheard her say something about going into work. Less chance of one of the Sons seeing us, especially since I heard Hawk say he was calling a church meeting. They'll all be preoccupied."

"So what do we do?"

"You are going to get us a van. We can't just kidnap her on the back of this rat trap you call a motorcycle."

Birds brow creased. "What's wrong with my bike?"

"For starters, it looks like it could use a good mechanic." Rosalee was used to the bikes most of the Sons rode, but then again, they owned a shop so they took pride in their rides. "Get a van, and I'll call you later, tell you where to meet me. I have a feeling this bitch will be easy pickings. And there is no doubt, that when Hawk finds out we have her, he'll do anything to protect her ... including sacrificing himself."

"Then what?"

Rosalee narrowed her gaze. "What do you mean? My revenge against Hawk will be complete and Viper will be devastated. Although, I'll still be far from finished with Viper."

Bird stood to his full six-foot height. He could certainly use a little meat on his bones. Rosalee shivered in revulsion. It was definitely time to cut this scum loose.

"I was talking about our bargain, witch."

Rosalee moved so fast, Bird didn't have time to blink as he flipped over the seat of his bike and landed on the tarmac. "Call me witch again and see what happens, Bird."

"Fuck!" He rubbed the back of his skull, coming away with a bit of blood on his hand. "You're a crazy, bitch."

"Don't forget that for one minute, Bird."

"If you're going to make me your mate, we may need some ground rules. Starting with you flipping out. It ain't cool."

Rosalee laughed. What a fool. Thank goodness he didn't know she didn't have the ability to turn him. Besides, there was no way she'd saddle herself with this freak.

"Yes, Bird, I'll keep my word when this is all said and done and you will get to become a vampire, just like me," she said, sarcasm dripping from her words. "Now get your sorry ass out there and find me a van to stow the little brunette away in. Nondescript, asshole. I don't need something with loud graphics on the side. Now, I need to get back to the townhouse so I don't miss Hawk's lady love leaving for work. I'll follow her and call you when I know where to have you bring the van."

Bird brushed the dirt from his ass before stepping over the seat of his bike, then started the engine. "I should have a van within the hour."

"Good. Then wait for my call. Now get the hell out of here."

Rosalee turned and ran the short distance back to the house, just in time to see Kaleb exiting the front door as he shoved his arms into his motorcycle cut. Stopping on the cement stoop, he turned, kissed the brunette on the lips, then headed down the stairs toward where he left his new ride. Rosalee smiled at the thought of his old chopper. Rest in peace. Kaleb kicked up the center stand, turned the key and hit the electric start. The bike rumbled to life. He took one last look at the brunette as he snapped on his skull cap, gave her a wink before perching his sunglasses on the bridge of his nose, then headed off down the road.

Rosalee watched as the brunette entered the house and shut the door behind her, the soft click of the lock sliding into place carrying to her ears. She'd wait her out, follow her to work, and hopefully find the perfect opportunity to take the bitch. Kaleb would no doubt come to her rescue ... and then he'd finally take his last breath. Good riddance to one of Vlad's descendants.

KALEB GLANCED OUT THE WINDOW of the clubhouse meeting room, waiting for the others to arrive. Cara continued to sit by Tamera's bedside. Another day and the change should be complete and the woman's pain finally gone. He couldn't help but feel a bit sorry for the redhead, even if she had caused her own problems by feeding from Grayson. Going through the transformation without a mate by your side, couldn't be easy. Sure, Cara had been there for her every step of the way, but it simply wasn't the same. His true sympathy, though, rested with his VP. What a hell of a fix he had gotten himself into. Saddled to a woman Kaleb would bet he barely knew.

When it came to women, and playing the field, Grayson was far more of a womanizer than Kaleb or Kane. He jumped ship quicker than any of the Sons and yet, women never seemed to mind. They flocked to him like seagulls looking for a crumb. Grayson always had an overabundance of willing candidates. Kaleb supposed his laid-back and jaunty outlook had a lot to do with it. When it came to most matters, he conquered them with a smile and not a care in the world. Kaleb knew first hand though, appearances could be deceiving. Grayson might have been built slightly smaller than both he and Kane, but the vampire knew how to throw down and not one of the Sons could keep up with him. He had watched Grayson fell much bigger men. That boy packed one hell of a punch and knew how to fight. Even relished a good brawl.

The door opened and Kane walked through, taking his seat at the table. He might not have voting rights, but he'd always be a respected member. Maybe one day Kaleb would see about reinstating some of his rights. After all, he was a Tepes and, as so, should have his say in all club matters. But Kaleb wasn't about to give his twin the power to hold a position at the head of table again, not as long as he remained club pres. He supposed his ego had something to do with it, but now that he wielded the gavel, he wasn't about to hand that back to Kane.

"How's Tamera doing?"

"She's a trouper. She's almost made it through the change and hasn't hardly bad-mouth Gypsy. How the fuck does that happen? I swear Cara chewed me a new ass through the entire process." Kane chuckled. "Even if I was the one to save her life."

"Sounds like her."

"You know you like her, Hawk. You might as well admit it."

Kaleb rolled his eyes. "Just keep your woman under control, Viper, and I'll like her that much better."

"So what's on the agenda?" Viper leaned back in his chair and linked his fingers behind his head, his straight, black hair reaching his shoulders.

Though twins, they often times looked nothing alike, at least that was Kaleb's belief. His hair was nearly as long as Kane's, but his waves gave it a shorter appearance. He supposed in size and build they were much the same. But facial features? Kane's cheekbones were sharper, his cheeks more hollow, giving him the more fierce look of the two. Kaleb supposed it had something to do with him being hours younger and Kane making himself protector all these years, even if Kaleb hadn't asked for it.

"Rosalee, as always, and bringing on new prospects, along with a few other matters."

Kaleb wasn't ready to share the information with Kane just yet about Suzi. He'd hear when the rest of the Sons did. He was sure to take shit from his twin as much as he gave over Cara. Kaleb supposed he even deserved it.

"You talk to Red ... tell him about the vote?"

Kane nodded. "I did. He's none too happy about it. Said he had given us forty percent of the cut, and that was more than generous for us to continue our loyalty to his club."

"Fucker has it backward, Viper, and you know it. He's to show us his loyalty. He needs to be put in his place."

"I can't argue that." Viper leaned forward again, placing a forearm on the table. "That's why Cara and I are going to see him following today's meeting, followed by a trip to the nursing home to visit her grandfather. It will be just a meet and greet between Red and me. I'll see that he knows his place, but I'll also keep that line open. I think once this all blows over and we discover who the fuck is helping Rosalee, we need to revisit that vote."

"I'll take it into consideration. I'm not saying we can't still use them as a puppet club. However, they might be more useful to us if we talked about patching them over. That way, loyalty is no longer a question."

"You might be right."

Kaleb grinned at his twin. "I'm always right, bro. But for now, let's keep patching them over between us. First agenda, we need to find your ex bitch and whoever the hell is working with her and cut their fucking heads off.

"I couldn't agree more," Anton said as he walked into the room. "Any idea where she's hiding out yet?"

"No doubt in Lane County, Blondy. She ain't going far from her prey ... me," Kaleb added.

Shortly thereafter, the rest of the Sons started filing in and taking their seats around the table, talking amongst themselves. Everyone was in attendance except for Grayson. As VP, he was required to attend all meetings. He wasn't about to let the vampire slide because of the unfortunate turn of events.

"Blondy," Kaleb got the secretary's attention. "Where the hell is Gypsy?"

"I'm right here, Hawk," Grayson said as he walked through the door. "No fucking reason to get all bent out of shape."

"I wasn't sure where the hell your head was these days."

"I moved out, Hawk, that has nothing to do with my loyalty to this club."

"And your duty to help your mate?"

Grayson flopped into his seat. "I won't even dignify that with an answer. Now can we get onto business and get the subject off me?"

"You're an ass, Gypsy," Anton said.

"Duly noted, Blondy," Grayson all but growled. "Go ahead and write that in the minutes."

"I see you two roommates are getting along famously." Kaleb chuckled. "But yes, we do have business to discuss."

The room quieted as he stuck the plate with the gavel. "First and foremost, let it be known that Grayson has taken on a mate without club approval as you are all already aware. I put it to a vote that there be no disciplinary action given due to the circumstances. Shall we take it to a vote?"

"Yay," Joseph, the Sergeant in Arms, replied. "I second the vote."

Once everyone agreed to allow Grayson's slight to go without retribution, Kaleb moved on to the second order of business. "Prospects. Do we have any hangarounds worth bringing up?"

"There's a guy at the Rave who seems pretty cool. Goes by the name of Rocker," Grigore said. "Not sure of his real name. Got into a heated exchange with an idiot on Disco Biscuits and Rocker was quick to see if I needed him when about four of this jerk's friends thought to take me down. Short of it, the crew of imbeciles backed down and I thanked Rocker for his interference. We've been friendly since."

"You willing to sponsor him, Wolf?"

He shrugged. "Yeah, I think he could be good for the club. He's loyal. I've seen him in a few other skirmishes. He can hold his own."

"All those in favor of making Rocker a prospect?" The "yays" traveled the table. "Anyone else?"

"I know a guy named Constantine Dalca, goes by the name Lightning," Alexander said. "Lives around the corner from me, bought his last bike from the shop. Fucker has no fear."

"You willing to sponsor him, Xander?"

He nodded.

"Then all those in favor of Lightning becoming a prospect?" Again the approval traveled the table. "Then we have two new prospects. Bring them to the clubhouse for a meet and greet."

"We any closer to finding that primordial bitch?" Alexander asked. "I'd certainly like to hear she lost her head after trying to divest me of mine."

"She's still our top priority, Xander. Trust me, no one wants to catch her more than me," Kaleb said. "I still want all eyes out there looking for her and the rat that's helping her. She will eventually slip up, and even Mircea won't be able to rescue his wicked stepdaughter this time."

When no more was said than voiced approvals on the matter, Kaleb cleared his throat. "We have one more item to table, then we can call it a meeting."

Nervous tension twisted his gut, in fear of the vote going against him. He couldn't think of one reason to be denied, but one negative vote would cost him his lifetime with Suzi. All members had to agree, and once voted upon, it couldn't be brought back up for revote.

"Everyone here knows Suzi Stevens, probably fed off her, and the fact I made her my personal donor." Most nodded, though no one commented, so he continued, "I plan to take her off the market for good."

"Just what the hell do you plan to do with her, Hawk?" Grigore asked. "I doubt she's done anything worth taking her out. Or did she do something grave like reveal what we were to an outsider?"

"Nothing like that, Wolf." Kaleb toyed with the gavel, then looked each one in the eye, ending with his twin. Finally, he said, "I plan to take her as my mate."

One of Kane's brows rose. "That's rich ... you who gave me so much shit over my mate."

"This is different, Viper."

"How so, bro? I loved Cara, and the way I see it, that's no different."

"Because I'm doing it by club rules and asking for the vote."

Kane leaned back. "You know I had no choice. It was that or let her die."

"So you're going to hold my prejudice against me in my own desire to take a mate?"

His twin smiled. "Just busting your balls, Hawk. Besides, I don't get a vote. If I did, it would be in your favor. If you love her, then I'm all for her becoming your mate. I'm sure Cara wouldn't give any arguments."

Kaleb ran a hand down his lightly whiskered jaw. "I don't suppose. Do I get any arguments from the rest of this motley crew?"

Anton was the first to speak up. "Take it to a vote, Hawk. We'll be happy to take you off the market. With you, Viper and Gypsy—"

"Fuck you, Blondy," Grayson said. "No one is taking me out of the game. Viper and Hawk may be pussy whipped, but that redhead in there is mate in name only. Not going to argue that point with any of you."

"So she's free to take on lovers?" Anton asked.

"No fucking way. She gave up that right when she bit my sorry ass."

"You're a hypocrite, Gypsy."

"What the hell is your interest, Blondy? You wanting to fuck my mate?"

The table moved a half a foot as Anton bounded out of his chair and braced his hands on the surface as he leaned toward Grayson. "I would never touch another's mate."

"Then we don't have a problem." Grayson stared down the blond vampire.

Kaleb struck the gavel against plate. Anton retook his seat and silence descended about the room. "This isn't about your problems, boys. Take it up outside. Let's put this to a vote so that we can get out of here and on with the real issue at hand, the bitch primordial wanting to take my head. All those in favor of Suzi Stevens becoming my mate?"

"Yays" traveled about the room, and to his relief, not a single "nay." Kaleb should have been scared shitless about taking a mate and ending his days as a single vampire. Instead, he couldn't wait for Suzi's shift to end so that he could tell her in person. His smile rose as he struck the gavel against the plate again.

"Then this meeting is adjourned."

As the vampires filed out of the room, he accepted the well-wishes and congratulations of his fellow MC brothers. Never did he think he'd see the day he'd take on a mate. And damn if he wasn't happy about it.

CHAPTER TWENTY-EIGHT

K ANE TRAILED CARA AS SHE HEADED DOWN THE HALL OF THE
Pleasant Care Nursing home, on the way to see her grandfather, his mind still on his meeting with Red. The president of the Knights had a big hard-on for his twin. Kane couldn't very much blame the man since Kaleb was instrumental in cutting off his channel to the guns they were running. He supposed that Red would still try to run them through Oregon, though skirting the Sons stomping grounds in hopes of not getting caught. Should that happen, he warned the man, then there would be an all-out war, with no hopes of fixing it.

Red wasn't exactly taken by the idea of patching over to the Sons of Sangue as Kaleb had suggested. Though Kane came up with some viable reasons why it might be good for both clubs, Red couldn't get past the idea that it was more beneficial to the Sons as his beloved MC, the Knights, would disappear. Patching over and making vampires out of another MC would increase the Sons numbers, making them stronger. They'd control all of Oregon as well as Washington. Of course, Kane had yet to let Red in on the vampire end of the bargain. That could come later. But he supposed Red was correct, they stood to benefit a lot more from the union. He'd give Red time, but in the end, Kane was pretty sure he'd be able to persuade the man into his way of thinking.

349

But first, they needed to find the rat.

Red might not be convinced there was a dirt bag in his camp, but Kane would bet his own life on it. Someone was aiding Rosalee in her vengeance and goal to see his twin dead. Someone had to help her string the steel cable across the road. And someone had to be feeding her inside information. Not a single Son could be guilty of such a betrayal. Every one of them hated Rosalee as much as he, if not more so, besides the fact they had nothing to gain from crippling their own MC.

Cara entered the doorway to her grandfather's room, turning his thoughts to his mate and the fact that Kaleb had expressed his desire to take her high school best friend as his mate. Cara would be thrilled. Kane hadn't so much as breathed a word, knowing that Suzi might want to tell Cara on her own. Three women in the clubhouse though? Kane shook his head. He'd no doubt be spending more time on the road.

"Cara." Her grandfather's smile was immediate, as was the love that shown in his eyes.

His mate kissed his weathered cheek and placed the piece of peanut butter pie on his dinner tray that they stopped to get at Tom's Deli on Main Street. His pleasure at the sight of the sugary treat was evident as he immediately reached for it.

Cara gripped his hand, the flesh thin, leaving the purple veins sticking out in contrast. "Not until after you eat your supper, old man. You know the rules. Otherwise, I stop bringing it."

He chuckled. "You're a cruel woman."

She laughed, and Kane resisted the urge to reach out and pull her into his embrace. Nothing warmed his heart quicker than to see her truly happy. Damn, he loved his woman. Even having seen her for the first time some ten years back, he never could have imagined the depths of his feelings now.

"If I were cruel, I wouldn't have brought the pie at all." She sat on the edge of the bed, while Kane walked over to the window and leaned against the ledge. "How are your nurses treating you?"

"Bah, you know them. If I didn't use the damn call button, they'd leave me here to die."

"I know better than that, Grandpa. These nurses love your cranky old ass, though I'm not quite sure why." She smiled at him.

"Hey." He chuckled. "Watch your respect, young lady. You aren't too old I can't turn you over my knee, you know."

"No, but you're no longer strong enough to do it. Besides, you're a blowhard. You've never once raised your hand to me."

"You never once gave me reason to. I think that piece of shit mother of yours did more than you ever deserved." His pale blue eyes moistened. "You were a good kid. Still are."

"Suzi stop in to see you tonight?" Cara asked, her brow furrowed. "She's supposed to be working, but I didn't see her on my way in."

"She was here about an hour ago. Brought me my meds." The old man rubbed his nape. "Damnedest thing though, I asked her for a blanket and she never sent an orderly back with one. She's not usually forgetful."

"Maybe she got busy."

"I'm sure that's it. She dropped her phone on the way out." He pointed a gnarled finger at the bedside table. "I put it up there for when she comes back to take my vitals. The woman who came to get her seemed like she was in an awful hurry. Maybe something bad happened to that poor woman's relative."

"What did she say?" Kane asked, something raising the hair at his nape.

Cara's grandfather turned his light gaze to him and shrugged. "Just that she had some sort of emergency and needed her. The two went hurrying out of here and I haven't seen her since."

Kane stood from his perch on the window sill. "What did she look like?"

"She was a tall one. About six feet if I were to guess. Dark hair, nearly black eyes. Pretty woman, big boned. Looked like she might be Italian."

Cara's grandfather had described Rosalee to a T. Kane hoped to hell he was wrong. "Think carefully. It might be important, Grandpa."

"What is it?" Cara asked.

"I hope it's not what I'm thinking, *mia bella*," Kane said, before returning his attention to the older man. "I need to know exactly what she said."

He twisted his lips in thought, then as if a light bulb had gone off, he replied, "She said, 'Nurse, come quick ... my brother-in-law is about to lose his head."

"Jesus!" Kane blasphemed.

"Kane?" Cara questioned.

"Grab Suzi's phone." He gripped the elder man's hand and shook it. "You've been a big help. But I'm afraid we have to run."

"Go." He waved them off. "I'm about to dive into that pie anyway."

Cara trotted after Kane down the hall, barely keeping up with hm. "What is it? You're scaring me."

"You should be, *mia bella.*" Kane gripped her hand and squeezed her fingers as they headed for the front of the nursing home where they left his Fat Boy. "If I'm right, Rosalee has your best friend and she's about to use her as a bargaining chip for Hawk."

"How's she doing, Blondy?" Kaleb asked as Anton walked into the living area of the clubhouse.

Anton ran his hands down his face, and truth be told, he looked a little worse for wear. Kaleb couldn't help but wonder what had the big man bugged. He usually didn't allow anything to get beneath his skin. Out of all the Sons, though largest in size, he was the most centered. Nothing seemed to ever bother him, when it didn't involve club business. Kane and Cara left following the meeting to catch up with Red, then planned to stop by the nursing home to visit with Cara's grandfather. Suzi came to mind and the likelihood of the pair running into her.

Kaleb couldn't help wonder if she might tell Cara about Kaleb's proposal. Kane's mate would no doubt gloat with her *I told you sos,* but Kaleb no longer cared. Even Cara couldn't ruin this for him. For the first time in a long time he was pretty damned content with his life and the promise of a future with Suzi. A silly grin crossed his face as he looked back to Anton, who took a seat across from him at the bar, oblivious to Kaleb's good mood. He had agreed to hang back and take care of Tamera in Cara's absence, since there certainly was no counting on Grayson.

"She's holding her own. She just drifted off to sleep. If I were to guess, I would say another twelve hours and she'll be through it. Who's going to teach her to feed?" Anton asked.

"Probably Cara and Kane since Kane offered to take on the responsibility."

"Man." Anton brushed his overgrown, blond bangs from his eyes and blew out a breath. "I can't help feeling sorry for her, you know?"

"You understand Gypsy didn't ask for this, right?"

He nodded. "But that doesn't excuse the way he's handling it. He's being such a ass. And that cute little redhead isn't even furious with him. She blames herself."

"I can't argue that Gypsy needs a lesson in manners, but I'm not so sure I would've handled it any better." Kaleb rubbed his nape. "Cara asked me to do something, make Gypsy step up to the plate. But, man, I just couldn't bring myself to punish him for what clearly wasn't his fault. Like you said, even his mate isn't pissed at him. How the hell does that happen?"

"Doesn't matter." Anton's lips became a hard line. "That woman is suffering in there all by herself. I'll see this through with her. She needs to know that someone cares, offer her comfort that Cara can't. I came out here to tell you that I'll hold her through the night until the pain passes. Cara and Kane can teach her to feed."

"You tell Gypsy about your plans?"

"He's already proven he doesn't care." Anton growled low. "At this point, neither do I. It was his decision to make her go the change without a male vampire to help her through. You and I know that Cara can't offer that comfort and only a male can alleviate some of that pain, absorb it into ourselves."

"You think that's wise, Blondy?" One of Kaleb's brows rose. "Regardless of his actions, she's still his mate."

Anton shrugged. "Fuck him. Let him try to take me to task for it. Someone has to step up to the plate. I'm not fucking her, just going to hold her and help her get through the rest of it. You know as well as I do, the mate can make the change more manageable and he's the one who decided to let her take on the pain all by herself."

"The mate, Blondy, can make it more manageable. That's the way it's supposed to be," he reminded Anton.

"But her fucking mate isn't here. Looks like I'll have to be stand in."

"And if I tell you no?"

Anton braced his hands on the bar that separated the two of them. "I'll do it anyway."

"I thought you might say that." Kaleb took down a couple glasses from the cupboard and poured them each two-fingers of the amber whiskey. He held his up glass to Anton. "If this causes a problem between you and Gypsy, then you two will solve it like men. You will not drag the club into your beef with each other. Deal?"

"Deal." Anton clicked his glass with Kaleb's, then they both downed the fiery liquid.

The main door opened, Kane and his mate walked in. The look on his twin's face caused him immediate concern. "We got problems, Hawk."

Kaleb didn't like the way the hair rose at his nape, telling him something had happened he wasn't going to like. Had the two run into Rosalee or did the meeting with Red go sour? "What's up?"

Cara walked past the men to the rear of the house, leaving them to discuss business as she went to check on Tamera. Kane walked over to the bar and eyed the whiskey. Kaleb reached for another glass, then filled the tumblers. Kane laid a cell on the bar between them, his hand still covering it, then downed the Jack.

Sliding the phone in Kaleb's direction, he said, "This belongs to Suzi."

Kaleb narrowed his gaze. "Why do you have her cell?"

His twin's concerned gaze held steady on his. "She's missing, bro."

"What the fuck are you talking about, Viper?" Kaleb tamped down his rising panic. "She's at work."

"She's not there, Hawk. Cara and I checked. Questioning Cara's grandfather ... someone came into the room to retrieve Suzi. He described Rosalee to a T. Told Suzi she needed her right away because her brother-in-law was about to lose his head."

"What the fuck?"

Kaleb sucked in a breath, poured himself another glass of the whiskey, and downed it, reveling in the fiery liquid. He slammed the tumbler on the bar. The whiskey burned his esophagus, roiling his gut. His breathing damn near stopped. Had he just led Suzi to slaughter by his declaration to take her as mate? Had Rosalee somehow overheard? The bitch had probably followed him to Suzi's house.

"We have to find her, Viper. I will fucking kill your ex if she so much as lays a finger on her."

"We can leave Cara here with Tamera—"

"No," Anton spoke up. "You three go. Suzi may need Cara. I'll stay with Tamera."

Kane eyed Anton at his declaration, though wisely did not comment. At the moment they had bigger issues than worrying about a possible blowup between Sons.

Suzi's cell vibrated on the bar, drawing all eyes. The caller ID displayed Caller Unknown. Kaleb snatched it up, slid the lock and took the phone to his ear.

"Who the fuck is this?"

"Why, Hawk, is that anyway to talk to your sister-in-law?"

"Cara is my sister-in-law, you bitch. What did you do with Suzi?"

Her tsk, tsk sounded through the earpiece and he might have thrown it if he hadn't needed to listen to what she had to say. Only she could tell him the whereabouts of his woman. And right now, he was in the mood to take someone's head. That someone was Rosalee. She'd not get out of this alive, not if he could help it. Tonight it ended. It would either be her head or his.

"Come alone and she lives."

"Where?"

"The same spot you ended my Alec's life, you will lose yours." Kaleb heard a man's chuckle in the background. No doubt the Knight rat bastard. "If you bring anyone else with you, then it will be Suzi's head that is taken. Do I make myself clear?"

"Perfectly."

"Don't play me for the fool, Hawk. You know I'll smell Kane or any of the other Sons long before you get here. They can't come close enough to save your sorry head. You want your desired little mate to be saved ... then do as I say," she said, then the line went dead.

"What do you want us to do, Hawk?" Kane asked, his acute hearing no doubt picking up on the other side of the conversation. By the looks of Anton's face, he had heard every word as well.

"You heard the bitch. If I don't go alone, Suzi will lose her head. I can't chance it."

"Hawk," Kane warned, "if you go alone, you will lose yours ... and possibly Suzi will die anyway. Rosalee is a merciless bitch."

"I will not endanger Suzi's life. I'll make Rosalee release her first." Kaleb walked around the counter, and drew Kane into a bear hug. "I love you, Viper."

Kane slapped him on the back, then fisted the material of his tee. "If this goes south, know that I will personally kill Rosalee and her worthless father, Mircea. I will get restitution."

Kaleb stepped back and smiled. "I know you will, bro. But I have no intention of dying today. This ends now. Your job? Convince that bastard stepfather of hers that she deserved what the hell she got."

"You got it. I love you, bro." He pulled Kaleb in for another quick hug.

Kaleb stepped back. "Now let's cut the theatrics. I'll call you when it's done."

Walking over to Anton, Kaleb gripped his hand, and bumped his shoulder with his. "You take care of Gypsy's mate, help her through this. And don't let Gypsy give you any shit over it, you hear?"

"You'll be back to ensure he doesn't, Hawk," Anton replied, clearing his throat from what sounded like emotion.

Kaleb grabbed the keys to his new bike and headed for the club entrance, steeling his jaw. His focus was single-minded, killing a primordial bitch ... or die trying.

CHAPTER TWENTY-NINE

ANE PULLED INTO THE GRAVEL PARKING LOT, FLIPPED THE center stand Kaleb rolled his brand new black denim, Night Rod to a stop in the gravel parking lot, near the shed where Alec had held Cara captive some six months prior. He balanced the bike between his jean-clad thighs and stared into the forest. The now-dead vampire had sliced her throat from damn near ear-to-ear, forcing Kane to make the decision to turn her. His twin had made the sacrifice which cost him his P patch, though Kaleb would bet Kane hadn't once regretted his decision.

Cutting the engine, silence descended about him. Other than the sounds of birds taking flight and the scurrying of forest critters, his hearing didn't pick up anyone or anything else in the near vicinity. He could smell Rosalee, though, over the scent of pine and knew that she was near. He couldn't help but second-guess his decision to go it alone, it no doubt being a suicide mission. But he couldn't risk Suzi's life, and there was no way any of the vampires could've come within a mile and have Rosalee's olfactory nerves not privy to the fact.

Kicking down the center stand and stepping over his bike's black, leather seat, he hung his helmet on the rubber handle grip, then headed for the path leading into the thick of the woods. As he drew closer, he caught Suzi's unique scent as well as that of someone he couldn't quite put a face to. He had smelled the odor before, and knew the rat in cahoots with Rosalee had to have been near him at one time or another. The person riding her coattails was no doubt someone he had done business with in the past and probably felt he had a score to settle.

Soft muffled voices traveled to his ear the nearer he came to the shed. He could easily pick Kane's ex by the sound of her grating voice. The egotistical bitch thought to take him down, but he sure in the hell wouldn't go easily. Kaleb had yet to hear even a whimper from Suzi, giving him no indication if she was still alive, though he doubted Rosalee would be so stupid as to kill off her one bargaining chip. Just as he rounded a bend in the path, and the old, graying shed came into view, Bird stepped from the doorway, a cocksure smile on his face, telling him that Rosalee had indeed detected his arrival.

The son of a bitch.

Kaleb had known one of the Knights had sold them out. But the VP? The man Red had trusted most to sit at his right? Kaleb's desire grew to rip his head clean from his shoulders. He wanted to wipe the condescending look from his face ... pull his beating heart from his chest and shove it down his throat. One thing was a definite, no matter the method, Bird would not draw breath come tomorrow. If nothing else came out of this death trap set for him, Kaleb would take Bird to hell with him ... kicking and screaming the entire way.

"Nice of you to show, Hawk." Bird chuckled, then spit in the dirt to the right of his own boot. He wiped a grimy hand across his thin lips.

Just the thought of those hands anywhere near Suzi brought out the animal in him. He wanted to rip the bastard's throat out with his fangs. Kaleb stopped a few feet short of him, not trusting himself to keep from following through with his desires.

"I don't think I was given much of a choice, ass wipe. Where the hell is Suzi?"

"Here." Rosalee stepped from the shed, her hand fisted tightly in Suzi's hair, shoving her toward Bird. Suzi's sneakers caught on a limb, half buried in the dirt, and stumbled in the VP's direction.

Rosalee towered over Suzi, easily manhandling her with her size and strength. The bitch shoved her again. Bird caught her before she went face-first into the dirt. Every muscle in Kaleb tightened, his willpower at the snapping point. Bird gripped Suzi's shoulders and forced her to her knees so that she faced Kaleb. Gray duct tape covered her mouth, while her hands were bound with a white zip strip. Rage simmered in Kaleb's gut, burning slow and hot. His gaze heated as his gums ached with the lengthening of his fangs. If Rosalee even so much as gave him an inch, Bird was a dead man.

"The choice is yours, Hawk." Rosalee regained his attention. "I will spare her life for yours."

"Then let her go, bitch. I came as you requested. Alone." He glanced briefly at Suzi, who frantically shook her head, eyes wide, tears making dirty tracks down her cheeks. "Cut her loose, and I'm all yours."

Her lips quirked to one side. "You must think I'm some kind of stupid. I let her go and what leverage do I have?"

"You and I both know, alone, my strength doesn't compare to yours as a primordial. You can outrun me, Rosalee. I have nowhere to go that you won't catch me. But I promise you this, I'll still put up one hell of a fight, and your man over there"—Kaleb jerked thumb toward the scum still holding Suzi—"won't make it out of here alive. Now, let her go."

Rosalee's dark reddish-brown hair glinted in the sunlight peering through the trees as the slight breeze picked up and brushed tendrils across her tanned flesh. The woman was stunning, he'd give her that. She no doubt had men, and vampires alike, vying for her attention and the sole reason she was able to get scumbags like Bird to follow her every directive. All Kaleb saw now was the hideous, black-hearted person she hid beneath the exterior to everyone but the Sons of Sangue. Each and every one of them would rather kill her on sight, than humor her.

Rosalee glanced at Bird, and with a quick nod of her head, said, "Let her go."

"Seriously? I say the bitch dies anyway."

"Cut her loose, Bird." Rosalee glared at the greasy haired biker, giving him no room for argument. "Don't question me, or I'll let Hawk make good on his promise to take you out."

Bird leaned down, caressed Suzi's shoulders beneath her scrubs, and licked the shell of her ear. "Today's your lucky day, doll. Too bad. I could've had some real fun with you."

Suzi shivered and Kaleb growled, tamping down the beast inside wanting to tear the man limb from limb. Curling his hands into fists at his side, he bit back the urge to bleed him dry. Kaleb would be no good to anyone if he acted on impulse. He needed to get Suzi the hell out of here first.

"Sorry, doll," Bird said, right before he gripped the edge of the tape and ripped it from her mouth.

Suzi cried out, the skin around her mouth instantly reddening, little beads of blood drawing to the surface in spots. Kaleb steeled his jaw, a muscle ticking in his cheek, but stayed his position. Any movement from him could cost Suzi her life. The VP of the Knights reached into his pocket and pulled out a switch blade. With a click, the knife sprung free and he cut through the white, plastic zip strip binding her wrists as easily as if only string bound her, telling Kaleb how sharp he kept the blade. Suzi stumbled to her feet, looking as if she meant to run into Kaleb's protective hold, and damn if he didn't want her there. But he shook his head for her to stay her position.

"Don't do this." Suzi glanced at Rosalee, though Kaleb knew her pleas fell on deaf ears. "I can't lose him. I'll do anything."

"You're breaking my heart, sweetheart." Rosalee laughed. "But I suggest you accept my hospitality. My beef is with the Tepes boys. You just happen to be my means of getting Hawk here. I swear the boy has more lives than a cat."

Rosalee approached Suzi, framed her face within her palms, and forced her to look into her obsidian gaze. Thankfully, Rosalee meant to hypnotize her. "You'll forget the last few hours and every-thing you've seen. Turn around and head for the road and don't look back. Return to work, little girl."

Without question, he watched Suzi turn and head for the road, her gaze unfocused. She'd no doubt wake from the stupor Rosalee placed her in a few short miles down the road, and wonder how the hell she got into the middle of the forest, with no recollection of leaving the nursing home. Kaleb was thankful that Rosalee took the initiative, though it was more likely out of consideration for herself than Suzi. Kane's ex was way too selfish to hypnotize her for any other reason than to erase her own memory from Suzi's mind.

"What's to stop you from going after her once you kill me?" Kaleb asked, gaining back the witch's attention.

Rosalee shrugged. "I don't suppose my word is good enough."

"Not in the least, bitch. You and I both know it could take her over an hour to get back to Pleasant by foot."

"Killing her at this point gains me nothing, Hawk. She won't remember me, won't remember being here, and once she finds out that you lost your head ... she'll be heartbroken. Much more fun to watch her suffer over your loss."

"Will my death finally satisfy you?"

Rosalee shrugged.

"Look, take my life and end this here. My death will serve your purpose in making Kane suffer. Go back to Italy and let him live in peace."

"You know I can't do that."

"Why the fuck not? You'll never get him back."

"Because I'm his mate!" Her face reddened as her ire rose. "You and I know that's for eternity."

"Then take it up with your stepdaddy. He granted Kane the right to take on a new mate. Even he knows what an evil bitch you are."

"Face it, you're a dead man, Hawk." Bird cackled, drawing Kaleb's murderous glare. "You won't mind me having a little fun with Suzi—"

His words were cut off by Kaleb's fist wrapping his neck, dangling him in air. His legs kicked as his fingers tried desperately to loosen Kaleb's hold to no avail. Kaleb would have easily crushed his windpipe had Rosalee not intervened and gripped the hair at his nape in her vise-like grip. Bird dropped like the sack of shit he was to a pool at Kaleb's feet, clutching his injured throat. She forced him to his knees in the dirt, stones digging into the soft material of his jeans. She stood so close that her legs brushed his shoulders. Kaleb knew she could easily remove his head from his shoulders with hardly any effort. If he didn't keep her focus elsewhere, he'd be dead in mere seconds.

Bird scrambled to his feet, stumbling as he did, his hand still covering his bruised throat. "You, son of a bitch," he rasped. "I'm going to enjoy watching Rosalee kill you."

"What's in it for you, Bird? Why make a pact with the devil's spawn?"

"To be like you." He spat at the dirt, just inches from Kaleb's knees.

"Shut the fuck up, Bird," Rosalee warned the biker.

"Why? Not like he'll be alive to tell anyone." He used the toe of his boot to kick dirt at Kaleb. Stones and dirt clods pebbled his chest.

Kaleb struggled to no benefit in Rosalee's iron-like grip. "You best hold on tight, bitch. If I get loose, I'll send you both to hell with Alec."

Her fingernails pierced his flesh and dug into the muscle of his rotator cuff, smelling the fresh blood trailing from his shoulder. Kaleb bit back the grunt of pain, not wanting to give the satisfaction of letting her know she caused him pain.

"Just think, Hawk," Bird went on, not heeding Rosalee's warning, "you die and I get to have immortality."

"And just how do you think to accomplish that, you ass wipe?"

Rosalee's nails twisted in his flesh. Kaleb cried out, not being able to contain the anguish.

"Rosalee promised to turn me."

"You really are an idiot. I almost feel sorry for you." Kaleb chuckled, his humor bubbling up from his gut. "Rosalee can't turn you. Only a male of our species can turn a human into a vampire."

Rosalee tightened her grip, her bone-like claws wrapping his clavicle. Much more and he feared her ripping his clavicle from his body. The scent of his blood filled the air.

"Son of a—" Kaleb grit his teeth, trying instead to focus on the dumbfounded look on Bird's face. The man had clearly been duped by Rosalee for her own gain. But then, Kaleb highly doubted she did anything without benefit.

"He speaks the truth?" Bird asked, his brows meeting over the bridge of his nose.

Kaleb heard Rosalee's exasperated sigh. "I might have missed that tiny little detail."

"So I've been helping you all along, for what? A good piece of ass?"

"Oh please, there was nothing good about that piece—" Kaleb's insult cut short as Rosalee tightened her grip on his shoulder bone, ready to hear it snap at any moment. "Shit!"

"I needed you, Bird." She paused long enough to twist her nails into the muscles, tearing at the tendons. Kaleb cried out again. "Now, I don't."

"I suggest if you want to live, you let the boy go," came a fourth party, a deep pitch Kaleb was unfamiliar with.

Kaleb caught a whiff of a primordial other than Rosalee. The strong stench of Kaleb's fresh blood likely kept Kane's ex-bitch from detecting the intruder's approach. The timbre of the man's voice rose the hairs at his nape, telling him they should fear the man behind it. Kaleb glanced about the clearing, seeing no one. Sniffing the air, he tried to pick up the scent again, something other than that of his own blood, but failed. Rosalee loosened her grip just enough that Kaleb broke free and rolled from her reach. The witch stood perfectly still, her gaze darting about the forest as if even she feared the evil that lurked in the shadows. Standing, Kaleb's gaze snapped about the thickening of pines, seeing no one. When he turned to look at Rosalee, her wild gaze continued to case the area. Whoever lurked in the shelter of the forest clearly had the primordial bitch worried.

Bird, on the other hand, still focused on the fact he had been duped and wasn't going to make vampire status. "You bitch!" He cursed. "I should—"

A deep blue streak moved through the clearing, faster than Kaleb's eyes could track. Bird now laid face-first in the dirt, neck at an awkward angle, no longer drawing breath. Next to the prone body stood a man, easily towering a good couple inches taller than Kaleb, his long, blue-black hair hanging lose about his face. Broad shouldered and heavily muscled, the man stood sizing Rosalee up, paying Kaleb little mind.

White fangs stood out in contrast against rich red lips as he smiled. "My dear niece. Pray tell, dear, what dastardly plan did you have devised for my grandson? Surely, you didn't mean to try and end his life?"

She stumbled back a foot. "You're dead."

"Last I checked, the tomb was empty." The man's smile widened. Even Kaleb had trouble believing what ... who stood directly in front of him. "But you, my dear, deserve nothing less. I should kill you outright."

"Vlad?" she whispered.

"In the flesh." He raised his arms in a Christ-like pose. Then, in the blink of an eye, Rosalee dangled from his fingertip. Jesus! His forefinger pierced the flesh beneath her chin and all six-feet of her dangled from that one finger stuck through her flesh.

"I assure you I'm just as strong and healthy as the day I supposedly died. Now, unless you want your head sent back to your worthless father on a pike, I suggest you collect your things and return to Italy before I change my mind. Tell Mircea, the cowardly bastard, I'll be by to see him shortly. I'll allow him to decide your fate, you insolent little brat, for daring to take my grandson's head."

He dropped Rosalee to her feet, blood leaking from the hole left by Vlad's finger. She stepped back from his reach, though his great grandfather had already proven should he desire to take her in his hold again, she couldn't back up far enough. Her limbs trembled, proving Vlad scared the bejesus out of her and rightly so. Hell, the man scared the shit out of him and Kaleb was his flesh and blood.

"Go!" Vlad's voice rose to a near deafening pitch, spurring Rosalee into action.

She took to the forest on long legs, disappearing into the foliage within seconds. Kaleb glanced back to Vlad, still shocked by the man who stood next to him. How the hell was that possible? His great grandfather placed a hand on his shoulder, Kaleb's wounds already nearly self-healed from Rosalee's nails.

"Suzi..." Kaleb voiced, suddenly worried that Rosalee might yet take her life. "I need to make sure she's safe."

Vlad clapped him on the back. "Trust in me, son. I took care of your woman. She is worth your life?"

Kaleb nodded.

"I thought as much." Vlad glanced to Bird lying prone in the dirt. "Let us return to the clubhouse, you'll find your woman there. I think it's time to meet my other grandson."

"I brought my bike. I don't..."

"I have no use for cars, motorcycles or otherwise. I'll go the way of the forest and meet you there. See if you can beat me on that contraption of yours." His grandfather winked at him, then turned to leave.

"Vlad?"

He looked back at Kaleb. "How long have you been here ... in the States, I mean?"

A smile warmed his tanned handsome face. "Long enough to know Rosalee was up to no good."

And with that, he was gone. Kaleb stared into the forest for long moments before turning and heading to his bike, still not quite believing what the hell just happened. Vlad's return. He couldn't help but wonder if it were a good thing ... or a very bad thing. He sure hoped the eldest primordial approved of the life Kane and he led. Kaleb didn't relish the idea of any of his friends or family winding up on one of Vlad's pikes.

CHAPTER THIRTY

KALEB WALKED INTO THE CLUBHOUSE, HIS EYES TAKING BUT A second to adjust to the lighting. Kane sat on the sofa with Cara tucked under his arm, chatting with Vlad, who sat across from them as if it were the most natural thing in the world. Cara laughed at something his great grandfather had said. He stood watching the scene before him, the whole thing surreal. He still couldn't believe that Vlad was not only alive, but looked as young and healthy as he and his twin. He could even see the resemblance. His great grandfather, however many times removed, looked more like Kane than Kaleb due to them both having the straighter hair, though Vlad's was at least a good six inches longer. The Romanian ruler certainly didn't look as if he had aged in the past four hundred plus years.

His next thought was of Suzi, who he hadn't spotted upon his arrival. She wasn't among those in the front area of the clubhouse. Anton stood to his right on the opposite side of the bar while Tamera sat on a bar stool just a few short feet away. Kaleb could see the change had completed sooner than they had thought and that she didn't bear any lasting effects. The redhead was downright stunning. Grayson could have done much worse for a mate. When he glanced back to the living area, Vlad took in his wild gaze with a smile.

"She's here, son."

"Where?" Kaleb asked about the time Suzi exited the bathroom.

"She doesn't remember much," Vlad said. "Which is probably a good thing."

He hated the hesitancy he saw in her beautiful warm eyes. How much of her memory had been erased by Rosalee? He couldn't stand the idea that she might not remember their morning together or the fact she had agreed to be his mate. Being that a very powerful vampire had hypnotized her, it was hard telling how much damage Rosalee had done. Hell, for that matter, Kaleb had no idea what Vlad might have done. After all, he had said that he had taken care of her, but hadn't elaborated how.

"You okay?"

Suzi nodded, wetting her lips with her tongue. "At least I think so. I remember leaving for work this morning. Next thing I knew, I was here with Kane and Cara."

"You do remember this morning then?"

A smile lit her face and centered in her eyes as her cheeks reddened.

"You haven't changed your mind?"

Suzi shook her head. "Why would I want to do that?"

Kaleb opened his arms and she ran into them. He easily enfolded her within his large embrace, never wanting to let her go. *Damn!* He had almost lost her. He hadn't been able to breathe, let alone think when Bird had his fucking grimy hands on her. He wouldn't morn the dirt bag's loss. Rosalee, on the other hand, he wished would've met the same fate. But for his own reasons, Vlad had spared her life, sending her back to Italy and her stepfather.

Kaleb fisted the hair at Suzi's nape, tipped her head back and kissed her, one filled with possession and desperation. Her small hands slipped around his waist and gripped the soft material of his tee, holding onto him as if she felt the same sense of anxiety. Never had he been so scared of losing someone. He didn't care that they had an audience. He only cared that Suzi was in his arms, alive and well. Kaleb wanted to pick Suzi up and carry her to his room, more than ready to make her his for all eternity.

Anton cleared his throat. Kaleb pulled back out of respect for his soon-to-be mate. She didn't need to be the center of a bunch of gossipy vampires ... even if Kaleb didn't care what the hell they thought of him.

"Your rooms that way, Hawk," Anton said, a smirk on his face, pointing his thumb over his shoulder toward the back of the clubhouse.

"Fuck you, Blondy. I'm fully aware of that. Don't you have some place better to be? Like throwing back a few beers with your new roomy?"

He chuckled, not offended in the least. "I think I'd rather stay here and get to know your granddaddy."

Vlad rose from the sofa, his sheer size filling the room. The man certainly knew how to command a presence. He strode over to the bar, grabbed the half-filled whiskey bottle and downed what was left of the contents. He then tossed the empty bottle into the receptacle at the end of the bar. Bracing his hands on the surface, his black eyes centered on Anton. Hell, even Anton was small in comparison.

"This isn't your mate." It wasn't a question, but damn near sounded like a threat coming from Vlad.

Anton's Adam's apple bobbed in his throat. "No, sir."

"You going to let this woman come between you and a brother?"

"It isn't my intention." Anton toyed with the cap from the whiskey bottle between his thumb and forefinger. "Gypsy wasn't stepping up to the plate to see her through the change. Someone needed to be there for her."

"Cara was, from my understanding." He crossed his muscular arms over his chest and held Anton's gaze. "Kane filled me in when I noted the newly turned mate."

Anton shrugged. "You and I both know I had the ability to take away some of her pain."

"It's my fault," Tamera spoke up, squaring her shoulders as she looked up at the large, intimidating vampire filling the space beside her. "I take full responsibility for my actions."

"You can't take responsibility for Anton. His actions are his own." He paused, his hot gaze pinning her. To Tamera's credit, she didn't so much as blink. "Are you prepared to be held accountable for Grayson? It's in my power to punish him for his insolent behavior. Regardless how it came to be, you're his mate. How he handled the unfortunate turn of events is inexcusable. Are you saying he doesn't deserve to be reprimanded and that should I see fit to punish him, that you'll take said punishment in his place?"

Tamera glanced down at the folded hands in her lap. "I will."

One of Vlad's brows rose. "Very well. A female without a mate is not allowed within our race. I placed the rules in place many years ago and they aren't to be taken lightly. Grayson has one year to claim you. If he does not, then I give you to Anton."

His gaze moved to the large blond vampire. "Do you dare to disagree with my decision?"

"If Gypsy doesn't claim her as his mate ... then I will."

"You'll not touch her. For if I hear that you acted inappropriately, I will return and you will rue the day you disobeyed me. Grayson is to be given one year, understood?" When no one offered an argument, he continued, "Then let it be known that what I have decreed this day will be carried out, in one way or another. This woman will be mated to one of you."

Anton's gaze traveled to Tamera, who still bowed her head. Kaleb detected the heat in Anton's gaze. There was no mistaking that he wouldn't mind Grayson shirking his duty and claiming Tamera as his own.

"Then if there is nothing else, I will take my leave. I fear I need to see that my gutless brother punishes that contemptuous brat of his. I still haven't seen restitution for her causing my grandson's death."

"You know of that?" Kane asked.

"Dear boy," he patted Kane's cheek, "you may not have seen me, but I was never far away. I always knew what was going on."

"Then you know of the cartel?"

He nodded. "I believe you and your brother will take care of the humans responsible?"

"We have a plan in place, a barkeep who is willing to hand over the key players to us."

"Good." He smiled. "Then see that they pay. A life for a life, Kane. I'll accept nothing less."

"Absolutely."

Vlad turned, pulled Kane into a hug and slapped him on the back. He then framed his face in his hands. "You do me proud, grandson."

He walked over to Kaleb next and wrapped his muscular arms around him. Stepping back, he placed a large hand on Suzi's shoulder. Vlad looked like a giant next to her.

Glancing back to Kaleb he said, "Waste no more time. She should've been your mate some time ago. Don't be a fool and chance losing her to mortality."

"I don't plan to."

"Good." He nodded, then smiled, his teeth impossibly white against his red lips. "Then my job here is done … for now." He turned without so much as glancing back, and walked from the clubhouse, his broad shoulders barely clearing the door frame.

Kaleb looked at Kane and whistled. "Jesus! I'd hate to be Rosalee when he gets to Italy."

Kane was the first to chortle, followed by the lot of them. After the day Kaleb had had … it felt damn good to share in the humor.

KANE AND CARA HAD TAKEN Tamera to the Rave to teach her to feed and Hawk couldn't be happier to finally get some alone time with Suzi. Hell, he was beginning to think he was going to have to kick Anton's sorry ass to get him to return to his own fucking farmhouse. He was sure Grayson being there had something to do with his reluctance to leave … that or the cute redhead he helped transition into vampire. When Vlad had first made the demand that if Grayson didn't step up to the plate within one year's time, that Anton take his place, Kaleb was sure the large blond would back down in a moment's time. Instead, he'd looked Vlad straight in the eye and agreed to his terms.

For fuck's sake!

He sure in the hell hoped Anton did not have a thing for Tamera. No telling how Grayson might react, knowing a brother homed in on his territory even if Grayson was being a complete ass about it. Kaleb was positive, even though his VP didn't want the redhead. Grayson wasn't going to be open for someone else to take his place. Grayson may not appear to be the jealous type, but he did have a short fuse for a temper. And one of his brethren thinking to sneak and take what was rightfully his, might just light that fuse.

Suzi caught his attention as she fidgeted by the foot of his bed, bringing his focus back to what really mattered. *Her.* Let Anton and Grayson sort out their own fucking mess. He had other plans for his night, and it sure in the hell didn't involve figuring out two grown vampires' love lives. His soon-to-be-mate sat hesitantly on the edge of his bed, her eyes wide and not full of desire like he preferred them. He needed to get her mind on the physical and off the idea what was to come later. He would absorb every damn ounce of pain for her if it were indeed possible. Kaleb didn't plan to leave her side once during the change.

He pulled his tee over his head and dropped it to the wooden flooring, her gaze traveling to his pecs before trailing lower to his abs. She drew her lower lip between her teeth, telling him he had her heading in the right direction. Getting her mind off the change might not be so much of an issue after all. Suzi had always been very sexual, which he loved about her. She had no problem going after what she wanted. The scent of her rising desire wafted to his nose.

Kaleb sauntered over to the bed, stopping just within reach. "You're so beautiful, *piccolo diavolo.* You steal my breath away."

Suzi dipped two fingers into the front of his jeans and pulled him toward her. "Make love to me."

"With pleasure, sweetheart." A grin split his face. God, how he loved this woman. "I'm all yours."

Her heated brown gaze held his as her pink tongue darted out and trailed the line of hair leading from his navel, disappearing into the top of his jeans. Kaleb sucked in a breath. He had wanted to take it slow, show her how much he loved her. But his cock had a mind of its own. His need for Suzi turned into desperation, in all probability due to the fact he had almost lost her.

Kaleb placed his hands over hers, gripping her tiny wrists within his large hands and pulling her to her feet. He easily divested her of her shirt, his heated gaze taking in the red lacy brassiere covering her small, pert tits. God, she was perfect ... and she was his. Working the button of her pants, he shoved them past her hips, where they pooled at her feet. She stepped out of them, leaving her in a matching red lace thong. Her hand found the button on his jeans, then slowly slid the zipper over his cock. She reached inside and pulled him free, causing Kaleb to growl.

He wasted not a moment as he lifted her from the floor. Her lean muscular legs wrapped his waist, bringing her center flush against his abs. Pulling the red scrap of lace to one side, he guided her onto his erection and swiftly entered her. Suzi gasped, wrapping her arms around his neck as she began rocking on his cock. Kaleb knew he wouldn't last. He had wanted this woman for far too long, even if he was too damn stubborn to admit as much. Suzi's hooded gaze centered on his mouth and the lengthening of his fangs. Tilting her head to the side, she gripped his nape and urged him forward.

Kaleb didn't hesitate as he sank his canines into the silky flesh with a soft pop, tasting the sweetness of her blood. Suzi moaned, her breath coming in shallow pants. He could tell her orgasm wasn't far off. And damn but it wouldn't take him long to follow her over that peak. Turning, he backed her against the door and anchored her against the wood to get better leverage. His fingers dug into the soft flesh of her ass as he started sliding in and out of her at a swift pace, continuing his communion as he did.

Her arms tightened about his nape, her heart beating heavily against his chest. Kaleb withdrew his fangs and licked the wounds to aid in healing, just as she cried out. His name tumbled from her lips as she fought to regain breath. Kaleb shoved into her, his balls tightening with each thrust, then growled as he reached his own climax. He leaned his forehead against the top of her head, attempting to catch his own breath.

Life was good.

Kaleb couldn't remember a time he had ever thought as much. Wrapping her tightly in his hold, he carried her to the bed where he set her atop the sheets. He handed her his tee, which she quickly pulled over her head. The soft material pooled about her. Kaleb tucked himself back into his jeans, then joined her on the bed. He leaned against the headboard and pulled her against his chest so that she sat between his spread thighs and her back rested against his chest. He could feel her heartbeat.

"I love you, Suzi." He leaned down and whispered into her ear, "Everything about you. Your spirit, your tenacity, your courage, the love you had for my nephew and for keeping his secret. But most of all, the way you never gave up on me."

She snuggled more fully into him, taking his arms and wrapping her middle with them.

"I may have wished otherwise, Kaleb"—she looked over her shoulder at him, and he laid a brief kiss upon her lips—"but I've always loved you ... though I didn't always like you. Down deep, I could never truly hate you."

"You make me a better person." He placed a kiss in the crook of her neck where moments ago he had fed. "Are you glad that you told Kane about his son earlier?"

She nodded. "He needed to know. Ion loved his father so much that he feared disappointing him. Ion would've been happy to know that his sexual preference wouldn't have mattered to Kane ... or you for that matter. I just wish he would've lived long enough to know that."

"Kane and I will get our retribution."

"Don't you dare do something stupid, Kaleb Tepes. I couldn't bear to lose you."

His arms tightened around her. "I am yours, Suzi, now and forever. I will never jeopardize that."

He then brought his tattooed wrist to his mouth and bit. Red blood began to flow from the twin holes down his wrist. He held his arm out to her. Suzi stared at his offering, then gripped his large wrist in her tiny hand.

"Are you ready to be mine?"

"Now and forever," she said, then took the wrist to her mouth and drank.

ABOUT THE AUTHOR

A daydreamer at heart, Patricia A. Rasey, resides in her native town in Northwest Ohio with her husband, Mark, and her lovable Cavalier King Charles Spaniel, Todd. A graduate of Long Ridge Writer's School, Patricia has seen publication of some her short stories in magazines as well as several of her novels.

When not behind her computer, you can find Patricia working, reading, watching movies or MMA. She also enjoys spending her free time at the river camping and boating with her husband and two sons. Ms. Rasey is currently a third degree Black Belt in American Freestyle Karate.